Grady Gilbert

Googles God

Dale Slongwhite

Williams & King Publishers

DEDICATION

Dedicated to David whose belief in my work keeps me writing.

NONFICTION BOOKS BY THIS AUTHOR

Silently Guided: A Journey of Faith into Hearing Loss
and Deaf Ministry

Saved for Service: The Arturo Santos Story

Fed Up: The High Cost of Cheap Food

<u>Co-authored with Sandra Doran</u>

Gathering: A Search for Balance and Fulfillment

ACKNOWLEDGEMENTS

Where do I begin? Many people read or listened to portions, asked about the well-being of the characters as if they were real, laughed and snickered in all the right places. Let me take a stab at remembering you all. I'm sure to remember someone after this book goes to print. Please forgive me in advance.

Mallory DePalermo, the first reader, editor, and encourager;
Deby and Mick Hazelwood who read original drafts and gave encouragement;
Sandra DAscencao who did a wonderful job of copy editing, suggesting a few plot points that added greatly to the story, and completed the first layout;
Anne Marie Monzione who introduced me to my first literary agent;
Joanne Wojtyto, Bonnie Fesmire, Karen Spruill, Chintana Ahlund, writing partners who listened to first drafts;
Marcia Williams, a great friend and publisher;
Saritza Hernandez, literary agent in a workshop who harshly critiqued my manuscript, forcing me to come up with a much better beginning;
Sandra Finley Doran, David Slongwhite, Laurel Slongwhite, Holly Finley David, Carol Robertson, and Dori Pope who eagerly awaited the printing;
Karen Slongwhite Greene who created the cover, the website, the registration process for the launch, and other marketing material.

"If done properly, being a pastor is a walk in the park. Jurassic Park, but a park."

Mark Gungor

CHAPTER ONE

Grady Gilbert pushed back the pine branches draped across the hand-made wooden sign. He squinted in the dusky shadows and still couldn't read it. He fumbled in the pocket of his jeans until he found his iPhone and flicked on the flashlight app.

WILSONS CORNER BIBLE BELIEVING CONGREGATION

Why'd that crappy car have to run out of gas in front of a church? He hadn't been inside one since his grandmother died the summer after eighth grade. For three summers, he spent three weeks with her on Daytona Beach. He loved everything about his visits except for Sundays. She made him go to this standing/kneeling/arm-waving service in a small, packed store-front building. The only thing that got him through the morning was anticipating the potluck lunches the ladies miraculously produced after the dreaded service. His mouth watered at the memory.

Blueberry cobbler, barbeque meatballs, date bars, homemade rolls. His stomach rumbled. Did all churches have ladies who put out a spread like that?

He glanced back at the Pontiac, gasless, half in a ditch, and turned to look forward where trees arched over a gravel road and disappeared into darkness. Would anyone even be at the church on a Wednesday evening?

What the hey. He needed help and no cars had come by in the last...who knew how long...he'd been waiting to flag one down. Gambling with the darkness it would have to be. Decision made, he turned away from the main road and caught his sweatshirt on the rough side of the sign. The tear sliced through the middle of the UCF logo. *Great!* First college ripped from him, then home— if you wanted to call it that. Now his favorite sweatshirt. What else could go wrong on this miserable day? Best get walking and pray someone was at the church.

Grady took one step and banged his head on a tree branch. "Shit!" he said, then caught himself. He was on holy ground and better watch his language. He didn't want to ruin his chance of begging a tank of gas from someone in Wilsons Corner Something Or Other.

Being tall had its advantages, other than constantly knocking into low-hanging light fixtures, or in this case, low hanging branches. He'd reached 5'10" by eighth grade, and because of it, most people meeting him for the first time thought he was older. Now five years later, he was 6'3" and that commanded a lot of respect the shorter guys he knew never garnered.

A twig snapped beneath Grady's feet. Small animals scurried through the trees, squawking and chittering. His Nikes scuffed dry leaves, making them crinkle like torn paper. A movement to the left caught his eye. At first, he didn't see anything and tried to convince himself the movement was only leaves rustling in the breeze or just his overactive imagination. Then in the darkness he detected a movement—a flicker, a flick, a twitch of a white tail not twenty feet away. He squinted and made out the silhouette of a deer. The doe raised her head. Her jaw moved back and forth, up and down, without opening her mouth.

He stared until she leaped into the brush out of sight. Grady smiled. The deer was a good omen. The breeze picked up, carrying with it the minty aroma of pines, the musty smell of decaying vegetation, and a tiny hint of hope.

CHAPTER TWO

Mae-June Yearling parked as close to the church as she could. Quite a few cars for a Wednesday night, she noted. On the one hand, she felt glad so many parishioners had come out to meet the new pastor. On the other hand, she wasn't convinced his credentials fit the needs of the Wilsons Corner Bible Believing Congregation. And he was so young. He'd just graduated from Gordon Conwell Theological Seminary in Massachusetts. Wilsons Corner needed someone with experience. They hadn't even met him in person, just interviewed him on the computer somehow. Mae-June knew people could talk a good talk, but when you met them face to face, they could be totally different than you imagined. The new pastor was fortunate, though. As the church secretary, Mae-June knew the ins and outs of running the place. He would do well to listen up and learn from her years of experience.

She reached into the back seat of her Ford Focus and grasped her grandmother Myrtle's antique crystal serving plate with her date bars sealed with a new kind of wrap that actually stuck to the glass. She'd only discovered the wrap last week and was mighty pleased the date bars were protected and fresh. Her grandmother had willed her this one valuable item—the serving plate. God rest her soul; she'd passed away at the age of 95 after breaking a hip and spending her last three years in a wretched nursing home. Even now, five years later, Mae-June shivered when she thought about the urine-smelling sheets, the blended food, and the Alzheimer's roommate who called Mae-June 'Mom' and tried to sneak out with her at the end of each visit. Kind, unselfish people such as her grandmother shouldn't end up in that kind of place.

Mae-June stepped away from the door and closed it with her hip. A sense of pride filled her as she crossed the church parking lot with her state fair prize-winning date bars. Women begged for her recipe, but she wasn't about to give it out. She herself had to cajole Grandmother Myrtle for the ingredients. Miss Cora, bless her heart, would probably bring brownies from her "Aunt Betty's secret recipe." Mae-June wasn't fooled. Aunt Betty was definitely Betty Crocker and the secret recipe was on the side of the box. Sprinkle the pre-packaged mix into a bowl, crack a couple eggs, pour in a little water and you were good to go. Nevertheless, she liked Cora. Cora was not one of the troublemakers Mae-June would have to warn Pastor Decker about.

Wilfred Wheeler peeked out the window beside the door to the fellowship hall. His black and red flannel shirt was tucked into a pair of jeans hiked up by red suspenders. The jeans rode below what he called his Barrel Belly. Beer Belly was more like it, but Mae-June wasn't one to point out the sins of others. The least Wilfred could have done on such an important night was dress up a little. She herself had spent more time than usual dabbing powder on her nose, adjusting her plaid skirt, straightening the collar on her tan pull-over sweater, and pinning up her gray hair in a bun. You didn't get a second chance to make a first impression. No matter how young and inexperienced the new pastor was, she wanted him to think positively of her.

Wilfred pushed up his square black eyeglasses with a hand reflecting a life of manual labor. A grin nearly cracked his face in half. Mae-June knew what this one-sided grin meant. Forget it, she thought. She wasn't the least bit interested in Wilfred. She'd nursed one husband through to his end and had no plans of re-living that experience.

Wilfred disappeared from the window. The door flung open and Wilfred stepped out, his bald head reflecting light from the lamp post, glowing like a harvest moon. "Mae-June, ain't you prettier than a glob of butter melting on a stack of wheat cakes."

She raised her chin, ignoring the compliment. "Has anyone heard from Pastor Decker?"

"Pastor Joe. Said to call him Pastor Joe. Phoned 'n hour ago. Passing through Knoxville. 'Spect he'll be pulling in mighty soon. Here, let me carry ..." Wilfred reached for the date bars.

Mae-June drew the dish protectively towards herself. As if she'd let that bumbling fool put his paws on a valuable antique platter. "Doin' fine, Wilfred. Doin' just fine." She breezed past him into the fellowship hall and stopped short. The decorating committee had done an excellent job for once. Pastor Joe probably wouldn't even notice the peeling pea-green paint on the cement-block walls or the yellowed linoleum with the pattern scuffed off. Purple streamers arced from beam to beam. Purple and white balloons floated from the chairs. Lavender and white plastic tablecloths graced the tables. Even the plates, cups, and plasticware matched the décor. "Well, I'll be," Mae-June said.

Arlene Tooley stood beside a large glass bowl with grapes painted on the side. She was spooning lime sherbet into red punch.

"Isn't it a little early?" Mae-June asked, already knowing it was. "Why, he might not be here for another fifteen or twenty minutes. That sherbet's gonna melt."

Arlene's hand began to shake. Her eyelids blinked an unknown Morse Code message. Mae-June set her date bars beside the punch bowl and took Arlene's trembling hand. "Now, now," she said. "Don't you worry. We understand. Those of us with more experience will take care of it."

The last thing she wanted was to discourage Arlene Tooley. She'd just started coming back to church after a long absence— five years or more. There were rumors someone had said something to upset her, but Mae-June wasn't sure who or what they said. It didn't take much with Arlene. Some people were so sensitive. You had to tip-toe around them so as not to get them upset.

"Dessert over here, Mae-June." Chipper Mangrove's hose swished against her bulky thighs as she passed. A woman that size shouldn't be wearing a dress with gigantic red flowers. Maybe she was trying to look like a garden. Chipper looked more like a complete arboretum. Mae-June almost snorted, but she wasn't about to enlighten the woman.

"Hold your horses." Mae-June let go of Arlene's hand and picked up the date bars. "I know where the desserts go. Do we have enough food?" Based on what she could see, Mae-June didn't think the ladies had been very generous. At this rate, Pastor Joe wasn't going to be very impressed.

"Cora's bringing her aunt's brownies." Chipper winked and giggled. "Louise is in the kitchen putting together finger sandwiches. We'll have plenty by the time everybody gets here." Chipper sashayed into the kitchen. Her dress couldn't have swayed more if she'd been square dancing.

"This is a *big* day!" Wilfred said from behind Mae-June.

"I suppose," Mae-June said. "Although I'm not looking forward to training another pastor." This would be her fourth, no, fifth new pastor since she became the secretary. Wilsons Corner didn't seem to hold their attention for long.

"But you do such a good job." Wilfred lifted the corner of the wrap covering the date bars.

Mae-June slapped his hand. "Wilfred Wheeler, take your hands off those date bars. They haven't even been blessed yet."

Wilfred licked his finger. "Mm," he said. "Mmm. Got a tiny taste of those date bars and, heavens to Betsy, they are mighty good!"

Mae-June glared at him, opened her mouth, but he spoke first. "I'd best be watchin' at the winder for the pastor." He snapped his suspenders, turned, and settled himself beside the door.

CHAPTER THREE

Up ahead, Grady spotted yellow lights shining through the skeleton of trees and illuminating the outside of Wilsons Corner whatcha macallit. Stained glass windows cast a kaleidoscope of color onto the lawn. In a large lit room, a crowd of people milled about. Some stood with their noses pressed to the window, shading their eyes, and scanning the parking lot and sidewalk leading to the door.

Something was up. Grady hoped he could speak to one person without drawing too much attention to himself or before someone asked if he was saved. He hoped they would ask if he was hungry. He wasn't going to lie. He was starving. His plan was to ask for a lift to the nearest gas station, buy a couple gallons and something to carry it back, pour it into the Pontiac's fuel tank, and be on his way. *His way*. Where was his way? What was his destination? He had no idea.

He stepped from the shadows and crisscrossed the lot between vehicles. A bald man poked his head out of the door to the large room and looked around. He wore a red and black flannel shirt and jeans held up by suspenders. The man pushed up the nosepiece of his square black glasses and raised a plastic cup to his lips.

Grady waved. "Hey, my car —"

The man whipped the cup from his lips and juice spilled onto his plaid flannel shirt. "He's here!" he called into the room and hobbled down the sidewalk. By the time he reached Grady, his breath came in gasps. He grabbed Grady's hand in his own beefy paw and shook enthusiastically. Grady's whole arm flopped like a fish on a dock. "Name's Wilfred," the man said. "Wilfred Wheeler."

"Hey," said Grady. "My name's—." Before he completed his introduction, a noisy crowd swarmed out the door and encircled him—a bunch of old men with canes, a young mother with twin girls, and three white-haired old ladies. Someone slapped him on the back, someone else tried to shake his hand. Wilfred Wheeler placed a hand on his back and drew him towards the entrance.

Grady swallowed hard. This was the friendliest church group he'd ever met, yet he felt uneasy. Was this a cult planning to capture him? Even as his mind objected, his feet climbed four steps and entered a gymnasium-like room with tables and chairs. The place was decorated in purple and white. Off to the side, fruit and sandwiches and cookies and a few different types of dessert bars filled up a whole table. His stomach leaped at the sight. He hoped they would invite him to eat before he escaped. The Twinkies and Coke he'd had for lunch hadn't held him very long.

Wilfred Wheeler directed Grady to a chair and then approached a microphone close to the food table. He raised his hands in front of him, prayer-like, then said, "Let's hear it for

Pastor Joe!" He clapped, and soon everyone joined in, including Grady.

Wilfred pointed to Grady clapping and chuckled. He dropped his hands and said, "Let's bless the food so we can eat. I knows most of ya'll are so hungry your belly thinks your throat's been cut." He bowed his head and the group silenced. Grady observed the folded hands, the bowed heads, the closed eyes, and he mimicked them. If that's what it took to grab a plateful, he was game.

"Dear Lord," Wilfred Wheeler said. "Thank you for Pastor Joe's safe arrival. We pray for your guidance in all he does. Bless this food. May it strengthen our bodies, so we get the energy we need to do your work. Amen."

At the sound of *Amen*, the chitchat in the room resumed. Grady stayed seated at a table watching kids dash for the food table and ladies remove cellophane wrap from food dishes. An old lady with hair white and curly as a newborn lamb stood by the sandwiches, hand to chin, obviously debating her choice. A second woman wearing a white blouse firmly tucked into a plaid skirt, pushed the gray streak in her black hair behind her ear. She placed carrot sticks, potato chips, dip, and two date bars on her plate. The Lamb Lady finally took a finger sandwich off one plate and a second sandwich off another. Grady chuckled. As if choosing a sandwich should be so difficult. Together, the women approached him.

"We made this for you," Lamby said. She dropped her lashes and giggled.

"Thanks," Grady said. He took the plate and stuffed a tiny sandwich into his mouth.

The ladies watched him chew as though they'd never seen anyone chew a sandwich before. He chewed slower with great emphasis in the up and down movement. He wished he could imitate the deer, but his jaw didn't go sideways the way hers did. He swallowed and said, "You didn't have to fix me a plate, but I sure am glad you did. I was starved."

Plaid-Skirt Lady shoved Lamby Lady aside with her hip. "These," she said pointing to the corner of the plate she held. "These are my prize-winning date bars. We usually run out. I wanted to be sure you had a couple of them." She handed him the plate with such gentleness, you would have thought it was made of fancy glasswork, not just an ordinary paper plate.

"I'm not used to this special treatment," he said.

"Better get used to it," Lamby said. "We plan to take good care of you."

"Aha," Grady said. He set down the plate and swiped the back of his hand across his lips. Take care of him? He didn't like the sound of that. The ladies watched in horror at the hand swipe. "My bad," he said. "I couldn't find—" Lamby handed him a purple paper napkin and he wiped his hands and lips until every last crumb was gone. "You know," he said, "I should probably be on my way."

"Not yet," Plaid-Skirt Lady said. "We've got a little welcome for you."

Now his belly was full, Grady eyed the door. He hadn't spoken to anyone about the gas situation yet. Maybe he'd sneak a word with Wilfred or perhaps just sneak out the door.

A little boy, not more than five, touched Grady's leg. "You're tall," he said. His skin was milky white, his red hair was slicked down with some sort of goop, and his eyes were a sharp blue.

Grady patted the boy on the head. "I'll bet you'll be this tall someday," he said.

"I don't think so." The boy clasped his hands together behind his back and swayed to and fro. "My teacher says I have to be tall to play basketball. Do you play basketball?"

It was a simple question, but it struck Grady in the heart. "I used to be on a team," he said. "In college." He remembered back when he was a junior in high school, the tallest kid in his class and full of optimism about the future; especially when Coach Amos retired Otis Chapman as the point guard of the basketball team and gave him the position. Too bad a college basketball scholarship depended on good grades. "You have lots of time to grow," he told the boy. "Sometimes it happens all at once. That's what happened to me. I was just a scrawny kid and all of a sudden I got to be a big kid."

The boy grinned and dashed off announcing, "Pastor Joe said I have lots of time to grow! It happened to him!"

Pastor Joe? Grady raised the last forkful of the prize-winning date bars to his lips when Wilfred Wheeler tapped on the microphone and pointed a long-blade knife in Grady's direction. "We're going to cut the cake now. Will you do the honors?"

Grady chewed the date bar quickly, his mind seeking an explanation for all the attention.

"Come on up," Wilfred said. He rotated the knife in a circle. When Grady didn't move, Wilfred left the mic and set the knife down beside Grady's plate. "I'm sure you can cut a cake for us, can't you, son?"

Grady looked at the knife, then at Wilfred, then at the rest of the group. If cutting the cake meant he could eat a piece, he'd cut the cake then be on his way. He picked up the knife gingerly and stood slowly. The group broke into laughter and clapped. With much bravado, he sauntered over to the cake table. Dark blue flowers ringed the edge of the white frosting. Letters in lighter blue spelled out the words: *Welcome, Pastor Joe.* He raised the knife over his head with both hands, bent his knees, leaned forward. Again, the crowd laughed. He lowered the knife, cut through the center, turned, and bowed.

"Well done!" A man towards the far wall called.

"Thank you," Grady said in his best Elvis impression. "Thank you very much." He swaggered to his seat, hoping the cake was chocolate.

Lamby and Plaid Skirt rushed to the cake table. One cut the cake into pieces a bit too small for Grady's sweet tooth and placed each one on a purple plate. The other stuck white forks into each slice, and a couple of kids delivered them to the tables.

Wilfred tapped Grady on the shoulder. "I'm going to introduce you and then you're up."

"Wait!" Grady waved both hands. "Listen, all I need is a little gas for my car. I ran out at the end of your driveway."

"No problem," Wilfred said. "We'll take care of it after this." He ambled to the front of the room and tapped the microphone.

Grady's heart pounded louder than it had in the woods. Something niggled at the corner of his brain. Something about what the boy said, what the cake said, and what Wilfred said.

When they offered him sandwiches and chips, he thought they were just being friendly. Now it seemed like something more.

Those who had been milling around visiting found empty chairs and sat down with expectant smiles. Wilfred Wheeler's bald head reflected the lights in the room. He stood in front of the microphone and yelled, "Allow me ..."

The microphone squealed a gut-piercing noise. Men and women screamed, a baby to the left howled, and Wilfred jumped back two feet. Grady didn't flinch. The squeal was no louder than the concerts he attended.

"Sorry," called a policeman who pushed his chair away from a table and jumped up.

Blood rushed to Grady's head. He wondered why a cop was present. Did they expect a riot? Was he here to protect the congregation *from* something or protect *someone* from the *congregation*? Had Matt the Rat somehow tracked him here all the way from Orlando?

The cop dashed to a large black speaker in the corner, squatted in front of it, turned some dials, and swiveled round to give Wilfred a thumbs up.

Wilfred nodded back, tapped the microphone again, drew his bulky, chapped lips up close to the mic. "Testing 1-2-3," he said. He gave the thumbs up to the cop still squatting by the speaker. "Thanks, Irving," he said. "Let's try again. Good evening. Let's welcome our new pastor straight from Gordon Conwell Seminary. May I present to you Pastor Joseph Decker." He gave an exaggerated bow. His outstretched hand pointed to Grady.

Grady looked around, waited for Pastor Joseph Decker to step to the mic. No one stood. In fact, more people than not were looking at *him*, and Wilfred Wheeler was signaling to *him*. Grady pointed to himself and shook his head. Suddenly he was hot, perspiring, wobbly in the knees. Something was wrong, terribly wrong. Wilfred nodded. Grady shook his head again. Wilfred came over, grasped Grady's elbow, and half dragged him to the front.

The pleasant laughter from the audience did little to quell Grady's nerves. Sweat beads formed on his forehead and dropped into his ears. His hands shook. All spit evaporated from his mouth. He had to set the record straight. He wasn't this Pastor Joe. He'd run out of gas. He was just a runaway looking for some peace. He hadn't been in a church in years and didn't even know if he believed in the Bible, never mind God. Maybe he'd hold back on the last part, lest someone try to convert him. Wilfred adjusted the mic, nodded at Grady, and stepped aside.

Grady stood awkwardly in front of the mic. "Thanks," he said, his voice a squeaky octave above his usual tone. Fragments of sentences bounced around in his brain like lottery balls in a bingo-looking cage. He doubted they would make sense even if he could catch them. He shoved his trembling hands into the pockets of his jeans as he stepped from one foot to the other.

Focus on one person in the audience Professor Jackson had said in debate class. Someone with a friendly face, someone who seemed receptive and nonjudgmental. Pretend you were speaking only to him. Pretend no one else mattered. The second hand on the clock made a silent full circle as Grady searched the crowd for his savior. He found him in the middle of the third row—the freckle-faced boy with reddish-brown hair who'd asked him about playing basketball. Everyone else dissolved into a hazy mist and Rusty hair stood out in clarity. The boy placed both hands under his thighs on his metal chair and stared without blinking at Grady. Grady focused on two of the boy's large freckles beneath his left eye.

"Good evening," Grady said. He cleared his throat. "It's good to be here. I've waited a long time for this night."

Again, the congregation clapped. Someone shouted, "Amen, Brother!" And from somewhere in the middle of the haze, someone else shouted, "So have we!"

Laughter … Grady heard the laughter. It flowed around Rusty hair, casting an otherworldly glow on the boy. Grady relaxed a little. The group seemed friendly enough. How hard could pastoring be? You didn't have to punch a time clock. Didn't have to report to anybody. Just visit sick people. Listen to other people's problems. Heck. Oops, maybe words like 'heck' weren't allowed from a pastor's lips … by golly, God knows he'd had enough problems in his nineteen years to give advice on just about any topic you could name. "I look forward to getting to know each of you," he said.

He raised his hand above his head in a sort of victory motion, then stepped back. The clapping went on for another two or three minutes. All the clapping and cheering for him felt good. He thought about the deer. His omen. He was, indeed, a lucky man.

CHAPTER FOUR

Grady checked his watch. 9:15. Only the cop who was tending the sound equipment and a few ladies cleaning up in the kitchen remained, along with Wilfred. One woman's legs made a swishing sound as she walked past Grady. Another woman asked the Plaid Skirt woman for the date bar recipe. She said no.

The cop left the sound equipment and approached Grady. He grasped Grady's hand in a firm shake. Grady's arm stiffened with guilt, and the cop chuckled. "Officer Irving Welch, here," he said. "Don't let the uniform scare you, Pastor. I'm a member here and just didn't have time to go home and change after my shift. Wanted to be here to give you a proper greetin'."

Grady tentatively squeezed his hand a little bit tighter. "Thanks, much obliged," he said.

Wilfred interrupted before Irving got in another word. "Come on," he said and placed a hand on Grady's shoulder. "Let me show you the parsonage."

Grady nodded goodbye to Irving, stood a little straighter and followed Wilfred out the door of the church. He wasn't sure what a personage was, but he was willing to find out. As far as pastoring, he knew as much about that as he did a personage, but he could google it. Google knew everything.

"It isn't much," Wilfred said. "We fixed it up best we could."

They rounded the back corner of the church and there stood a yellow cottage. Gold lantern-type lights on either side of the door lit up the brick walkway. Bushes with red berries extended from the front stoop to either end of the house. Three cement steps led to a solid oak door with four frosted glass panels on the top half.

Grady stared until Wilfred nudged him. "Come on. Let me show you the inside." Wilfred walked up the steps, unlocked the door, and handed the keys to Grady. "Welcome home, Pastor Joe." He bowed slightly and gestured for Grady to enter before him.

Slowly, Grady walked up the stairs and stepped into the living room. Slowly, he scanned all he could see. A small brown leather couch and an end table took up one wall, a fireplace took up another. Under the bow window on the front wall was a two-shelf bookcase jammed with books. Two wooden rocking chairs sat in front of a square cut-out in the wall with a tiny kitchen on the other side. A two-seater table with fresh flowers was pushed into a corner near a gas stove.

"It's small," Wilfred said.

"It's the nicest place I've ever lived!" Grady said before filtering how Pastor Joe might have reacted.

"After the wedding, your bride can put her own touch on things. You know women!"

Grady laughed and opened his mouth to object, to say he had no intention of marrying any time soon but caught himself just in time. *He* might not intend to marry soon, but apparently, Pastor Joe did.

"You're probably exhausted after driving from Massachusetts," Wilfred said.

"Massachusetts? What do you mean Massachusetts?"

"I thought you came straight from seminary."

Grady gulped. "A few stops in between," he said.

"Okay, then. Now don't forget, you'll need to turn in your sermon title and scripture by noon tomorrow. We're all anxious to hear your inaugural sermon."

Sermon? All Grady wanted was to crawl into bed and sleep for a week. "When?" he asked. "The sermon … and where?"

Wilfred laughed a hearty laugh, one that jiggled his over-sized belly. "Sorry about that! I didn't even show you the church! Can't miss it. To the right of the fellowship hall. Stained glass windows. Big wide steps. Double doors. 10:30 Sunday morning." He coughed, made a fist, and raised it to his lips as though he were tooting a horn. "Irving and I have this bet. Now don't tell me what you're gonna be preachin' about. He thinks one thing and I think another. But don't tell me now." His eyes twinkled.

"Let's all be surprised," Grady said. Thursday, Friday, Saturday. He'd have to come up with a topic by tomorrow and spend the next few days writing. *Great,* Grady thought. That's what got him in this mess—too many D's last semester. But hey, nobody would be checking footnotes. Challenging, but he'd come up with something to pass as a sermon. Thank God for Google!

Wilfred clapped Grady's shoulder. "Good idea," he said. "I wouldn't want Irving to think I cheated or nothin'." He turned to leave and then looked over his shoulder. "Almost forgot." He reached into the breast pocket of his flannel shirt and withdrew a folded paper. "There's a computer back in the study. Here's the password. All the information about the e-mail account is here, too. Only you and Mae-June have access to the account."

"Mae-June?"

"Your secretary. She didn't introduce herself to you? She's the one who makes the date bars." Wilfred licked his chapped lips. "Prize-winning date bars."

Plaid-Skirt Lady was his secretary. Great.

"You got the check she sent, right?"

"Yeah, Yeah. Of course."

"Very good. Just something to get you started."

Grady nodded, already regretting saying he'd received the check. It wouldn't have been a lie to say no, and if he had said no, they probably would have issued him another one. He could have cashed it and been on his way in the middle of the night.

"By the way," Wilfred said, "the phone in the church office rings four times and then transfers here. You don't have to answer it if you don't want to. After it rings three times in here, it goes into voice mail in the office."

"Okay," Grady said.

"So, is there anything else I can do for you before we call it a night?"

"Yeah," Grady said. "Gas for my car."

Wilfred snapped his fingers. "Almost forgot. Come on. I keep a spare gas can in my truck for times such as these." Together, they headed out the door.

Wilfred whistled at the sight of the Pontiac. "Classic," he said. "You must have had some big job in Boston when you were in seminary to afford this baby."

Not wanting to start off his career as a pastor with a lie, Grady decided to lead with the truth. A stripped-down version of the truth, but the truth, nonetheless. "1956. My stepdad got it from a friend. Rebuilt it."

Wilfred examined the Pontiac from bumper to bumper, whistling and rubbing the shiny surface. "You help him?"

"No." Grady stepped from foot to foot pretending to be cold.

Wilfred placed a gentle hand on the roof and turned to Grady. "And after working on this classic he gave it to you? Wow! He must think highly of you."

Grady choked. Yeah, as if. Right about now Matt the Rat was probably sending out search dogs looking for him just to get his car back. But what'd he expect? He kicked Grady out. How did he think he'd get anywhere without a car? Grady hoped the darkness hid his flushed face. He scrambled for a truth or a half-truth. He wasn't about to say he stole it. Then his eyes set on the Florida license plate. He settled on a lie. "My step-dad sold it to a guy in Florida. He asked me to deliver it … one of these days. Tennessee being closer to Florida and all."

Wilfred didn't move and Grady studied his shadowed face, hoping he'd buy the story. Wilfred nodded slowly. "Oh," he said. "Makes sense." He patted the car roof and said, "Let's fill 'er up."

Sprawled on the couch in the yellow cottage, Grady unpacked the events of the day. He didn't want to remember all of it, but the scene played itself in his mind like a 3D movie. He didn't feel guilty about taking Matt the Rat's car. Served him right after what he said and did. All over nothing. "It's my life," Grady mumbled to the room. "Flunked a couple tests and lost the basketball scholarship. Not the end of the world." Matt the Rat didn't have to go ballistic. It wasn't any of his business, when you thought about it.

Grady rubbed his shoulder and the side of his face. Maybe he should have slugged Matt the Rat back. Nah. Taking the car hurt him worse. But his mother. He'd left her alone with him. Grady could only hope she'd find her own way of escape.

Sermon … what the heck was he going to talk about in a sermon? *Language*, he reminded himself. *Watch your language.* Didn't want to be excommunicated before he'd even begun. Even though he was exhausted and wanted to forget the sermon, Grady felt drawn to the bookcase under the front window. He rolled off the couch and sat cross-legged on the floor in front it and read the titles. *Amazing Grace* by Phillip Yancey. He didn't have the slightest idea what grace was, never mind why it was so amazing. *Forgive to Live* by Dick Tibbits. It would be hypocritical to deliver a sermon about forgiveness. He'd never forgive that idiot Matt.

He slid a copy of the Bible from the middle shelf—the first time he remembered holding one in his hands. The cover had the authoritative smell of leather. The pages were so thin, he had a hard time turning them. He flipped through. Names of people and places jumped out. Adam, Moses, Lot, Jericho, the Red Sea. He'd never heard of any of them.

Then he noticed something about a deer. He folded over the corner of the page and fell asleep on the floor dreaming about a white-tailed deer eating a piece of cake. The face of the deer morphed into a man and Grady knew it was Pastor Joe. Pastor Joe exhaled blue curly-cue letters. Grady watched each letter float towards him, then through him. Y-O-U-F-R-A-U-D.

CHAPTER FIVE

Mae-June reached into her kitchen cabinet and pulled out a china dessert plate. She arranged the two remaining date bars on it and folded the plastic wrap around the plate. She opened the refrigerator and placed the plate to the left of the coffee creamer on the second shelf. One for lunch tomorrow. One for lunch on Friday. Maybe she should have wrapped them separately. Oh well, it was too late to think about that now. *Wait a minute!* She had an idea. Why not start things off right with that whipper snapper pastor. She'd give them to him.

She stood there a moment staring absently at the contents on the shelf. Something was not right, and it wasn't in her refrigerator. She closed the door. The idea buzzed in her head like a pesky mosquito trapped in her bedroom on a warm summer night. It was the party for the pastor. The ladies had done a good job with the function hall decorations. Clean-up was smooth and quick. And Pastor Joe seemed pleased. He especially liked the date bars. Nevertheless, something was not right.

The reception had been too long. That was one thing. Stick a microphone in front of Wilfred Wheeler and he'd wax eloquent. As if he had something important to say. As if anybody cared to listen. A few people did, now she thought about it. Irving Welch, for one. But, as the saying goes, birds of a feather …

Wilfred. The audacity of that man. Tried to sneak a date bar even before the blessing. How had Sylvia, bless her soul, put up with him … how many years did they say at her funeral last year? Mae-June couldn't remember exactly, but she figured it was nearly half a century. Half a century with Wilfred Wheeler underfoot in your kitchen and hogging the blankets on your bed was more than Mae-June could have stood. That's for sure.

She walked over to the sink, squirted a bit of pink dish soap on a sponge and ran it under the hot water. She washed every crumb off grandmother Myrtle's dessert platter. Her date bars had been the hit of the evening. Again. Maybe the cake baker had been jealous that Mae-June's date bars had stolen the limelight. The cake was atrocious. The blue letters on top were hardly legible. Mae-June had to read them twice to figure out what they said. Looked like a first grader wrote them. And the cake was too dry. Way too dry. Way, way too dry. She wondered who made it. She'd have to poke around and find out. She'd be sure whoever it was didn't embarrass themselves at the next big event the church hosted.

Still, something was not right. More than the cake. Mae-June snapped out the kitchen light and made her way to the bedroom. She sat on the edge of her bed and removed her shoes. Back in the day, she could wear heels and dance all night. Now, after three hours of simply walking, she had to sit down. She rubbed her feet, flinching when she hit a particularly tender spot. Something was not right, but it wasn't her shoes or her feet. She hobbled down the hall to the bathroom.

She squeezed the perfect amount of Crest onto the bristles of her electric toothbrush and raised it to her mouth. The movement of her hand caught her eye in the mirror of the medicine cabinet. Her veiny, wrinkled hands gave away her age. They didn't match her face. Years of expensive face creams and care with the sun had left her face almost wrinkle free, but her hands told the truth. She'd been on the planet four score and…oh what good did it do to count.

No matter how her hands looked, Mae-June was proud of all they'd accomplished. Those hands could play *The Holy City* on the piano like no one else in the church. Those hands could type a letter faster than a pastor could dictate. Those hands had cleaned vomit from her dying husband's lips. They'd stroked his face and assured him she'd be all right after he was gone when, in fact, she wasn't all right at all. Not that she allowed herself the luxury of letting anyone know.

Those hands had raised a son, Jimmy-Lee, Jr. Spanked him when he deserved it. Caressed him when he didn't. There was one thing those hands had not done—wave goodbye to Jimmy-Lee, Jr. when he snuck out in the middle of the night. How long ago now? Five years, she guessed. Without a word or backward glance.

She wondered where he was. What he was doing with his own hands. She prayed he remembered his upbringing and remained a good boy; but even more so, not that she would say it aloud, she hoped he would come home.

Mae-June rinsed her mouth, dried the toothbrush on the lace-edged hand towel looped through the brass ring mounted on the wall beside the sink. She snapped off the light and returned to her bedroom.

Mae-June hated to think it, but the problem might be Pastor Joe. The congregation appointed a search committee that had chosen him. Lord knows, if she'd been on that committee, she would have brought them to their senses. She had spoken to him on the phone since his hire. Twice.

The church treasurer needed his address so he could forward a "just to get you started" check. Which, in Mae-June's opinion, was unheard of. Gifting money to someone before they worked a day on the job was outrageous. No one paid Mae-June in advance of her work. Trusting a perfect stranger with hard-earned money was a huge risk. And what would the Lord think about them advancing money to Pastor Joe? It was the Lord's money, after all. The congregation worked hard and, in good faith, slipped their money into the offering plate. They probably needed it more than that young man.

The second time Mae-June had spoken to him on the phone, they'd talked a good fifteen minutes or so. She'd warned him about the troublemakers and volunteered to fill him in on what needed fixing, and she didn't mean janitorial fixing. He seemed too self-assured when he didn't have a clue what he was in for. In person, he was the exact opposite. He appeared like he didn't know what anyone was doing, never mind himself. Almost outside the circle of reality.

She'd try to give Pastor Joe the benefit of the doubt even if her gut was telling her otherwise. She'd been trusting her gut before the new pastor was born. Right now, her gut was screaming something was wrong. Nevertheless, he was here to do the Lord's work, and far be it from her to be a stumbling block to that mission.

Mae-June slipped on her flannel nightgown with the tiny blue flowers and lowered herself with some difficulty to kneel beside her bed. "Dear Lord," she prayed. "Help this transition be smooth for all of us. Help young Pastor Decker, I mean Pastor Joe, to be a fast learner. Give me wisdom and discernment so I know what to teach him first. Give me patience as I work with him. May his sermons touch the hearts of those who need it. Amen."

She crawled into bed and covered herself with the faded yellow and green quilt her mother had made as a wedding gift. She fingered the fabric Mama's fingers had touched, praying for Mama's wisdom. When she finally fell asleep, she dreamt of Pastor Joe standing behind the pulpit with blue cake frosting coating his lips. From the front pew, she kept wiping her lips, hoping he'd get the idea something was wrong. Instead, the blue frosting slowly spread across his face. In the dream, she thought, "He'll be the hardest one yet to train."

CHAPTER SIX

Joe Decker heard *Beep, beep, beep* like a truck backing up. Then a soothing voice crackled from somewhere. *Dr. Greene, dial extension 251. Dr. Greene, extension 2-5-1.* His throat felt dry, closed off. He tried to swallow and gagged. Slowly, he willed his eyes to open. He was in a bed with silver bars on the sides. A silver pole outside the bars. Clear tubes snaked their way from the silver pole to his hand.

An unfamiliar face appeared above him. A woman's face. She wore glasses. Her brown hair was pulled away from her face. She smiled. "Mr. Decker?"

He nodded. The motion shot a bullet of pain down his neck. He winced.

"Mr. Decker, my name is Rita. I'm your nurse today. Do you know where you are?"

Joe thought back to the last thing he remembered. He was driving. A large green sign.

Knoxville, 10 miles. A phone call. Who was it? Oh yes, a man. Wilfred Wheeler. Wilfred Wheeler from Wilsons Corner Bible Believing Congregation.

"Tennessee," he whispered to Rita. "Knoxville."

"Very good," Rita answered. "You sound as if you could use some water." She lifted a paper cup and adjusted the bendable straw. She slipped a hand under his neck and helped him raise his head.

The water was cool, yet it burned his throat. The second sip was easier. He gulped water until he coughed. Rita took the cup away. She dabbed the side of his mouth with a brown paper napkin.

"What happened?" Joe let his head drop back onto the pillow, his strength zapped from the simple act of supporting his own head.

"What do you remember?" Rita asked. She tugged at his sheet and blanket, lifted them up and let them fall onto his body, delivering a cool draft of air.

"Driving," he said.

"Yes. On I-75."

"Looking for a route heading south west." He thought hard. What happened after the Knoxville sign and after the phone call?

"Then what happened?" Rita prodded.

"I don't know," he answered. *A flash of a tree. Brake, brake. BRAKE! A squeal of tires. Lights flashing.*

Rita leaned on the silver bars that imprisoned him. "The police say you lost control. Went off the road. No skid marks."

Drop. He dropped something. The phone. Bent to reach for it. Swerve. Slide. He pressed the brake pedal. It wouldn't move.

Jammed. PHONE UNDER THE PEDAL! Blackness. "Anyone else?" he asked. "Did I hit anyone?" If he'd killed or injured anyone, how would he ever live with himself?

"No. Just you." She patted the blanket. "You only did damage to yourself. Compound fracture of the femur. Shattered ankle. Cuts and bruises. You've been in surgery. The doctors have patched you back together. You'll heal just fine. No worries."

He nodded, using every brain cell he had to comprehend her words, the gap in memory, and the sense of it.

"I need to check on my other patients," Rita said. She reached for a cord on his bed and placed it within his reach. "If you need me, just press the button."

He listened to her rubber-soled shoes squeak across the tiled floor and out into the hallway. His room was neither dark nor light. Grayish. He didn't know if it was day, night, or morning. He didn't know how long he'd been here or if the hospital had contacted anyone. How could they, he thought with a start. How would they know who to call? The googled directions to Wilsons Corner Bible Believing Congregation had been on the passenger's seat. Probably thrown out the window in the crash. Roxanne? Would they have called Roxanne? God, he hoped not. He hadn't told her about this trip. Had been waiting for the right moment. Which never came.

His parents were still in the Congo. They wouldn't be flying in for another three weeks for the wedding. *The wedding!* How was he going to stand at the altar? How was he going to hold Roxanne in his arms on the dance floor while the band played Whitney Houston's "I Will Always Love You"? They'd spent hours choosing a first dance song. He'd like one she didn't like, then she'd declare she found the perfect song and he'd hate it. All that time wasted. He wouldn't be dancing now.

And the honeymoon! How was he going to …? He tried not to think about it.

Joe pressed the buzzer. When Rita's voice sounded over the intercom, he asked, "Do you know where my cell phone is? I need to make a call."

"I'll be there in a minute," Rita answered.

While Joe waited, he composed his explanation to Roxanne. He would tell her the truth, but in what order, in what voice tone, and the big question—*why?* He'd plotted three scenarios before Rita's so-called minute delivered her to his doorway.

"Mr. Decker?" she said. "Your phone did not come in with your personal belongings. I'm guessing it was lost in the crash."

Joe leaned up on one elbow. "I really need to call my fiancée. She has no idea where I am."

"We do have your wallet," Rita said. "You can charge a call using your bedside phone."

He dialed Roxanne's number and it rang once, twice, three times, four times. He pictured her fumbling in her purse for her cell phone. He told her to buy a purse with a built-in pocket for a cell phone, but she liked the multi-colored leather shoulder bag she purchased in Tijuana on vacation with her parents some time ago. Fumble past car keys. Fumble past a couple packets of tissues. It seemed she always needed them for something—to catch a sneeze, dab at her lipstick, bandage a paper cut. Fumble past gas station receipts. Fumble past lipstick and blush and a miniature-sized bottle of hairspray.

"Hello?" Roxanne's voice was anxious.

"It's Joe."

"But this isn't your number," she said. "Some weird area code I've never seen before."

"I lost my phone," he said. "I'm in—"

"Phewf." She laughed. "For a minute there, I thought something had happened. I'm so glad you called. I've had such a busy week, I didn't even have time to call you. I went up to Danvers with the girls. For our fitting. I told you, right?"

"Yes," he said. "I was —"

"Ashley's dress came in a size smaller than she ordered."

"Roxanne!"

"But the tailor said he could have it ready in time for the wedding."

He was going to have to interrupt her. Once Roxanne got going, the only way to de-rail her was to interrupt. Having grown up as an only child raised by parents who believed in proper etiquette, interrupting was difficult for Joe. Roxanne had grown up in a family with eight children. Interrupting and talking over each other was the norm. He wasn't sure he'd ever get used to it.

"Roxanne! I'm in the hospital! I was in an accident."

Silence.

He hated it when she gave him no option but to be rude. Sometimes, even now, a little more than a month from the wedding, he wondered about their relationship. Roxanne was fun-loving; laughing with her made him feel high. But pastoring was serious business. He probably shouldn't laugh as much as he did when he was with Roxanne. He wasn't sure if she would enhance his ministry or be a hindrance.

"But you're okay?" Her voice was tentative.

"Broken leg." He pushed himself up in the bed and moaned with pain. "The nurse says I'll mend in no time."

"Did they bring you to Mass General? I'll be right over."

"That's the thing." He closed his eyes, placed a finger over his right lid. The dreaded moment. "I'm in Tennessee." He waited for a response. When the hum of silence was more than he could tolerate, he said, "Roxanne? Are you there?"

"I don't understand," she said. "I don't remember you telling me you were taking a trip to Tennessee. How long did you plan to be gone? There are so many last-minute details for the wedding. I can't do it alone."

"I know," he said. "I know." Why hadn't he told her? Any reason he conjured up now seemed thoughtless. After all, his life would soon become her life, too. He should have discussed it with her. They should have decided together, but there was no time. It all happened so fast. "I should have told you," he said. "We should have discussed it."

"Discussed it?"

He heard the hesitation in her voice.

"I got a call. A few days ago. I didn't want you to know until I had worked something out. Church in the Meadows canceled out. I've secured a position at Wilsons Corner Bible Believing Congregation."

It took him a moment to decode the squeak that traveled from Boston to Knoxville. "What? Are you talking about that tiny church in that tiny town a million miles away? Tell me you didn't. You turned that down months ago, I know you did."

"I think it's going to work out," he said. "Maybe I turned it down too fast. The Lord leads—"

"But what about me, Joe? What about me?"

He had never heard this tone in her voice. Anger mixed with hurt mixed with disbelief mixed with probably more emotions than he could identify.

"We're in this together. We'll make it work," he said.

"Not if you don't even consider my input in a major life-altering decision."

"I do … Roxanne? Are you there? Roxanne?"

CHAPTER SEVEN

Thursday morning, Grady awoke uncertain of his surroundings. At home he slept on a single bed mattress on the floor, no sheets, wrapped in a blanket. Wherever he was now, he was sleeping in a double bed, an actual bed, with clean white sheets, two blankets, and a white bedspread with little knots of fabric all over it. He hoisted himself up on one elbow and looked around. He was facing a dresser with his jeans draped across the top. A picture of Jesus with a child on His lap hung above the dresser.

Slowly the memory of last night came back to him. Running out of gas. A blow-out party for him. Falling asleep on the floor. The cake dream. Crawling into bed at some point was hazy. He remembered bumping into unfamiliar furniture on his way to the bedroom. He smiled, placed his hands behind his neck, and lay back on the pillow. Thursday morning. Nothing to do but get his sermon title to the secretary. *Lessons from a Deer.* That's what he'd decided on. He'd figure out the details over the next three days.

This job was going to be a cake walk. No wonder he dreamt about cakes.

At 8:00 a.m., he wandered into the kitchen and opened the refrigerator. Stocked. He wondered if he was still dreaming. Milk, orange juice, apples, bread, peanut butter, jam, eggs. You name it, it was in there. He opened the cabinet to the right of the sink. Cheerios. Wheaties. Grits. On the shelf above the cereal, he spotted cans of Progresso Chicken Noodle Soup, Chef Boyardee Ravioli, boxes of spaghetti, jars of sauce. This was amazing. He wondered how often they stocked the place, and if he could add stuff he liked to the order. He fixed himself a bowl of Cheerios and milk, carried it to the living room, plopped onto the couch, and flicked on the television.

"… Floods across the plains."

Click.

"Stretch one knee out. Bend. You've got it."

Click.

"… now to our correspondent at the White House."

Click. Click. Click.

Grady settled on the movie *My Cousin Vinnie*. He'd seen it half a dozen times and knew what was going to happen. Setting down the remote, he spooned cereal into his mouth and watched Vinnie's girlfriend give expert testimony on tires.

Tires … cars … the Pontiac. Grady chuckled, imagining the expression on Matt the Rat's face, then fear smothered the humor. He choked on a Cheerio and coughed until he thought he'd never catch a normal breath again. What was he thinking taking Matt's first love? The guy had spent months under the hood tinkering away and then months on the outside replacing bumpers and mirrors and burnt-out brake lights.

Why had he stolen—no, borrowed—that car? Sitting on a comfortable couch in the peace of the yellow cottage after a good night's sleep, he had to admit taking the car hadn't been the best decision he ever made. But how would they find him? He shoveled another spoonful of Cheerios into his mouth. Yeah, how would they ever find him?

Vinnie's girlfriend chawed her gum, and Grady flicked off the TV. He set the cereal bowl down on the coffee table and checked his watch. 8:30. How would he spend the rest of this glorious free day? He'd have to do something about a sermon at some point. Tomorrow. Tomorrow he'd write up something about that deer. No need to worry about it today.

He decided to check out the rest of the personage to see what secrets it held. He tossed the cereal bowl and spoon into the sink and began his investigation. In one closet, he found a basketball. He picked it up and headed outdoors to the parking lot where he'd seen a hoop.

He dribbled under his knees, behind his back. He studied the basket, set up for the next shot, bent his knees, flicked his wrist. The ball bounced off the backboard, circled the rim, dropped through the net. "Yes!" he shouted, sweat sliding off his nose, dripping onto his upper lip. He sniffed, caught the ball, dribbled a distance he judged to be half-court if there'd been lines painted on the pavement. He pivoted, set up for another shot.

Out of the corner of his eye, he spied a woman standing on the grass off to the right of the basket. She looked vaguely familiar. He held the ball against his side with his right arm. "May

I help you?" He wiped the sweat off his face with the bottom of his shirt.

"Pastor Joe?" Her voice was hesitant, yet her demeanor was of one under control.

Her black hair streaked with grey near her ears was held in place by long, black bobby pins. She wore a grey tweed suit similar to the one his mother recently turned over to Goodwill.

"That's me. Pastor Joe. Pleased to meet you."

"We met last night. I'm Mae-June. Your secretary."

"Oh yes," he said, recognition dawning. Plaid Skirt Lady. He strode towards her, wiped his sweaty hand on his old gym shorts and extended the hand towards her. She looked at it and raised her chin a little higher. This old lady was the master of the stink eye.

"I've been waiting in the office," she said, her voice high and accusing. "Isn't that what we decided when you called last week?"

"Oh, oh." He stepped from one foot to the other, bobbed his head. "Sorry. My bad. In all the confusion, guess I forgot."

"Forgot?" Her left eyebrow twitched, and her voice lowered a notch. "How could you forget your first day at a new job?"

Grady dribbled the basketball at his side, faster and faster. "Of course, of course. I'm so sorry. Look, I'll get on some clothes and be in the office in a few—" He turned and sprinted to the yellow cottage feeling her eyes bore into his back.

Back in the personage, he pulled on jeans and an Orlando Magic t-shirt. He smoothed down his hair in the mirror, took a look at the t-shirt and decided it wasn't the best thing to wear on his first day. He rummaged through the duffle bag, produced two balled up Disney t-shirts and one from the university basketball team. *Great.* At the bottom of the bag, he found a pink three-button golf shirt—a Christmas gift from his mom. It still had the tags on. Although he originally wondered why she had chosen a pink shirt, now he was glad she had. He picked it up, shook it out, ripped off the tag, ran his hand down it to smooth out the wrinkles. It would have to pass. He let the front door slam shut behind him and jogged across the parking lot.

The church door Grady had entered last night was locked. He skipped down the steps into the parking lot, remembered what Wilfred Wheeler had said, and looked to the right. Ah, big wide steps, double doors. That was the door he was supposed to go in when he preached on Sunday. Maybe it was unlocked now. He jogged over to it, yanked open the door, and stepped inside a large lobby. Straight ahead were two sets of double doors and on either side of him was a hallway. One hallway was dark but the other was lit. He heard someone in the room closest to him. Mae-June, he presumed, but before he relinquished himself to whatever she had in mind, he decided to peek inside the double doors. Must be the actual church.

Slowly, Grady opened the door and tiptoed to the front. Dim emergency lights gave the place an eerie feel. He counted ten rows of pews divided by two aisles. The pews cast elongated shadows on the walls and carpet. In front of the pews was a raised platform with a lectern in the middle and behind it, three heavy wooden chairs with velvet cushions. Behind that was a floor to ceiling velvet curtain, like something you'd see at the movie theater or on the stage of a school play. A piano dominated the space on the left between the front row and the raised platform, while a small organ complemented it on the right.

Grady climbed three steps to the raised platform and crossed over to the lectern. *His* lectern. He grasped it with both hands and looked out over his people-less congregation. He was supposed to speak to them in just a couple of days? What in the world was he going to say that would not blow his cover? Who was this Pastor Joe he was supposed to be imitating? Lucky these people didn't know Pastor Joe very well either if they thought he was the man.

One of the doors in the back opened and Mae-June stuck her head in. "Oh, there you are," she said.

He gripped the sides of the pulpit tighter and his knees trembled. A one-person congregation petrified him. What was he going to do on Sunday? Over the next couple of days, he'd have to practice climbing the two steps and standing behind this pulpit and looking out over this church. "Yeah," he said with the quake in his voice. "Just seeing what it looks like from up here." She didn't look fooled and he didn't blame her.

Mae-June sat primly behind her desk and gestured to the guest chair on the other side of it. Grady eased himself into the chair, feeling awkward and unsure, like when he got called into the principal's office. Mae-June's desk was stacked with papers, unopened envelopes, and a small pile of pink index cards.

"Pastor Westbrook reviewed the cards on Monday mornings," she began without preamble. "But since you are just getting here on Thursday, I think we should do it today."

Grady eyed the cards, hoping Mae-June would explain their significance without his having to ask. When she didn't volunteer any information, he said, "I'll review the pink cards."

She picked up the cards and handed them to him. Score one for Mae-June, he thought. He set them down on the edge of her desk. Her eyebrows wrinkled.

"What?" he said. "Can't I just leave them there 'til we're done?"

Her eyebrows rose. "I suppose," she said, a little huffy in Grady's opinion.

Didn't she report to him? She was acting more like the teacher who monitored detention. What would Pastor Joe do, Grady wondered. Should he try to grab back control? No, he'd sit tight. See how the rest of this session went. He didn't want to alienate her. She could be an asset to him by filling in the blanks of how he could succeed at this job—or she could be his downfall by recognizing his lack of ... lack of ... his lack.

She leaned back stiffly with a tight-lipped expression. "After Pastor Westbrook reviewed the cards, he looked over the weekend mail." She pushed the pile of unopened envelopes across the desk.

He had to hand it to her—she was organized. And the way she kept bringing up Pastor Westbrook's name, Grady wondered if she mighta had something going with the man. Whatever. He needed to get on Mae-June's good side. He'd have to be a combination of the old Pastor Westbrook and the new Pastor Joe, neither of whom he'd met, but she seemed to have a handle on both of them.

"Going forward," Mae-June said, "we'll meet on Friday afternoon and I'll give you the schedule for the coming week."

Schedule? Pastors had schedules? Grady opened his mouth to say 'aye, aye captain,' then decided against it.

"Do you have a question?" she asked.

"No, ma'am." He flapped the air between them. "You're doing a fine job. Proceed."

"Okay then. This morning we'll go over the agenda for the board meeting, which is next Tuesday." She slapped a paper in front of him. "I typed up the agenda based on the tabled items of last month and what you and I discussed on the phone last week. I'm sure you'll find everything in order."

"Board meeting?" he asked. "Who will be there?"

"The board," she said dryly.

He laughed. She didn't. He bit his lip. "I mean, like anyone I met last night?"

"I don't know who all you met last night," she said. "Most of them were there. You'll see the names on the top of the sheet where I listed who was there last time and who was absent."

He glanced at the names and only recognized Wilfred Wheeler and Mae-June. "So, like, what if I have changes?" he asked.

"Pastor Westbrook trusted my work. You should have no changes. But if you do, Tuesday morning is fine." She took a deep breath, let it out. "You're different than I expected," she said.

"Oh, really?" Grady picked up the pink cards, tapped them against the desk, made sure all the corners lined up. "How's that?"

"Your hair. Your clothes." She pointed in apparent disapproval. "You never said anything about basketball when we talked on the phone. Forgetting to start work? You seemed so eager to take the reins."

Grady looked down at his shirt. The best he had. Clothes would be a problem. He patted down his hair. A trim would help pull off this charade.

"You don't seem as serious in person." She folded her hands and placed them on her thighs.

"Trust me," Grady said. "I'm definitely serious about making my time here a success."

Mae-June's voice rose a bit. "Nevertheless, we'll be a team. You and me. You have a lot of good plans. Things I thought should have been instituted around here a long time ago."

She laughed. He didn't. She clamped her lips together, slapped a yellow paper down on the desk. He read the word SCHEDULE in large font at the top of the page. "I always print your schedule on yellow paper," she told him.

"Yellow paper," Grady repeated. "Pink cards." He leaned forward, elbow on one knee, thumb and forefinger pressed into his bottom lip and started reading the schedule.

"Tomorrow morning you have the Blue List," Mae-June instructed.

Another color?

She slapped a blue paper down on top of the yellow paper beside the pink cards before he had a chance to read but a few lines. A list of names, addresses, and telephone numbers covered the entire blue page.

He waited for an explanation. She paused longer than he could stand. He raised his head and looked at her with questioning eyes.

"Visitation list," she said. "Members who haven't been to church in a while because they supposedly are too ill."

She emphasized the words *members* and *supposedly* in such a way he knew she was making a point, but he wasn't sure what the point was.

"Monday morning you have marital counseling with the Riddles in the morning. As I said, Tuesday evening is board meeting. Wednesday evening is prayer meeting."

"Riddles?" he said. "Is it a riddle or is someone's name actually Riddle?"

She glared at him and spoke as if each word were in a column of words, not a sentence. "Their name is Riddle. Back to your schedule. On Thursday—"

Grady descended into MTTYL, or mittle, as he pronounced it. He had perfected the method in high school. *Make Them Think You're Listening.* He planted a pleasant smile on his face, a look of sincere interest in his eyes, and tightened the muscles in his neck and upper back so his head wouldn't droop. From that point on, Mae-June morphed into Ferris Bueller's teacher, and all he could think about was riddles.

What does the sea otter use for money? Sand Dollars.

What city has no people? Electricity.

What stays in one corner but travels around the world? A stamp.

After a length of time he could not quantify, Grady heard the words *credit card* and immediately snapped to attention. "For pre-approved church business." Mae-June said. She pushed the credit card across the desk. "Save the receipts so I can reconcile the bill each month."

"Uh, huh," he said, curbing his eagerness to grab his plastic ticket to freedom. "Got it."

Pre-approved church business. New shirts and a haircut didn't need pre-approval, he decided. Or, better yet, should he just take it and drive away? No, that wouldn't be ethical.

"Any questions?" Mae-June asked.

"Yeah, actually." Grady stretched his arms as far over his head as he could and yawned. He noticed her look of disapproval. "How do I go about ordering food for the kitchen?"

"What do you mean?" Her mouth contorted into an indescribable shape.

"Food. The cupboards are stocked, but I prefer chocolate Cheerios to plain Cheerios. Who do I tell about that?"

She placed both hands on the edge of her desk as if holding on for dear life. "You can't be serious."

Grady's face flushed.

"You do your own shopping," she said. "That was just a welcome gesture."

"Oh, I—"

"Let me show you to your office." She pushed her chair away from her desk.

Grady stood and meekly followed her down the hall. How was he supposed to know about the food? She couldn't hold that against him, could she? Mae-June turned the knob on the last door on the right. Grady noted the plaque on the wall beside it that read *Pastor's Study.* It was a corner office with two walls of windows overlooking woods. Outside, the sky was the color of Marge Simpson's hair and halfway between the building and the first stand of trees, a small brown rabbit munched on a bed of wilted white flowers.

Inside, a brilliantly waxed desk was arranged to take in the view of both windows. There was nothing on the desktop except for a phone with four square clear buttons and one red button. On the edge of the desk was a brass nameplate engraved with PASTOR JOE.

He had an office with a view! He wanted to hide out in here forever to enjoy the peace while awaiting the paycheck.

Mae-June studied him a moment, then without a word, she retreated, closing the door behind her. Grady slid into the high-backed chair behind the desk. He swiveled right and left a few times, feeling important, then he picked up the pink cards she'd given him and read a few out loud.

"Karl Blackstone's doctor said he needs a partial knee replacement. Pray God will heal him, so he won't have to have surgery."

"Suzanne Simms' daughter is giving her a hard time. She's 16. Pray she will see the error of her ways and give her heart to the Lord."

"Albert Jason has been reconciled to his father. Our prayers have been answered! Praise the Lord!"

Gossip. That's all this was. People's private goings on with the word 'prayer' thrown in. He wondered how Suzanne Simms' daughter would feel if she found out a group of people was praying she would become someone else. Or what Albert Jason's father would think if he knew people he didn't know knew all about him. Grady opened the top drawer of his desk and tossed in the pink cards. Deal with that later. Not sure how. Did Google have anything about pink cards? He'd have to check.

The mail. Luckily, three were ads—a Piggly Wiggly Grocery Store, Ace Hardware, and one that appeared to be a ladies' dress shop. He trashed those and placed the three unopened white envelopes into the top drawer along with the pink cards. On the edge of his desk sat a marble open book with a clock etched on the top of it. 11:00.

He snoozed. He played solitaire on his iPhone. He wandered to the window and gazed at the pastoral scene. Funny. He'd never made the connection between a pastoral scene and someone being a pastor. He wondered how words got their meanings. Who was the first one to come up with the term *pastoral scene*?

At noon Grady heard a knock on the door. He tossed his iPhone into the top drawer with the pink cards and grabbed the schedule Mae-June had printed on the yellow paper, not to be confused with the Blue List. He grabbed a pen and called, "Come in."

Mae-June entered with a wooden tray. "I made you quiche for your first day." She set the tray on his desk. Two slices of some kind of egg pie. *Quiche?* A sectioned orange, some type of red juice, and two date bars.

"I was going to have the date bars myself," she said. "But I thought you'd appreciate them. They're better the first day. But then, you had two last night, so you know how good they are." She stepped back with her hands folded in front of her.

"Thanks," he stumbled. "Wow. Homemade food. So much better than school cafeteria or canned." He reached for the juice and sipped.

Her brow furrowed. "I assumed you had an apartment in seminary. Cooked your own food."

He choked on the juice. "Yeah, yeah. So busy. Just so busy." He dismissed her point with a wave. "Breakfast in my apartment. Lunch in the cafeteria. Supper, half here, half there."

"I suppose Roxanne is a good cook. That's important. She'll be expected to entertain. Maybe have parishioners over."

"We'll see, won't we?" he said with a straight face.

Mae-June's eyes darted from side to side. "Enjoy your lunch," she said, stepping towards the door. "Don't get used to it. See you in my office at 1:00 as planned."

"Looking forward to it." He picked up the fork, cut off about a third of the quiche and stuffed it in his mouth.

CHAPTER EIGHT

Grady had suggested they meet in his office after lunch. He wanted the upper hand, but Mae-June insisted she and Pastor Westbrook had always met in her office. She was in control, not him, he thought, and the smirk on her face confirmed it. He grimaced but decided it wasn't worth the fight.

"So," she said. "What do you think of the agenda?"

A cactus sat on the corner of her desk and Grady decided it was an appropriate choice of plants for Mae-June.

"Agenda? I left it in my office." He stood. "I'll go get it." He jogged out the door and down the hall to his office. *Keep it together. Do what you gotta do. Just think of the peace in that cottage. Just think of hiding in your own office behind closed doors. Just think of that paycheck in a couple of weeks. Focus.*

He snatched the paper from his desk and returned to Mae-June's office. "It looks like I open with a devotional," he said. He'd have to look up that word on Google.

"Yes," Mae-June said. "After that, Sally Greenwood reads the minutes from last time and Cornelius Wiggly will give the treasurer's report. Don't be shocked at the numbers. People in this church, they squeeze a quarter so tight, the eagle screams."

"Uh huh." Grady decided not to ask what that was supposed to mean. Nothing on the agenda made much sense to him. He concentrated on the odd last names—Riddles and Wiggly. "Music," he said. "What's that all about?"

Mae-June brightened. "Glad you asked. Some people think we should change the type of music to attract more young people. We don't have young people in this church so what's the point? I think we should plan a program to satisfy the people we have, not the people some people hope to have. The whole thing is ludicrous if you ask me."

"What do you mean no young people?" He thought back to Wednesday night. There was that rusty-hair kid. He heard a baby cry. He assumed the baby had a young mother or father. Was there no one within fifteen years of his own age besides those people?

"Just what I said."

He cleared his throat. "Okay, then. So how do people want to change it?"

"Not many do."

"Let me reword that." He took a second to think about it. Slowly, he uttered the words, "Of those who want to change it, of which there are not many, how do they want to change it?" Grady sat with his elbows on his knees holding the agenda with both hands.

"That awful contemporary stuff they call Praise Music. Nothing but Rock N Roll repeating, repeating, repeating the same words over and over and over."

"Just guessing," he said. "But I gather you don't agree."

"Do you?" Her eyebrows disappeared beneath her bangs.

He thought. And thought. And thought. "I'll keep an open mind."

"You're in charge, so don't let them bully you." Mae-June shook the paper, sending a blast of irritated air to muss up Grady's hair.

In charge. Glad she admitted it. Grady Gilbert, in charge. Well, Pastor Joe in charge. He decided the best thing to do since he was in charge, would be to change the subject. "What's this about the water fountains?"

"Another waste of the coffers," she said.

"Coffers?"

"You know, like in the Bible and Josiah and the coffers. Money—the offerings. Some people want to put water filters on the church fountains. I think it's just because Bud Waters is into some pyramid scheme selling water filters. I'm sure we can shoot that one down."

"I'll check it out," Grady said. "Take a sip. See what I think." Bud *Waters* sold *water* filters. What was with the names in this place? For that matter, *Mae-June*, who had a name like that?

"How'd you get your name?" Even as Grady uttered the last word, he regretted asking Mae-June a personal question.

She glared at him, seemed to be thinking. "Well, yes, I'll tell you. I was born at either 11:59 p.m. on May 31 or 12:01 a.m. June 1. There was a dispute between my mother and the midwife."

"Oh," he said, all he could think of as a reply.

"Back to the water filters. Do you think the Lord's money should be used on water filters?"

If Mae-June's eyes were laser beams, Grady would have been fried for sure. So that was the game, huh? He knew how to play this. He'd won at this game with his teachers and parents. This he called the *Yeah Game*. Say what they want to hear until they let their guard down, then slowly lead them over to your point of view. "I can see your point." He spread a charming smile across an innocent face. That smile had gotten him out of more than one detention. That smile had melted his mother's heart. He kept his voice smooth. "Thanks, Mae-June. So glad you're here to fill me in on these issues."

Her left eyebrow twitched. She looked skeptical. She drew in a deep breath, exhaled loudly. Her face relaxed slightly. That's all he needed. Baby steps. He could woo her in one baby step at a time.

Grady felt his cell phone vibrate against his hip. Glad for the interruption, he grabbed it from his pocket and pressed it to his ear. "Hello?"

"Grady! Grady! I've been so worried!"

"Mom?"

"I let it go as long as I could. Gave you time to cool off. Gave you time to settle down. I thought you'd be back this morning …" Her whimper escalated to a cry and culminated in a howling.

"I'm fine." He rose from his chair and walked towards the door.

"But where are you? Matt is so worried—"

"About his car, not me." Grady suddenly became aware his voice was a snotty kid and Mae-June was staring and listening intently. He held up his hand to her and mouthed, "Back in a minute." He slipped out of her office, closed the door behind him, and leaned into the hallway wall.

"Matt has never cared about me. Only half cared when he wanted to get it on with you."

Instantly, his Mom fell silent. She could turn her hysteria on and off as fast as Grady could turn the charm on and off.

"That's not true, Grady. He loves you. Both of us."

"He sure has a strange way of showing it."

"You've got to understand his background. Where he came from. He's doing better than his father did with him. Besides." She paused. Her voice lowered. "You took his car. His pride and joy."

"You think I don't know he cares more about that car than he cares about me and even you?"

"That's not fair," she said.

"It's the truth. I'm sorry I took the car. Really, I am. But how was I supposed to leave if I didn't take it?"

Her voice tone changed from whiney and pleading to firm and commanding. "He wants it back. *Now.*"

"How am I supposed to get it back?"

"You've got to come home."

"Forget it, Ma. I'm not coming home." He punched the End button, jammed the phone back into his pocket, and looked up to see Mae-June, wide-eyed, standing in the doorway.

"Is everything all right?"

"Yeah," he mumbled, turned his back, marched down the hall, out into the bright sunshine, back to the safety of the little yellow cottage he now called home.

CHAPTER NINE

Friday. Blue List Day. Grady picked up the blue paper from his desk and snuck past Mae-June's office while she was on the phone. He jumped into his Pontiac, *his* classic Pontiac. He liked the sound of that. Liked the feel of the steering wheel beneath his fingers and the pedal beneath his foot. Liked the engine's power. Liked the power *he* felt behind the wheel. He drove to the end of the driveway where Mae-June couldn't see him. He put the car in park and looked over the Blue List.

Fifteen people! Was he expected to visit them all? He checked their ailments. Someone had a tonsillectomy. Must be a kid. He'd skip that one. When he put the address of another one into WAZE, it was 15 miles away. Forget that one. He made a random decision on the rest and decided he'd aim for three people. Three lucky people would get a visit from their pastor today.

He set the WAZE app for the first address, Myra Mosely, whose name was listed near the bottom of the page. The age and ailment columns were empty. He slipped the car into drive, pressed the pedal to the metal and left a storm of stones when he pulled from the driveway onto the blacktop.

"Who's there?" The voice that responded to Grady's knock was old and frail.

The house was heavily draped in vines. There was no way the occupant could see out any windows. He'd rung the bell three times before he heard the voice. He leaned closer to the door and called, "Pastor Joe. The new pastor from Wilsons Corner Bible Believing Congregation."

No answer, but he heard the tap of something slowly advancing. Very slowly. Nearly five minutes later, someone unlatched a chain on the top of the door, then slid back a bolt in the middle of the door and turned the handle. He saw the edge of a red walker, and then Myra Mosely backed up to open the door. Answering the door took forever. How long would the visit take?

"Come in." Her voice trembled as much as her hands on the walker.

Grady hesitated. This might be more than he bargained for. But after coming this far, after he'd identified himself, how could he run away? It wasn't his intent to show the church in a bad light, after all, they had already been good to him. He stepped inside and the odor of cats hit him before his eyes adjusted to the dimness. A gray and white one slithered around his legs, an orange tabby peeked at him from a doorway, and he heard meowing coming from another room.

Slowly, slowly, the room materialized. Before him stood the oldest person he had ever seen. A flowered housecoat with snaps hung from her rounded shoulders and on her tiny feet were dirty pink slippers. Patches of grey hair fringed a dried apple face with a few long white hairs stippling the chin. Lively, bright blue eyes peered from the face—eyes that seemed to belong to a much younger person. Eyes that didn't quite understand how they had been planted into such an old body.

Leaning heavily on her walker, Myra Mosely beamed at him. "Pastor Joe! To what do I owe the privilege? No one has been to visit me for nearly two years!"

Two years? Maybe that's why her name was on the bottom of the Blue List.

"Come in, have a seat."

She shuffled behind the walker with tortoise-length steps. Grady fought the urge to pick her up and carry her down the hall. She led him to a darkened living room and settled herself into a red vinyl recliner with the stuffing poking out from dozens of pinprick holes in the arms. He checked out the room for a place to sit and realized his only choice was a swayed-back sofa covered with newspapers, a book, and two more cats—a calico and one as grey as Myra Mosely's hair. He pushed aside the newspapers and perched with only a couple inches of his butt on the couch.

Myra Mosely tittered. "I'm so pleased you're here. Oh my. I haven't had company in so long. Of course, there's the girl who brings my groceries, but she doesn't stay long. And she isn't really company. I could make you a cup of tea. Would you like tea?"

Based on the trek from the front door to Miss Myra's chair, Grady calculated the time it would take for her to walk to the kitchen, make tea, and come back with it. Probably be tomorrow. "No thanks," he said. "I'm fine. But tell me about you. How are you?" The white cat crept across the couch on its belly, pulling itself along with its front paws. It settled against Grady's back and purred loudly.

"Me? I just can't get over it. You've come to visit me."

"Yes, I have." Grady nodded and looked around a room that probably had been decorated fifty years ago and never updated. Probably dusted around the same time. "So, what's new?" Too late he realized how ridiculous that was. "Forget that. Tell me about yourself, Miss. Myra. Tell me about your involvement in the church. Tell me about your life."

"Okay." Her bright eyes lit up even more than Grady thought possible. "I used to sing," she said. "In church. I sang solos." She hummed a few bars then sang a chorus of crackly words. "A … MA zing Gra … ce … How … swwweeeet … the … sssssound …th …at ssssaaaaved a … a wretch li ike MEEEEEE." She laughed. "How did you like that? Of course, I was more in tune back in the day."

Grady clapped. "Very good, very good. Never heard a better rendition." He dismissed his lie with the thought there were different kinds of lies. Those intended to hurt. Those intended to compliment. Those intended to keep a secret. Like at Christmas. You could lie about presents and it didn't count against you. "You have lots of cats," he said, deliberately changing the conversation.

"I do, I do. Eight in all. They're my children. I never had children. My husband was killed during the war. I never married again."

"The war?"

"Korean War. He was a jet fighter. Shot down. There. Look at that picture. Wasn't he handsome in his uniform?"

Grady picked up the gold frame she pointed to on the end table beside her chair. Between the dust and the darkness of the room, he could barely make out the smile of a young serviceman. "Handsome, indeed," he said and set the picture back on the table. "What was his name? How did you meet?"

"Norman," she said. "Norman Mosely. Oh, we were so young. I was nineteen and he wasn't much older. But I knew he was the one. They had trains full of servicemen back then. We used to meet the trains in Chattanooga when they stopped for short breaks. We'd sew on buttons if they needed it. Bake them snacks. I remember I made cookies that day. Sugar cookies. I offered him some and he said all he really wanted was for me to write to him."

She giggled then, and Grady could imagine this leather-faced woman as a blushing teenager sweet on a serviceman.

"We wrote each other for six months. Then he got leave and came to see me." She leaned forward and lowered her voice as if to conceal the secret from anyone who might be listening. "We snuck out of the house, this very house. My parents' house, God rest their souls. We snuck off and got married. I went back with him to the base in Texas until they shipped him out."

"So how long were you married?"

"Not even a year." She spoke as though the words were glass and if she uttered them too loudly, they might shatter.

"I'm so sorry," Grady said. "What a story."

"Oh, don't be sorry, dear. It was the best time of my life. I have so many wonderful memories."

She smiled, remembering. Grady sat respectfully watching her face come alive—as alive as her eyes had been from the beginning of the visit.

When she returned to the present day, he asked, "Would you like to come to church this week? I could pick you up."

She laughed. "I don't see how I could."

"Maybe that girl who delivers your groceries could help you get ready."

"I'll think about it," she said. "Maybe. Give me time to think."

On the porch, Grady stood with one foot on the bottom step and one foot on the step above it. He looked back and pondered the progression of life, how it moved on without stopping to ask if you wanted to stay in the spot you found yourself at any given moment. That old woman was young once. She snuck out of this house in the night to see Norman. Grady was nineteen, the same age as Norman when he was a jet fighter in the Korea.

Grady shook his head as he ambled to the Pontiac. It was lucky he hadn't been born in the 1930s when he might have been drafted or seen the service as his only way out. He might have been dropped in the middle of the Sea of Japan and eaten by sharks or drowned. The thought made him nauseous. He was glad to be alive in this year in Wilsons Corner, Tennessee.

CHAPTER TEN

B ack in the car, Grady checked the Blue List. So much for visiting three people today. He only had time for one more. He ran a finger down the list and recognized a street name he'd passed a mile or so back. Theresa Murdoch. Nothing was written beside her name. He didn't have a clue as to her age, her ailment, or why she was on the Blue List, but she was close by, so Theresa Murdoch it would be. He cranked up the radio until the car was rocking. He pounded out the rhythm on the steering wheel and mouthed the words to the song.

When he parked in front of the brown two-story with a white picket fence across the front yard and stepped out, Grady still felt the vibration of music. It took a minute for him to realize the source of the music was not coming from his car, but from the back of Theresa Murdoch's house. *Ring the doorbell or investigate the music? What the heck. Music. He deserved a little reprieve from the Pastor Joe role.* He ambled down the driveway on the right side of the house. The sound grew louder as he approached a detached garage.

He entered through a side door, stood in the shadows, and watched three boys two or three years younger than himself. The one who played an electric guitar shook a curtain of dirty blonde hair out of his eyes, revealing a large, hooped nose ring. The one on the drums sported a tattoo of a devil on his neck. The one on keyboard looked too innocent to be hanging around with the other two.

Ah, to be as free as these guys, Grady thought. To not have a care in the world except hang out and jam. He caught himself. He'd only been a grown-up for a couple of days. Besides, if that meant being young in Orlando under Matt the Rat's thumb, forget it. He'd continue wearing a mask of deceit in Tennessee.

They didn't notice him until they finished the second song.

"Dude." The guitarist shook the hair from his eyes. "Who are you? What are you doin' in here?"

"Me?" Grady placed a hand on his chest. "I just came to visit Theresa Murdoch. She's on the Blue List."

"That's my grandma," the drummer said. "What the hell's the Blue List?"

"The sick people. I'm the new pastor of Wilsons Corner Bible—"

The guitarist snickered. The kid on the drums laughed. The keyboard kid's mouth dropped open.

"You Pastor Joe?" The guitarist lifted the strap of his guitar over his head and set it down.

Grady nodded. "How'd you know?"

The guitarist wrinkled his nose. "People talk," he said.

"How old are you, man?" the keyboard kid squeaked.

"Not kidding and none of your business." Grady sat on a nearby stool. "Keep playing. You're good."

The drummer and the kid at the keyboard exchanged looks. "Now you're kiddin'," the keyboard player said. "Adults don't like this, never mind wannabe pastors."

"I don't lie," Grady said. "I'm a pastor, 'member?"

"So you say," the drummer said. He brought his sticks down on the drum and played a rat-a-tat-tat.

The guitarist swaggered over to Grady, his hands in the back pockets of jeans with slits in the knees. He wore a black hoodie and a gold chain. "Michael. Name's Michael." He extended his hand. "What'd you say your name was?"

"Grady …" *When would he stop bringing up the name of his old self and naturally respond with his new identity?* "Pastor Joe," he said with as much confidence as he could muster. "Middle name's Grady. Sometimes I use it."

Michael nodded, stood with one knee bent, all his weight on the other leg. "So, why'd you move to this God-awful speck of earth? Most of us are figurin' out ways to make it outta here."

Direct. Grady liked that. No beating around the bush with this kid. He shrugged. "They needed a pastor. I was available. Seemed all right at the time. You live here forever?"

"Yeah." Michael snickered. "How long will it take you to figure out this ain't no place to call home?" He brightened up. "Hey, we've got a singer, too. Melissa. Why don't I see if she can come over? You never know." He pulled an iPhone out of the back pocket of his jeans and pressed a couple buttons before Grady had a chance to answer.

"Yo. It's Michael. Get your butt over here. We're jammin' with a pastor."

Pause while presumably Melissa responded.

"No, I'm not lyin' to you. Get over here."

"You're the pastor of Wilsons Corner Bible Believing Congregation?"

Grady wasn't sure if Melissa's pretty face showed contempt or disbelief. The ends of her blonde hair looked as if they had been dipped in red paint. The left side was long and ragged, and the right side was shaved in a chevron pattern. A red plaid skirt barely covered her buttocks. The outfit was made minutely more modest by the black tights she wore underneath. She topped this off with a black shirt with long sleeves and a hole for her thumbs. On the back of her hand was the tattoo of a yellow and black butterfly. She lowered her chin and perused him up and down. She swept her hand in front of her neck in a cutting-type motion. "You're kidding."

"Really." Grady hoped he sounded convincing. "Just arrived Wednesday night."

"So, like, my mother goes to that church," Melissa said. "Suzanne Simms. Couldn't get me near that place."

Suzanne Simms? Why did that name sound so familiar? The prayer list! So this was the sixteen-year-old giving her mother problems ... because of a butterfly tattoo? Suzanne Simms wanted the church to pray over that? What would the broad do if she faced a real crisis?

"So, does anyone like know you're like over here with us sinners?" Melissa crossed her arms over her flat chest.

"Actually, I came to visit his grandmother." Grady pointed to the drummer.

Melissa snickered along with the boys in the band. "I won't tell if you won't tell," she said. "Or else they'll think you're going to hell right along with us. You know they think we're all going to hell, right?"

Grady didn't answer. Only a few days ago people would have thought the same of him.

"Well?" she demanded. "They do." She swished around and approached the microphone.

All three boys hurried to take their places. Michael strummed a few bars, nodded at the drummer and keyboard kid and they were off, all of them strumming or tapping, or racing up and down the keyboard, and belting out words unintelligible over the sounds of the instruments. If Grady thought the place was rocking before, he was convinced now that old Myra Mosely could probably hear this concert from her house a mile away.

When they finished the performance, Michael said, "So, Pastor. Pick up that tambourine next to you and join us." He flashed a sarcastic grin to his bandmates.

"Yeah, sure." Grady shrugged. "Why not." He picked up the tambourine and joined the others performing for an audience of zero. He slapped the tambourine on his thigh, against his other hand, and over his head. He could get used to this. Yeah, this was the place he'd come when things got too stressful.

After three songs, Michael opened a dorm-size refrigerator and handed out cans of Coke. Grady gulped a quarter of the can then pointed it at the drummer. "So, what's your name?"

"Alex," the kid said.

Grady waited for more, but when Alex didn't reveal any other details, he turned to the keyboard kid. "And you?"

"Keith."

"So," Grady asked. "Why not? Why won't you come to church, Melissa? And what about you three, Keith, Michael, Alex?"

The boys shook their heads without replying.

"You're kidding, right?" Melissa popped a piece of peppermint gum into her mouth. "My mother used to make me go, but I've got better things to do with my time than have a bunch of old ladies monitor my every move."

That stung. He might have been involved with the church for only a day or two, but he felt connected. "Maybe it's changed since you stopped coming."

"I doubt it," Melissa said. "People don't change overnight."

Grady thought about that. Maybe she was right. Maybe not. Maybe now he was the pastor, he could make some changes that couldn't have been made otherwise. Maybe destiny brought him here. Maybe it wasn't a mistake he ran out of gas right in front of Wilsons Corner Bible Believing Congregation. Besides, he wouldn't mind having more people near his age in the church.

"What would it take," he asked, "for all of you to come to church . . . just once?"

"I ain't goin' no matter what." Alex drew designs in the condensation on his soda can.

"I might go." Keith tapped out a rhythm on the stool Grady had vacated. "If you let us perform."

Michael and Alex snickered. Michael leaned against the wall and crossed his ankles. "That's a good one, man," he said.

"What would you sing?" Grady asked.

"What difference does it make?" Alex said. "It ain't happenin'."

"Maybe it will," Grady prodded. "What would you play?"

"I dunno," Michael said. "We'd come up with somethin'."

Melissa sneered. "Yeah, we'd come up with somethin'. I'd do it just to see the look on my mother's face. Drums and keyboard and guitar in that 'holy' place." She drew quotation marks in the air when she said 'holy.'

"Practice up," Grady said. "We'll talk next week."

Alex shrugged. "Maybe," he said. "We'll talk about it."

CHAPTER ELEVEN

On Saturday Grady stayed in bed until eleven, ate cereal as a breakfast and lunch combo, played a little basketball, and figured out what he was going to preach about. Granted, it wasn't going to be a long sermon, but heck, people would probably be glad. He doubted they wanted to be stuck listening to him babble the morning away when they could be doing things that were definitely more fun.

In the evening, he googled 'sermons' on YouTube. He watched half a dozen and imitated the arm movements, the cadence of the words, the holding of the Bible. He went to bed just after 10:00, ready for the next day.

On Sunday morning, he pulled a pair of khakis out of his duffel bag. *Wrinkled. Great.* He hadn't seen an iron anywhere in the personage, but even if he had, he wouldn't dare try it. He'd probably burn a hole in the seat, or worse yet, the crotch. Instead, he hung them in the bathroom with the shower running for half an hour and hoped the steam would get the wrinkles out. At 10:10, the trousers were in much better shape than when he'd stuck them in the bathroom. He pulled them over his feet and up his legs and realized they were damp. No more time to waste.

Damp or not, ready or not, the time had come. He left the personage at 10:20 with his scribbled sermon folded and stuck in his shirt pocket.

"Morning, Pastor!"

Grady almost didn't recognize Wilfred standing at the top of the wide stone steps outside the double doors to the church. The brown polyester suit, white shirt, and gold tie of miniature crosses were a step up from Wednesday night, albeit straight out of another generation.

"Oh, hi!" Grady replied.

"Let me show you where your robe is kept." Wilfred opened the door to the church and led Grady down the hallway past Mae-June's darkened office. Grady was glad to hear he would be wearing a robe to conceal the clothes he knew weren't formal enough.

Their feet clattered on the tile floor. Large black and white pictures in matching black frames lined the walls. Grady stopped to examine the first one. A gold plate affixed to the bottom of the frame identified a serious-looking man, head tilted slightly to the left, mutton chop sideburns, John Lennon type rimless glasses as Pastor George Estabrook, 1917-1927.

"Come on down here." Wilfred gestured from further down the hallway. He was pointing to a frame.

Grady read each gold plate as he passed. Pastor Joseph Pickler, 1928-1935; Pastor Amos Hood, 1936 - 1956; Pastor Emmett Feathersworth 1957 - 1969; Clark Hawkins, 1970 - 1990. He skipped a few decades and stood beside Wilfred staring at an empty frame.

"Soon your mug'll be ahangin' on the wall aside all these great men," Wilfred said.

Grady attempted a smile, but it came out as a sort of sneer. *A great man? He didn't even qualify as a mediocre boy.*

"We'll take your picture after church." Wilfred puffed out his chest. "I'll take it. I'm a very good photographer, if I may say so myself."

"No, no, no." Grady shook his head. "Let's hold off on the picture taking." There was no way he wanted this church to be able to identify him when he left after pocketing the paycheck. "Couple weeks anyway."

Wilfred slapped Grady's shoulder. "You one of them humble ones? Don't want your picture ahangin' on a wall? Think it's tootin' your own horn? Nah. It's just appreciation on our part."

Grady shrugged. He'd just have to figure a way to dodge the camera when the time came.

A young woman in a red dress with a black belt and a black hat sporting feathers passed them. Wilfred tipped his head. His face was stern. Grady expected an introduction, but Wilfred kept quiet.

Two little girls trailed behind the red dress woman—the twins he'd noticed when he arrived on Wednesday. They were miniatures of their mother in red dresses, black belts, and black hats with feathers. All three smiled the same smile as their black patent leather shoes clip-clopped past. The parade of red dresses made Grady dizzy. For a moment, he thought maybe he was so nervous his eyes weren't focusing properly. He glanced back to make sure he'd seen what he thought he saw. One of the girls was looking over her shoulder at him.

"Come along, Betty Lou," the mother said. She looked at the other twin. "Good girl, Betty Jean."

Betty Jean and Betty Lou? Grady could only imagine what the woman's name was. He watched as she opened a door. Heavy-handed organ music poured into the hallway. da-DA! da-DUM! It reminded Grady of an old-fashioned horror movie. He felt trapped in the narrow hallway with the triplicate red dresses, the Dracula music, and the empty picture frame he would do anything to not have filled. He prayed, he could not believe he was doing it, but he prayed, the morning would soon be over.

"Your robe is in the closet in your office." Wilfred stepped across the hallway and opened the door.

Grady followed Wilfred into the office, and again, a sense of peace flooded over him. He loved his office. Even more, he liked the sound of it. *His* office. The place from which he would rule his little kingdom.

Wilfred opened a door Grady hadn't noticed before and pulled out what looked like a graduation robe, but much fancier. The silver fabric sparkled in the sunlight from the window. The sleeves were tight around the wrist, but so wide you could hide a watermelon in each. A black velvet stripe straddled a zipper from the neckline to the hem. Wilfred held it open and Grady slipped his arms into the sleeves. He spread his arms wide and checked himself out in the full-length mirror hanging on the inside of the closet door. He could rule the world in this outfit, forget ruling one kingdom.

Wilfred velcroed a stiff white collar around Grady's neck. "I don't know what you did in seminary, but our previous pastor wore his collar whenever he left the parsonage." Wilfred smoothed the shoulders of the robe and nodded his approval.

Grady felt like he was wearing a neck brace. He turned his head stiffly to the left, then right. *Wear this thing all the time?* Wilfred had to be kidding! "Whatever happened to the previous pastor?" he asked.

"Pastor Westbrook. He wanted to pastor a larger church," Wilfred said. "He moved to Nashville. There's a retired pastor in the congregation who's eager to meet you."

"Yeah? Who's that?" Grady shook his arms to loosen the billowy fabric where it clung to his lower arms.

"Pastor Oscar," Wilfred said. "He'll be sitting in the third row on the organ side. White hair, black glasses, gray suit. His wife plays the organ. Miss Cora. You'll see her join him once you start to preach."

Grady doubted he'd see much of anything when he stood up to preach. He hoped the rusty haired boy sat close to the front.

"Pastor Oscar retired from Missouri and settled here," Wilfred continued. "He's a graduate of Gordon Conwell, too. He can't wait to talk to you. He says it's probably changed a lot since he graduated!"

"Gordon Conwell?" Grady asked. "Where's that?"

Wilfred slapped him on the shoulder and laughed. "Come on. It's almost time."

Grady made it through the first part of the Mass. *No, that was a Catholic service. What did these people call this gathering? Service? Vespers? Temple? What was the name of the place? Oh yeah. Wilsons Corner Bible Believing Congregation. Strange.*

He remembered the dreaded church experiences from visiting his grandmother, and for the first time, was glad she insisted he go. That long-ago memory gave him at least a bit of a clue of what to do. When the people in the audience stood, sat, or kneeled, he followed. At one point when he knelt, the robe caught on the back of his sneakers, and he nearly catapulted headfirst right off the stage when he stood.

The program leading up to his sermon dragged on with people popping up all over the place to praise the Lord for all sorts of naturally occurring daily activities. One woman found lost keys. The delay meant she just missed a three-car pile-up on the freeway. *Amens* and *Praise the Lords* followed her story. A man was hired by the gas station off County Road 33. *There was a gas station on County Road 33?* Grady wished he'd found it before running out of gas so he wouldn't have ended up petrified standing at the front of a church.

Another man praised God that after six months out of work, he'd found a job and could now pay tithe. Grady wondered who tithe was and why this man felt an obligation to support him. So much for preaching a short sermon so everyone could vacate early. This sharing part was taking up all the time.

Finally, at 11:52 a.m., Wilfred stood and with much bravado introduced Pastor Joe. "Pastor Joe is a recent graduate of Gordon Conwell Seminary ..."

Gordon Conwell Seminary? He supposedly graduated from Gordon Conwell Seminary? The same one Pastor Oscar wanted to talk to him about? He'd make sure he avoided him after church.

"He focused his studies on developing small group ministries," Wilfred continued. "He is a third-generation pastor, having grown up in the Congo where his parents were missionaries. He will be joined by his wife in …" He turned and nodded at Grady. "…Five weeks, is that right?"

Grady's tongue affixed itself to the roof of his mouth. All he could do was nod. He'd have to figure out this marriage snag at a later date. For now, he needed all of his effort to stay calm.

"So, we'll be losing him for one week for their honeymoon …"

Holy Crap! This was getting more difficult by the moment. "And without further ado, Pastor Joseph Decker!"

As Wilfred left the stage and Miss Cora slipped off the organ bench to join her husband in the third row, Grady willed his knees to support him. Only three steps from chair to podium. Lectern? Pulpit? Whatever the name, it was a large wooden item open in the back with shelves visible only to those sitting behind it. As Grady approached, he took a cursory inventory of its contents. A basket of chains; a Mason jar of pennies with a few pieces of silver mixed in, a box with the word ENVELOPES on the side with a mess of papers inside. The mishmash comforted and elevated him somehow.

He grasped the outer edges of the podium tightly, pasted on a smile, and searched the audience for the rusty-haired kid. He found him seated directly behind a tall, big-boned man sitting beside a short squat female. Grady mistook the woman for a child. She seemed tiny compared to the man. Then he noticed the plastic cat-eye glasses hanging by a gold chain around her neck and figured she must be his wife. They made an odd couple.

Grady could hardly see the kid behind the man. In fact, the only thing he could see was an ear that made a moving target, but he focused on it anyway. It was time. This was it.

"On Wednesday," Grady began in his most authoritative voice, "just as I arrived, it was dark. The sun had already gone down." He pointed with a stiff arm toward the window and many people looked in the same direction. "As I walked from the far end of the parking lot, I saw a deer in the woods. She didn't see me, and I watched her chomp on leaves." He imitated the up and down, back and forth motion of the deer's mouth.

Many in the congregation laughed. Grady grasped the lectern tighter, thinking they were laughing at him. *Weren't church people serious?* Then the laughter died down, and as he looked from face to face, he realized they were smiling at him. They liked what he was saying.

Buoyed and empowered, he straightened up and plucked the Bible from the center of the podium. "It reminded me of something I read in the Bible." He held out the Bible in one hand and raised his other hand high above his head. He set the Bible down and opened to the folded-over onion-skin page. The small print made it difficult for him to find the right words. His hands were sweating, and the thin, crinkly paper stuck to his fingers. He heard people moving in their seats. He looked up and they all were staring at him, waiting. He dropped his eyes to the page again, and finally found the word 'deer.'

He drew a finger under each word as he read, "Then … will … the … lame … leap … like … a deer … and the … mute … tongue… shout for joy."

"Amens!" Echoed off the walls of the church.

"Oh yes!" From the far-right corner.

"You preach it, Brother!" From behind the pretty red dress lady and her twins Betty Lou and Betty Jean.

Grady's chest expanded like the Grinch's at the end of the movie. *His heart grew three sizes that day.* Grady gained momentum. "I watched that deer BOUND!" he shouted. "I tell you, BOUND over bushes and branches, over twigs and underbrush. Nothing stopped it." He pounded the podium. "I couldn't have followed the path she took. I would have been scraped and scratched, caught up at every turn. But here —" He held up the Bible and jabbed a finger on the page just as he'd seen preachers do on YouTube. "Here it says the lame will leap like a deer."

The audience erupted once again in "Amens!" And other such accolades.

He was the voice of authority now. They looked at him, nodded their heads, believing he held the truth. "Who hasn't been lame?"

"No one, Brother!"

"Who hasn't wished they could leap like a deer?"

"You got that right!"

"Who wants to leap like a deer one day?"

"I do!"

"I do!"

"I do!"

Arms raised to the heavens and swayed back and forth.

Grady glanced at the clock hanging on the far wall. 11:59. He couldn't think of anything else to say. He'd made his point after seven minutes. "If you believe the Bible, some day you will!" He raised and lowered both arms a couple of times in a "Rah! Rah!"

gesture, turned and sat down in the high-back wooden chair in the center of the stage.

Total silence.

Grady looked up in alarm. People were consulting their watches, whispering to each other, then slowly they reached for the songbooks in their pews. The organist raced to her post, and at the first Dracula note, they all stood and began singing, "On a hill far away, stood an old rugged cross …"

Grady searched the stage for a songbook, but none was to be had. He stood awkwardly swaying from one foot to the other, opening and closing his mouth in what he hoped looked like word formations.

As the organist held the last agonizing note, Wilfred jumped onto the stage. "May the Lord be with you!" he shouted.

"And with you!" the audience responded in unison.

Wilfred pointed to the three steps leading from the stage to the main floor. Grady took the hint and descended. Immediately, a flood of people surrounded him.

"You make the Bible so plain!" someone said.

"Short and to the point," said another.

"Just the way I like it."

"I never heard that verse explained that way," said another.

"You were preaching right to me."

With each word of praise, Grady's ego floated higher. If only Matt the Rat could see him now. He'd be ashamed of his last cutting words. *Loser. You'll never succeed at anything you try*. He was succeeding at being a preacher right now. The people had spoken.

CHAPTER TWELVE

All Grady wanted to do was rip off the clerical collar, strip down to his boxers, grab a Heineken he'd bought with his fake ID and watch the Miami Dolphins decimate the New England Patriots. Unfortunately, the church had other plans for his Sunday afternoon—and the next Sunday, and the next Sunday, and the next Sunday, on into infinity. He was to have lunch in a family's home. Once he made the rounds, he'd start the cycle all over again.

He prayed—the second time in one day—that his hosts this week, Pastor Oscar and Miss Cora, were football fans, but he doubted it. He also prayed he could field the Gordon Conwell questions. He googled Gordon Conwell on his phone and tried to memorize a few facts.

"Ride with us," Pastor Oscar said. "We'll bring you home afterward." They were standing on the steps of the church. Pastor Oscar's white hair glistened in the sunlight. Grady had never seen such pure white hair. He wondered if the man bleached it.

"That's okay," Grady insisted. "Might as well learn my way around. I'll just follow you." What he really meant was he planned to make as quick an escape as possible. Maybe, with any luck—or answer to prayer, he'd make it back to the personage for the second half of the game.

Pastor Oscar took a right out of the parking lot and Grady followed. So much had happened in just a few days that when the tires hit the blacktop, Grady felt as though he were emerging from Alice's rabbit hole. He liked the security of the alternate reality hidden behind the trees and the so-called real world made him feel queasy. It seemed bright and artificial.

Pastor Oscar drove at least ten minutes before taking a left onto an unnamed road. They passed a field with rolled hay bales, a hand-written sign at a crossroads advertising EGGS FOR SALE, and a professional sign beside the egg sign pointing to KRISTY'S CAMPGROUND.

Lucky thing he'd run out of gas when he had. If he'd traveled another half mile, he'd probably still be wandering around looking for help. Or he would have run into the one on, what was it the guy said in church? Oh yeah, Route 33.

Pastor Oscar put on his blinker beside a tall tree covered with green vines. His car disappeared into the leaves despite the fact Grady did not see a road. Nevertheless, he followed and discovered the road was more of a path, unpaved and rutted. He slowed down to 5 mph and jostled along, at times hitting his head on the ceiling. The trees fell away, and he drove into an open field. Straight ahead sat a log cabin with two rattan rockers on the front porch. Behind the cabin, a lake stretched as far as Grady could see. The sun twinkled off the water and momentarily blinded him. Pastor Oscar pulled up in front of the cabin and turned off the engine.

Grady pulled up beside him, opened his door and stepped out. "Wow! What a place!" he said.

Pastor Oscar smiled. "I wanted you to see it," he answered. "You're just starting out in the ministry, and I have a few words of advice for you. Just a sec …" He opened the car door for his wife and helped her out. "First, find yourself a good wife and take care of her." The couple laughed and clasped hands. "But by the sound of it, Pastor Joe, you've already done that."

Both Pastor Oscar and Miss Cora grinned at Grady. He blushed and looked away. It wasn't Pastor Oscar's comment, it was the holding hands. Based on the grown-ups he'd known, he'd come to believe love and caring belonged to the young. After a few years, people just tolerated each other or got a divorce or, like his mother, stayed with someone for monetary security. These people had to be in their 70s, or even older, and they seemed to *like* each other.

The three of them fell into step and approached the house.

"I'm eager to meet Roxanne," Miss Cora said.

"Roxanne?" Grady pulled at the clerical collar, which was causing an irritation that probably looked like a hickey.

"Your fiancée," she said.

"Oh, Roxanne! Yes, you'll meet her soon enough." Grady cleared his throat and searched his brain for a way to change the subject.

Fortunately, Pastor Oscar began to speak. "The second piece of advice I have for you is to get out of the parsonage as soon as you can."

Grady stopped walking and stared in disbelief. "Get out of the personage? It's a nice place."

"That's the problem," Pastor Oscar said. "If you get too comfortable in parsonages and live in them your whole life, where are you going to live when you retire? You've got to build up equity, son. Buy a house sooner rather than later."

Retire? He'd only just begun the first real job of his life! Couldn't he bask in the gloriousness for more than a few days of living in his own place, relish a real paycheck, and have people believe what he said was important? *Retire?* He wasn't about to think of that just yet.

Pastor Oscar unlocked the door and stepped aside so first his wife entered, followed by Grady, then himself. Grady tried to hold back his awe, but a sort of gaspy sound might have leaked out. The entire back wall of the house was glass. Double sliding glass doors led onto an enormous deck. In the middle of the deck, two lounge chairs with cushions that looked like something you'd see in Hawaii stood side by side with a small glass-topped table between. A kayak was tied to a tree by the shore.

"Have a seat," Pastor Oscar said. "I'll change, then start a fire."

Grady pulled back from his trancelike view of the lake to focus on the room. Half a dozen chairs formed a semi-circle around a fireplace with a stone chimney extending to the peak of a high, high ceiling. In one corner, an open staircase led to the exposed second floor. Upstairs, a railing looped around a hallway and he saw several doors with panels of etched glass.

All of this could be his if he didn't live in the personage? He chose a seat in front of the fireplace, immediately sinking into its comfort. He wasn't sure he'd want to or be able to move when Miss Cora called them for dinner. Yet again, by the aromas from the kitchen, he'd find a way.

Pastor Oscar returned with an armload of wood. He'd changed into khaki slacks and a polo shirt. Kneeling in front of the fireplace, he slid the wood into a small bin beside the hearth. He drew back the metal screen, crinkled newspaper from the pile beside the woodbin, and stuffed it in the bottom of the fireplace. "So, what do you think?"

What did he think? Grady choked back a laugh. For the last couple of years, since his Mom married Matt, they lived in a second-floor apartment with no yard. Through the rickety walls and floorboards, he could hear the neighbors in constant battle. Before that, he and his Mom lived in a rusty trailer, one room in a boarding house, and a bunch of other places he chose to forget.

"So?" Pastor Oscar knelt on one knee in front of the fireplace and turned to look at Grady. "What do you think?"

"How much money do you need to buy a house like this?" Grady asked.

They sat in an alcove off the kitchen at a round oak table, each with a view of the lake. A flock of birds descended for a landing. They beat back their wings, extended their feet on top of the water, skidded about a yard, then settled down and floated as if it had been an easy landing.

Pastor Oscar took hold of his wife's hand and the two of them extended a hand to Grady. He looked from one to the other, confused, then tentatively reached out and touched fingers.

They wrapped their fingers around his, closed their eyes, and lowered their heads. Grady followed their example.

"Dear God," Pastor Oscar whispered. "We humble ourselves before you. We thank you for Pastor Joe and the talents he brings to our congregation. Bless him in his work. We now thank thee for this bountiful meal you have given to us. Bless the hands that prepared it. May we do your will with every ounce of energy this food bestows upon us. Amen."

Miss Cora responded with a hearty, "AMEN!"

They both looked expectantly at Grady. He was more concerned with the baked ziti cooling off and his glass of lemonade warming up than to interpret their stares. "Looks mighty awesome," he said, reaching for the ziti. The aroma caused his stomach to growl in anticipation.

They passed rolls, ziti, green beans, and tossed salad. Serving spoons clanked against dishes. Grady heaped his plate and plunged a fork into the green beans. Eating as a family around a table with homemade food instead of canned ravioli or cereal or a peanut butter sandwich, felt surreal. No yelling at the table or TV commentators in the background. He'd never seen a home with the view of a beautiful lake. He'd had no idea people actually lived like this, except on TV.

"So, son." Pastor Oscar cut a salad tomato. "Tell me about our alma mater. What's new? I heard Dr. Ouerbach finally retired at 90. Is that true?"

Grady was glad for the forkful of salad he'd just stuffed into his mouth. He pointed to his lips as a way of explanation as to why he was holding back an answer. He chewed slowly, his mind whirring. "That's right," he finally said. "I forget how many years they said he taught. Longer than I've been alive, anyway."

"He certainly was getting up there." Pastor Oscar split open a dinner roll and slathered it with butter. "Age is relative, I suppose. Old age is a little older than one currently is!"

Silence enveloped them as they chewed. It was Miss Cora who spoke next. "When we were there, they offered courses for women whose husbands were seminary students. I enjoyed that quite a bit." She sipped her lemonade. "They encouraged us to learn to play piano and organ, so I took lessons. We had one class in hospitality, another in running children's ministries. I imagine all that's been changed." She leaned forward and chuckled, her eyes on Grady. "With women entering the ministry now, what do they teach husbands to do?"

Pastor Oscar and Miss Cora laughed heartily, and Grady joined in. He thought it was a rhetorical question until the laughing stopped and they both stared at him, forks poised above plates.

"Well," he said. "Well. I wouldn't know, would I? I was the one enrolled and not the spouse."

"Good point." Miss Cora nodded and lowered her fork into her ziti.

Grady needed to divert the attention from Gordon Conwell Seminary before they asked a question he couldn't fudge. Something uncontroversial. Something simple. Something about them. "Do you have children?" he asked.

Miss Cora's face paled. She set her fork on the edge of her plate, raised her cloth napkin, and dabbed at her lips.

Pastor Oscar placed a hand on her arm. "We did," he whispered. "We had twin sons who died shortly after birth. Today they can save preemies, but back then medicine hadn't made such advances. The boys weren't even three pounds ..."

In the following silence, Grady blushed, tore off a too-big chunk of dinner roll with his teeth, and searched for an appropriate response. The only thing he could come up with was, "I'm so sorry." Too late he realized he'd said it with a mouthful of bread.

Miss Cora looked up tentatively. "We named them Matthew and Mark, like the Gospel writers. People might say it was God's will my babies died. What do you think, Pastor Joe?"

Grady blinked. Up until the last word—Joe—he'd just been a sympathetic listener. Now he was drawn into the conversation, expected in fact, to know the mind of God. A God he hadn't given much thought to until a few days ago.

"I tried to tell her God doesn't work that way," Pastor Oscar said. "But she still grieves, and it's been thirty-five years."

Thankful for Pastor Oscar's lead, Grady had a starting point. "I agree with your husband, Ma'am. God doesn't work that way. But I don't think it's wrong to be sad over losing someone. In this case, two someones."

A tear spilled from Miss Cora's left eye, slithered past her nose, and dripped off her chin. "I wonder if I show a lack of faith when I'm sad. Maybe God doesn't think I trust Him." This time she didn't look at her husband and he didn't offer any clues for Grady to respond. The longer the silence lasted, the clearer it became to Grady that it was probably Pastor Oscar who thought her faith was weak. Now he was in a real quandary—comfort the woman or support the man.

"I suppose," Grady started, then paused. He raised the lemonade glass to his lips. Gulped half the sweet liquid. Cleared his throat. "I suppose it's what you do about that sadness. I mean, if you're sad because it's a sad situation, God will understand. I'll bet he was sad when Adam and Eve ate that damn apple." Once again, he was glad for his foray into church life at his grandmother's insistence.

The Oscars exchanged glances. They were probably surprised he knew so much. Wait. If he was a pastor, he'd probably know all this and a whole lot more. "But if that sadness turns to madness and you blame God," he said, "that's another story."

Miss Cora peered into Grady's eyes with such intensity he had to look away. "All I wanted was to be a mother," she said. "I feel so empty. What was my life worth …"

"*What your life was worth?!*" Grady leaned forward, his shirt hovering dangerously close to the red sauce on the ziti. "Look at all you have. This wonderful house. A husband who actually loves you. If you want to talk about what's a life worth, come home with me and I'll introduce you to my mother and Matt the … her husband." He cut into a salad tomato with such force, he was afraid the scraping sound he heard was the plate being sliced in half.

Miss Cora looked at him with a funny expression he couldn't interpret. "I suppose," she said.

"You mean in the Congo?" Pastor Oscar asked.

The *Congo*?! "Yeah, in the Congo. As for kids, you're probably lucky you didn't have any. They can be a pain in the ass."

Pastor Oscar and Miss Cora gasped. Grady replayed the words in his head. "My bad," he said. "I meant to say 'neck.' Kids can be a pain in the neck."

CHAPTER THIRTEEN

Mae-June plunged her reddened hands into the nearly scalding water of her enamel kitchen sink and found the sponge floating beneath mounds of suds. Trust. That was the problem.

She swiped the sponge across a fork twice, rinsed it, placed it tines up in the plastic dish drainer, and searched for the butter knife hiding beneath the cloud of cleanser. She had every right to be suspicious until Pastor Joe earned her trust.

Trust. Who did she trust? Pastor Oscar was old school, but a good man. Would she have trusted the committee if they'd asked Pastor Oscar to come out of retirement to lead the church? Probably not. What they needed was a pastor who fell between Pastor Joe's age and Pastor Oscar's age. Seasoned, but not, well, to keep with a food metaphor, overcooked.

She glanced at the rooster clock affixed to the wall above the two-seater Formica table. 2:50. Ten more minutes. She'd hold herself back ten more minutes before calling Cora. She'd calculated how long it would take to drive to their home from the church—18 minutes; how long Pastor Oscar would brag about that cabin he'd built—9 minutes; how long it would take Cora to put the meal on the table—30 minutes; how long Pastor Oscar would take to bless the food—3 minutes; how long it would take to consume the meal while conversing—26 minutes. And dessert? She shivered. Aunt Betty's secret recipe for sure. Would they invite Pastor Joe to stay and chat? Would he volunteer to help with kitchen clean-up? Mae-June tossed in an extra 15 minutes and added it all up. $18 + 9 + 30 + 3 + 26 + 15 = 91$. One and a half hours. She'd make it two. She doubted a young man would last much longer than two hours talking with old folks. She'd seen the two cars pull out of the church parking lot at 1:00. At 3:00 on the dot, she picked up the phone and dialed.

"Hello?" Cora answered in a voice Mae-June judged as childlike.

"It's Mae-June. What did you think of the new pastor?"

"Hello, Mae-June," Cora said.

Mae-June rolled her eyes. Cora's voice was on the edge of sugary sweet.

"Just a minute," Cora said. "He's leaving now. I need to say goodbye."

Mae-June heard a clunk as Cora set the phone down on the counter. She heard the tip-tap of heels growing fainter and the muffle of cheerful-sounding voices. The tip-tap of heels grew louder.

"Yes, Mae-June. How are you?"

Cora sounded more chipper than Chipper herself. "What'd you get out of him? What do you think?" Mae-June asked.

"He's nice," Cora offered. "Here, let me hand the phone over to my husband."

"No!" Mae-June shouted. She wanted an honest woman's take, not a pastor's. Particularly not the one who would have to eat crow if the pastor didn't work out since he was the chair of the search committee.

"Mae-June! How are you?" Pastor Oscar's commanding voice came through the lines so loud, Mae-June jerked the phone away from her ear.

Mae-June pictured Pastor Oscar's shock of white hair and his angelic white teeth holding his ruddy face in place. She switched to her professional voice. "Hello, Pastor Oscar. Just checking in to be sure Pastor Joe is all settled in. Wondering if he needs anything, but I understand he just left. What a shame." Mae-June twisted the cord of her telephone receiver around her fingers, untwisted it, wrapped it around her wrist.

"No, No," Pastor Oscar assured her. "He's fine. All taken care of."

"How'd it go? Did he say much?" Mae-June edged closer to what she wanted to know.

"Chitchat," Pastor Oscar said.

"I know you wanted to talk about Gordon Conwell."

"Yes, yes. We touched on that. As I suspected, Professor Ouerbach retired."

"Nothing else?"

"Sat by the fire a while." Pastor Oscar laughed. "Boy, can he eat! Spread the word to wherever he's going next Sunday. He put away two helpings of everything Cora set out and still had room for a big ole hunk of her Aunt Betty's secret recipe!"

Mae-June smacked her lips, opened her mouth, closed it. Her lips parted on their own volition and words emitted she hadn't vetted in advance. "You think he's up to the task? Is he seasoned enough for us?"

Pastor Oscar's voice grew more serious. "Seasoned? I wouldn't call him seasoned. No one is seasoned straight out of the seminary. It takes time and experience to be seasoned."

"But should we be his guinea pigs?" Mae-June asked. She heard the exasperation in her own voice, took a deep breath, steadied herself. "I don't understand why the committee chose such a young man."

Pastor Oscar's voice came as close as Mae-June had ever heard to becoming annoyed. "The search committee felt his qualifications were excellent. That's all there is to it. Give the boy a chance. Not even been in Wilsons Corner a week and you're already stirring up trouble?"

"I am not stirring up trouble. I'm just being aware, is all. I mean, after all. That sermon. Surely, you have something to say about that."

Pastor Oscar was silent long enough for Mae-June to wonder if they'd been disconnected. "A little short—"

"A little short? That's all you've got to say?" Mae-June hated it when people accused her of being huffy. Unfortunately, she heard the huffiness in her voice now.

"Yes, it was a little short."

Pastor Oscar had always been too gentle. What would it take to rile the man up? To take a stand? To say he'd been wrong all along and Pastor Joe was too young and inexperienced? "Well, then," she said. "All I'm saying is I want to see our church served well. That's all I'm saying."

Pastor Oscar backpedaled. At least that's what his voice conveyed. "And that's exactly what the committee wants," he said. "Now don't you worry. I'm confident we have chosen the right man. Promise me you'll trust our decision and give him a chance."

Trust. There was that word again. "Trust is earned," she said.

"And haven't I earned your trust?"

She thought about this a bit. "I suppose," she finally said.

"Then give the boy a chance. And if it will ease your mind a little, I'll talk to him. I'll stop by the office tomorrow. What's his schedule?"

No problem answering that question. Mae-June memorized the pastor's schedule every week. "Counseling with the Riddles at 9:30. Why don't you drop by after lunch?"

That evening, Mae-June knelt beside her bed and prayed. "Dear God, I don't mean to bother you again. I'm just concerned about the well-being of the congregation. I prayed you would guide us to the new pastor. But I think Pastor Oscar just bulldozed the committee because of Pastor Joe's alma mater. Pardon me for saying, Lord, but I don't know if you sent us the right man."

CHAPTER FOURTEEN

J oe Decker had cabin fever. Hospital Fever would have been more accurate if there were such a term. He was tired of being confined to one room with the occasional limp down the hall with the help from the physical therapy guy. The over-bleached sheets scratched his skin. The lukewarm food arrived in indefinable scoops. Daytime television consisted of talk shows geared to women, quiz shows intent on making fools of the contestants, or, God forbid, those imbecilic 'daytime dramas'.

He had not suffered through Greek, hermeneutics, and eschatology only to waste his brain on this frivolity. He should be at Wilsons Corner Bible Believing Congregation by now. He had intended to call on Thursday right after speaking with Roxanne, but her reaction to the situation concerned him. They needed to talk things out. She was due at any minute. He didn't want to tell the church he was good to go if Roxanne was not. She had been expecting to stay in Boston and to keep her job as a guide for the Duck tours. She wanted to stay close to family.

That was his first choice, too. When he landed the associate pastor position at Church by the Meadows in Concord, they had celebrated. When the Board of Elders reneged, he panicked. With the wedding a few weeks away, he needed a job. Roxanne depended on him. He was a professional. He had a Master of Divinity degree. Roxanne had a job, not a profession. She had her sights on raising a family.

Joe believed the old adage that when God closed one door, He either opened another door or opened a window. Wilsons Corner was Joe's open window.

He was dreaming he was preaching in the Old North Church; standing on the high enclosed pulpit. Men in red coats marched slowly and solemnly down the aisle, beating their drums in harmony with the cadence of their steps. Rat-a-tat-tat.

One if by land. Two if by sea.

One if to stay. Two if to go.

From his position, he couldn't see the lamps in the white steeple of the church. One or two? Stay or go?

"Joe?"

He tried to roll over in bed, but something held him fast. His leg. Something weighed down his leg.

"Joe?"

He recognized Roxanne's voice. Slowly he opened his eyes. She looked beautiful—dark hair to her shoulders, the olive skin of her Italian mother, brown eyes that revealed the emotions of her heart. She was slight of build, but her spunk could put a man in his place very quickly. It was that spunk he feared today.

"Come here," he said. He stretched one arm towards her. "Give me a hug. I need a hug."

She crossed the room, bent over the bed, and hugged him. It was a friendly hug, not what he expected, not what he needed. She pushed away from him and looked for a place to sit.

"Here," he said. He patted the bed beside him.

She ignored him and sat in the uncomfortable-looking, wooden chair across the room.

"Bring it closer," he coaxed.

Roxanne stood, dragged the chair half the distance between them. If he weren't in so much pain, if he didn't need her support so much, he would have laughed. Her stubbornness was one of the qualities that attracted him to her, but not when it was used against him.

He remembered the first time he saw her. He'd never been to the northeast and had just arrived at Gordon Conwell Seminary from Abilene Christian University in Texas with his newly minted Bachelor of Theology degree in Biblical Studies. Before the semester started, he ventured into Boston with his roommate, Jack Bennington. Of all the tours they could have chosen that day, they chose the Duck tour. Roxanne was the guide.

"Welcome aboard!" she said in a voice that immediately grabbed his attention. "Today I will be your guide for an unusual journey through the streets of Boston, and of course, a splash down into the Charles River. Where is everyone visiting us from today?"

"Chicago!" shouted a woman in the rear. "Dropping my daughter off at Harvard." She patted the head of a teenager beside her who reddened and sank lower in her seat.

"Texas!" Joe called from the second row.

"And what brings you he-yah?" she asked.

It took Joe a minute to de-code 'he-yah.' He smiled at the accent. "Attending Gordon Conwell Seminary."

"If the Duck turns over in the river," she joked, "will you say a prayer for us?"

"No problem," he said.

Jack Bennington nudged him. "Get her number," he said.

The driver edged away from the curb and merged into traffic, and Roxanne held onto the bar on the back of the front seat as she faced the ten passengers and began her lecture. "To our right, you see the Mother Church, the world headquarters of the Christian Science Church. The building was completed in 1894 in just 13 months' time. It is reminiscent of the Romanesque style of architecture. The exterior is New Hampshire granite. Note the beautiful opalescent glass of the stained-glass windows. The church seats about 900 people. And the organ is one of the largest in the country with 2,825 pipes."

They passed Boston Common, the Swan Boats on the pond in the Public Garden, Beacon Hill, and the science museum. Pedestrians quacked as they passed and the passengers shouted, "Quack! Quack!" in response. As they splashed into the Charles River, Roxanne pointed out the sculling boats, Harvard boatyard, the Hatch Shell. And all the time Joe tried to think up ways to get her number. He ended up paying for three more Duck tours before she finally gave it to him. He knew right then and there she had a strong personality.

In his hospital bed, Joe tried to catch her eye, but she wouldn't look directly at him. "How was your trip?" he finally asked. Lame, he thought.

"Joe." She raised her eyes to the ceiling. They glistened. She blinked. "What happened?" she asked. "The Church in the Meadows. Wilsons Corner. The accident. We can't have a relationship if you don't trust me enough—"

"I trust you," he interrupted.

"Okay, then. You trust me. Let me start again. We cannot have a relationship if you don't honor me enough to draw me into the decision making. You can't expect I would just pull up roots and move a million miles away without even talking about it."

"I thought—"

"What? What did you think?"

What did he think? He wasn't sure. He'd moved from the Congo to Texas then to Boston not knowing anybody. He thought since they were moving together, it wouldn't be a problem. "I thought we'd start a life together," he said.

"I don't know." She fixed her eyes on something over his head.

A cold feeling spread from his heart. "What?" he asked. "What don't you know?"

She shook her head, her eyes brooding. "The whole thing." She lowered her eyes then raised them to look at him. "Wilsons Corner. You made a major decision without even consulting me. Being a pastor's wife. Is this how it will be? Me following whatever you decide God is telling you? I won't have a say in my own life?"

He reached out his hand, but she kept hers folded under her Mexican purse. He drew his hand back. "I'm learning, too," he said. "I was scared. I knew you were depending on me. I panicked when Church of the Meadows called. I felt like a trapeze artist who had let go of one bar. There wasn't a net, and I had to grab another bar before I fell."

"Did you have to grab the first bar?" she asked, the ice in her voice beginning to melt.

"I had no way of knowing if there'd be another bar," he whispered.

"How can you expect me to have faith if you don't?" she asked.

He had no reply. No one had ever questioned his faith before. Instead, he changed the subject. "The doctor said they'd be transferring me to the rehab wing. Maybe even by tomorrow."

Roxanne paced the room, arms folded across her chest, her eyes dark and moody. Joe watched her, hesitant to say anything. Better to give her time to process the whole thing.

Roxanne stopped by the window and looked down at the parking lot. Without turning to face him, she asked, "What did the church say when you told them about the accident?

Joe felt his Adam's apple rise and fall. "I didn't," he said. "I didn't call. I wanted to talk to you first. To see if you and I can work something out."

"It seems to me you have already decided what you're going to do. Now give me the number. I'll call." Meekly, he picked up a scrap of paper on the tray beside his bed. She snatched it from his hand and left the room.

CHAPTER FIFTEEN

The first thing Grady did when he left Pastor Oscar and Miss Cora in his rearview mirror was rip off the clerical collar and toss it in the back seat. When he returned to the personage, he stripped down to his Mickey Mouse boxers, tipped back a Heineken, and flipped on the television. The Miami Dolphins were up one entering the third quarter. He plopped onto the couch, stretched his legs across the coffee table, and pounded his fist into a throw pillow. "Go! Grab that ball!" he shouted at the television. "Down the field! Down the field! Go! Go! Go!" He stood, stamped his feet, pointed at the screen. "Touchdown! Way to go! Way to go!"

He took a long draught of his beer, looked around his domain and nodded. Life was good. Yes, very good, indeed. It was remarkable how life could change dramatically in less than a week if you had a little faith and stepped out into the unknown. If he had stayed living in that stinkin' house in Orlando, where would he be? Not watching football in his boxers, that's for sure. Matt the Rat hogged the television most Sunday afternoons watching reruns of Bonanza, Gunsmoke, and Rawhide. This was where he belonged.

During a commercial break near the end of the quarter, he padded barefoot into the kitchen for another beer, pleased that on his way home from Pastor Oscar's, he'd found a small convenience store that actually sold beer on Sundays and (after he donned his white collar) they hadn't even asked for ID. It was a stupid law—not selling beer on Sunday or to anyone under twenty-one. You could vote or go to war at 18—even get married, but they didn't want you having any fun until 21. Where was the sense of that?

As he pulled open the refrigerator door, he heard a ringing. He'd read about refrigerators giving off a dinging noise if you left the door open too long, but this noise upon opening was new to him. He grabbed the beer, slammed the door, and still heard the ringing. The phone! Wilfred had told him a phone would ring in here if no one answered in the office. Wilfred said he didn't have to answer it, but on a Sunday afternoon? It might be important. What the hey. He picked up the receiver. "Hello?"

The silence stretched a bit too long. He almost hung up, then a soft, tentative female voice spoke. "Is this the church office?"

Grady glanced down at his ridiculous boxers as though she could see him. He reached for his throat, searching for the sacred collar he'd tossed in the back seat of the Pontiac. "Actually, this is the personage."

"Oh," she said. "My name is Roxanne Newman."

Roxanne, Roxanne, ROXANNE! Pastor Joe's fiancée! "Oh, yes, Roxanne. How are you?

In the other room, loud cheering and whistling erupted. Grady walked to the cutout in the wall to see which fans were the ecstatic ones. He couldn't tell from this angle.

"Hello?" Roxanne said. "I can't hear you. There's lots of people talking. Do you have people there?"

"Sorry," Grady said. He walked to the other side of the tiny kitchen. "Is this any better?"

"Yes. I'm calling to let you know on the way down to Tennessee, Joe was in a car accident."

Yes! Grady thought with a fist pump. Please say he died. Oh yeah. The problem could be solved with this one simple phone call! Oh yeah. Oh yeah.

"His car was totaled. They brought him by ambulance to the hospital."

And? Grady was all ears now. Who cared about football!

"He has a broken leg, a shattered ankle, and other minor injuries, but he's going to be all right."

Grady's shoulders slumped like a deflated balloon.

"He's been in the hospital a couple of days. They're transferring him to rehab tomorrow. He wants you to know that's why he didn't show up on time. He's not sure when the doctors will say it's all right for him to start work."

"Tell him to take all the time he needs," Grady insisted. "Three weeks would be good. Four weeks would be even better. Whatever he needs." He held the phone to his ear with his shoulder, popped open the Heineken, titled his head back and gulped half the can.

"Thank you," Roxanne said. "That's so kind of you. I'll tell Joe what you said and I'll be back in touch to let you know his progress."

Back in touch? "Just a sec," Grady said. "Let me give you my cell phone number. That way you can call me directly and keep me posted."

"Okay," she said. "Let me get a piece of paper."

Grady heard footsteps and the rustling of paper, and then Roxanne's voice. "Okay. I'm ready."

He recited his phone number, and she said, "I'm sorry. I didn't get your name."

His name? His name? Should he say Grady or Joe or make up a totally different name? How was he going to keep all his identities straight? Things were getting complicated. Then he thought of a brainstorm. "Joe," he said. "Just like the new pastor we've been waiting for."

"What a coincidence!" she said.

"Yeah," he said. "What a coincidence." He was about to hang up when he heard her sniffle. "Roxanne, are you all right?" he asked.

"Yes." Yet her voice conveyed otherwise. "No. Maybe. I don't know."

Grady set the beer can down on the kitchen table and hoisted himself onto the counter between the sink and stove. He didn't know what to make of a Yes, No, Maybe, I don't know answer. His experience with women was limited. He'd only had one girlfriend, Emily Pratt. She was a short girl who could whip any kid in the school in tennis. The kids nicknamed her Whippet. She had these little muscular legs and could pivot back and forth on the court like nothing he'd ever seen. But she wasn't emotional.

She was a no-nonsense, facts-only person. In the eight months they dated— most of junior year— he'd never seen her cry. She hadn't given him much insight into the female brain.

"It's more than the accident." Roxanne's sniffles grew louder. "Just a minute."

Grady heard more rustling then she blew her nose loudly.

"Sorry," she said. "I didn't even know Joe was going to Tennessee. Do you believe it? We're getting married in about a month and I didn't even know. When was he going to tell me?"

Grady waited for her to answer her own question. When she didn't, all he could offer was, "I don't know."

"Me neither," she said. "He said he was waiting for the right time. What's that supposed to mean?"

"I don't know," he said, shrugging.

"He was supposed to be the Assistant Pastor of the Church in the Meadows in Concord. We weren't moving anywhere. I've always lived in Boston. I don't want to leave. How could he do this?" The sniffles dissolved into sobs and another loud honk of nose blowing.

"Maybe he could still get that job by the meadow," Grady said hopefully.

"Church in the Meadows," she said. "That's the thing. He says they called two weeks ago. He's known for two weeks! They miscalculated their budget and can't afford to hire another assistant. I'm sorry to be dumping on you. I just don't know who to talk to. But you ... Joe, what's your position there?"

Position? A few days ago, he didn't have one. For four days, he was a pastor. What was he this evening? What was it she said Joe was supposed to be in the meadows church? "Assistant Pastor," he said.

"Oh." She sounded surprised. "So, it's a large church then? They have a pastor and an assistant?"

Grady didn't know where the cut-off was between large and small churches. Wilsons Corner was bigger than the storefront church his grandmother attended, but smaller by a long shot than the Baptist churches in and around Orlando. "Medium," he said.

"Anyway," she said. "You're a pastor so you have experience counseling people. So, do you mind if I tell you about it?"

Grady said, "Sure. No problem. I don't mind." He looked down at his feet dangling about a foot from the floor. He flexed and unflexed his toes. "So, how'd he get the gig down here?"

"Weren't you involved?" she asked. "Don't you know?"

Yikes. Almost a giveaway. Think fast. "Not really," he said. "I've kind of been out of the loop."

"Oh," she said. "Joe interviewed by Skype a couple of months ago. We talked and he decided not to take it. My family lives in Boston, and we're really close. I love my job. But then when the position at Church in the Meadows fell through, he called down there. I guess you've been having a hard time getting a pastor. Anyway, they did another phone interview, he says, and hired him on the spot."

"It's something to love your job. Few people can say that. What do you do?"

"I narrate Duck Tours of Boston. I can't narrate a Duck Tour of Boston in Tennessee."

"Duck Tour?" He was beginning to like this Roxanne. Not in a romantic way, of course.

He didn't even know her. But he found her upbeat, open, honest. Something about her voice. He wasn't sure what, exactly. He already felt closer to Roxanne Newman than he ever had to Emily Pratt.

"It's a replica of a WWII amphibious vehicle they refurbished to give tours through the city. Our big finale is a splashdown into the Charles River. Big cities have them." She sighed. "I never imagined myself married to a pastor. Then I met Joe. He says he got this 'call' from God. I don't even know what that means. How did you become a pastor? Did God call you?"

Actually, in his case, it had been a deer. "Well," he said, letting the word linger. He caught sight of the Bible he'd used that morning. "Interesting story, really. I actually preached about it this morning." Maybe he could get Roxanne to talk Joe Decker out of his 'calling.' If this dude stayed in Boston, things could get back to the new normal of the last week.

"It's one thing to change your career path," she said, "but don't you think you should consult your future wife before accepting a calling?" She spoke as if the last word were curdled milk.

Grady shrugged. Roxanne didn't hold back her feelings. "I suppose," he said.

"What is the church like? What is the town like? Is there even a mall there?"

"The church is fine," he said. That didn't reveal much, but he couldn't think of a better word. "They gave me a welcome party when I arrived. It was nice. There's one woman whose date bars won some kind of prize at the fair. As for a mall, I haven't seen one."

Her sigh sent wave after wave of staccato tones through the telephone connection. "Great," she said. "Prize-winning date bars and no mall. A real happening place." She sniffed. "Joe says it was a good thing I wasn't with him. He says I might have been killed. He says God intervened."

"I guess so," Grady said. But he was only thinking of himself. He hoped God intervened Joe Decker straight back to Boston. Wilsons Corner Bible Believing Congregation would be none the wiser.

CHAPTER SIXTEEN

Monday morning Grady awoke with a start. Something had happened the night before. Something important. Something he had to remember. Yes! Roxanne. Roxanne called. Joe Decker and the car accident. This put an interesting twist on Grady's plans. He really hadn't put much thought into where Pastor Joe might be and why he hadn't shown up as expected. Just thought he, himself, had caught a lucky break. Now, he had to keep Pastor Joe away for a little while or at least get out of Wilsons Corner before the man showed up. Grady realized he needed to keep up communication with Roxanne. Yeah, that was it. Keep talking to Roxanne. She'd keep him informed and he'd be able to ride this wave right into the beach before jumping off.

He was still thinking about Roxanne and Pastor Joe when he entered his office in the church an hour later. A man and a woman occupied the guest chairs. The woman was crying, and the man sat stoically looking out the window.

Grady slid to a stop, hand still on the doorknob. "May I help you?" he asked, unable to hide his surprise.

The woman boohooed into a tissue and the man turned to Grady with cold eyes. When he spoke, his voice was even colder. "Mae-June said our appointment was for 9:30 and it's already 10:00."

9:30. Appointment. Mae-June. Oh yes! Grady snapped his fingers. Those people. What were their names? *Why did the bee get married? Because he found his honey.* The Riddles! Marriage Counseling. Grady closed the door and tried hard to contain a smirk. These guys were older than his mother. Probably closer to his grandparents' age!

He dropped into his chair, grabbed hold of his desk, and pulled himself closer to it. "I'm sorry," he said, eyes darting from man to woman. "An emergency came up." Sleep, that was an emergency, wasn't it? He tried to remember if he had combed his hair.

The couple remained silent. Grady looked from one to the other, trying to figure out what he was supposed to do. *Did Adam and Eve ever have a date? No. They only had an apple.* The minutes ticked by as the tension in the room built up. It was Mrs. Riddle who broke the silence.

"He says he's leaving me. He says we have nothing in common anymore." She covered her mouth with the soggy tissue.

Grady pulled a wad of tissues from the box on the corner of his desk and handed them to her. He looked at Mr. Riddle and decided to start with the basics. Heart pounding, he fought to keep his voice calm. "Let's start with introductions." Palm upraised, Grady extended an arm towards the husband.

"Ralph Riddle," the man grunted.

Muffled by the tissues, came the words, "Rose Riddle."

"So." Grady dragged out the word as long as possible. "Ralph and Rose, how long have you been married?"

"What's that got to do with anything?" Ralph growled.

Rose raised her face from the wad of tissues, looked sideways at her husband, and inched to the far side of her chair.

"Just trying to get a handle on things," Grady said. "See what the problem is. I mean, if you said two years, I'd say one thing, but if you said twenty, I'd say something else."

Ralph scratched his nose, looked puzzled. "That what they teach you in seminary? Recite page fifty for newbies and quote page a hundred for old folks?"

Grady leaned back in his chair, swiveled to and fro. The wheels squeaked. "No," he said. "Matter of fact, I don't have any memorized speeches from seminary. What I'm going to say comes from my own experience. What I know to be true."

Ralph snorted. "What do you know? This your first job? Looks to me you're as lost as last year's Easter egg."

Last year's Easter egg?

Rose dropped the tissues onto her lap. "Not fair, Ralph," she said. "Give 'im a chance." Ralph half raised out of his seat, his face scrunched into a scowl. "He ain't even hitched. What does he know? Life ain't nothin' like book learnin'."

"Let him speak," Rose insisted.

Grady waited for Ralph to settle down. "Okay," he said, "See, my friends in high school, they were in love. Huggin' in the hallways. Doin' what you'd call makin' out in cars. Couldn't get enough of each other."

Just the hint of light went on in Rose's eyes. The right side of her mouth almost smiled. "Us, too," she said. Ralph played hockey—"

"He doesn't want to hear this!" Ralph's hand zig-zagged through the air between them.

"Actually, I do," Grady countered. "Go on, Rose."

Ralph's eyes turned heavenward and he guffawed. "Here we go," he said. "Here we go."

The light in Rose's eyes brightened ever so slightly. The right side of her lips tugged upwards. "Remember, Ralph? Your red Mustang? We spent a lot of time in that."

Ralph harrumphed. "That was thirty years ago," he reminded her, his eyes at half-mast.

Grady knew pink splotches were spreading across his own hot cheeks. He coughed. He really didn't want to picture it. "What else did you do besides that?"

Ralph folded his arms across his chest. "I don't remember."

Rose edged an inch or two towards Ralph. "I do," she said. "When we were first married, I use to prepare a special meal on Friday night, and we ate by candlelight."

"Go on," Grady prompted.

"On Saturday," Rose continued, "we did housework together."

Ralph glared at his wife. "So, you think if I pick up a broom, everything's gonna be all right?" He turned to Grady. "I work overtime in the factory so she can stay home and take care of the kids. Now she wants me to clean the house?"

"I didn't say—"

"Which factory would that be?" Grady interrupted.

Ralph grumbled, shifted in his chair. "Zellwood Furniture Parts," he said, his voice a few notches below the disgust he had previously demonstrated. "We make parts for different furniture manufacturers in North Carolina. I run the lathe, mainly work on wooden legs."

"Sounds pretty dangerous," Grady said. "Working on a lathe." He didn't know what a lathe was, but he presumed it was a machine and most machines were dangerous.

"That's the point!" Ralph leaned forward, hands on knees.

Grady noted the man's dirty fingernails.

"It ain't easy," Ralph continued. "Guys get hurt in there all the time. I could go somewhere else. But why do I stay? More money, that's why. So's, I bring in more money for her." He thrust his thumb in Rose's direction.

Grady held Ralph's gaze. "You must love her to make such a sacrifice." He wanted to laugh. He'd used this trick against his mother many times. Take her own words as cues and twist them for a different meaning. As a matter of fact, he'd done something similar to Mae-June yesterday. Or was it the day before? Time was blending into one long train of activity.

Ralph snorted. He stood, placed one hand on his forehead, the other on his hip and paced the room. "I do love her," he said. "That's not the point."

"What is the point?" Grady asked. He glanced at his watch. Waited for either Ralph or Rose to speak. Neither did. "Pastor Oscar and Miss Cora hold hands," Grady said. "Do you hold hands?"

"Oh, for God's sake, this is ridiculous!" Ralph stopped by the window, placed both hands on the sill and stared outside. "We're not teenagers."

"But you were happy as teenagers," Grady said. "Sit down, Mr. Riddle. Hold your wife's hand."

Ralph Riddle looked ready to explode.

"I wish you would." Rose looked hopeful. "We used to do things together." She sniffled. "Now it's like you don't care."

"What I regret is you nagging me. 'Come to the table, Ralph.' 'Play ball with your son, Ralph.' 'Help with the dishes, Ralph.' 'Come to church, Ralph'."

"What I want is for you to spend time with your son, Ralph. Before he grows up. Moves away. I don't want you to regret it."

"Is it baseball?" Grady interrupted.

"What?" Ralph turned from the window.

"Baseball. Softball. Basketball. What type of ball do you play with your son?"

"I didn't say I played."

"Do you?" Grady asked. "Like to play ball?"

"He used to play softball in high school," Rose offered. "Along with basketball. He was pretty good at both, too."

"Life isn't about fun and games," Ralph snapped. "It's about work. It's about responsibility. It's about paying your bills. Don't you understand, Rose? I'm busier than a one-legged cat in a sandbox."

"I like to play basketball and softball," Grady said. "Maybe I can join you some time." He wondered what it would be like to play sports with a father. His own father was long gone before Grady started walking, and Matt the Rat was nothing but someone to put a roof over his head. Both Mr. and Mrs. Riddle stared at him, speechless.

"Just sayin'." Grady opened his top drawer. Picked up a stapler. Opened and closed it a few times. Staples fastening nothing at all dropped to his desk. The Riddles seemed to be hypnotized as they watched the staples pile up.

Ralph said slowly, "Ralphie would like that, too, I imagine."

"Tell you what. How about we plan a church picnic, and we have a softball game? Would you play?" Grady turned his attention to Ralph, waiting for an answer.

Ralph shrugged. Stuck out his bottom lip. "Maybe," he finally said. "I guess. Yeah. I'd come and play softball."

"It's too cold," Rose said. "We can't have a picnic in this weather."

"I know," Grady answered. "In the spring." Already he was planning ahead. Staking his claim on leading Wilsons Corner Bible Believing Congregation. "What would you bring, Rose?" Grady fiddled with the pile of staples, making different shapes, sweeping them into a pile, designing a new formation. "If we had a picnic, what would you bring?" Before she answered, he turned to Ralph. "What's your favorite thing Rose makes? What should she bring to the church picnic?"

Without hesitation, Ralph said. "Those frosted brownies with nuts. You haven't made them in a long time. Yeah. That would be good."

"Okay," Rose said. "I'll bring the frosted brownies."

"They sound delicious!" Grady said, his eyes brightening. "Do I have to wait 'til a church picnic or will you make some for me sometime?"

Rose's cheeks flushed. She lowered her head, studied her hands. "I s'pose I could bring you some."

"Cool beans," Grady said. "Now, Ralph, sit down. Hold your wife's hand."

"What?" Ralph looked incredulous.

"Sit down," Grady said, pointing to the chair Ralph had vacated.

Ralph checked his watch. "We've gotta get going."

"Just sit down," Grady said calmly and firmly.

"You were half an hour late. We have things to do." Ralph gripped his wife's upper arm, urging her to stand.

"We're almost done," Grady said. "Now sit down."

Slowly, Ralph lowered into his chair. Rose offered her hand and Ralph stared at it. He grabbed it and dragged it back to his leg. "Are you happy now?" he asked.

"I think it's a start," Grady answered before Rose had a chance to open her mouth. "But before you come back, I'd like the two of you . . . " He couldn't get himself to utter the words he wanted to say lest his mind conjured up an image he didn't want to see. He settled on a phrase he'd heard in an old black and white risqué movie. "I want the two of you to get to third base by tonight." He studied them to see if they got the message.

Both looked shocked.

"That would be my first suggestion," Grady said. "If you don't like that idea, I think you should carry through on your word, Ralph. I think you should leave tonight. Do you have a place to stay?"

"You think he should leave me?" Rose reached for more tissues from the box on Grady's desk.

"I didn't say that," Grady said. "You're the one who said he wanted to leave you. I mean, what the hey. Stay or go. Make a choice." He picked up the stapler and shot five staples across his desk.

"Idiot!" Ralph clutched Rose's hand tighter and pounded his other fist near the Pastor Joe nameplate. "Come on, Rose, we're going home. I can't believe this joker."

"Just giving it to you straight, man. Just giving it to you straight." Grady stuck his index finger inside the clerical collar, stretched it out a little.

The Riddles watched Grady adjust the collar. All three sat quietly. "Time," Ralph finally said. "Maybe we should just give this a little more time. Try out third base and see you again next week. What could it hurt?"

Rose gasped.

"Sounds like a plan," Grady said. He rose, walked to the door, and opened it. "Make an appointment with my secretary for next week, same time."

They left, holding hands and smiling.

What do you call two birds in love? Tweethearts.

Grady plopped into his desk chair, pushed himself away from his desk and burst out laughing. He laughed and laughed and laughed and laughed. Third base! How had he ever come up with that one for a couple of old farts?

CHAPTER SEVENTEEN

Grady fed junk mail into the shredder beside his desk. Advertisement after advertisement. Timeshare postcard. Application for life insurance. *We're pleased to inform you* ... It was a stupid exercise, this shredding. Nothing but busywork. If Mae-June hadn't insisted he complete this task, he would have been off to practice with the band. He was pretty excited about meeting them last week. It was difficult to keep up the facade of pastor with them—he just wanted to relax, be as carefree as they were. He wondered what they would think when he hightailed it out of this Podunk town. He wouldn't let himself think about it. He had to do what he had to do. Let the chips fall. Move on with his life. What a bunch of clichés. Life was just nothing but clichés when you stopped to think about it.

"How's it going?"

Grady's hand missed the slot in the shredder and the *You've been selected* postcard fell to the floor. He bent to pick it up and noticed Pastor Oscar in the doorway. He wore a blue three-button polo shirt with a pin-stripe blazer and khaki pants with a perfect crease. His white hair was combed straight back with no part. His smile was warm and accepting. He looked so . . . Grady searched for a word. *Confident. Official. In charge. Put together.* That was it. Put together in any kind of way you could think of.

"Hey," Grady said. He stood and extended his hand. "Come on in." He pointed to the chair opposite his desk.

In three strides, Pastor Oscar made it to the chair and sat down. In a dignified way, Grady thought. The man sat dignified. Grady shimmied up in his own chair, attempting to mimic the confidence and put together manner of Pastor Oscar.

"I stopped in to see how you were doing." Pastor Oscar crossed one knee over the other and folded his hands on his knees.

"Fine," Grady said, hoping he sounded more confident than he felt. His voice caught on the word and he coughed. He grabbed a tissue from the box Mrs. Riddle had practically emptied this morning.

Pastor Oscar's eyebrows rose as did the corner of his lips. "Oh? Then you are doing better than I did with my first church."

Grady leaned back in the chair. He swiveled from side to side. He opened his mouth to speak. Closed it. How much to reveal? How much to ask? He liked this man. Wanted to trust him. "What happened in your first church?" It was a safe topic, and luckily, his voice sounded normal to his own ears.

"Where to begin," Pastor Oscar said. He chuckled and Grady couldn't help but smile. "I didn't have a secretary. You're lucky to have Mae-June."

Grady rolled his eyes before he could catch himself.

Pastor Oscar held up a hand. "I know," he said. "I know. She can be a little bossy at times. Thinks she needs to ..." He drew imaginary quotation marks in the air. "Train you. Just overlook that and do what you've already been trained to do. You remember Dr. Horowitz's class on the day-to-day duties of the pastor?"

Pastor Oscar smiled and seemed to be waiting for something. Grady manufactured a smile and nodded.

"Just put into practice what Dr. Horowitz taught. You do all right in that class?"

Grady shrugged. He wanted to be as confident as Pastor Oscar, but at the same time, he wanted to be honest with someone he admired and someone who actually wanted to help him. "About the same as my other classes," he said. "No problem, really."

The light in Pastor Oscar's eyes dimmed for a second. "No need to be modest," he said. "I spoke to Dr. Horowitz. He said you did some outstanding work in that class."

Grady licked his lips, rolled closer to his desk, opened the top right drawer. He took out the stapler and began releasing staples into a neat little pile in front of him. Was Pastor Oscar testing him? Grady preferred multiple choice tests, not fill-in-the-blank tests with one right answer. He was pretty good at eliminating and guessing. If you paid attention, lots of times one question revealed hints or answers to upcoming questions. But this wasn't school, so he had another method of deflecting attention from himself—keep the other person talking about himself. "Back to your first church," Grady said. "What happened?"

"Yes, of course." Pastor Oscar slapped his knee. "Mae-June will keep you organized. I didn't have that luxury, and back then, I wasn't very organized. So, this one time I had to officiate at a wedding. The next day I had a funeral for a couple who had died in a boating accident if I recall correctly." He stopped, studied the floor, tilted his head. "It's been a long time. Maybe they drowned. Anyway, something to do with water. That's not the point. I was new to the parish—three weeks, maybe a month. There I was, up there at the wedding calling the couple I was marrying by the names of the couple I was going to bury the next day." His face reddened and he shook his head. "Nobody corrected me until I asked them to repeat after me to say their vows. 'I Kathy,' you know how it goes."

Grady nodded, eyes locked on Pastor Oscar. He felt his shoulders relax.

"Even now I get embarrassed thinking about it," Pastor Oscar said. "The mother of the bride stood. Indignant, she was. 'They are very much alive,' she called to me from the front row. 'You are trying to marry two dead people.'"

Grady laughed. "I haven't done anything that bad."

"Yet," Pastor Oscar interjected.

"Yet," Grady repeated. He knew the consequences of making a serious mistake would be more to him than the reddening of a face half a century later. He'd be sent packing immediately. And for that matter, he could be packing for jail! Was impersonating a pastor a crime?

"How about we talk about preaching?" Pastor Oscar's voice changed. Sweeter. Gentler. As if he were talking to a child.

Grady thought about the deer. It was a pretty good analogy. He hoped no one had complained to Mae-June or Pastor Oscar. "Was there a problem?" he asked.

"Well." Pastor Oscar seemed to be searching for a word. "The deer illustration was good. Very good. I appreciated that."

"Okay." Grady flicked a few pieces of confetti-like paper off the shredder onto the floor.

"You were enthusiastic in your presentation."

"And?"

"It was a bit short." Pastor Oscar raced through the words.

Grady had to repeat the words in his head to understand. "Hmm," he said. "I thought people would appreciate short. When I went to church with my grandmother, everyone was excited to have more time for Sunday afternoon."

Pastor Oscar looked puzzled. He placed his forefinger over his lips and studied Grady. "Hmm," he said. "Hmm." He removed his hand. "Your grandmother?" Before Grady could reply, Pastor Oscar said, "No mind. Twenty – thirty minutes is a short sermon to this congregation. If you want a short sermon, keep it to that. These people are used to 45 minutes to an hour."

An hour! Grady didn't see how he could come up with twenty to thirty minutes!

"Just remember," Pastor Oscar said. "I'm here for you. Use me as a resource. What can I help you with?"

Grady relaxed even more. He hadn't known he was tense until the tension began to dissipate. "I'll try to extend my sermons," he said. "But there are a few other things."

"Yes?"

"Board meeting, for starters. Mae-June made up the agenda. Do I have to stick to it? I'd like to make some changes. Can I do that?" Grady picked up the agenda Mae-June had typed up and handed it to Pastor Oscar. Before the retired pastor could answer his first question, Grady came up with another and another. "What's the deal with the water fountains?"

Pastor Oscar laughed. "You've got a good heart, Pastor Joe. A caring spirit. I see you're worried about stepping on people's toes. You're the leader now. Remember that. You've got good instincts. Trust your gut and your education. I spoke to Dr. Drexel and Dr. Horowitz about you. Dr. Drexel said you aced the Pastoral Leadership class. Go ahead and make the changes. Bring them to the board tomorrow and we'll vote. That's why it's a committee. Checks and balances. Bring your confidence to the table. Dr. Drexel said you were top of your class— prepared and confident. He told me about that weeklong seminar you held. How good you did. If you could handle that with grace, a board meeting should be easy."

Trouble is, Grady wanted to say, I wasn't there when I supposedly presented that seminar or took those classes. He wished he could simply recall Dr. Drexel's words. Unfortunately, he hadn't heard them in the first place.

"Thanks," Grady said. He felt close to this man and looked forward to getting to know him better.

CHAPTER EIGHTEEN

Joe Decker stabbed into what he guessed to be meatloaf swimming in half congealed brown gravy. The mystery of rehab food. When they transferred him to the rehab wing, he'd hoped the food would taste better. So far, it didn't seem so.

He placed the bite into his mouth, chewed as little as possible and gulped it down. Maybe the scoop of mashed potatoes would taste better. He unwrapped the pat of butter and placed it on top of the potatoes. It balanced there like a snowboard perched on the edge of a slope, and it didn't melt. Unappetizing. Yellow Jell-O wriggled in one corner of his tray and lukewarm coffee in the other. He'd have to remember this during hospital visitations. During seminary, he had sympathy for the folks he visited. Now he had empathy. At least he wouldn't have to put up with it much longer. The therapist said he'd be discharged soon.

Today had been a rough day. The physical therapist pushed him too far. By the time he'd trudged down the hall to the nurse's station on metal crutches, he was sweating from the exertion. While the physical therapist held him upright, one of the nurses—Alva or Alma or something like that—had quickly rolled over an office chair for him to plop into and catch his breath before he trekked back to his room. Only a broken leg. There was nothing ONLY about this.

"Are you finished with your dinner?" A teenager stood beside the door fiddling with the net covering a mound of dark brown hair. She wore the pink uniform of the kitchen staff.

"As much as I'm going to eat," he said.

She approached the bed cautiously and reached for his tray.

"Are you from around here?" Joe asked.

She nodded, her cheeks flushed. "All my life," she said.

"I was just passing through," he said. "Do you have any idea how far we are from Wilsons Corner?"

"Mm-hmm," she said. "I have kin down that way. I'd say … maybe … I'd say forty minutes or so. Maybe more. But definitely less than an hour."

"Thanks," he said. He glanced at her name badge. "Emma-Jean. Thanks, Emma-Jean."

He picked up the television remote and clicked through the channels until he found Wheel of Fortune. "I'll buy a vowel," said the man in the first contestant station. "E."

"There are five Es," said Pat Sajak.

A bell dinged and Vanna White sashayed across the stage in a shimmery pastel blue evening gown. She turned lit-up squares to reveal the E's.

He must have dozed. The next thing Joe knew, a nurse was cranking up a blood pressure cuff on his bicep. He smacked his lips to moisten his dry mouth. "Oh," he said, scooting up in bed and wincing in pain. "What time is it?"

She removed the stethoscope from one ear and said, "Eight thirty. Here, let me take this reading and then we'll see what I can do to make you more comfortable."

More comfortable? He doubted there was anything. Except to help to him think up words to calm down Roxanne. He wasn't happy about the way they'd left things the other night. She hadn't been in touch all day.

The nurse ripped the Velcro apart on the blood pressure cuff, folded it up, and stuffed it into its place on the wall. "So," she said, "What can I do to make you comfier?"

Joe checked out her name badge. *Stella.*

"Stella," he said. "Will you see if my phone's in working order? I've been expecting a call from my girlfriend, fiancée … actually. She hasn't called and I'm wondering if my phone is off."

Stella picked up the phone on the nightstand just out of Grady's reach. "There's a dial tone," she said. "Tell me about your fiancée." She tugged on his blanket and sheet.

"What would you like to know?" Joe turned the volume down on the television.

"Let's start with her name," Stella said brightly.

"Roxanne," Joe said. "Beautiful dark hair. Blacker than black. Black with a sheen. It's long. To her shoulders."

Stella smiled, encouraging him to continue.

"Her parents are both Italian. Her grandparents on both sides are first generation born in this country. She's got that Italian nose …" He fingered his own nose. "And eyes so brown the pupils blend in. She's short, but don't think that makes her a pushover. I've seen her put men twice her size in their place. Me included."

Stella laughed. "What does she do for work?"

"She's a tour guide on the Duck boat in Boston. You ever been on a Duck tour?"

Stella shook her head. "I've never even heard of it."

"It's this thing," Joe said. "An old World War II vehicle they drive down the streets in Boston, then it goes right into the Charles River and they steer it like a boat."

"How interesting," Stella said. "Sounds fun."

"It is," Joe answered. "Big cities have them. Miami. San Francisco. Philadelphia."

"She must love that job," Stella said. "So unusual."

Joe smiled, nodded his head. "Yeah, she does."

"What will she do once you settle here?"

Joe's smile evaporated. His shoulders drooped. "I don't know," he said. "We'll have to see." He brightened a little. "It's not a career or anything. She didn't have to go to school to do it."

Stella patted his hand. "I'm sure it will all work out," she said. "Now see if you can get some rest."

He dreamed Roxanne drove a Duck boat from Boston to Tennessee. Traffic jams formed on the highway since the vehicle couldn't travel very fast. People lined the road to gawk. A television helicopter hovered overhead broadcasting the spectacle live over the Internet. He watched her progression on his computer from his bed in rehab. He was bandaged head to toe, with only his eyes exposed, blinking. He wondered how he could possibly eat. In the dream, he remembered it was a dream, so eating didn't matter.

At the Tennessee border, Roxanne sped up. From his hospital bed, Joe tried to scream at her to slow down. That's where he'd gone off the road. But his mouth was covered with bandages and all that came out was the sound of an angry cat. Now the Duck rolled and careened down the hill.

He woke himself up screaming "No! No! No!" He panted, swiped a hand across his sweaty brow, and forced his breathing to slow. What did the dream mean—or did it mean anything? In the Bible, men had dreams. It meant God was speaking to them. Is that how he should take this dream? If so, what was God trying to tell him? Move? Don't move? What was the precipice?

CHAPTER NINETEEN

On Tuesday, Grady awoke at 7:00 a.m. A personal record. He had gotten used to sleeping until 9:00 or 10:00 at least. He yawned, stretched, and looked around his bedroom with contentment. Tomorrow would be a week since starting his new job. Things were going well. He wondered how he'd spend his day. He had the board meeting tonight. Certainly, they didn't expect him to work all day, too. After all, he was on duty all day Sunday. Give a guy a break.

Explore the area, that's what he'd do. See if he could find some stores. Use the credit card Mae-June had handed over for 'church business' as long as he got 'permission' ahead of time. Who was she kidding? He was the pastor, not her. Besides, he needed a better wardrobe for this job. And she'd been critical of his hair. He'd go out, buy some clothes, get a haircut, and hope upon hope they had an arcade where he could slip in a few quarters.

Sometimes he spent six hours a day playing CALL OF DUTY. Before last week, he hadn't skipped a day in over a year. Strange. The desire to play had suddenly evaporated. Partly, he surmised, because of that clunky thing in the study of the personage Wilfred called a computer. It was a dinosaur. It had nowhere near the capacity or graphics needed for CALL OF DUTY.

Grady plunked himself down on the couch with his cell phone and googled church board meetings, devotionals, and praise music. He read a number of articles and listened to some praise music on YouTube. He then picked up the draft of the minutes and agenda Mae-June had given him. He compared her agenda to what he read online, re-organized the order, and scratched out some items altogether. One site said to assign a certain amount of time for each agenda item and stick with it. He scribbled '10' beside some items, '15' beside others. Another site said a regular monthly board meeting should be no more than two hours. He adjusted the times. Mae-June and Pastor Oscar said he was in charge, so that's what he would be—in charge. As the very last item on the agenda, he added *schedule church picnic and softball game*. He e-mailed the changes to Mae-June and asked her to have them ready for the board meeting. He then googled 'nearby malls' and left the personage before Mae-June could snag him.

The mall, he noted, was twenty miles north. The next time Roxanne called, he'd be able to answer her question about the mall. Once he was on the interstate, Grady pulled the Pontiac into the left lane and gunned it. He shot past the middle-laners as though they were creeping towards a drive-through window. He made it past 80 mph, a sense of freedom engulfing him. He wanted to keep driving. To head north. Mae-June was too much like an overbearing parent, and Grady wanted to be on his own.

Despite the fleeting thought, he took the mall exit and circled until he found the entrance to the Food Court. He was looking for the arcade and he knew the most likely place for one was there. The aroma of fried food engulfed him the minute he opened the door, and *Bingo!* There was the sign pointing to a room between the pizza place and a Chinese buffet.

A young Asian girl standing outside *Fast and Good Asian Food* offered him Sweet and Sour Chicken on a toothpick and he weaseled two out of her. An acne-faced boy in the next booth, *Best Yogurt in Tennessee*, held out a minuscule spoon of frozen yogurt in a tiny white paper cup. Grady swallowed it in one swig, took another, and a third. He left the bewildered boy and headed for the arcade.

Multi-colored lights flashed in the dark interior. Dings and dongs echoed from wall to wall. Shadows floated past him— students ditching school like he used to do. He'd spend the day in the arcade at the mall, strut home at the expected time, glowing with pride over earning the new record score, greeting his mother with a hug and kiss, lying about acing a test.

The arcade was familiar territory.

He slipped two quarters into a machine, grabbed the controller, and waited for his first prey to materialize along the moving blue screen. His brain and hand went into automatic mode. Grady pulled the trigger at just the right moment and blood spurted across the screen. One enemy down.

The screen changed from hallway to railroad track. An enemy sniper jumped from a mountain, automatic weapon poised, but Grady was faster on the draw. He riddled the life-like character with bullets. Blood dripped from each wound, but the guy refused to die. Grady grabbed another controller. A knife appeared. He jumped on the enemy, stabbed him in the back repeatedly until he finally died. The machine dinged and dinged and dinged, joyfully adding up his score.

He fed quarter after quarter into the machine, his psyche going deeper and deeper into the make-believe world of the battle. Sometime later, he heard a little girl's voice from the doorway.

"Mommy, there's our pastor."

Grady heard but didn't comprehend the words. He grabbed the control, intent on the screen, his mind focused on the game. He felt tapping on his left leg, then on his right. He looked down. Two clones stood beside him—one on the left and one on the right. They had blonde pigtails, a few freckles on their noses. They wore identical brown corduroy elastic-waist pants and orange shirts with ruffles at the neck and edges of their sleeves. A second little voice said, "Hi, Pastor Joe."

"Betty Lou! Betty Jean! Come here this instant!"

As the fog of the alternate world slowly lifted, Grady looked to the door and there stood the pretty young mother who had clip-clopped past him in the church hallway. She had one hand on her hip, and with the other, she pointed a finger from the floor in front of her to the girls.

He looked back at the girls, then knelt in front of the death machine. "Well, hello, Betty Lou, Betty Jean." He said the names randomly without looking at them specifically. He wondered how their own mother told them apart. "Let's go see your mom." He took the girls by the hand and led them from the darkness into the lighted mall.

"I didn't expect to see anyone I knew way out here," Grady said, grinning.

"Apparently not," said the mom. Her chin raised ever so slightly. The girls wrapped themselves around her waist and legs.

Grady's voice changed from Grady the Video Game Master to Pastor Joe the Compassionate Shepherd. "I don't think we've officially met. Joe Decker. You can call me Pastor Joe." He extended a hand. She didn't take it.

"I know who you are," she said. She protectively patted each girl's shoulder.

"But *I* haven't met *you*." He admired her spunk. Sassing the pastor. He smiled his most charming smile.

Her shoulders relaxed and she exhaled deeply, considering him for a moment. Finally, she spoke. "Dixie Talbot," she said.

"So, what brings you to the mall today, Miss Dixie?"

"Play group every Tuesday." She pointed at the girls, then glanced at her watch. "We'd better go. It's all the way down the other end."

Grady shoved his hands into the pockets of his jeans and fell into step beside her. "I'm buying some new clothes and getting a haircut. Apparently, I don't pass the Mae-June test."

Dixie laughed. A hearty, sincere laugh. "Who does?" she said, wiping her eyes. She stepped onto the down escalator. The girls stepped onto the stair behind her, separating Grady from their mother.

Grady wondered what she meant by that—*Who does?*

The escalator rolled them into an alcove designed strictly for children. A swarm of preschoolers climbed on yellow plastic slides, sifted sand in a turtle-shaped sandbox, and danced in circles holding hands. Betty Lou and Betty Jean raced to the dancing group and joined the circle.

Dixie purchased a coffee from a vending machine and found a seat in a quietish corner. Grady sat beside her, but not too close. She even smelled pretty.

"What did you mean by that?" he asked. "You said 'Who does.'"

Dixie held the Styrofoam cup with both hands and blew on the coffee. She took a tentative sip. "Mae-June is my daughters' grandmother. She believes I seduced her son Jimmy."

"So ... you're Mae-June's daughter-in-law?"

"We never married. He took off when he found out I was pregnant. He never contacted me or Mae-June again. She lost her boy, and she won't have anything to do with what she calls his bastard children. Won't even admit she's their grandmother."

Grady mulled over this information. Weren't church folk supposed to be holy and better than the rest of society? What about forgiveness? What was that book he'd spotted in the personage? Something about forgiving to live.

"Where's Jimmy now?" he asked.

Dixie shrugged. "Wilfred knows but he's not telling."

"Wilfred? What does he have to do with this?" Grady rested his forearms on his knees and stared at his Nikes.

"Wilfred Wheeler is Mae-June's brother-in-law. Her sister Magnolia is married to Wilfred's brother Zeke. They had a falling out with the church. I don't know what it was about." Dixie stood and called, "Betty Lou! Play nice!" Betty Lou stopped her playing momentarily, nodded, then skipped over to the turtle sandbox.

"Anyway," Dixie said after she sat down. "Rumor has it Jimmy's kept in touch with Zeke and Magnolia. If so, Wilfred knows. He rents their upstairs apartment."

Grady replayed this information, not sure he was getting it right. Mae-June's sister was related to Wilfred Wheeler who might know the whereabouts of the father of Dixie's twins whose grandmother was Mae-June, his secretary, and the unrevealed grandmother of the twins. Was that it? He wouldn't swear to it in a court of law.

"So," Dixie said. "What skeletons do you have in your closet, Pastor Joe?"

He glanced up quickly. The way she said 'skeletons in your closet' made him wonder what she knew about him. And the way she said 'Pastor Joe' almost sounded like a come-on. Not that he would have minded, but weren't pastors supposed to be celibate? Wait. That was the Catholics. Pastor Oscar was married and had encouraged him to find a good wife. Oh right, and supposedly he, as Pastor Joe, was getting married in a few weeks. Maybe it was just celibate until marriage.

"Skeletons?" He shrugged. "Nothing but being fired from a few jobs and having a drunk stepfather."

"Drunk stepfather? I thought your parents were missionaries in the Congo." She stood, walked over to a trash bin and threw away her empty coffee cup. When she returned, she sat a bit closer to him. She waited for an answer.

"Actually," he said, thinking fast, "my father died ... of ... of ... a snake bite. That's why we came back from the Congo. My mother remarried."

She placed a warm and reassuring hand on his forearm. "I'm so sorry," she said. "About the snake bite and about your stepfather."

"Thanks," he said, manufacturing sad eyes.

She giggled. "But how did you have time to get fired from a few jobs? Did you work in seminary? I thought that would have taken all of your time."

Grady drew his arm away from her hand. Somehow a lie seemed less bad if physical contact wasn't involved. "Yeah, but..."

A smiling young woman blew the whistle suspended from a lanyard around her neck. A literal saved by the bell, Grady thought. Another woman held the end of a clothesline and the woman with the whistle grasped the other end. They both wore red pullovers with yellow emblems. The group of children ran to the spot beside the escalators. They jostled for a place between the women, grabbed hold of the clothesline, and waited for their mothers.

"Good luck with the haircut and clothes. You should try something blue. It will bring out your eyes," Dixie said. "Nice talking with you."

Grady smiled. "'Til next time." He studied her hips as she walked away. Dixie Talbot mesmerized him.

She stopped just before reaching the clothesline and turned back to him. "Hey, the girls and I are going to Madison Farms on Saturday morning. Wanna come along?"

"Sure," Grady said. He had no idea what Madison Farms was, but he needed a break and he wouldn't mind spending time with Dixie.

"I'll pick you up at 9:30," she said.

"I'll be ready."

As the stylist cut Grady's hair and while he was picking out trousers and a couple of dress shirts, he replayed the conversation with Dixie in his mind. Mae-June not seeing her son in five years. Maybe that's what made the woman so grouchy. What if she could see him? What if Grady could find the guy and bring him home? But if he did, would Jimmy want to reconnect with Dixie? Grady wasn't sure he wanted that to happen.

CHAPTER TWENTY

Mae-June unlocked her office door and immediately hooked her keys to the strap of her leather shoulder bag. Everything in its place. She had no desire to waste time searching for her keys at the end of the day. She had tasks to complete at home.

She opened the second drawer on the right side of her desk, set the purse inside, and closed it. What would this day bring? Unlike the weekend and the day before, she had an optimistic feeling she couldn't explain. Something felt right. Couldn't you be optimistic without a reason?

She turned on her computer. As it came to life, she dialed into voicemail, picked up her pen, poised it over the message pad. She'd learned her lesson with Pastor Courtney, a good twenty years ago. He was a good man, a good preacher, but he constantly lost the messages she personally placed in his hand and he claimed she never gave them to him. Now, she used message books, four messages to a page. When she ripped off each individual message, a yellow duplicate remained in the book. She'd dated the covers and lined them up chronologically in a box in the supply room. There were twenty years of logged phone messages.

He was the first pastor she'd worked with. Over the last twenty years she'd been holding Wilsons Corner Bible Believing Congregation together, she'd seen four pastors come and go, and now the fifth, Pastor Joseph Decker, had just arrived. She doubted he'd last long. Pastor Westbrook, his predecessor, left to pastor a larger church. Not surprising. This little church was but a steppingstone in his career.

Before that, was Pastor Martin. The man thought the sun rose just to hear him crow. He was a poor match for the congregation. She knew it the minute he walked in. He was a short man who wanted to prove he could fill a big man's shoes. Only *his* guidance could save his sinning congregants from hell. She agreed they were sinners. Then he let it slip he thought she was in the same category. She smirked when she thought of his leaving. He had no idea of the pull she had or why he was asked to leave after only nineteen months.

Pastor Martin never could have filled Pastor Lester's shoes anyway. Pastor Lester led Wilsons Corner for ten years. Ten wonderfully organized delightful years. He appreciated Mae-June. Took her in as his confidante. Respected her opinion. No pastor before or after held a candle to Pastor Lester. Pastor Joe could be a success if he listened to Mae-June, but if he didn't … She cluck-clucked. Nevertheless, she felt happy this morning. Positive. Something good was around the corner.

Without her at the helm, this church would be in dire straits. She kept it humming. Any question regarding how things were done, who did what, who to contact in town and who to stay away from, she could answer it. Permitting? Jackson Grant, Town Hall. Printing needs? Andy at McNall Printers, Westmoreland, two towns over. Catering? Main Street Deli gave the best service with the best price.

Who not to call? She had answers for that, too. Plumbing? Kettle Plumbing employed inferior thieves. Electric problems? Albert Somers had been good, but he retired and left the business to his incompetent son. Funerals? Guy Fletcher. He thought all caskets should be lined in gold no matter the budget of the one left behind.

First message on the voicemail, Suzanne Simms. "Mae-June, do we have a board meeting tonight or are we skipping this month since Pastor Joe is just arriving and isn't up to speed?"

Mae-June shook her head. "Yes," she said to the empty room. "If you read your bulletin this week, you would know the answer to that question." She didn't waste the message pad for that. She wrote it on her legal pad as Action Item #1. "Follow up with Suzanne Simms."

Next message. "Hello, this is Fred Pilot. It's time for the annual maintenance of your copier. I'm calling to schedule an appointment." She wrote on her legal pad. "Call Fred Pilot."

Two hang-ups. Annoying. Probably kids fooling around.

"Hi, Mae-June. This is Sally Greenwood. Will you please put in the bulletin we'll be having a tea for the ladies three weeks from Saturday at 4:00 p.m. Everyone should wear a fancy hat."

A tea? Mae-June decided right then and there she'd be out of town that day. She had no reason to sit around wearing a gaudy hat sipping tea pretending to be high society. Note number 3. Add Tea to the bulletin.

Her computer waited patiently. She typed in her password and logged into her e-mail. A few names popped up right away—more bulletin announcements, she presumed. And an e-mail from Pastor Joe. She'd set up his e-mail and password last week. She was glad to see he was using it. That might be a benefit of working with a young man, someone more technologically savvy than the three older pastors she'd worked with. Her happiness quotient ticked up a notch. She clicked on his message.

"Here are the changes for the board agenda."

Mae-June frowned. Changes to the agenda? She'd typed up the agenda after they last spoke. The day he spoke so horribly to his mother. He'd stormed off and hadn't indicated he wanted any changes. What could he have possibly come up with in the meantime?

She'd already run off a dozen copies. Annoying, but she'd have to write in the changes. Her happiness quotient dipped a full step. Resting her chin in her hand, she pushed up her bifocals to see better and leaned closer to the screen. "Move water fountain issue to #1 after the treasurer's report." Crazy. What difference would that make?

"Under Praise Music, type 'sample.'" What was that supposed to mean? *Sample.* As if you could sample music like you do a cookie or new drink. "Add a Picnic?" She scanned the rest of his changes, an indescribable heaviness in her gut. It might be better to wait until he arrived before making the changes. Yes, that's what she'd do. This e-mail had to be a mistake. Besides, she'd already printed the agenda along with the treasurer's report and secretary's report. It would be wasteful of the Lord's money to use more toner and paper over an error. She'd wait. She set the copies of the agenda on the corner of her desk and moved on to the next task.

"Hey, Mae-June, how's it going?"

Mae-June's shoulders jerked and her fingers came down hard on the keyboard. "Irving Welch, don't you sneak up on me ever again! You may be an officer of the law outside of these walls, but inside these walls, *I* keep order."

Irving hunched a little, and the overhead light glinted off the revolver snapped to his belt.

"Sorry. I thought you heard the door." He pointed to his right.

"I was concentrating." She swiveled in her chair to face him. "What can I do for you?"

"Prayer warriors," he said. "I'm here for prayer warriors."

Mae-June inhaled sharply, raised her arm, checked her watch. "Is it that time already?"

"Sure is," Irving said.

Mae-June jumped to her feet. "I didn't see Pastor Joe come in. Let me check his office." She pushed past Irving, opened the door, and hurried down the hallway. She grabbed the door handle to Pastor Joe's office and tugged. The motion wrenched her shoulder. The door was locked. She peeked through the narrow panel of glass that took up one-third of the right side of the door. The office was dark. Good grief. Could he possibly be playing basketball again?

Mae-June scurried down the hall, her arms pumping briskly back and forth. She pushed open the door to the outside. No pastor on the basketball court. She picked up her pace. Down the steps, through the grass around the corner. No car in front of the yellow cottage. What in the world?

A crick in her side kept her from hurrying and she hobbled back to her office. Hopefully, he was on some church business, an emergency. She'd have to speak to him about this. She needed to know his whereabouts at all times.

Pastor Oscar was standing beside Irving when she entered her office. "I'm sorry, gentlemen," she said. "He's nowhere on the premises. I'm sure he's on his way. I'll unlock the boardroom for you."

By 10:30, half an hour after the meeting was supposed to start, four more members of the prayer warriors had gathered in the boardroom. Irving opened Mae-June's office door wide enough to poke his head in. "Do you have a number you could reach him at?" he asked. "If not, we're heading out."

"He didn't give me his cell phone," Mae-June said, embarrassed at her own negligence. Then she raised her index finger and reached for her message book. "Wait a minute! We spoke last week before he arrived. I wrote his number in the message book." She licked her finger, flipped through the book. "Wednesday. No. It was further back than that. Tuesday? No." She flipped back a few pages. "Here it is!" She was triumphant.

She picked up the phone. Dialed two numbers. Looked back at the message. Dialed two more. And so it went until finally, the phone started ringing on the other end. She raised her thumb in victory at Irving.

"Hello, this is Pastor Joe …"

"This is Mae-June," she said indignantly. "Where …"

"…I am unable to take your call at this time."

Mae-June slammed the phone down. "Voicemail."

"You should have left a message," Irving said.

"Why bother. He's on his own time schedule." So much for an optimistic feeling, Mae-June thought. She nodded her head in Irving's direction. "You might as well leave." She tried to smile, although she wondered if it looked more like a grimace.

At noon, Mae-June pulled out the brown bag she'd tucked in the drawer with her purse. She placed the office phone on automatic forward to voicemail and crossed the hall to the boardroom. That's one thing she insisted upon—an uninterrupted lunch break. Stress while eating caused all kinds of digestive problems.

She bit into her turkey and cheese on rye and chewed slowly. Just the perfect amount of mayonnaise and mustard. That was the trick to a good sandwich— what and how much you slathered on the bread. You could make or break a sandwich in one simple step.

Where was Pastor Joe? When he came back, she'd insist he keep his cell phone on at all times. This waiting and wondering was like a parent waiting for their teenager out past curfew—the kid better have a good excuse. She hoped he was all right.

Luckily, her Jimmy hadn't been much trouble as a teenager. She rolled her eyes and puffed out a breath. A fragment of bread flew from her mouth, landing a foot away on the table. She retrieved it, smashed it onto her napkin as though she were putting out a cigarette, not that she smoked or ever would.

Jimmy was a good boy until Dixie set her sights on him. Mae-June wondered where he'd gone and if he'd ever come back to her.

By 3:00, Mae-June was losing hope. Her optimism had dipped after lunch and faded away within the last half hour.

"Afternoon, Mae!"

The last person Mae-June wanted to cope with was Wilfred Wheeler. Most afternoons he found some reason to stop and check on her. She didn't turn from the computer. "Mae-June," she said. "You know I hate it when you call me these made-up things you come up with. How would you like it if I called you Wil?"

He chuckled from way down in his belly. "I'd like it just fine if you called me any which way. Here … I'll give you my number so's you can call." He reached for a pen with a silk carnation glued on top that she kept in a vase on her desk amongst a bouquet of silk daffodils, rosebuds, and hyacinths.

"I've got your number, Wilfred," she said.

"Sure 'nough," he said. He eased into her guest chair and let out a sigh that sounded like he was letting air out of a balloon. "Pastor Joe check in yet?"

Mae-June took her eyes off the computer screen, crossed her arms, rolled her chair to face Wilfred across her desk. "No," she said. "No show, no call, no message."

"Hmm," Wilfred said. He placed a hand on the wooden chair arm and re-positioned himself. "Wonder what's up."

"Something or nothing," Mae-June said.

"What do you mean?"

"He's either got an emergency, which I doubt, or he's off somewhere fooling around."

At 6:30, Mae-June heard the engine of Pastor Joe's car and the squeal of brakes as he stopped outside her window.

This had better be good, she thought.

CHAPTER TWENTY-ONE

W"here have you been?" Mae-June stood just outside the conference room door holding a stack of stapled papers. Her voice hit a high note Grady didn't know was humanly possible. He winced.

"You missed the Prayer Warriors. You missed half a dozen phone calls. You changed the agenda, obviously without thinking. I knew it was a mistake, so I stuck with what we discussed." She held up a stack of papers. "I'm ready with the copies."

Grady took a copy of the agenda and glanced through it. He shook his head. "I need those changes."

Mae-June looked as though she'd been slapped. "There is absolutely not enough time."

"There was. Anyway, I believe in you, Mae-June. You are the most efficient worker I've ever seen." He placed a hand on her shoulder, smiled, and waited.

For a second, she looked like she was going to absorb the manipulated compliment. "If this was so important, why weren't you around all day so I could ask you questions?"

"I e-mailed you." He grinned and shrugged.

"Where were you?"

"Didn't you notice my haircut?" He looked over his right shoulder, then his left. "I took your advice. You wanted me to look more professional, right? I really appreciate your guidance."

"Well," she said. "You do look better. But I'm not happy—"

"With your talent, Mae-June, you'll have it done in no time." He turned and walked down the hall without looking back. As he passed the water fountain, he stopped to take a sip. Nasty stuff. Downright nasty. He was glad it was on the agenda tonight. He'd take care of it before someone contracted a waterborne virus and keeled over.

Pastor Oscar was standing near a pot of coffee with two other men when Grady entered the board room. He beamed at Grady, crossed the room, shook his hand. "I see you've weathered another day."

Grady shrugged.

"A little snafu with Mae-June today?" Pastor Oscar raised the coffee mug to his lips. The smile he hid behind his raised cup twinkled in his eyes.

Grady shifted from one foot to the other. "I went out for a haircut cuz *she* thought my hair was unbecoming of a pastor. What do you think?"

"Pastors come in all shapes and sizes and each of them reaches a different group of people. That's why good pastors come and go. Keep it up. You'll do fine." Pastor Oscar tapped

Grady on the upper arm, and Grady warmed to his touch. "Hey, let me introduce you to a few people you haven't met yet."

"Sure."

Pastor Oscar extended a hand in the direction of a man wearing a navy-blue turtleneck under a maroon sweater. "This is Cornelius Wiggly," he said. "And this is Hilton Alabaster." Pastor Oscar gestured to the man beside Mr. Wiggly.

Hilton Alabaster wore a brown corduroy blazer over a black three-button shirt. He sported a mop-like white mustache that would have covered his mouth if he hadn't been smiling so broadly.

Cornelius reached out to shake hands, but before he made contact, Hilton clutched Grady's hand in a crushing grip. He shook it like he was hooking a fish intent on getting away. "So pleased to meet you. Welcome."

"Thanks," Grady said, half seasick from the arm pumping.

Soon they were joined by Wilfred Wheeler and a woman who introduced herself as Sally Greenwood.

Grady noted the time as 7:00 p.m. and said, "I'll start with a devotional for church leaders. Have a seat."

The board members scraped out chairs and sat around the long conference table. Sally Greenwood rummaged through her purse, then stopped and looked at Grady. "Shouldn't we wait for the others? Mae-June's not even here with the agenda yet."

"She'll be here straight-away," Grady said. "She's still making copies."

Sally's forehead scrunched into ridges. "She's running late? Mae-June always has the agenda completed hours in advance. She's always on top of everything."

Grady contemplated how to respond. If he blamed Mae-June, it would only hurt himself. They would be forced to take sides and Pastor Oscar was the only one who knew him well enough to side with him.

"I made some last-minute changes," Grady said.

"Oh." Sally sat beside Cornelius Wiggly and returned to rummaging in her purse.

"There's Betty Newman," Hilton Alabaster said. "And Paul Quinley."

"Paul isn't on the board anymore, Hilton," Cornelius Wiggly said with very little patience.

"Hm," Hilton said. "Hm." He scratched behind his ear.

"We'll start on time," Grady said. There were rules. He'd read about them this morning on the Internet. Start board meetings on time. Never allow them to run for more than two hours. He intended to stick by the rules.

"They'll catch up." Grady picked up a printed sheet. "I found this devotional for church leaders. I thought it was good." He paused. "Especially for me."

The board members chuckled, and Grady began to read. "It's from the Christian Life Resources. 'Why is it that I don't seem to live the Christian life I want to live? I want to live for my Savior, serve Him in all I do, let others know about His love. But so often … the good I want to do I do not do, but what I hate I do …'"

Betty entered and quietly took a seat between Hilton and Sally. Grady nodded and continued to read. Then he prayed. "Be with us, God. Help us make good decisions. Amen."

"Very good," Hilton said. "Encouraging. Very encouraging."

"Amen," Pastor Oscar said, and the others uttered their *Amens*.

"Sally, will you give us the secretary's report and then . . ." Grady consulted his notes. "Mr. Wiggly, the treasurer's report? By that time, Mae-June should have printed our agendas."

Sally stood. She was a petite woman in her 40s with bottle blonde hair. No denying it—a two-inch brown strip straddled her part. She cleared her throat and read. "Our last meeting was on September 6. It began at 7:00 p.m. and ended at 11:30 p.m."

"It was a long night," Hilton said.

Grady shook his head. No way were they running past 9:00 tonight.

"After Pastor Oscar brought us the devotional and prayer, we heard my secretary's report and Cornelius's treasurer's report. Mae-June raised concerns about some members wanting praise music introduced into the church. After 56 minutes we tabled that discussion and vote until this meeting. We discussed the water fountain filters for 29 minutes and tabled the discussion and vote until this meeting."

They got to be kidding. Did the board ever actually decide anything? Grady thought. He didn't hear another thing until Hilton raised a motion to accept the minutes as read.

"Aye," they all said.

Cornelius Wiggly stood. "Treasurer's Report," he began. "At this time, we have $27,000 in the building repair fund..."

"Wait a minute, wait a minute, wait a minute." Grady raised his hand in a 'stop' gesture. "How much will the filters cost?"

"We have four water fountains in the church," Wilfred said. "At $100 apiece, that would be $400, plus $100 installation fee. I could install them and wouldn't charge a thing."

"Do it," Grady said. "The drinking water is disgusting. Do we want people getting sick or what?" He scanned the faces of the board members. All looked stunned except for Pastor Oscar who looked amused.

"We have to discuss it," Sally said.

"Seems it's been discussed," Grady said. "Let's get it done."

"But Mae-June …"

"Is one vote," Grady persisted. "Let's vote. If it's close, we'll let her cast a vote. Who thinks the water in this building tastes good?"

No one raised a hand.

"Who thinks there's something we can do about it?"

All hands raised.

"Good," Grady said. "Who's in charge of maintenance?"

"I am," Wilfred said.

"Schedule it as soon as possible," said Grady. "Next item."

"Schedule what?" Mae-June rushed in and slapped an agenda in front of each board member.

"Filters on the water fountains," Wilfred said tentatively.

Mae-June set an agenda in front of Grady. "We need to discuss this," she demanded, looking him in the eye from a distance of no more than two feet.

"You did," Grady answered. "Last time. This meeting is one of action." He rubbed his hands together like two sticks. He half expected a fire to ignite.

"But …"

Grady cut her off. "Have a seat, Mae-June. There are more pressing matters to discuss." For the next hour, Grady rushed them through conversations and votes with Mae-June objecting to the pace. That didn't deter him. He looked at the others, asked if they had comments or questions and if they so much as paused for a nanosecond, he said, "Okay, moving along …"

"What's this about a church picnic?" Sally asked.

"Thought it would be a good idea." Grady shrugged. "Get the folks together. Play games. You know, a picnic."

Mae-June and Sally exchanged disapproving looks. It was Mae-June who spoke up. "At this time of year? A month and a half before Thanksgiving? Are you crazy as an outhouse rat?"

"Now, now," Pastor Oscar said. "Let's not get carried away. How about we table it until after the holidays and maybe schedule something for the spring?"

Mae-June raised her eyes to the ceiling and spoke under her breath. "Let's table it for a month of Sundays."

Grady glanced at the clock on the wall over Mae-June's head. 8:45. All that was left to discuss was praise music. Could they do it in fifteen minutes? Grady hoped so. His TV was calling to him.

"Praise music," he said. "What's the problem?"

Mae-June exploded. "What's the problem? Really? What's the problem?"

"Now, now." Pastor Oscar reached across the table for her hand, but she quickly pulled it to her lap. He drew his hand back.

Mae-June gave the same stink eye to everyone around the table that Grady had witnessed the day before. "Once you let go of one little standard, the next goes, then the next and the next. Pretty soon you have mayhem. That's all I'm saying."

Grady took out his phone and pulled up a song he'd found that morning on YouTube. Without a word, he pressed a key and slow piano music filled the room. Then Chris Tomlin began to sing. "Amazing Grace how sweet the sound that saved a wretch like me. I once was lost, but now I'm found, was blind, but now I see …" His voice became louder, pleading. "My chains are gone. I've been set free."

When the song ended, no one spoke. Sally reached into her purse, took out a miniature packet of tissues, and drew out two. She dabbed her eyes with one and blew her nose with the other.

"That was beautiful," Hilton said.

"That was praise music," Grady said.

"Not all of it is like that," Mae-June insisted. "It's a slippery slope."

"If it slopes into the arms of Jesus for our young people, I'm all for it," Pastor Oscar said.

"What young people?" Mae-June asked. "We have no young people."

"Maybe that's the point," Grady said. 8:59 p.m. "Let's take it to a vote."

Five yes. Four no.

"Passed," Grady said just as the 9:00 alarm on his phone chimed. "Meeting adjourned." He stood. He was exhausted in body, mind, and spirit. The day seemed more like a week. He walked out the door and didn't look back despite the objections of some of the board members.

CHAPTER TWENTY-TWO

Wednesday morning Grady lie in bed rehashing the events of Tuesday. He had handled the board meeting like a pro. Unlike the month before, they had actually voted on a number of issues and made progress. He was thankful to Google for that. Timing the discussions and keeping the meeting to two hours was a great method.

He relaxed against his pillows and tried to remember every enjoyable detail of the conversation with Dixie. What a shock to discover those twins were Mae-June's grandchildren and she refused to acknowledge them. Maybe the girls were better off not knowing the prickly cactus personality of their grandmother; then again, everyone needed grandparents. He was sure thankful for his. What could he do to help rectify that situation? He should just stay out of it. No, he shouldn't. Mae-June was his parishioner and so was Dixie, and for that matter so were the twins and their father Jimmy. A pastor was supposed to help the people in the congregation, right?

Where to start? Not with Mae-June, that's for sure. Not with the little girls, and he wasn't sure how Dixie would take it if he got involved. He'd start with trying to locate Jimmy.

Grady rolled over and grabbed his cell phone charging on the nightstand beside his bed. He logged into Facebook and searched for a Jimmy Yearling. Five results popped up. Two were older bald men. One did not have a picture associated with his private profile. Two were possibilities. He clicked on the first one. The guy lived in Colorado and worked as a ski instructor. He listed his high school alma mater in Boulder, Colorado. Unlikely, unless this was false information.

He clicked on the last Jimmy Yearling. Right age. Said he was born in Tennessee. He was in a relationship. Hmmm. Grady wondered what that was about. He scanned the employment history and discovered he was currently employed as a furniture salesperson and delivery driver in Oak Harbor. He brought up Google maps, typed in directions to Oak Harbor from Wilsons Corner. Forty-five minutes. Assuming, this was the right Jimmy Yearling, his "hiding place" was less than an hour away? For five years, or whatever it had been, he was this close and he hadn't been in touch with anyone?

Jimmy Yearling had an open profile on Facebook. Grady clicked on messages and typed, "Are you the Jimmy Yearling who once lived in Wilsons Corner? I have some information for you." He had no idea what "information" he would supply if Jimmy responded, but he felt Jimmy was more apt to reply if he thought it was important.

"Wrench." Wilfred reached his hand out from beneath the water fountain outside Pastor Joe's office. The pastor wanted the water filter's installed, so he'd do it. He had some free time, so why not. Besides, he got to see Mae-June earlier in the day than usual.

Mae-June picked a tool from Wilfred's toolbox and handed it to him.

He peeked out and handed it back. "This is a screwdriver. A wrench looks like, I guess to you it probably looks like … you know … say, a hand mirror with no glass."

The sound of metal against metal echoed down the hallway as Mae-June pushed one tool against the other. "It's not here," she said, irritated.

Wilfred rolled himself farther out from beneath the water fountain. "It's …"

"Oh, here it is." Mae-June shoved the wrench into Wilfred's hand, and he scooted back under the water fountain. "I don't understand why you're in such a rush to install these water filters. We've existed just fine for years. I think you should wait until he's forgotten about them and moved on to more important matters."

Wilfred grunted.

Mae-June bent over so that her green polyester skirt brushed against his elbow. "What'd you say?" she asked.

"Dishonest," he said, sliding out. He waved the wrench towards her. "I'm not going to be dishonest with Pastor Joe. Now take this. We've got one more to go and then we're done here."

"*You've* got one more to go," she said. "*I've* got more important things to take care of."

"Wait a minute," Wilfred called to her retreating back.

"I've got to get back to work. I'm busier than a moth in a mitten."

The phone rang as Mae-June stepped into her office. She grabbed the receiver from the opposite side of her desk, then walked around it and sat down. "Thank you for calling Wilsons Corner Bible Believing Congregation," she answered in her most professional voice. "Mae-June speaking. How may I help you?"

"Hello? Oh, I was wondering if Joe was there." The voice was that of a young woman, a hesitant, unsure-of-herself young woman.

"Pastor Joe isn't here right now." Mae-June rested the phone against her shoulder and picked up her gold letter opener with the ceramic handle Pastor Westbrook had given her one Christmas. She sliced into an envelope. She removed the water bill from the envelope and slipped the invoice into the "Bills to be Paid" folder. "I can take a message if you want."

"This is Roxanne Newman."

Mae-June set down the letter opener and grabbed the receiver off her shoulder. "We are so looking forward to meeting you, Roxanne!"

"You are?" The voice sounded even more uncertain than before.

"How are the wedding plans coming along? You must have everything just about settled by now."

Silence. "Yes," she said. "How did you know about the wedding?"

"Pastor Joe told us, of course. Made sure he'd have time off for his honeymoon before he took the job."

"Really?"

"Why does that surprise you?" Mae-June fiddled with one of her pearl earrings.

"To tell you the truth, I'm just learning about all this now. He accepted the position without consulting me."

Mae-June should have been surprised, but she wasn't. This went along with everything she'd deduced about Pastor Joe from observing him. "Well, she said. "Isn't this a fine kettle of fish."

"What?" Roxanne asked.

"Never mind," Mae-June said. "What do you want me to tell him?"

"Joe?"

"Yes, Joe." Maybe Roxanne was a good match for Pastor Joe after all. Great. A green pastor with ditzy wife.

"That's why I'm calling," Roxanne said. "He's still in the hospital but I have an update."

An update? In the hospital? Joe was in the hospital? An update? What did she mean by an update?

"Joe is doing a little better."

"What do you mean, Dear, Joe is doing better?"

"Joe was in a car accident. He's been in the hospital and was just transferred to rehab."

Mae-June gasped. "No, we haven't heard. I had no idea. How bad is it?"

"That's why I'm calling. He doesn't expect to be in rehab long, and he's wondering if he could move into the parsonage once he's out."

The door to the office opened and Wilfred entered. "I've got…"

"Sshh!" Mae-June waved her hand in Wilfred's direction.

"Sorry," Wilfred whispered. "I didn't know you were on the phone."

Mae-June's eyebrows slunk into her eyelids. "SHUSH!" she said, wagging her finger. Wilfred clamped his lips shut and tiptoed to Mae-June's desk. With exaggerated effort on being quiet, he lowered himself into her guest chair. The cushion on the chair made a gasping sound, and Wilfred smacked it. "Quiet!" he whispered.

Mae-June turned her back on Wilfred and resumed her professional voice. "Sorry," she said. "Someone just came into the office. I didn't hear all you said."

"Can he move into the parsonage when they discharge him?"

Mae-June was pretty good at weeding through the garbage people said and figuring out what they meant, but this request baffled her. "Dear, he already moved in. Of course, he can return to the parsonage." A hum traveled through the line. "Roxanne? Are you there?"

Wilfred scooted forward in his seat. He tapped Mae-June on the shoulder. She partially turned to him and he mouthed the words, "Roxanne Newman?"

Mae-June nodded.

"I have to go," Roxanne said.

"Rox—" Mae-June started but Joe's fiancée had already hung up.

Mae-June whirled around in her seat. "Could you have waited a few seconds, Wilfred? Yes, that was Roxanne. Roxanne Newman. As in Pastor Joe's fiancée."

"What'd she say?" Wilfred drummed his fingers on the corner of Mae-June's desk. "What'd she say?"

"She would have said more if you hadn't interrupted!" Mae-June rolled her eyes. "One of these days, Wilfred Wheeler. One of these days."

"So?"

"Pastor Joe was in a car accident. He's in a hospital or rehab somewhere." Mae-June glared at Wilfred. "She would have said more if you hadn't interrupted."

CHAPTER TWENTY-THREE

This won't go over well." Alex McAllister tossed the hair out of his eyes. As he moved, his nose ring flashed in the light cast by the tableside lamp. With his drumsticks, he attacked his drum set with the intensity of one attempting to squash a pesky fly.

"I'll take care of it," Grady promised. "Just do as I say and we'll be okay."

"I know those people," Melissa Simms said. She thrust one shoulder forward, raised her eyebrows and sneered. "Remember? My mother? She, like, goes there."

"But you don't know me," Grady said.

Melissa folded her arms and tapped her foot. "But we've known these people our whole lives and you've only been here … I don't know how long, but it isn't long. That I know."

Grady stuttered his answer. "I have power over Wilsons Corner." He hadn't meant to say power. Now that he'd said it by mistake, he liked the sound of it. *Power. He had power over people. A* lot of people, in fact. He stood in front of them at church. He sat across from them in his office, in their living rooms, at their dining room tables, at board meeting. He told them what to do and they hung on his words as though they were delivered on heavenly stone tablets.

"Yeah, right," Melissa scoffed. She clucked her tongue and sashayed to the microphone. "So, what are you waiting for? Pick up that tambourine and let's get started."

Grady remembered a phrase scrawled on a pink card. *Suzanne Simms' daughter is giving her a hard time. She's 16. Pray she will see the error of her ways and give her heart to God.* The kid was a twit. No wonder her mother handed in that prayer request. Who did Melissa think she was, overruling his power? Grady snickered.

"What's so funny?" Melissa demanded.

"Nothin'," Grady said. He grabbed the tambourine and took his place behind Alex. He could picture Suzanne and Melissa going at it day after day after day. Every time he turned around, Suzanne was giving him some kind of trouble. Board Meeting. Sermon critique. Phone messages. He was glad Melissa, at least, gave it back to her mother. They were two of a kind.

Michael Turner strummed his guitar strings, jumped forward, raised his chin and the fretboard towards the ceiling. He increased the tempo, his fingers racing across the strings. The garage vibrated with the music. Grady felt the music in his gut, in his leg, in his hands. It obliterated any thoughts. Banging the tambourine against his leg, he swayed his hips and tapped his feet to the beat of the music. He couldn't wait to debut this teen band to the Wilsons Corner Bible Believing Congregation.

After an hour of band practice in the garage, Grady jogged down the driveway toward his car. He'd almost reached it when he heard someone calling for Pastor Joe. On the porch of the brown two-story house stood a woman with a gray ponytail. She wore well-fitting jeans and a green paisley blouse tucked in with a leather belt. Grady couldn't reconcile the sexy jeans with the gray ponytail. The woman looked young and old at the same time.

"Yes?" he answered.

"I'm sorry I missed you last week," she said. "I'm Theresa Murdoch. The boys said you were looking for me." She nodded her head towards the garage. "I had a cold. I'm glad you didn't come. I'm over it now. Want to come in?"

"Sure," Grady said. "Yeah, I could do that." He took the six cement steps two at a time.

Mae-June would be happy he'd crossed another name off the list.

Theresa Murdoch held the door open with a smile. Two skylights beamed sunshine into a kitchen/family room combination. A glass case in the corner held four shelves of baby dolls that looked like they'd been there a long time. A faded, but clean, red, white, and green braided rug lay in front of the fireplace. Grady heard a rustle off to his right and turned to look. An aging black lab with a white chin stretched its front legs, opened its mouth in a wide yawn, stood, wagged its tail, and limped to Grady.

"Hey, boy." Grady rubbed the dog's head.

"Actually, she's a she," Theresa Murdoch said. "She's fifteen now, so she doesn't get along as well as she used to. Lemonade?"

"That would be nice," Grady said, thirsty after playing with the band.

"Have a seat." Mrs. Murdoch took two tall glasses from the cupboard, plunked in ice cubes, and poured the lemonade.

Grady chose a rocking chair with a braided pad that matched the rug. The dog plopped down by his side.

When Mrs. Murdoch returned, he accepted the offered glass and gulped down half of it.

"Do you live here alone?" he asked.

Mrs. Murdoch laughed. She sat in the swivel rocker across from him. "Oh no," she said. "Definitely not alone. My mother is in the other room. I'll introduce you in a bit. She's sleeping right now. My husband is at work." She glanced at the clock. "He'll be home in about an hour if you stay that long." She smiled hopefully.

"Probably not." Grady placed his empty glass on a coaster on the magazine table beside him.

Theresa Murdoch said, "My two grandsons live here, too. I think you were with them in the garage?"

"Really? I didn't know two of them were brothers." He thought back to the introductions. None of the kids had the same last name.

"Michael and Alex are brothers," Mrs. Murdoch said. "Different fathers."

"So, their mother is your daughter?"

"Yes," Mrs. Murdoch said. "Mae-June probably told you the story." She dropped her chin and studied the braided rug.

"No," Grady said slowly. "I don't remember hearing anything."

"I'm surprised." She drew a circle in the condensation on her glass of lemonade. Grady waited until Mrs. Murdoch looked up from her circle drawing and spoke. "My daughter is in rehab." Her lips were tight. "Drugs." She forced a smile.

Grady sensed the words were hard for her to form. "Sorry," he said.

"Not the first time. Not even the second." She stood with a flourish, placed her glass on the table. "I think I hear my mother in there. Let me check. She'd love to meet you." She hurried across the room, opened the door to a darkened bedroom. "Mama?" she whispered. "Are you awake?"

Grady didn't hear a sound, but Mrs. Murdoch gestured to him from the door. "It's the new pastor, Mama," she said in a voice you'd use with a child. "He's come to visit you. Isn't that nice?"

It seemed to Grady the darkness of the bedroom neutralized the bright light of the family room. For some unexplainable reason, his shoulders tightened, and his stomach screamed, *don't go in there or I'll rebel.* In dread, he crossed the room and entered behind Mrs. Murdoch.

It took a few seconds for his eyes to adjust to the darkness. When they did, he was facing a twin bed with a tiny lump extending halfway down the middle. Was there a broom under the covers, he wondered? A beautiful quilt of flowers covered the lump and part of the pillow. A few sprouts of hair seemed to be placed on the pillow.

Mrs. Murdoch stroked the hair with a featherweight touch. "Oh, Mama," she crooned. "This is Pastor Joe." She pushed the quilt down a few inches.

At first, Grady thought he was viewing a Halloween mask. The face was thin, the skin pulled tight, delicate as tracing paper. Like if he touched her, she'd split. Her mouth, open in a jack-o-lantern smile, exposed four teeth on the bottom and three on top. A film covered her pupils. Grady gasped, then gulped.

Mrs. Murdoch took his hand and guided it to the top of her mother's head. "She's blind. I want her to know you're here."

Grady cringed and fought the urge to pull his hand away and run. He thought the woman with the cats who married the pilot, Myra Mosely, was old. This lady won the old contest by a mile. "So," he said, and his voice cracked. He swallowed and started again. "So nice to meet you." A twig of an arm reached from beneath the quilt and touched his leg.

"She says thank you," Mrs. Murdoch said. "She's having a birthday in two weeks." Her voice changed to a baby voice when she addressed her mother. "Aren't you, Mama? Two weeks from Thursday. 99. You'll be 99."

The Pontiac roared into the church parking lot as the sun dipped close to the tree line. Grady was ready to grab a bite to eat, plop on the couch, and turn on the tube. He noted with surprise a few cars, and then he remembered … prayer meeting … That jerked him back to reality.

He parked in front of the personage and ambled over to the church. He entered from the back. He recognized Wilfred Wheeler, Irving Welch, Pastor Oscar, and Miss Cora. Three white-haired ladies sat together in the front pew on the right side. He remembered their faces from church but didn't know their names.

"No!" One of the ladies was saying.

"When?" asked another.

"We don't know," Pastor Oscar said. "His fiancée called and told Mae-June this afternoon. We don't know the extent of his injuries or when he'll be back."

"Hey, sorry I'm late," Grady said. He pulled at the clerical collar, which was getting annoying after wearing it since 9:30 this morning. He sauntered down the aisle. Miss Cora gasped. The three old ladies whipped their heads around faster than Grady would have guessed them able to. Irving Welch said, "What the—"

"Pastor Joe?" Pastor Oscar sounded incredulous. "What are you doing here?"

Grady poked himself in the chest with both hands. "What do you mean? Isn't it prayer meeting night? Mae-June said it was prayer meeting night."

"No," Pastor Oscar said. "I mean yes, it's prayer meeting night. But your car. The accident. We were told …"

Grady approached Wilfred and Irving. "Huh?" he said. "What are you talking about?"

Pastor Oscar stepped closer to Grady. "Roxanne Newman called this afternoon. She said you were in an auto accident and in the hospital."

Grady's heart nearly stopped. "Roxanne? I gave her my cell phone so she wouldn't call the office." He rushed on to correct himself. "I mean bother Mae-June."

Irving looked at Wilfred. Wilfred looked at Pastor Oscar. The three white-haired ladies exchanged glances, and Miss Cora said, "But if you were in the hospital, why would she call you to tell you?"

Grady bit the side of his lip. Good question. "I don't know," he said. He felt his eye twitch. *Quick! Think!* "Wait! I think I know what she was trying to say. Mae-June must have misunderstood. I'm not the only Joe in the world. See, we have this friend named Joe and I'm sure that's who she was talking about. Our friend. Named Joe." He clapped his hands. "Yes, our friend, Joe, is in the hospital. Broken leg. Car accident. So, then, let's get this party started, shall we?"

"Party?" asked one of the white-haired ladies.

"Prayer meeting. Let's start prayer meeting, shall we?"

Confused glances bounced from one face to the next. Slowly those standing sat down. Grady approached the first white-haired lady and extended his hand as he had become accustomed to doing. Her arm and hand shook as she raised it to his. He grasped it firmly and she winced. "Sorry," he said. "Sorry." He lessened his grip and she smiled painfully.

Although her skin was a little saggy around the eyes and chin, she looked remarkably good, particularly compared to Myra Mosely and Theresa Murdoch's mother. Her hair looked like what you'd see in a cartoon when someone's hair is all shampooed up. She had hearing aid buds in both ears, and her glasses hung from a gold chain onto her white sweater.

She smiled broadly and said, "I'm Sophie Jenkins. Been coming to this church since I was a little girl."

"Pleased to meet you," Grady said.

He moved on to the next woman and extended his hand. Her hair was a blunt cut with no curls at all. He thought it would have been better if she and Sophie Jenkins mixed their hair together and came out with something in between.

This woman did not offer her hand. Instead, she kept her arms folded just under her bosom and glared at him warily. "I hope you're better than Pastor Westbrook," she said.

"Oh?" Grady drew back his hand and stuffed both hands into the pockets of his new church-financed khakis. He rocked back on his heels. "What didn't you like about Pastor Westbrook?"

"He was never available," she said. "I called and called for a pastoral visit, but he never came to see me. I think pastors should visit their parishioners. What are your plans?" She looked at him as if she doubted he'd come to visit her, but no harm in asking.

"Actually, I visited two people today. Myra Mosely …"

"Myra Mosely!!!" the woman spoke the name in horror. "How does she rank over me? I come every week. Myra Mosely hasn't been to church in … God, I don't know how long. So, if I stop coming, just hang around my house, you'll visit me? Is that it?"

Sophie Jenkins put her hand on the woman's arm. "Now, now, Millie, he just arrived a couple of days ago. Give him a chance."

"Next week," Grady said. "I'll visit you next week, deal?" Millie harrumphed and turned away.

Grady moved onto the third lady. She leaned forward grasping a walker and breathing heavily through her mouth. Her hair was yellowed white, flattened on one side as though she'd been sleeping. She had to be over 400 pounds and wore a flowered sack of a dress that extended almost to her ankles. She wore white ankle socks and black nurse shoes. "Gabriella Bryant," she wheezed. "You can call me Gabby."

She didn't offer her hand and Grady didn't offer his. "Pleased to meet you, Gabby. And the rest of you, I already know." He grinned and nodded at them. "What shall we pray about tonight?"

Silence for a minute as all six individuals stared at him. Finally, Wilfred spoke up. "You mean who wants to have an opening prayer?"

It was Grady's turn to stare back. How could you have an opening prayer at a prayer meeting? Maybe you had an opening prayer, then middle prayer, then closing prayer? He hadn't googled prayer meeting. Why would he? Seemed pretty straightforward. He hesitated. "How does this usually go?" he asked.

Gabby gasped the answer. "Wilfred back there …" She thrust a shoulder in his direction. "He usually does opening prayer. Then the pastor gives the lesson."

"Lesson?" Wasn't this called prayer meeting?

Millie said, "Of course, lesson!"

Grady's cell phone rang and he jerked. He turned away from the group and grappled with the phone a second or two. He was glad for the diversion. This prayer meeting thing with a lesson was too confusing. The phone caught on his pocket and somehow, he pressed the speaker button. Matt the Rat's voice boomed into the room.

"Grady? Where the heck are you? Your mother says you aren't coming home. Get your sorry —"

Sophie Jenkins choked and started to cough. Everyone stared at Grady in horrified shock.

Grady felt faint and he knew his face was red. He raised the phone to his ear. "I'm sorry, sir," he said. "This is Pastor Joe and *you* have the wrong number." He clicked the off button and switched the phone to vibrate.

He laughed weakly as he wiped the sweat from his brow. "Always happens at the wrong moment. Guess that's why you call it a wrong number." He chuckled nervously. No one responded.

Sophie's mouth still hung open, as did Miss Cora's. Grady clapped his hands together. "Let's get this prayer meeting started. Wilfred, would you like to pray first?"

"What about the lesson?" Gabby asked.

Grady's shoulders drooped.

Gabby clutched her walker like a weapon she planned to plunge into his heart. "You don't know how to run a prayer meeting?"

Eyes stared at him expectantly. Droopy eyes behind Millie's round rimless glasses. Confused eyes from Miss Cora. Reproachful eyes from Gabby's sunken eyeballs. Sympathetic eyes from Wilfred's wrinkled face.

The phone vibrated on Grady's hip. BZZZ. He felt trapped between Matt the Rat's insistent calling and the expectations of these people. The room became hot and blurry. He needed … he needed … prayer.

"Actually," he said, licking his lips. "There is much to pray about. It would be wasteful to present a lesson when what we need is prayer." He stood a little straighter, gained a little confidence feeling inspired. He was, as Mae-June had stated, in charge. "We need to pray for everyone on the sick list. We need to pray for … me … that God will instruct me in my duties. What else?" Sweat trickled down his brow and he hoped no one noticed. BZZZ. He refused to look down, afraid he would see sweat rings spreading from his armpits onto his chest. "What else? Certainly, you know more about the needs of this congregation than me."

Two minutes of silence followed. The slowest two minutes of Grady's life.

"I suppose we could pray for my sister's grandson," Gabby suggested. "Even though I don't care for the boy. One of those smart-mouth types. He needs prayer where he's headed."

"Good," Grady said. "Very good. Who else?"

Miss Cora tentatively raised her hand. Grady nodded. "I need forgiveness," she said. She looked at him knowingly. "I think you know what I'm talking about. But that's all I want to say."

Gabby, Millie, and Sophie turned simultaneously and looked at Miss Cora. They turned back in synchronization then raised their eyebrows at each other. Their movements seemed choreographed. Grady almost laughed.

"We should thank the Lord you weren't in a car accident," Wilfred said.

"I'll second that," Grady said. "Okay, then. Who would like to pray first?"

"I don't like to pray in public," Millie said. Her lips clamped shut like they were super glued together.

Sophie sighed loudly. "Just say skip when it comes to you. Let's just get on with it. Whatever *it* is."

"Shall we kneel?" Grady suggested. BZZ from his pocket.

The ladies exchanged glances yet again.

Grady looked at the row of white-haired ladies and then at the row behind them. Kneeling was out of the question for these ladies. "Okay," he said. "God can hear you from whatever position you happen to be in. If you want to … or can … kneel. If not … whatever …"

When those who could kneel, knelt, and those who remained seated had stopped rustling around, Irving Welch volunteered to start.

"Dear Creator of heaven and earth, of man and woman and child, of birds in the air and of fish in the sea, of all that is great and all that is small, we praise you."

Grady sighed. He hoped it was soft enough so no one heard. He peeked through one eyelash. Gabby was giving him the evil eye, but everyone else looked reverent. He snapped his eye shut and concentrated on listening to Irving.

"We know you can perform miracles, Lord. We ask you to perform a miracle, Lord, for Gabby's sister's grandson. He's made some wrong choices, Lord. He's let the evil one—the snake that roams the earth—into his heart, Lord."

Irving's voice, melodic and steady, seemed hypnotic to Grady. He felt drowsy. A buzzing filled his ears and a flash of light lit the back of his eyelids. He felt himself wilt and heard the bang as his head thunked the pew in front of him.

Everyone gasped. Irving stopped praying. Grady forced his eyes open and all eyes fell on him. He rubbed his forehead. "Carry on," he said, closed his eyes, and bowed his head.

Ten minutes later, when his knees ached and his thighs burned, Grady was sorry he'd said kneel. Irving finished with an earnest 'Amen' and Sophie started another long diatribe.

CHAPTER TWENTY-FOUR

What do you mean he wasn't in a car accident?" Mae-June pulled the sheets up to her neck and slunk lower in her bed. She was on the telephone, but still, there was something about wearing her nightgown and talking to Wilfred that made her uncomfortable.

"I'm telling you," Wilfred insisted. "He's fine. Led the prayer meeting tonight."

"But Roxanne said—"

"He said they have a friend named Joe and that's who was in the accident."

Mae-June opened her mouth, shut it. Opened it again. Shut it again. What exactly had Roxanne said? In an accident. In the hospital. Could he move into the parsonage when he was discharged. It didn't make sense. Pastor Joe was already in the parsonage, although he called it the personage. Was his friend moving in, too? For how long?

"I don't understand," Mae-June said. "I specifically asked if Pastor Joe was in a car accident. You were there, Wilfred, tell me if I'm wrong. What did you hear me say?"

"I heard you," he said. "Yes, that's what you said. But I'm telling you."

"Now do you believe me?" Mae-June asked.

"About what?"

Mae-June clucked in disgust. "This doesn't sound strange to you? I have no idea what's going on, but I'm going to get to the bottom of it one way or another."

"There's another thing," Wilfred said.

"Really? And what is that?"

"Pastor's cell phone rang just as prayer meeting started. He must have hit a wrong button or something cuz a man's voice, a really mad voice, yelled something about Grady coming home."

"What's that supposed to mean?"

"Pastor said it was a wrong number, but by the way he reacted … the whole evening was odd. Here's another thing. He fell asleep when Irving was praying and you're not going to believe this. He actually lost his balance and knocked his noggin' on the pew." Wilfred spoke and laughed the words.

"There's something going on with that boy. I told you right from the beginning."

"Okay, Mae-June, I'll admit, it was strange."

"Converting to my side, are you?"

"There are no sides. There is a simple explanation to all of this, and time will tell."

"All's I can say is sometimes I think that boy's only got one oar in the water."

Mae-June's mind would not shut off. She rolled over in her

queen-size bed, punched her pillow, rolled back. The 1200-count Egyptian cotton sheets wrapped around her legs trapped her in a cocoon. She fought with the sheets, kicked her legs, rolled again. Darn Pastor Joe. She needed eight-hours of sleep to contend with her job and Pastor Joe was once more depriving her of it. She didn't know how people did it—subsisted on five or six hours of sleep a night. They must have easier jobs than she did. Mindless, repetitive tasks. Her job required she be on her game eight hours a day. Many days required even more.

She exhaled loudly through the side of her mouth, stretched one arm across the nightstand and pulled the chain on the Tiffany lamp she'd inherited from her mother. She threw back the comforter and sheet, slipped her feet to the floor, felt around for her slippers.

Pastor Joe. Why did Roxanne say he was in an auto accident? Pastor Joe said he wasn't. Maybe Roxanne was lying. She said Joe broke a leg. Wilfred said he walked into prayer meeting just fine. Then Pastor Joe claimed they had a friend named Joe. But that didn't make sense. The name Joe wasn't an unusual name, but how many Joes did she know?

Mae-June shuffled across her bedroom. Removed her robe from its hook beside the closet. Slipped her arms through the sleeves. Cinched the belt.

Joe. She had an Uncle Joe. He died in 2007 from a heart attack at the age of fifty-nine. So unnecessary. If he'd taken better care of himself—quit eating so many hot dogs and smoking those nasty cigars—he most definitely would have lived longer. But she hadn't liked him anyways. He was an automobile mechanic and smelled like grease and oil. She scrunched her nose thinking of it.

Joe. There was the owner of the shop who printed the church bulletins each week. She'd been dealing with him ever since she'd taken on organizational challenges and control of Wilsons Corner Bible Believing Congregation.

Joe. Did she know another Joe? She padded down the hallway to the kitchen. Snapped on the light. Squinted in the brightness. She limited the bedroom to a 25-watt bulb. The kitchen light had a 75 watt. Wow. During the day, she hadn't realized how bright the kitchen could be.

Tea. Maybe chamomile tea would induce sleep. She filled her teapot with tap water, set it on the burner, dialed the knob to high. A blue flame sprang to life, lapped at the bottom of the pot.

Joe. Were there any church members named Joe? In her mind, she flipped through the index cards she kept on each church member. A, B, C, D, E. F. Yes. Joseph Finch. Should she count him? He hadn't been to church in many years. He should be removed from the roster if he wasn't going to support the church. Hmph. She supposed whether he came to church or not wasn't the point. The point was she was trying to figure out what the chances were of Pastor Joe and his fiancée having a friend named Joe.

The teapot whistled. Mae-June lifted the lid of the glass jar where she kept her chamomile tea bags. She retrieved one and set it in her favorite mug with the lilacs on the inside, over the lip, and halfway down the side. She'd purchased it in the gift shop when she'd visited Rock City two years ago. She poured the boiling water into the mug and carried it to the table. She blew on the tea, sipped gently, and wondered if tomorrow would bring clarity.

What a day. What a week. Grady fell onto the couch, beer in his hand, feet on the coffee table. Roxanne's phone call had almost blown his cover. He'd given her his cell phone for a reason. He'd have to be more insistent with her. But how? He didn't want her suspicious. *A friend Joe.* How many Joes could he invent? What did he think he was doing? How long could he keep Mom and Matt the Rat under wraps?

Marriage. That had been the theme of the last couple of days. Starting with Roxanne. What was he supposed to tell her? Go ahead and marry the guy just because you promised you would? It seemed to him that Joseph Decker deciding to move to Tennessee without asking her opinion was a deal breaker. That dragged Roxanne into a life she didn't want. Why was she asking him anyway? Oh yeah, because he was a pastor—or whatever he had told her.

And then the Riddles. He snorted and wondered what they were doing right about now. Wondered if they'd taken his advice. Wondered if he'd hear from them again. And Matt the Rat. Why hadn't Mom left him years ago? She allowed the guy to mess up the both of them.

Oh yeah. And that old lady. What was her name? He drummed his fingers on the arm of the couch. Swigged the beer. Myra Mosely. That was it. Myra Mosely. A lady who lived her whole dang life remembering a few futile months with a pilot. Unreal. And Dixie who didn't get married. Raising those two kids by herself. What a life. She seemed up to the challenge, though. Grady couldn't picture himself raising kids. Never mind alone.

His head felt on the verge of exploding. He needed rest. He let his thoughts settle on Dixie herself. Pretty Dixie. Nice Dixie. His eyes grew heavy and he drifted into sleep with one leg draped over the sidearm of the couch.

Grady was dreaming he was a telephone operator with an old-fashioned switchboard like the one in EPCOT in the giant silver earth. Zillions of calls came in at once. He jammed wires into the appropriate receptacles and connected call after call.

"Hello, please connect me to the church office."

"Hello, this is Ralph. Gimme Rose."

"Hello, is Pastor Joe there? This is Roxanne."

In the dream, he hesitated. He didn't want to connect Roxanne to Pastor Joe. "Roxanne? Wouldn't you rather talk to me than Pastor Joe?"

"Aren't you Pastor Joe?"

He didn't answer her question and the switchboard lit up again. He connected call after call until, finally, he had all the cords in the switchboard connected. They snaked around each other in a jumbled mess. And still, he heard the persistent ring of a telephone. How could that be when all lines were in use?

He rolled off the couch, hit his ankle on the coffee table, knocked over his half-filled can of Heineken. The warm liquid poured onto his socks.

Grady yelled into the empty room, glanced at his watch. 3:15 a.m. He needed a minimum of four more hours of sleep. He lurched up, grabbed the edge of the couch cushion, heard the ring of a phone again. This wasn't part of the dream. The kitchen phone was ringing. He raced to the kitchen and grabbed the receiver. He heard sniffling. "Hello?"

"They took him away."

It was a woman. A very distraught woman whose voice he didn't recognize. In the background, he heard a siren. Loud at first. Then fainter and fainter until there was silence.

"Who?" he asked.

Was this Mom? Had something happened to Matt? Did he die before they'd uttered a civil word to each other?

"My husband."

He decoded the single word from the garbled sound coming through the phone line. He rubbed his eye with the back of his hand. His brain was slow on the uptake, but all of a sudden, he recognized the voice. "Miss Cora?"

"The ambulance," she sobbed. "Took him. Heart attack. Will you come?"

The night was blacker than black. Misty droplets splattered on the windshield. When Grady turned on the wipers, they squeaked dust across the glass. When he turned them off, the droplets obscured his vision. "Either rain or don't rain!" he yelled into the night. "None of this halfway shit!" He clutched the steering wheel tightly and leaned forward, his body rigid, the muscles in his back screaming for release. He flicked the wipers on and off manually, the automatic settings not right for the occasional plip plop of the drops. He passed the field with the rolled bales of hay. In the darkness, only the ones closest to the road were visible; they looked like sleeping elephants.

Heart attack. How could Pastor Oscar have a heart attack? He looked fine. Healthy. Straight back. Confident walk. Positive speech. He loved his wife. He had a nice house on a lake. A good man. Why would God take a good man like him and leave behind Matt the Rat?

Grady braked at the stop sign. His headlights lit up the handwritten EGGS FOR SALE sign. No traffic in either direction. At this hour, he wasn't surprised. Matt. What if it had been Matt? Would he be feeling as knotted up inside? No. That thought made the knot clench tighter. What kind of stepson was he to be more upset over a stranger having a heart attack than the husband of his mother? What would she do if Matt died? She'd be destitute on the street, or Grady would have to take on the responsibility of caring for her. He couldn't move her into the personage.

But Pastor Oscar wasn't a stranger. Grady hadn't known the man long, but he wasn't a stranger. Grady imagined Pastor Oscar as what a father should be. What a pastor should be.

He signaled with his blinker even though there were no cars in sight. He turned under the low-hanging trees and bumped along Pastor Oscar's dirt driveway. The porch light was on. Miss Cora leaned against the railing hugging herself.

Miss Cora looked older and frailer than the last time Grady saw her. He jumped out and helped her into the front seat.

"He got up to go to the bathroom," she whispered. "I must have fallen back asleep. Then I heard a noise. A bump. I thought he dropped something. A book, I thought. Sometimes he reads in the night." Her voice faded out.

Grady took his eyes off the road for a second, checked to see if she was okay. Tears soaked her cheeks. Snot trickled from her nose. She didn't notice. Grady felt around on the floor for a napkin left over from a drive-through lunch. He handed it to her and hoped there wasn't any ketchup residue on it. She dabbed at her eyes, wiped her nose, and wrung the napkin tight in her hand.

"I couldn't open the door. He was wedged." Miss Cora hiccupped and dabbed at her cheeks with the wadded napkin. "I dialed 911. One of the firemen had to break down the bathroom door to get him." She reached over and grabbed Grady's hand. "I called you. I knew you would come. You've been so good to us."

Grady's stomach churned. His mind raced. He blinked rapidly.

"What if he dies, Pastor?" Miss Cora turned her head slowly with eyes so wide the whites glowed in the dark. "What if he dies because I didn't wake up in time?"

Grady pulled into the hospital parking lot. He was glad they finally arrived. He didn't want to think about Pastor Oscar dying. And he had no theological or philosophical answer to her question.

By now it was 4:00 a.m. and he felt wide awake. He thought of his mother. As a certified nurse assistant, she made trips like this every night back in Orlando. She was the mother, and that's what mothers and fathers did—worked and took care of their kids. Now he wondered how she stood it all those years, working all night, catching a few winks in the morning, cooking meals, cleaning, washing clothes. Nobody else helped her around the house. He felt guilty for waking her up during her brief hours of sleep to complain about some petty thing or to beg money for pizza or whatever seemed important at the moment. Sometime when it was safe to do so, he'd write a letter of apology. Maybe send her a couple bucks every once in a while, to help out.

Lights blazed as though it were mid-day. Silver letters spelled out COUNTY HOSPITAL over a glass entryway. A helicopter landed on a concrete square with a red X.

Grady waited until the propellers slowed down along with the noise. He jumped out of the car, ran around to the passenger's side, and opened the door. Miss Cora did not move. He reached in and enfolded her elbow with his palm. She swiveled like the tin man in the Wizard of Oz. One stiff leg clunked out of the car. Next leg out. She stood. He grasped her arm and aimed towards the door marked ENTRANCE.

Grady's throat felt like he imagined a snake would feel after swallowing a whole rat. He hated hospitals generally, and this was worse. He had no idea if Pastor Oscar was dead or alive and what he was supposed to do in either case.

In the lobby, he saw a sign pointing down a corridor to the EMERGENCY DEPARTMENT. He half dragged Miss Cora in that direction. They passed a darkened gift shop and several wheelchairs lined up against the wall. A few high-pitched dings sounded over a loudspeaker and a professional monotone voice said, "Dr. McDermott, Dial 1 please. Dr. McDermott, Dial 1."

They turned a corner and entered the waiting area. Grady scanned the room. A woman sitting alone in one corner coughed continuously into a tissue. An older gentleman paced from one end of the waiting room to the other, hands in pockets, a worried look on his face. A young couple sat close together with a sleeping toddler sprawled over both of them. On a television screen in the corner, a model strutted across a stage. The camera zoomed in on a diamond necklace she wore.

Grady steered Miss Cora across the room to a glass window with a sign reading CHECK IN. A tired-looking receptionist slid the window open.

"Oscar," Grady said, and realized he hadn't a clue if Oscar was his first name or his last name.

Miss Cora leaned closer to the window. "Oscar Petronella," she said. "They just brought him in."

The receptionist tapped on a keyboard, consulted a screen. "Room 3," she said. She pressed a button. A buzzer sounded and the door to their right opened.

Grady walked through the door, his supper creeping up his throat. Miss Cora shuffled beside him. From behind one curtain, a woman screamed, "It hurts! It hurts!" A calm voice soothed, "Yes, the doctor has called into the pharmacy …"

Someone overtook them dressed in blue wheeling a stretcher with a woman who had tubes attached to her arm. Her face was pale, and she appeared to be sleeping or unconscious.

Grady's stomach clenched. He wasn't up to this pastoring thing. He needed to make his identity known. *No!* Miss Cora needed him. He'd buck up, cross the divide of kid to adult and comfort her as well as he could. What Miss Cora needed was a pastor. Grady would do his best. He stopped in front of a curtain with a sign on the wall indicating it was Room 3.

"This is it," he said. With a trembling hand, he drew back the edge of the curtain and peeked in. A doctor and a nurse hovered over the bed. Pastor Oscar's face was almost as pale as the white sheets. He was hooked up to oxygen and other things. His eyes were closed.

The doctor turned around, offered his hand to Miss Cora.

"Are you the wife?" he asked.

Miss Cora nodded. "This is my pastor," she said, her voice trembling.

"Dr. Ferguson." He shook Grady's hand and nodded. "We were just going to take him down for some tests to see the extent of the damage. You can wait here. There's coffee down the hall."

Grady didn't think he could swallow even if he wanted coffee.

The nurse wheeled the gurney past them and out the curtain. With a burst of strength, Miss Cora grabbed one of the silver bars encasing her husband. "Wait," she said. "We need to pray. Pastor Joe?"

Grady's shoulders twitched. His eye twitched. The side of his mouth twitched. Dr. Ferguson, Miss Cora, and the nurse stared at him. Grady coughed, placed an arm around Miss Cora's shoulders, closed his eyes. "God, Pastor Oscar needs you right now. As does his wife. As do I. Give us strength. Amen."

They waited a lifetime for Pastor Oscar to return from the tests and another lifetime for the test results that followed. Grady felt queasy. He fought the urge to bolt from the hospital. Instead, he dozed in a chair, bought a coke and M&Ms in a vending machine, visited the restroom more than once, and occasionally thought up something to say to Miss Cora. She didn't seem to mind his silence or his treks down the hall, and she seemed to appreciate the few things he said.

When the doctor returned to deliver the test results, Grady understood nothing. Catheterization, beta something or other, and another word that sounded like "scream." Miss Cora wept. They waited an hour for an available bed. Finally, Miss Cora and

Grady followed the nurse wheeling Pastor Oscar's bed down the hall into the Coronary Care Unit.

"He loves you, you know." Miss Cora grasped Grady's elbow. They passed under a clock indicating the time was 2:14 p.m. "He told me. The other day he said, 'That Joe Decker. He's something. If our boys lived, I can only hope they would have been just like him'." She squeezed his arm and attempted a smile.

Grady felt as if he had been stabbed. Pastor Oscar and Miss Cora were good people. They didn't deserve this. Not the heart attack. Not the sorrow. Not a fake pastor. If those babies had lived, Lord only knows they could have fared a whole lot better than a fake Pastor Joe Decker.

The nurse removed a silver clipboard from the end of Pastor Oscar's bed and placed it on the counter of the nurses' station. "She'll take care of you from here," she said to Pastor Oscar, whom Grady thought was asleep.

To Miss Cora, the nurse said, "The next forty-eight hours are critical, but he's in good hands." To Grady, she said, "Thank you, Pastor. Everyone should have the support you've shown to this couple."

The CCU nurse wheeled the bed into room 8 and connected wires and tubes from a control panel on the wall and a wheeling pole she'd brought in. "Mr. Petronella?" she said too loudly and too close.

Pastor Oscar's eyes fluttered.

"We've moved you to the Coronary Care Unit. My name is Tricia and I'll take good care of you today."

"I think you should go," Miss Cora said to Grady. "We'll be fine."

"You'll need a ride home," Grady said, and despite a valiant effort not to, he yawned. She tried to push him towards the door, but his feet stayed rooted to the linoleum.

"I'll call if I need you. How's that?" Miss Cora said, her eyes sad and tired.

Grady hesitated. He was so tired, he wasn't sure he could drive back to the personage. He would have preferred finding an empty room, hanging a DO NOT DISTURB sign on the door, crawling into bed, and having meals delivered to him, no matter how mushy and tasteless he imagined them to be.

"Go," Miss Cora insisted.

"Okay," Grady said. "I'll go."

The hospital had taken on a different tone since their arrival in pre-dawn hours. The waiting room in the Emergency Department was standing room only. A woman in a brown uniform labeled DIETARY pushed a crate-size silver cart full of trays with remnants of eggs, toast, and jam. Two men in white shirts and dark suits passed. Grady heard one say, "I thought he'd do a good job." The second one said, "The second candidate had—"

A half dozen shoppers poked through the merchandise of the now open gift shop. Two display carts had been rolled into the hallway, one with cut flowers in vases and another with stuffed animals.

The parking lot was filled now. Despite the sunshine, the cold air pierced Grady's lungs.

The last thing Grady wanted was to face Mae-June, but he decided he really should.

"I need to talk to you," Mae-June said when Grady entered her office.

"Me first." Grady ran a hand over a day's growth of facial hair.

"You look rode hard and put up wet," Mae-June said. "Your hair is a mess, you haven't shaved, it looks like you slept in that shirt, and …" She sniffed. "Goodness gracious, Pastor Joe, you stink."

Grady plopped into her guest chair and dropped his head to his hands. "All true," he said. "Miss Cora called me … I don't know when … two, three, something like that. Pastor Oscar had a heart attack. I picked her up—"

"Why didn't you call an ambulance!" she scolded.

"He went in the ambulance. She asked me to drive her—"

"Where is she now?"

Grady wished she would stop interrupting. All he wanted was to get the story out, grab something to eat, and call it a day. "At County Hospital. Coronary Care Unit."

"You left her there?" Mae-June yanked open the second drawer on the left side of her desk, grabbed her purse, and stood. She rustled through the purse huffing, finally locating her keys. "I can't believe you left her. At a time like this, she needs someone."

"But she said —"

Mae-June was gone, her heels clacking disgust all the way down the hall.

"What did you want to talk to me about?" he called. He heard a bang. She'd pushed open the door with such force, it hit the side of the building.

CHAPTER TWENTY-FIVE

When Grady visited Pastor Oscar on Friday, he was relieved the man's face had lost the pale ghostlike complexion of early Thursday morning. Miss Cora sat in a chair beside his bed knitting. The needles click-clacked as she looked up and smiled at Grady. "Look at him," she said. "Doesn't he look wonderful? So much improvement in a short time."

Grady nodded although he wouldn't have gone so far as to say *wonderful*. *A tad better* would have been more accurate. Nevertheless, he had almost canceled the trip to Madison Farms with Dixie, but with the good report about Pastor Oscar, he decided to indulge in some recreational fun.

Saturday morning, he sat on the church steps waiting for Dixie and the girls, eager in a way he couldn't describe. She arrived at 9:30 on the dot. Betty Lou and Betty Jean sat in the back seat of Dixie's 70's Oldsmobile Cutlass. The girls were strapped into booster seats playing with their Barbies. Dixie wore tight jeans and a leopard skin jacket as did the girls as did the Barbies.

All the matchy-matchy was curious but Grady held his tongue. "Tell me about Madison Farms," he said instead.

"You don't know about Madison Farms?" one girl asked.

"Mommy, why doesn't the pastor know about Madison Farms?" the other girl asked.

"Everybody knows about Madison Farms," the first girl said.

Dixie checked the girls' reflections in the rearview mirror. "Shush," she said. "Pastor Joe just moved here." She turned her attention to Grady. "Madison Farms is a seasonal place. It's where we get our pumpkins for Halloween and cornstalks to decorate. In summer, we pick strawberries. This time of year, they have a corn maze. The girls like the pen where they pet the baby animals. The main reason I'm going today is to pick out my Thanksgiving turkey. They'll tag it for me, and I'll come to pick it up the Tuesday of Thanksgiving week."

"Alive?" Grady was aghast. "You'll take the thing home alive?"

The back seat erupted in laughter. "They take the feathers off," one girl said.

"And the head," the other girl said.

"And they put it—"

"And the gizzards."

"In a hole in its belly."

"They do what?" Where he came from a Thanksgiving turkey was a frozen brick bought at the grocery store.

The girls laughed and wriggled their Barbies at each other.

"All right," Grady said. "If you say so."

For a while, they were stuck behind a mail truck stopping to stick a few ads or envelopes in rusty mailboxes on crooked poles. Dixie made several attempts to pass, but the mail truck either sped up or a car was coming the other way or there'd be a curve up ahead.

"I used to take a lot more chances," Dixie said. "Before I had the girls. What about you, Pastor Joe? Did you used to be risky— before you were a pastor?"

"Well," he said, looking momentarily out the window at a stream that followed the road. It wove in and out of the trees appearing and disappearing and once it tipped over a small waterfall. The other side of the road was mainly wooded with an occasional opening for a small home, log cabin, or trailer on blocks. "Yeah, I guess I did."

"Like what?" Dixie teased. She took her eyes off the road and smiled at him.

He thought of what he'd done at the mall the last time he saw Dixie. "I charged some stuff on someone else's credit card."

Dixie smacked the steering wheel and hooted.

"What, mommy?" one little girl asked.

"What's funny?" the other asked. "Tell us! Tell us!"

"Hush!" Dixie said. "This is a grown-up conversation. You go back to playing with those Barbies."

Nothing but silence in the back seat. Grady knew they were listening.

"What'd your mother do?" Dixie asked.

Grady stretched his legs, pressed his hands onto his knees and shrugged.

"Surely you remember. Did she ground you? Take away your allowance? She must have punished you," Dixie insisted.

Grady shrugged again as he imagined Mae-June grounding him to the personage.

"How much did you charge?" Dixie asked.

"I didn't keep track."

They rounded a corner and Dixie pressed on the brake. Vehicles collected in a sluggish herd. A man wearing an orange vest held a flag and directed most cars onto a dirt pathway into a field.

"We're here! We're here!" The girls chorused from the back seat.

When the man signaled for them to go, they bounced across the field with the girls squealing and cheering in the back seat. Dixie parked beside a van, and Grady opened the door and stepped out. He immediately wished he'd worn a warmer coat.

Dixie slipped into a white furry jacket and matching hat she pulled down over her ears. She opened the trunk, and Grady wasn't surprised when she took out two miniature coats and hats identical to hers.

Betty Lou and Betty Jean jumped out of the car. They shivered, hugged themselves, hugged each other. "Hurry, Mommy," one pleaded.

Dixie tossed one set to Grady. "Here." She pointed to the girl who ran over to him.

He held out the coat, she slipped her arms through, grabbed the hat, and pulled it down to her eyebrows. Grady knelt and buttoned the coat. She blinked, her eyelashes catching some of her bangs. She stood still and silent, but her eyes never left his face. Looking at this tiny human being, Grady couldn't help but think how vulnerable children were; how dependent they were on adults for their very survival; how scary it must be to have a parent's responsibility. He felt a pang of empathy for his mother—how hard she worked to keep a roof over his head and food in his belly. Had Matt seemed like the only viable option for survival?

The little girl took his hand, then her sister's hand. Dixie slipped her hand into Little Girl Number Two's hand and smiled at Grady. He smiled back. This would be a good day.

"How do you tell them apart?" he asked.

"Betty Jean has more letters in her name and more freckles on her nose."

Grady stopped walking, stood in front of the two girls and compared their noses. Dixie was, in fact, correct. One nose had six freckles across the bridge, and the other had about a dozen. He wouldn't have noticed this on his own, but now that she pointed it out, it was obvious.

"Okay," he said, getting back in line with the others as they walked towards the entrance. "But what if they're running away from you?"

One giggled. Grady checked the noses. Betty Lou.

"A mother knows her children." Dixie squeezed the girls' hands.

They walked through an opening in a barrier made of square hay bales stacked three high. The girls wriggled their hands away from the adults and ran straight for a fence made of wood where other children fed lambs, kids, and ducklings. Dixie paid an attendant for tiny cups of feed and handed them to each girl. She and Grady leaned on the fence and watched as the girls offered dime-size scoops of feed to the animals.

Grady couldn't help but smile. The girls really were cute. "You have a good time with them, don't you?"

"Most of the time," Dixie said, adjusting her hat. "Actually, they're the best thing that ever happened to me."

"Really," he said. "How's that?"

She held onto the fence with both hands and swayed a little. "I was headed down the wrong road … someone like you probably thinks I'm still on it."

"What are you talking about?" Grady let go of the fence and turned to face her. "I have a lot of respect for you. You're a great mother. You have your life together. I wish my life was as put together as yours."

Dixie tossed her head back and laughed so hard Betty Lou and Betty Jean ran over to the fence, a lamb galloping behind each.

"What's so funny?" Betty Jean called.

"Nothing, honey," Dixie said, still laughing. She waved them off. "Go back to feeding the animals. Once your cups are empty, we'll go on the hayride out to the turkey pen."

"Oh, goody!" Betty Jean squealed.

Both girls turned and bumped noses with a lamb. They looked at each other, laughed, and wiped spittle from each other's cheeks.

Once Grady and Dixie stopped laughing, she said, "Unreal. Look at you. You made it through college and the seminary. I got pregnant at sixteen and dropped out of high school."

Grady puffed out his cheeks. Once more he had almost given himself away. He needed to stay on guard.

"At least," she said, "I'm an example that if you make a mistake, you can turn it around and still be successful."

"That's true," he said, thinking of how he could turn his own life around. He glanced at the girls and then back at Dixie, deciding how to pose the next question. "How old are the girls?" he asked.

She chuckled. "Cute," she teased. "Trying to figure out how old I am. Twenty."

His mouth dropped open. "No way! I thought you were a lot older than me! You're so mature!"

Dixie chuckled. "Not everyone agrees with your assessment. Since we're revealing our deep dark secrets, let's begin with your age."

Grady kicked a pebble with the toe of his loafer. He shrugged his shoulders.

"Come on," she said. "It's not a hard question."

Betty Jean and Betty Lou opened the gate and dashed past them. "Beat ya!" Betty Jean called.

"Oh yeah?" Dixie crooked her arms and swung them as if she were jogging, but her legs were going in slow motion.

Grady shoved his hands into his pockets and walked behind, hoping Dixie would forget the age question by the time they got to the turkeys. He didn't want to lie, but at 19, there's no way he could have made it through college and the seminary unless he was a genius. He doubted he could fool anyone into believing *that!*

A matched pair of tan horses with dark brown manes and tails hitched to a wagon awaited them. They climbed aboard and found a place to sit on a hay bale. The driver called, "Hee-yah!" and the horses trotted down a rutted path through a field of pumpkins. The hooves of the horses clip-clopped along the packed dirt path. A red-tailed hawk swooped and squawked overhead. Four grey mockingbirds dive-bombed the hawk.

The driver of the wagon pulled on the reins to stop the horses. He pointed to the spectacle in the sky. "They're afraid the hawk is going to get their babies," he said. "See how they've ganged up on him."

When the birds flew past the tree line, the driver clucked and snapped the reins across the horses' backs, and they jerked forward.

Grady closed his eyes and raised his chin. Tranquility washed over him. There was only the smell of hay, the chatter of Betty Lou and Betty Jean, and the sun on his face. There was only this moment. He had no past. There was no future.

"What are you so mellow about?" Dixie asked.

Grady opened his eyes a slit. "Nothing," he said. "Just enjoying this day."

The girls jumped up and pointed. "There they are!" Betty Jean cried, pointing.

The driver stopped and Dixie jumped from the wagon. She circled each girl with an arm and pulled them down. Grady followed.

The whole process of picking a turkey baffled Grady. He'd heard of tagging Christmas trees ahead of the season, but tagging turkeys seemed barbaric. He'd rather not know where they came from when he carved them up on Thanksgiving.

At least thirty turkeys strutted inside the pen made of chicken wire as high as Grady's neck. Feathers ruffled, one chased another pecking at its rump. The first one ran off, the red thing hanging across its beak bobbling back and forth. The smell of the pen was repugnant. Suddenly roast turkey seemed unappealing,

"That one!" Betty Jean said pointing to the attacker turkey.

"No! That one!" Betty Lou insisted. "That one's fatter."

They all looked the same to Grady. At the moment, he considered becoming a vegetarian. Finally, Dixie and her two clones agreed on a turkey. In a swift action Grady couldn't follow, a man dressed in jeans, a blue flannel jacket, and leather gloves opened the gate, fought off the turkeys with a pronged instrument, and somehow affixed a tag to one of the wing feathers of the chosen turkey. He dashed out of the cage, the turkey nipping at the back of his legs and handed Dixie a tag with a matching number. "See you Thanksgiving week," he said.

"We'll be back," Dixie said to him and turned to Grady. "We could grab a bite to eat at the snack bar if you'd like."

Betty Lou and Betty Jean held hands and ran ahead giggling. Grady decided this was the time to ask the question he'd been pondering since he saw Dixie and the girls when he first arrived. "Just wondering," he said. "What's with the matchy-matchy outfits?"

Dixie stopped walking, caught his gaze for longer than he was comfortable, then said, "When I got pregnant, some people suggested an abortion. When I refused, they insisted I give up 'the baby,' which turned out to be *two* babies, for adoption. Why do people stick their noses into other people's business, Pastor Joe?"

"I don't know," he said, shrugging.

"I never considered either of those choices. I'm proud of my babies. I sew quite a few of our outfits. We dress alike because I want everyone to know they are mine and I am their mother." Her eyes glistened with unshed tears. "And I'm a *good* mother. I know I am despite what anyone says or thinks."

"I see that," he said gently.

A movement in the crowd behind Dixie caught Grady's eye. It was a woman and a teenage girl—Suzanne Simms and her daughter Melissa. Melissa had her arms folded over her chest. She tapped her foot and snarled at her mother. "You said …"

Grady placed a hand on Dixie's upper arm and guided her in the opposite direction. Dixie wrenched her arm free and skidded to a halt. "What was that about?" she demanded. "Don't you ever—"

"Sorry," Grady said. He lowered his chin in an apologetic gesture. He had to think fast. Something that wouldn't draw attention to Suzanne Simms yet satisfy Dixie. "A guy was about to run into you. Just got you outta the way."

Dixie looked from side to side and behind her. "Oh," she said doubtfully. "Thanks, I guess. Snack bar?"

"I'd love to," he said. "But I should get back. I need to write my sermon for tomorrow."

Grady jogged across the church parking lot, golden with twilight. He had done no sermon preparation at all. He had actually forgotten about it with all that went on during the week.

He slowed and shuffled through the brown, crinkly leaves on the grass at the far edge of the lot and entered the quiet of the woods where he'd first seen the deer. Seeing the deer again might inspire the Sunday sermon. It had been a magical moment—one he interpreted as good omen.

He heard a rustle in the woods. The deer? If so, was it running away? Maybe it was time Grady did the same. Maybe it was time to leave Wilsons Corner. The night he'd spent with Pastor Oscar and Miss Cora at the hospital had convinced him what he was doing was dangerous. He had no business counseling those in need. And what good were his prayers—a kid, really, who was only looking for a good meal and a dry bed? His parishioners deserved more.

But he would miss the church and the congregation. In Orlando, he had felt as if he didn't belong. In Wilsons Corner, he not only felt a part of the group, but the epicenter. He mattered.

Mae-June. Would he miss her? He thought about it a minute. Analyzed it from a few different angles. Yeah. Probably. In fact, he was sure of it. Despite her prickly personality, despite her suspicions of him, she was the anchor of the church. She put her heart and soul into her job. He suspected that below her gruff exterior, and not too far below, was a kind heart trying to do the right thing. Given enough time, Grady believed he could win her over. Maybe a little bit, anyway.

Wilfred Wheeler. He would definitely miss Wilfred Wheeler. He was a simple kind of guy. Uncultured. But his loyalty was unquestionable. The man had his back. Wilfred believed in him.

As for Pastor Oscar and Miss Cora, he would always remember the way they respected him. And Dixie and the twins.

He would certainly miss them. He was attracted to her and he felt it went both ways. In other circumstances, he'd ask her out for an official date.

He might not be sure where he'd head after this, but he was sure of one thing—he would look back fondly on his few weeks in Wilsons Corner, Tennessee.

Would they miss him when he was gone?

Grady sat on a fallen branch, looked up, and noticed the blinking of a plane and constellations he'd learned in a high school astronomy class. He recognized Pisces and remembered that in the beginning, this constellation was drawn with the fish swimming together as a pair. In the present day, they were drawn as if they were swimming away from each other. They represented him and his family. He was moving away from them, whereas once, long ago, they had swum together.

He saw Pegasus—four stars forming a box, three of the corners reaching out to other stars. In mythology, Pegasus was a white horse that climbed Mount Olympus and carried around Zeus's thunderbolts.

Grady wondered how he could remember things he supposedly learned years ago. In high school, he couldn't recall these types of facts for tests, yet now he could. He had been branded stupid by his classmates, by Matt the Rat, and by himself. But if he could remember now, all these years later, was he really stupid?

His fingers were a bit numb, his cold toes were immovable. Yet he didn't want to leave. He could hear the beating of his heart. *His heart.* How much longer would it beat? Not forever, as he'd assumed. What would he do with the moments afforded him by the beating of his heart?

He'd never really had goals before. Slept late. Played video games. Took out the garbage once a week. Avoided his mother unless he needed something from her. Life just was. Maybe you had to make life happen, not wait for it to come to you.

Grady stamped his feet and blew on his fingers to warm them up. He didn't want to leave his hide-out, but the cold forced him to go. He stood and pivoted slowly in a full circle, scanning the night for a sight of the deer. A twig snapped, but that was it. No sightings. Maybe another night. His heart felt full and empty at the same time.

His phone alerted him to a Facebook Message from Jimmy Yearling. "Never lived in Wilsons Corner. Sorry. Hope U find the guy."

CHAPTER TWENTY-SIX

Sunday morning, sauntering down the hall to his office to don the silver preaching robe, Grady noticed Officer Welch, Wilfred Wheeler, and Chipper Mangrove staring at something on the wall. "What's up?" he called. They swung around and stared at him with masks of guilt.

"Oh nothing," Chipper said.

"Now that's a lie," Grady said, his heart flip-flopping in his chest. If Chipper were not laughing or smiling, he knew something was definitely not right. He joined the group and faced the direction they had been looking when he approached. The wall. A new picture at the end of the pastor's row. A picture of him. A picture of him standing behind the pulpit with the Bible raised high in one hand. Under other circumstances, Grady would have been happy with the picture. He didn't look half bad. But in this circumstance, this was not good. Not good at all.

"Who took this?" he demanded.

Irving and Chipper stared at Wilfred.

"It's a great shot," Wilfred said. "You look natural behind the pulpit, don't you? Check out the lighting. I caught it just right."

"Take it down," Grady insisted. He reached across Wilfred to pluck it off the wall, and Wilfred blocked him.

"Did you want to have a picture taken at a professional studio?" Wilfred asked. He looked hurt.

"No, that's not the problem."

Chipper, Irving, and Wilfred waited for Grady's response, but he didn't have an answer for them. *Why not? Why not? Why didn't he want the picture on the wall? Excuse. Reason. Something.*

"Yeah," he finally said. "Check out these other guys. My picture is too casual. I need a professional picture."

"Until then we'll keep it up," Wilfred said.

"Whatever," Grady answered, planning to rip it off the wall some evening when no one was around.

Grady fidgeted behind the pulpit. Was it only last week he hadn't known a soul? The Riddles sat halfway down the center. Ralph had his arms crossed over his chest and Rose looked meek and nervous sitting beside him, but they were together. Mae-June sat in the first row on the left. She had a notebook open in front of her. Grading his performance most likely. Wilfred Wheeler came in a side door. He tried to sit down beside Mae-June, but she had blocked him with a stack of files and papers. He hesitated, but she made no effort to clear away the barricade.

Irving Welch was sitting in the back, his chin to his chest, his mouth half opened. Grady wondered if he snored. The three prayer meeting ladies sat towards the back. What were their names? Sophie. Millie. And? He couldn't remember the third one. Miss Cora's seat on the organ bench was empty, as was the row

Pastor Oscar occupied last week. Front and center sat Dixie and the twins. The little girls held onto the pew in front of them with both hands, swung their legs, and smiled at him.

The back door opened and Suzanne Simms entered. She scowled at him and slipped into the very last row. Had she seen him yesterday at Madison Farms?

"Even though most of you have heard the news," Grady began, "I feel compelled to make mention of it. Miss Cora will not be playing for us this morning. Pastor Oscar is in County Hospital. He had a heart attack and is in need of our prayers."

A gasp zigzagged through the audience, both verbally and in facial expression. Grady let the news sink in before he sat down. Wilfred Wheeler strode to the pulpit and raised both hands as though leading a choir. "Today we will be singing acapella." He interrupted himself and turned to Mae-June. "On second thought, would you be able to play for us today, Mae-June?"

Mae-June? Grady had no idea Mae-June played any instrument. Without a word, she rose from the pew and sat at the piano. She poised her hands over the keys, closed her eyes and breathed deeply as if willing herself into a trance. She came out of the trance like a racehorse at the gate—her eyes flew open, she thrust her right arm to the end of the keyboard and drew her fingers the length of it. Grady couldn't have been more shocked if Wilfred had sung an opera.

Just before Mae-June's fingers reached the furthest note on the piano, Wilfred said, "Please stand with me and turn to page 479."

Grady had placed a hymn book beneath his chair this week. He stood with the others and began to sing, "A Mighty Fortress is our God, a bulwark never failing . . ." Mae-June played loud and she played fast. In between verses, she played little ditties and started again. When she was done, Grady felt as though he'd run a marathon.

Wilfred left the stage and Grady strode to the pulpit. He scanned the audience and warmth flooded him. He cared about these people, he really did. He hoped the congregation took to Pastor Decker as much as they had taken to him. He hoped Joe Decker treated them well.

Grady cleared the emotion from his throat. "That was incredible, Mae-June," he said. "And we are grateful for your playing."

The *Amens* that followed were almost as loud as Mae-June's performance.

Grady gripped the pulpit with both hands. The silver clergy gown gathered at the wrists, but the sleeves were so long they billowed over themselves and over his hands to his fingers.

"When's the last time you looked at the sky at night?" he asked. "For me, it was just last night. I saw the constellation Pisces, the fish, and I remembered that in the beginning, this constellation was drawn with the fish swimming together as a pair. Today they are drawn as if they are swimming away from each other. The sky didn't change. The astronomers just came to see them in a different way."

Mae-June wrote in her notebook. Irving Welch's eyelids hid half his eyeballs. Betty Jean grinned and waved at him. He grinned back, started to raise his hand in a wave, thought better of it, lowered his hand.

"Pluto was considered a planet for a long time. But a few years ago, it got demoted to a dwarf planet. It's actually smaller than our moon. But things didn't change. Only our perception changed."

Grady felt excitement fill his chest. He raised both hands. "Scientists in South America have discovered an asteroid with rings. Its name is Chariklo. It orbits the sun between Saturn and Uranus. Science once told us rings only formed around planets. Another new discovery. Nobody knew it and then it was discovered."

Suzanne Simms, with a furrowed brow, rested an elbow on her knee and cradled her chin in her palm.

"God lives in the heavens," Grady preached. "Somewhere up there anyway. And nothing changes. But I'll bet He wants *us* to change. To be open to new ideas. To look at people in a new way. Sometimes we pigeonhole people. We see them do something and forever from that point on, we think that's who they are. We treat them as though they couldn't change. But all of us learn new things and we change by learning." He paused, studied the concentrating faces before him. "That's what I think anyway."

He nodded his head, turned, and walked to the tall wooden chair a few feet behind the pulpit. Wilfred Wheeler raced to the pulpit. "Now turn to page 95. Let's sing *God Who Stretched the Spangled Heavens.*" He glanced back at Grady with a wink and a smile, then circled his arms in a 'U' motion, inviting the congregation to rise. Mae-June tossed the notebook she'd been writing in onto the pew and raced to the piano. She played an elaborate introduction, and the voices of the congregation raised to the rafters.

Success, Grady thought. Another sermon down.

CHAPTER TWENTY-SEVEN

Cletus and Grace Jackson welcomed Grady into their two-bedroom ranch home for Sunday dinner. The kitchen, dining room, and living room were all one open space. A black marble L-shaped bar divided the kitchen from the dining area. Grace Jackson, a short, bulky woman, stood at the sink in the middle of the bar washing lettuce. When she shook the water from the lettuce, the skin hanging from her upper arms jiggled like an animal trying to escape. She wore sky blue elastic waist polyester pants and a baggy flowered top.

The timer on the stove buzzed and Grace hurried to it. She lifted the lid from a pot and a burning smell wafted through the room. Grace didn't seem to notice nor did Cletus.

"We're ready," Grace declared.

Cletus stood behind the chair at the end of the table, and Grace hung her apron on a hook beside the stove. She, too, stood behind a kitchen chair and gestured to another chair for Grady. He chose the last remaining place at the table set with a bowl, small plate, a knife, spoon, and fork.

"Let us give thanks," Cletus said, bowed his head, and was finished with the blessing before Grady had closed his eyes.

Grace's eyes sparkled as she turned to Grady. "We're so pleased to have you here."

"Thank you," Grady said, confused about the short blessing and what he was supposed to do since they were all still standing.

"We serve from the stove," Grace said. She picked up her bowl, then reached over and picked up the bowl in front of Grady. She handed it to him and indicated he was to follow her to the stove. She lifted the lid from the pot and scooped stew into Grady's bowl. "Bread and salad are on the table," she said.

Grady studied the contents of his bowl but had no idea what it was. Amongst the burnt specks, unidentifiable meat floated in a clear broth with an unidentifiable green vegetable. "Looks delicious," he managed to say despite the scorched smell and the unknown substances. He placed the bowl on the table and reached for the salad in a wooden bowl with metal tongs. He held the bowl over his small plate, held the tongs in his hand, and spied two small green bugs hiding on the back of a salad leaf. He set the salad down, thankful Cletus and Grace were still by the stove.

Grady waited for Cletus and Grace to get settled before commenting. "Interesting stew, Miss Grace."

She slurped a spoonful of soup and nodded a thank you. "It's Cletus' favorite."

"Looks good." Cletus slurped down three spoonsful like a starving child in a third world country.

Grady looked warily at the bowl in front of him. "So, what's in it?"

"Chitlins and okra." Cletus grinned, revealing a dime size

piece of okra stuck to his front tooth. He pointed his spoon towards Grace. "Like she said, my favorite."

Chitlins? Grady had heard of chitlins … pig intestines … but had never seen them. And okra? Slimy, bitter. He opened his mouth to say he wasn't really hungry when his stomach growled. Grace and Cletus exchanged a look and laughed.

"Eat up, pastor," Cletus said. "Sounds like you're hungry enough to eat the north end of a southbound polecat."

"Please pass the rolls and butter," Grady said.

Grace tilted back her head and laughed. Her chin jiggled as much as her arms had. She picked up the breadbasket, took a roll for herself and passed it to Grady. "We used to live in the big house," she said, pointing her chin towards the window. "For nearly twenty years, I'd guess. It got too big for us to manage and our daughter's family was growing—she has five children and she's pregnant again!"

"That's a big family." Grady concentrated intently on buttering his roll. The cold, hard butter ripped away pieces when he tried to spread it. Breadcrumbs sprayed over chitlins and okra like confetti. He took one bite before setting the roll on the side of his plate as he feigned intent interest in Grace's story.

"Yes, it is," Grace agreed. "So, we built this. It's perfect for the two of us. Our son-in-law takes care of the outside. We only tend a little garden. You're eatin' the last of the lettuce and tomatoes we harvested. Have to go back to store-bought for a few months. Not happy about that. What about you?" Grace asked. "Do you and Roxanne plan to have a big family?"

Grady choked on the bread.

"Do something!" Grace commanded Cletus.

Grady held up his hand and shook his head, his face morphing from flesh to pink to red. Finally, the coughing subsided enough for him to take a sip of sweet tea. "Phewf," he said after he swallowed. "*That* was something."

"Guess it was the big family question," Grace teased.

"Don't start," Cletus said. "Give the boy some peace."

"Actually," Grady said, regaining his composure, "we haven't talked about a family."

"Haven't talked about it!" Grace set down her fork and placed both hands on the table.

"My dear boy, when marriages break up, money and children are the primary cause. You haven't talked about it? Not good. Not good at all."

"Grace ..."

"No, Cletus. He needs to have this conversation for his own good. For the good of the marriage. For the good of his ministry. Go on, practice with us. Tell us what you'd say to Roxanne if she were sitting here and we were not."

Cletus set his fork down with a clang on the side of his salad plate. "Grace, this is between the pastor and his bride. Not our business. Now drop it. Let's enjoy our dinner, all right?"

Grace picked up her spoon, heaped it with chitlins and shoved it into her pouting lips.

Afterwards, with the lingering taste of chitlins on his lips and hearty hugs from Cletus and Grace, Grady slipped into the driver's seat of the Pontiac and turned the key in the ignition. What he needed was a drive-thru hamburger joint. He kept an eye open for one as he drove home. All the while, he thought about the kids conversation. If he really were Pastor Joe, and if he really were going to marry Roxanne, and they really were having the discussion about children, how many would he say he wanted?

Like he said to Miss Cora and Pastor Oscar, kids are a pain in the ass. They were a huge responsibility. His responsibility for the church members was different. Not like having kids. What would the Riddles' lives have been if they didn't have children? Maybe Rose would have gotten a job. And Ralph would have worried less about money. Maybe their marriage wouldn't be in a difficult place right now. Then again, what about Miss Cora and Pastor Oscar? She still mourned the loss of the twins after more than thirty years. Would she be happier with children? What about Dixie and her little clones? Dixie thought they were the best thing that ever happened to her despite the condemnation of Mae-June and others.

Children. How many would he want? How should he know? He was still half kid himself.

Grady was nearly home when his cell phone rang. One glance at the screen indicated Roxanne was calling.

"Hi!" she said cheerfully. "You probably heard Joe was transferred to rehab this week. He's doing excellent. Can you stop by? He'd like to talk to you about moving into the parsonage when they discharge him tomorrow."

"Tomorrow? Personage?"

"Yes, tomorrow. Isn't this exciting?"

Grady pressed the gas pedal harder, breezed past a 40-mph sign going 50. He slammed on the brakes, did a U-Turn in somebody's driveway, and headed to Knoxville Rehab.

Speeding up the highway, his brain went into overdrive. No,

no, no, no, no. Joe Decker had to be kept away until payday. He needed the cash. He worked for the money. He preached. He visited the sick. He held board meetings. He counseled couples on marital problems. He deserved to be paid, particularly after the last couple of days.

Grady heard a siren but wasn't sure which direction it was coming from. A glance in the mirror confirmed a police cruiser with lights flashing a few car lengths behind him. He pulled into the middle lane to give the officer room to pass. The officer pulled into the middle lane as well. Grady pulled into the slow lane. By this time the cruiser was less than a car length from the rear bumper of the Pontiac. The only option Grady had was to turn into the breakdown lane so the officer could pass and get to whatever emergency he'd been called to. The officer followed him, parked, and got out of the car. He was a hulk of a man, appearing even bulkier by his straight back stance, shaved head, and no-nonsense expression. Grady rolled down his window.

"So where are you going so fast this afternoon?" The officer growled.

Grady blinked rapidly. He drummed his fingers on the steering wheel. "On my way to the hospital." He stumbled over the words.

"Which one? You passed County Hospital two exits back."

"Knoxville," Grady said. He remembered his clerical collar and pointed to it. "I'm a pastor," he said. "One of my …" What was he supposed to call Pastor Joe? "One of my parishioners is hospitalized and calling for me."

"Last rites?"

"Actually, if I remember correctly," Grady said, "it's a left off

213

the exit, not a right. I'm not sure if it's the *last* right."

The cop's neck twitched. He analyzed Grady up and down. "May I see your license and registration, please?"

Grady opened the glove box, retrieved the registration, and handed it to the officer. He leaned towards the window to retrieve his wallet from the back pocket of his jeans. The officer walked back to the cruiser. Grady closed his eyes and took a few deep breaths. It seemed to take forever for the officer to return to the car.

"The address on your license and registration is Florida. You drove all this way to see a parishioner in Knoxville?"

Grady wiped sweat from his brow. "No," he said. "No. I'm the new pastor, I mean associate pastor, of Wilsons Corner Bible Believing Congregation. Haven't been here long. Haven't had a chance to get a new license yet."

"And this car is registered to Matthew McDonald. Who might that be, Mr. Gilbert?"

"My stepfather."

"Your stepfather? And why would you be driving your stepfather's classic Pontiac?" The officer backed away from the window and scanned the car front to back.

Grady gulped, searched for words. "He restored it for a guy who lives in …" What had he told Wilfred? Grady couldn't remember. "Kentucky. Rather than Matt the—Matthew drive all the way from Florida — I was headed this way anyway. So, the guy from Kentucky is going to pick it up here."

"Does this guy have a name?"

Did the guy in Kentucky have a name? Um—um— "Charlie Brown," Grady finally said.

"As in the Peanuts cartoon?"

"No, no. He prefers Chuck, actually." Grady felt so hot, his temperature was probably 108 degrees.

The officer studied him with a sneer and sauntered back to the cruiser. He returned in a few minutes with a ticket in his hand. "You were going 90 in a 70 mile an hour zone, Pastor. Keep it up if you want to meet your maker earlier than expected. If you plan on pastoring a while longer, I advise slowing down."

Grady glanced at the ticket. *$250*. A big chunk of his long-awaited paycheck. He turned mournfully to the officer. "Would it make any difference if I told you Officer Irving Welch was one of my parishioners?"

"No," said the officer and returned to his squad car.

CHAPTER TWENTY-EIGHT

Joe Decker pulled a comb through his thick black hair, made sure the part was straight and his cowlick under control. He looked at himself in the mirror. It was the best he could do. He smoothed down the collar of his short-sleeved, blue dress shirt. It had been impossible to get trousers over his cast, however, so he pulled on sweatpants. He glanced at his watch. Better get in bed under that scratchy sheet. He leaned heavily into the walker the rehab insisted he use unless someone was nearby to assist. Slowly, he made his way out of the bathroom, across the room and into bed. He sat on the edge. Leaned back a little. Dragged his leg up. Covered himself with the sheet. No one would be the wiser. A perfect pastor from the waist up.

He was eager to meet the other Pastor Joe, to get up to speed on what was happening in the church, what programs they had going on, what the members were like, whether the board was easy to work with. They'd have to decide what tasks would continue to fall upon the associate pastor. But before that, they had to decide on different titles or names for each other or it would get confusing with two Pastor Joes. Since the other Pastor Joe had been at Wilsons Corner longer than he had and was already known to the congregation as Pastor Joe, it would be prudent for him to keep the name. Pastor Joe wondered what he should have everyone call him.

When he'd spoken on the phone to the secretary—what was her name? Two months of the year, July-August? No. March-April? That sounded familiar, but not quite right. For now, he'd think of her as March-April until corrected. Anyway, he'd told March-April he'd like to be called Pastor Joe. She said she'd have a nameplate made for his desk. Funny she didn't say anything about the associate pastor by the name of Pastor Joe. Maybe she presumed he already knew. Maybe she planned to tell him and someone entered the office and interrupted her train of thought. Now that he thought of it, she seemed pretty busy, distracted.

What should he have the parishioners call him? Joseph? Too formal. He wanted to be more approachable than that. John? That was his middle name. It was fine for a middle name, but too plain, too many Johns in the world. Whatever he chose now would stay with him throughout his career. How about just his initial—J. Sure. That sounded good. He'd spell it out, though—J-A-Y. He'd be known as Pastor Jay.

That settled, Joe realized he was feeling a little nervous waiting for Pastor Joe. That was silly. Why should he feel nervous to meet the man who was his assistant? Maybe he just felt vulnerable beneath the sheets. This is not how he pictured himself being introduced to his first church.

A tall young woman with sleek black hair stood in the hallway outside the room Grady believed to be Joe Decker's room. She wore a burgundy sweater and black pants. Her lipstick was the identical color of the sweater. Grady nodded as he approached. He pointed to the door. "Is this Joe Decker's room?" he asked.

A look of relief spread from the woman's eyes to a softening of her cheeks, to a broad burgundy smile. "Yes," she said. "Are you Pastor Joe?"

"Yes," he said, surprised at how young she looked. "You must be Roxanne. I recognize your voice." Grady held out his hand, expecting her to shake it. Instead, she threw her arms around his neck and clutched him tightly.

"Thank you for coming," she said into his neck before she pulled away. "I feel so helpless far from home, knowing no one here. I'm so glad we've been able to connect. At least I have one friend."

One friend? Grady liked the sound of that, but at the same time felt a little awkward. She thought more of him than he was.

"As I told you on the phone," she continued, "Joe will be discharged soon. We hoped he could move into the parsonage. Is that possible?"

Grady stepped back from her. Not that he didn't like being hugged by a beautiful woman, but she was, after all, already taken. "I'm going to be in the personage another week or two—" he started.

"Is there a way you can make space for him?"

"Roxanne?" A voice called from inside the room.

Roxanne drew a hand across Grady's shoulder. "That's Joe. Come on in. Let me introduce you and see what we can work out." She stepped inside the door as Grady waited outside.

He heard her speaking animatedly to Joe. "He's here. The associate pastor. Joe."

Grady rubbed his forehead—he wasn't sure who Roxanne was talking to when she said 'Joe.' How was he going to handle this? He entered the room and stood close to the door, rocking back and forth on his heels. His voice sounded as if it belonged to someone else. "How ya doin'?"

"Better every day," Joe Decker said from his bed. He looked past Roxanne to the young man. They could pass as brothers— same dark hair and cowlick, brown eyes, cleft in chin, about the same height and build. The young man wore jeans, worn Nikes, a blue collared three-button shirt with the clergy collar fastened around his neck. Joe couldn't hide his surprise. He thought Wilsons Corner was more formal than this guy presented.

"This is Pastor Joe," Roxanne said. She gestured towards Grady. "And this is Pastor Joe." She gestured towards Joe.

"Actually, I've decided to be called Pastor Jay from now on," Joe said. "Too confusing to have two Pastor Joes in one church. You've had the name longer than me—"

"No, no. The name belongs to you," Grady objected.

"I insist. I am now Pastor Jay."

Grady checked out Pastor Jay. So, this was the man he had tried so hard to emulate—the famous Pastor Joe. The Congo-raised, Gordon-Conwell-graduate expert in all things religious. His dark hair was flat on one side and sticking up at the crown. He looked vulnerable with his leg in a cast almost entirely covered by the sheet. A bit of the sheet slipped away, and Grady saw sweat suit fabric. He'd been nervous to meet the high and mighty Joseph Decker, and now the guy was reduced to this?

"Have a seat." Pastor Jay gestured towards an uncomfortable looking straight-back wooden chair. His voice exuded confidence. Maybe even arrogance.

Grady felt inadequate in this man's presence. At the same time, he felt superior in a relationship kind of way. He wasn't sure he wanted to relinquish his congregation, his people, to this pompous guy, then he immediately felt guilty about classifying Joe Decker as pompous. He didn't even know the man.

"Sorry you're going through all this," Grady said. He didn't move from his spot in the doorway. "You in much pain?"

"Come in," Pastor Jay said. "Sit down." It was more of a command than an invitation.

Grady ambled to the chair, perched himself on the edge of it, placed his elbows on his knees, leaned forward.

"I've been eager to meet you," Pastor Jay said. "I didn't even know they had an associate pastor until Roxanne called about my accident and you answered! How long have you been at Wilsons Corner?"

"Not long," Grady said.

Pastor Jay bobbed his head in a nervous sort of way. In Grady's eyes, he'd gone from high and mighty to a shrinking violet in a couple of seconds. Grady wasn't sure why, but he straightened up, put on his best Pastor Joe persona, although it was kind of hard to do it in front of the real Pastor Joe.

Pastor Jay waited for Pastor Joe to elaborate on his tenure, but he didn't supply any other information. *Strange.* "I was looking forward to getting started," he said. "Interested to meet the people. What a setback."

"Tough break," Pastor Joe said. Pastor Jay waited, but the room filled with awkward silence. This Pastor Joe was a strange guy. No wonder they didn't want to promote him to head pastor. He wondered where the guy went to school. How in the world did he make it this far?

"Tell me about the congregation," he said. "From your perspective. I know what they told me. But that's not always accurate."

"What do you want to know?" Pastor Joe's leg jiggled up and down.

"Start by telling me about the people. The secretary. What's her name? What can I expect there? I spoke to her a couple of times."

"Mae-June," Pastor Joe said. Was that a smirk on his face? "She uses different color paper for different tasks. She prints the visitation list on blue paper and the schedule on yellow paper. She'll boss you around all right, but she's organized."

"Thanks for the heads up," Pastor Jay said. He glanced at Roxanne who stood by the window with her arms folded, a look of displeasure on her face. She wasn't happy about moving here, but she'd seemed happy with Pastor Joe. Spoke highly of him. But if this man was the best the place had to offer, maybe he should call Gordon Conwell. See if any other congregation was in need of a pastor.

Grady unconsciously stuck an index finger between his clergy collar and his neck and stretched his chin back and forth. "This dang thing," he said.

"Not used to it yet, heh?" Pastor Jay chuckled. "How long's it been?"

Grady stopped stretching his neck but kept his finger in the collar. "Been? Been what?"

"Since you've been wearing the collar."

"Couple weeks," Grady said.

"Couple weeks," Pastor Jay repeated. "I'm confused."

Grady's hand trembled slightly. He hoped Pastor Jay hadn't noticed, or if he did, maybe he'd attribute it to some kind of palsy or other neurological disorder. "I thought you meant this collar," he said. "*This* collar." He pointed with the hand not stuck between his neck and the stiff clergy collar. "This one's not like any I've had before. Nothing. I should probably return it. Defect. I think it's defective." He drew his hand out, placed it on the chair arm, tapped his fingers. He was aware of Pastor Jay studying the movement. The silence that followed seemed strained, and he wasn't sure why.

"I never heard of a defective collar," Pastor Jay said.

"Me neither," Grady said. "'Til now."

There was a knock on the door and a young woman in blue scrubs entered the room.

"Time for physical therapy," she said.

Grady shot out of his seat and headed for the door. "I'd best be going." Relief engulfed him. "'til next time."

"Wait," Pastor Jay said. "The parsonage. We need to talk about me moving into the parsonage. I'm doing better than expected. Might even be discharged tomorrow."

Grady skidded to a halt in the doorway. He stood for a moment staring into the hallway. A nurse walked by wheeling a pole with plastic bags of clear liquid swaying from the top of it. "Tomorrow?"

"I'm hoping to move into the parsonage."

Grady turned around slowly. "It'll take me some time to get it ready. I'll let you know if I can get it done by tomorrow."

CHAPTER TWENTY-NINE

S o, how'd it go?" Grady swiveled in his desk chair as … what was the guy's name? *Tweet. Tweet Hearts. Riddle!* Ralph Riddle entered for their scheduled appointment on Monday morning. "Where's Rose?"

Ralph thrust a thumb over his shoulder. Rose peeked out from behind him. With both hands, she held a brown purse. The corners of the purse were peeling, revealing a tan underbelly.

Grady laughed. "Didn't see you back there, Rose. Here, let me get the door." He strode across the room and waited while the Riddles moved past and deposited themselves into chairs. Ralph appeared ready for a fight with his arms crossed over his chest, head cocked to one side, and eyelids half closed. Rose looked like a kid caught cheating on an exam. Her eyes were focused on some spot on the floor. She clutched her purse handle as though she expected a burglar to dash past at any moment. She did not raise her head in response to Grady's greeting.

Grady's bravado smile wanted to go into hiding and allow a terrified grimace to replace it. He crossed the room and glanced out the window at a cloudless azure sky. He'd read on Google news that the weather was going to be perfect today—not too hot, not too cold, no humidity. The kind of day everyone wishes would last forever before winter set in. The kind of weather anyone would rather be outside. Grady made an instant decision and swung around. "You know," he said. "Rose, do you mind if I take Ralph aside for a minute? A man kind of thing. Won't take long."

Rose's fingers on the purse handle relaxed. The muscles in her jaw loosened. She raised her chin ever so slightly. Grady thought the sides of her lips twitched upward. She nodded a jerky assent.

"Come on, Ralph," Grady said, his confidence edging out caution. He flung open the door and jogged down the hallway without looking back. He hoped Ralph was following. When he reached the door to the parking lot, he grasped the push bar and turned around. Ralph was only a few steps behind. Grady beckoned him forward, exited, skipped down the steps. The basketball sat on the grass near the hoop just outside the parking lot. Grady picked it up, dribbled to what he'd been using as the free throw line. He jumped, flicked the ball upwards in a perfect arc. The ball hit the backboard, bounced back onto the rim, circled it, dropped through the net.

"Two points," Grady shouted. "Come on, Ralph, see if you can steal the ball." He swung around so that his back was to Ralph. Bending his knees, he dribbled in front of his legs, under his knees, behind his back.

Ralph stood on the grass, hands in back pockets of his green work pants. "Come on," Grady urged.

Ralph grunted. "What about Rose? Aren't we supposed to be talking about Rose?"

Grady dribbled toward the free throw line, hurled himself into the air, tossed the ball. Smooth shot right through the net. "Yes!" he said and clapped for himself. He grabbed the ball. "Sure," he said to Ralph. "You wanna talk about Rose?"

"Not really," Ralph said.

"Then get out here on the court." Grady actually felt relieved. Even after laughing half the week about his own third base comment, he wasn't sure he wanted to hear a report on how it went. First base, second base, third base, home run. He cringed at the thought of two old people engaged at any point in the game.

Ralph ambled into the parking lot. Grady threw the ball. It bounced once, shot up, hit Ralph in the chest. His eyes widened, he reached out and grabbed the ball before it could ricochet back to Grady.

"So that's the way you want to play, huh?" Ralph stood in place, dribbled with his fingertips, glared at Grady.

Grady bent forward, ready to pounce, arms poised to steal the ball. "Yeah," he challenged. "That's the way I want to play it."

Ralph swung around, keeping his body between Grady and the ball. He stood for a minute, dribbling, looking over one shoulder, then the other, fixing Grady with a stare. Slowly he backed up, inching towards the basket. Still crouching with arms out and hands upraised, Grady approached Ralph. As Ralph backed towards the inner court, Grady backed with him. They were close. Close enough for Grady to observe sweat beads pop out on Ralph's neck. Close enough for Grady to catch a cigar smell from Ralph's faded *Hometown Days 2011* t-shirt. Close enough for Grady to remember the only time Matt the Rat had attended one of his high school basketball games.

The school had won 27 games in the 30-game season, catapulting them into the Florida division finals. Teams from Tampa, Tallahassee, Jacksonville, Miami, and other cities traveled to compete in Orlando. Grady had begged Matt to come watch him all season. There was always some excuse. Too tired. Bleachers too hard, no back support. Gotta work.

When the team made it to the finals, suddenly Matt took an interest. More than an interest. For the two weeks leading up to the first game, he bragged wherever they went. "My boy here." He'd fling an affectionate arm over Grady's shoulder, something he'd never done before. "You should see him on the court. Led his team to the finals."

"I don't know about *led*," Grady objected. He'd made a few baskets, intercepted some, but *led*? That was a bit of an overstatement, and he hated being called Matt's boy. Matt wasn't his father.

Matt tapped him in the jaw with a fist and laughed. "No time to be modest," he said. "My son," he said to whoever happened to be listening. "I'm so damn proud of him."

The hype, the expectation, the loud-mouth bragging grew louder every day. Whereas before Grady was excited and proud about the possibility, he now grew nervous. Coach always said, "Do your best. Go out there, remember the rules, give it your all.

Whatever the outcome, sportsmanship and effort are what counts."

But with Matt, sportsmanship and effort didn't matter. The goal was winning. Being #1. Laughing when the other team was down.

As the day of the first game approached, Grady felt a tiny lump in his throat. It grew every day until it seemed to cut off his airway. His mother brought him to the walk-in clinic. They couldn't find anything, diagnosed it as anxiety, recommended he see a therapist to work out his problems.

"Wimp," Matt said.

The team lost the second game. Matt never again attended another game or talked about being proud of Grady or referred to him as *my son*.

Ralph and Grady sat in the grass under the hoop, knees drawn to chests, arms draped over knees. Sweat sliding off their noses. They panted, almost in unison.

"Phewf." Ralph gulped in air. "I haven't had a workout like that in a long time. You gave me a run for my money."

"You're not bad yourself," Grady said.

"A little out of practice is all."

"Nah. What they say about riding a bike. Same for basketball. Same for softball and other things." Grady raised his shoulders. "Love even. Once you learn, you never forget."

"S'pose," Ralph said. "But sometimes you need … I guess I'd say, sometimes you need a new bike."

"Just give the old one a chance," Grady said. "Oil the gears. Buy a more comfortable seat. Bring it inside when it rains. Might surprise you."

"S'pose," Ralph said again. "I could try. Never made it round first base. Stayed there all week."

"It's a start," Grady said. He was relieved not to hear the details.

The printer cartridge ran out. Mae-June trotted across the office to fetch a replacement from the supply closet. So many people had moved or gotten new phone numbers, she was busy updating the church directory. And she needed to add Pastor Joe. Of course, she would send the document to Andy at McNall Printers. She needed to proof it first. She didn't do well reading on the screen. Too much gave her a headache.

She zipped out of her office and nearly bumped into a mousy-looking woman. Short, slight-built, looked like a good burst of wind would blow her into the next county. Her hair was dishwater brown, frizzy on the edges.

Mae-June gasped. "Bless my soul," she said. "You nearly gave me a fright."

"Sorry." The woman dipped her chin to her chest.

Suddenly Mae-June remembered who this was. Rose Riddle. Came in last week with her husband to speak to Pastor Joe. Waste of time if you asked Mae-June. But then, some people might cling to a speck of encouragement while others might need a bit more.

"Mrs. Riddle," Mae-June said. "Rose. Right?"

The woman nodded.

"Pastor Joe didn't show up?"

"Oh no. He's here." Rose pointed to the doorway. "Outside with Ralph playing basketball. Not sure what's going on."

Mae-June said, "Let me see about that."

Rose led the way to the doorway and they both peered out. Pastor Joe and Ralph were walking towards them, shirts soaked, laughing like two old pals who hadn't seen each other in ages. Ralph slapped Pastor Joe on the shoulder. Left his hand there a few seconds.

"Good job out there," they heard Pastor Joe say.

"Hmmm." Mae-June voiced her disapproval.

"Heavenly day." A smile crossed Rose's face. "He hasn't laughed like that in a coon's age."

CHAPTER THIRTY

The minute the Riddles left, Grady dashed back to the house to neaten the personage. He put dishes from yesterday and the day before into the dishwasher. He gathered the heap of clothes in the corner of the bedroom, stuffed them into the washing machine. He picked up the books and Bible that had remained on the floor since last week and the week before during sermon preparation. He jammed them into the bookcase under the front window, noticed some were upside down, righted them, patted the backs of the books.

Okay. What else. He scanned the living room. Crumbs on the coffee table. Swept them onto the floor. Quilt in a ball on the couch. How had it been when he first arrived? Draped over the back of the couch. He shook it out, folded it, arranged it as he remembered it from the first time he'd entered the personage.

In the kitchen he mashed down the items on the top of the overflowing trash can, stretched the plastic bag and tied it. He hauled it to the dumpster between the church and personage. He swiped a dishrag across the top of the stove, picked at a hardened glob of jelly with the edge of a knife, pushed both chairs under the table.

The flowers in the vase on the table, long dead, littered the table with dried particles. Should he replace them with a fresh bunch? They were intended for Pastor Jay, after all. Forget it. He didn't have time. Pastor Jay would never know about the flowers.

The place was beginning to look half decent. Now for the bedroom. He'd decided to move all his stuff into the second bedroom, to tell Pastor Jay he'd lost his own rental and Mae-June said he could stay here a week or so. After he collected the monthly paycheck next Monday, he'd be on the road heading north. One week to go.

One problem. How was he going to get that check with Pastor Jay here now? For that matter, did he have a right to that check now Pastor Jay was here? When the guy was just a name without a face, it was one thing. Now they'd met and now he'd actually be living in the personage, who was entitled to the check?

Grady's shoulders drooped. Well, Pastor Jay was here, that much he had to admit. But he wouldn't be working. Grady would be working. Shouldn't he be entitled to the money? A little shady, but, hey, he earned it. If he was entitled to the money, why did he have a sick feeling in his gut?

Then another thought struck him. How was he going to keep Pastor Jay hidden for a week? He hadn't thought that far ahead. Just solved each problem one by one as it was thrown at him. But now, this was getting complicated. Problem one intertwined with problem two which snarled with problem three.

His heart raced. He slapped a hand over his chest. Was he having a heart attack? Maybe he should just sneak away tonight.

Bring Pastor Jay home ... home ... in a short period of time, he had come to think of the personage as home. He felt hugged living within its walls. Hugged. Kind of a sissy word. He'd never admit it out loud. He suddenly felt the same lump in his throat as he did before the basketball game his team lost back in high school.

Maybe he should settle Pastor Jay into the bedroom, and during the night, drive away. No. He couldn't do that. Pastor Oscar was still in the hospital. He couldn't leave Miss Cora alone at a time like this. And he couldn't leave before the Praise Team sang. The teenagers had practiced three times to perform in church. He couldn't let them down. And he couldn't leave before Mae-June handed over the check. He groaned in frustration. He had to stop thinking and just do. Right now he was due in Knoxville to pick up Pastor Jay. He grabbed his keys and headed out the door.

When Grady pulled up to the rehab entrance, he spied Pastor Jay sitting in a wheelchair near a window in the lobby. A nurse was holding the handles so he wouldn't roll away. The minute he saw the car, Pastor Jay pointed it out to the nurse who rolled him outside. Pastor Jay rose and hobbled to the car. He whistled, opened the door, and stuck his head in. "Some wheels you've got here. Man, oh man, you must have had a great sponsorship deal to make it through seminary and come out with this baby."

Grady opened his mouth to deliver a half-truth, but the nurse interrupted. "Careful," she instructed Pastor Jay. She put her hand on his head as he grabbed the frame and heaved himself into the back seat.

"Thanks for the ride," he said. "I can barely make it in here. I'd never manage in Roxanne's Mini Cooper."

Grady checked his rearview mirror and roared away from the curb. "I know. That thing is tiny. I can't believe she drove down here all the way from Boston."

"Whoa," Pastor Jay said with alarm. "Hey, hey, let's make it to the church in one piece. I just got out of the hospital, remember. I don't want to go back so soon."

"Sorry," Grady said, although he wasn't.

Pastor Jay chuckled. "Anyway, I hear you about Roxanne's car. That thing is not safe. Once we're married, I'll insist she buy an SUV or minivan." He paused, then brightened. "How would you like to go car shopping? My check from the insurance company came in."

"Today?" Grady gripped the steering wheel with sweaty palms.

"Whenever you have time."

"We'll see," Grady said. "I really want to visit Pastor Oscar."

"What's going on?" Pastor Jay asked. "I was hoping to meet him. We really connected during my phone interview."

"Great guy," Grady said. "Had a heart attack. That was rough, I'll tell you. His wife, Miss Cora, she called me in the middle of the night. I mean two or three or around there. They took him away in an ambulance, and I had to go over and get her and bring her to the hospital. Phewf. That was something."

Pastor Jay chuckled. "Life of a pastor," he said. Then his countenance became more serious. "I'm sorry to hear about the heart attack. Give him my best, okay?"

"Sure enough," Grady lied. No way was he going to tell anyone Pastor Jay was in town.

They rode in silence for ten minutes or more. Grady prayed silently he could somehow slip into the church parking lot and around the corner to the personage without Mae-June seeing him. He planned to drive really slow once he turned in at the sign by the trees. He wouldn't gun the engine when he made it to the parking lot. Mae-June once commented she always knew when he drove in by the sound of the engine and the squealing of his tires. He wouldn't squeal the tires. If she was still working, she wouldn't have a clue it was him.

Next problem. How to get Joe Decker up the steps and into the personage. Joe seemed to think he could manage fine, but Grady wasn't sure. If Mae-June was still working, they would need to negotiate the stairs faster than if she was already gone.

"Where's Roxanne?" Grady asked. "I hoped she'd be here to help get you up the stairs."

"I'm fine," Pastor Jay said. "I told her I'd call her at the Bed and Breakfast where she's staying once I'm settled in. I don't want her to see me struggling or falling. I need to be the strong one."

Grady searched his brain for an answer, but could not come up with anything.

A pick-up merged onto the freeway. Grady flicked on his turn signal, glanced in the rearview mirror, pulled into the left lane, and gunned the engine.

"Whoa," Joe Decker said. "What did you do before seminary—race in Daytona?"

Grady laughed. "Lot of power under the hood. Hard to keep it under control."

Pastor Jay winced. "Ooh. That hurts. Sorry. Tried to re-arrange my leg. Still painful. What else can you tell me about the church secretary? What's her name again?"

"Mae-June." Grady hesitated. Should he tell Pastor Jay what he really thought? He toned it down a bit before speaking. "She thinks she's in charge."

"Really?" Pastor Jay sat up straighter. "The secretary thinks she's in charge?"

"Oh yeah," Grady said. "Oh yeah."

"Thanks for the warning," Pastor Jay said. "I was thinking of going to the office a couple of hours this week. Meet her."

Grady hoped Joe did not see the vein pulse in his temple. "Not a good idea," he said.

"Why not?" Joe asked.

Good question. Why not? Grady almost felt sorry he'd tried to impersonate the guy. It wasn't impersonation exactly. He hadn't even known who Joe Decker was when all of this began. He hardly knew him now. It was more like play-acting what someone in a pastor's position might do.

"Did you hear me?" Joe's voice was kind, calm. He didn't seem frustrated by Grady's lack of an answer.

"Sure," Grady said. "Just concentrating on the road. Don't want to miss the exit." *Exit.* What if he'd taken a different exit on that fateful Wednesday night? One exit before. One exit after. How different his life would be.

Meeting Mae-June. What excuse could he come up with as to why Joe should wait to go into the office and meet Mae-June?

"It's supposed to be a surprise," Grady said. "But under the circumstances, it's probably better you know. See, they throw this big party for the new pastor. They'll have balloons. Cake with your name on it. Punch. Speeches. Make sure you make a fuss over the date bars. Mae-June makes them from scratch and she's mighty proud of them."

"You think it's best I don't meet anyone until that surprise party?" Pastor Jay asked.

"Definitely." Grady hadn't wanted to lie, but what could he do? He hoped he wouldn't have to stretch the truth too many times before he took his leave. "Definitely. This is our exit. We're almost there."

As he'd planned, he drove slowly into the parking lot. Mae-June's car was parked in her usual spot. Wilfred Wheeler's truck was beside it. What was it with those two? Wilfred came by Mae-June's office every afternoon. Mae-June seemed annoyed on the one hand, but like an embarrassed teenager on the other. Maybe he'd have to do some marriage counseling with them pretty soon … if he stayed that long.

Pastor Jay managed the few stairs into the cottage with no problem. Grady made him a sandwich, then announced he was on his way to see Pastor Oscar.

CHAPTER THIRTY-ONE

The first few trips to County Hospital to visit Pastor Oscar, Grady relied on Google maps. Today he surprised himself and remembered every turn. He pulled up to reserved parking, stuck the clergy sign in the window, checked his clergy collar, glanced in the mirror for his clergy face, and headed into the lobby.

He nodded at the senior citizen volunteering at the reception desk and pressed the elevator button for the third floor. He remembered every hallway and every turn. He felt comfortable knowing what was expected of him—speak words of comfort, maybe say a prayer. *Presence.* That's really all that was expected, the presence of someone who cared. He could do that. He could care. He was smiling when he entered Pastor Oscar's room.

"Pastor Joe," Miss Cora whispered from a chair with wooden arms and a large uncomfortable-looking plastic seat. She looked up from her knitting, appearing even more fragile than she had the last time he visited. "He's weak, but he's doing better. He's been looking forward to your visit. He only fell asleep a few minutes ago."

Grady did his best to mimic Joseph Decker's pastoral voice. "That's great news, Miss Cora." He bent and placed a firm arm around her shoulder.

She looked up at him, smiled, then averted her eyes once again. "He says you make him feel everything's going to be all right."

Grady wished he felt the same about himself. The continued calls from Orlando were unnerving. Just as he was becoming comfortable as Pastor Joe, Matt or his mother would call. The colliding of two worlds had no business intersecting. He wanted to focus on the now and not be dragged into the past.

"Have you had a chance to eat, Miss Cora?" he asked.

She shook her head. "I didn't want to leave him in case he needed anything."

"Go on down to the cafeteria," Grady said. "Grab a bite. I'm here now."

"No—"

"As your pastor, I insist." Grady spoke firmly, but calmly. "Go get something to eat." He withdrew the church charge card from his wallet. "Here," he said. "On me. Get whatever you want."

"I couldn't," she said, yet reached for the card.

Grady helped her out of the chair. "Sure, you can."

She smiled, her eyes tired. "If you put it that way," she said. She pushed herself up from the chair, hugged him, and left.

Grady sat in the chair she had vacated and for the first time took a good look at Pastor Oscar. He couldn't count the wires hooked to the man or the machines he was attached to. He looked years older than he had when Grady ate Sunday dinner with him and Miss Cora such a short time ago. His skin was pasty and his breathing shallow. He breathed in and there was silence. Grady grabbed the chair's wooden arms ready to jump up and call for a nurse when finally Pastor Oscar breathed out. Miss Cora might be optimistic and speak of progress. Grady didn't hold the same opinion. He stood, reached through the rails, and clasped Pastor Oscar's hand. The hand was unresponsive and cold, almost reptilian. Grady stood there for a long while wondering about the man whose hand he held. What kind of life had he led? What did it feel like to be old, to know you had no more chances, to be looking back instead of ahead?

Miss Cora had been gone half an hour or so when Grady decided he needed a break. He stepped out of the room and noticed a wall of windows down the hall to his left. He wandered over and studied the view. From up here on the third floor, Wilsons Corner didn't look half bad. He spotted a lake and wondered if it was the same one near Pastor Oscar's house. He doubted it since he'd driven in a different direction when leaving the personage. A narrow river led out of the lake and disappeared into a grove of pine trees. Grady caught glimpses of it every few hundred yards where the trees cut away.

Far beyond the lake was a small mountain. At first, he thought it was clouds or haze, but after studying it a while, he realized it was, in fact, a mountain. He tried to figure out what direction he was looking. Towards the mall or away from the mall. He'd have to find that mountain sometime, see what was up there.

Someone had left a wheelchair pushed up against the wall beside the door to Pastor Oscar's room. Grady glanced in the room, realized Pastor Oscar was still sleeping and eased himself into the wheelchair. He took out his cell phone and googled "games." He played Solitaire over and over and still Miss Cora was not back.

A nurse entered Pastor Oscar's room, then Grady heard the click of an intercom and a monotone command, "Code Blue, CCU. Code Blue, CCU." He turned. Men in scrubs, women in white lab coats, two men in suits raced from way down the hall towards him. Three nurses charged out of three rooms across the hall and joined the brigade. Grady didn't know why they were running or if it had anything to do with the announcement, and if so, what did Code Blue mean. Nevertheless, his heart raced.

Then the brigade breezed past him and entered Pastor Oscar's room. Grady's vision swam and bile rose in his throat. There were too many people. Half a dozen spilled out into the hallway, some grasped the door jamb and peeked inside.

Panic spread from his heart to his stomach, down his arms. Zombielike, he stood and joined the nurses peering in the doorway.

"We're so glad you're here, chaplain," a nurse said. "Go on in. At this point, you may be able to do more good than anyone else."

What did that mean? Grady couldn't process the words. He felt a shove and his legs obeyed the shover, not his own mind. He was closer to the bed than he felt comfortable. Someone shouted, "Stand back!" and placed two thick pads with handles on Pastor Oscar's chest. Snap! Pastor Oscar's body rose from the bed.

"Again!"

"Again!"

"Again!"

Grady watched wide-eyed as if in a nightmare. Whatever happened to Pastor Oscar improving? What happened … heck, what would happen to Miss Cora?

"Call it," someone said.

"4:10," someone else answered.

Slowly the team marched out, all except for one nurse. Grady opened his mouth to speak, but all that came out was a squeak. The nurse glanced up. "Chaplain," she said. "Did you know him?"

Grady bobbed his head stiffly. He cleared his throat. "I … am …" He felt a build-up of tears behind his eyes. *Men weren't supposed to cry. At least pastors weren't. Pastors were the strong ones, the ones who helped everyone else.* Before a dam of tears burst, Grady turned and left the room.

Grady watched from outside Pastor Oscar's room while the nurse shut down all machines and removed all tubes. Far down the hall, Miss Cora rounded the corner smiling, looking refreshed. He tried to look casual, but Miss Cora must have caught some negative energy. Her eyes widened and her smile quickly evaporated. Grady grasped her frail shoulders and pulled her to his chest. He cocooned her in his arms.

"Is he …?" she said, her voice muffled in his shirt. "Is he …?" This time more urgently.

"Yes," he whispered into her thin gray hair. "He's gone."

She pulled away from him and shrieked, "NOOOOOOOO!" He pulled her to himself again, and she fought to release herself.

He did not let go. Eventually, she stopped fighting and drooped into his embrace. He let her cry until she was spent and his shirt was soaked, then he loosened his grip on her. He kept one arm across her shoulders and led her into the room. Pastor Oscar lay on his back with his arms folded on a smooth sheet. He looked peaceful.

Miss Cora approached the bed, despair and disbelief stretched across her face. She reached out and touched her dead husband's cheek. "I shouldn't have left," she wept.

"There's nothing you could have done," Grady said.

She stood quietly for a while, then began to cry again. Through tears, she choked on words. Some Grady understood. Some were muffled in sobs. " ... married 42 years ... I heard him sing. Did you know he could sing?"

Grady shook his head.

"A baritone. He sang in the choir. I heard him sing and I knew he was the one for me." She dropped into Grady's arms and cried. "I'll never hear him sing again."

Grady had never seen someone die before. Never even been to a funeral. To see life extinguished before his eyes ... no word described it. One minute a living human being and then a last breath left behind a shell. A body without a soul.

Death wasn't something he had given much thought to. Why would he? His life was just a canvas with a background painted. How was he supposed to comfort Miss Cora when he was crying, too? What could he say? Where was Pastor Oscar now? People talked about heaven, hell, purgatory, reincarnation, angels, death as a sleep, or the end of everything forever. Which was it?

Believing was one thing when it was only philosophical, but when death smacked you in the face, it was important to know.

Late afternoon, just as Mae-June scanned her desk to make sure she hadn't forgotten anything important, Suzanne Simms strutted in and slapped Mae-June's desk.

"I have two things to tell you," Suzanne declared. "And you're not going to believe either one."

Mae-June wasn't sure whose visit she dreaded most—Wilfred's daily afternoon visit or Suzanne's once a week visit with some sort of gossip about somebody. Not that Mae-June didn't find it interesting, but still … it disrupted her efficiency.

"Have a seat," Mae-June said. This time she expected good news. Heaven knew she could use it after all that had been going on.

Suzanne had a perkiness to her step and a smile that could shatter glass. She settled herself gracefully into Mae-June's guest chair. "Which one first?" she teased. "The mall or the hospital?"

"Oh, I don't know." Mae-June threw up her hands. "Let's go with the hospital."

"My daughter Rita? You know. The older girl. Not the one I put on the prayer list. Anyway, she married that salesman? Remember? They moved to Knoxville last year. Well … Suzanne wriggled in her chair like a child with ADHD. "She's a nurse in the hospital up there. I shouldn't be telling you this, confidentiality and all. Anyway, she says they have a patient named Joe Decker."

Mae-June felt the muscles in her face go slack.

"Not only that," Suzanne continued. "He was brought into the Emergency Department as a result of an auto accident."

"It's ... not ... as if the name Decker is all that common," Mae-June said. "How many Deckers do you know?"

"Pastor is the only one. And get this. She was talking to him and he's engaged."

Mae-June felt the color drain from her face. "The name. The auto accident. Engaged. That's too much of a coincidence."

"I know!" Suzanne squealed in delight. "We are in the middle of a true-life mystery."

"Is Rita sure about this?"

"Positive. Absolutely no doubt." Suzanne leaned forward and clicked her fingernails on Mae-June's desk. "Somebody needs to investigate. Don't you think?"

Mae-June nodded. "Uh, huh," she said. "Uh, huh. You said there were two things. What was the second thing? I hope it's better than the first."

"Oh yes." Suzanne settled back into the chair. "No, it isn't better. It might be worse. The first could be a coincidence. The second is no coincidence."

"Go on," Mae-June said.

"I saw Pastor Joe in the mall with Dixie."

"No!" Mae-June covered her mouth with both hands. This couldn't be happening.

"Yes. Tuesday. I saw them. Together. In the mall."

No way was Mae-June going to let Dixie seduce another young, unsuspecting male. Not on her watch anyway. It was bad enough the church hadn't taken a stand nearly five years ago when Dixie got pregnant at sixteen. To make it worse, Dixie had no shame. The least she could have done was keep a low profile. But no. She flaunted that big belly like she was the Virgin Mary carrying Baby Jesus. And then to find out it was two, not one. That made it doubly bad. Those poor little bastard children!

In Mae-June's day, she would have been housebound for the duration of the pregnancy, then coerced to give it up for adoption. In fact, when Mae-June was pregnant with Jimmy, she was glad moo-moos were in style. That's all she wore to hide her bulging belly. She'd rather people didn't look at her and know what she had done to become with child. And that was after she'd been married for five years!

To make matters worse, the church gave Dixie a baby shower and she wasn't even a church member! She was just some young kid Jimmy picked up in the pool hall upstairs from Wilsons Corner Convenience Store. The ladies came out in full force presenting Dixie with a crib, a baby carriage, cute little matching girlie dresses, and disposable diapers. Someone even rolled up diapers and crafted them into a cake.

Disposable diapers! The expense! Mae-June had dunked Jimmy's poopy cloth diapers into the toilet, washed them, hung them on the line to dry. In winter, they froze like boards and she stood them up by the space heater to thaw. Disposable diapers! What an expensive waste.

As for the shower, Suzanne told Mae-June all about it after the fact. Mae-June hadn't attended. It would have been too awkward. She stayed home and dealt with Jimmy.

"I thought she was using something, Mama," he said. "Told me she was. I swear. She said she couldn't get knocked up. I never woulda done it, Mama, if I'd known."

Here Mae-June was, the church secretary, the ambassador to the community, and now this. Was the church board going to fire her? What would she and Jimmy do? They depended on that meager salary to survive since Jimmy Senior fell asleep at the wheel on a cross-country run delivering soybeans. His eighteen-wheeler rolled over. He came home in bad shape. Mae-June bathed and fed and brought him to the toilet for nearly a year before he died of an infection. The trucking company said it was his fault which left Mae-June with none of her husband's benefits. She couldn't lose her job. How would she and Jimmy make it?

"What are you gonna do?" she asked Jimmy.

"Get outta Dodge," he said emphatically.

"What do you mean?"

"It's not my fault," Jimmy said. "But her father's gonna pin it on me. He's meaner than a rattlesnake. He'll prob'ly have me arrested 'cuz she's underage."

Mae-June hadn't even thought of that angle of the whole mess. She'd raised her boy in the church, then along comes some floozy and botches up all her efforts.

"When?" she asked. "When are you leaving?"

"I'm packing right now," he said and strode down the hall to his bedroom.

She expected him to wait a few days, tell her his plan, how she could reach him. Instead, when Mae-June woke up the next morning, he was gone, leaving his cell phone behind.

As if things couldn't get any worse, Dixie started attending church. Every dang week. All three dressed alike. Mae-June could hardly stand it. Week after week she watched that unrepentant slut struggling to keep two babies quiet. Mae-June changed pews so she wouldn't have to look at them. Dixie never spoke to her and Mae-June kept her distance. She doubted those girls called her grandmother or if they even knew.

Suzanne stood to leave, then said, "I'm not sure, but I might have seen him at Madison Farms over the weekend. I definitely saw Dixie and the twins. She was with a man that could have been the pastor."

Mae-June waited an hour past her normal leaving time for Pastor Joe because there were things she needed to discuss with him. She decided she'd give it another ten minutes and then she heard the roar of that dang car of his in the parking lot. He'd said he was visiting a parishioner, but she wondered if that was true because visitation was reserved for Friday, not Monday, and he'd left right after the Riddles. Anyway, that was the least of her concerns. She needed to warn him about Dixie and confront him about the Joe Decker in Knoxville Hospital.

She heard his car door slam, the outside door open and close, his footsteps firm and confident striding closer and closer. He appeared in her doorway, his shirt wrinkled.

"I've got a few things to discuss with you," she said.

"I've got news, too," he said, his eyes puffy and red.

Mae-June didn't ask about his news, just charged ahead with her inquisition. "Are you aware there is a patient in Knoxville Hospital by the name of Joe Decker?"

His eyes widened. He inhaled loudly, then his tone changed completely. He laughed, an almost evil laugh.

"I think that's odd," she said, lifting her chin and sniffing.

"Odd, but not important," he said. "I thought you were going to tell me you were quitting or … I don't know what else. You said it was important."

"Quitting? Why would you think I was quitting? This church can't run without me!"

"It's just the way you said *important*." He tapped one foot, then the other. Back and forth. A rhythm of sorts.

She felt foolish all of a sudden. As if there just might be two Joe Deckers in the world. And maybe two Joe Deckers could be engaged. "Google it," he said.

"Google what?" she answered.

"Google my name. Joe Decker. Go ahead. See how many people there are in the world with the same name as me."

"I've never googled a name before," Mae-June said doubtfully.

"I google stuff all the time," he said. "As a matter of fact, I've googled Joseph Decker. One is an artist. One is a doctor. One is a lawyer."

She rolled her chair forward and back a few times. "Fine," she said. "Fine. Let's drop that one for now. Anyways, the other thing is Dixie."

"Go on," he said, his voice light.

"I don't know how much you know about Dixie." She stopped and waited for a cue.

"A little," he said.

"She doesn't have a good reputation," Mae-June said. "I just wanted to warn you. To protect you. Your reputation. She's bad news. Could ruin you."

He jiggled his leg up and down, faster and faster.

"You're engaged," she said. "Due to marry a nice respectable girl in a few weeks. That Dixie … Well, going to church doesn't make you a Christian any more than standing in a garage makes you a car." Mae-June leaned triumphantly back in her chair, crossed her arms over her chest. "That's all I'm saying."

"Car in a garage?"

Mae-June could tell by the confusion in his eyes he didn't get it. She pursed her lips tightly thinking of another way to break it to him. She was telling him this for his own good. "Do you see a man in her life?" she asked.

"I have no idea," he said.

Mae-June gripped the edges of her desk and leaned halfway across it. "Well, there isn't one. Those girls? Their mother was sixteen when she got pregnant. No father in sight. Yet she sashays around here like she's some sort of saint."

"What does this have to do with me?"

"You were seen cavorting with her."

"Cavorting? What does that even mean?"

Mae-June wrinkled her nose, shook her head. Was he really two grains short of a full silo? "You took her to the mall. Tuesday." There, she said it.

He out and out laughed. She cringed. This was no laughing matter.

"I did not take her to the mall. We happened to run into each other there. We spoke for a few minutes. That's all."

"Oh." *That Suzanne Simms. Starting rumors. Getting people upset over nothing. Wait a minute. Something else was going on here.* "Are you telling me," she said indignantly. "Are you telling me you spent Tuesday in the mall? That's why you missed prayer warriors and phone calls and left me here to re-do the board minutes? Is that what you're saying?"

He stood, leaned on one foot then the other, scratched behind his ear. "Maybe," he said, shrugged his shoulders, and headed for the door. Before he walked out, he turned back. "By the way," he said. "Who is the father of those children?"

Mae-June opened her mouth to say how should she know. But that was a lie. An out and out lie. She closed her mouth. Opened it again to say it was none of her concern. That was a white lie. It *was* her concern.

"When you walk through a briar patch," she retorted, "how do you know which briar scratched you?"

He blinked, shook his head, rolled his eyes. "I'll tell you some important news. Pastor Oscar died this afternoon. Miss Cora will hold calling hours tomorrow night and funeral on day after tomorrow. Put it out on the phone tree or however you get the word out."

Mae-June struggled to catch her breath. "When?" She finally gasped out the word.

He didn't want to answer. Maybe if the words were not spoken, they wouldn't be true. He realized how ridiculous that was. "A couple hours ago." The words felt heavy. "Can you send flowers, organize a meal afterwards, send it out on the phone tree or however you do it?"

He turned to leave. "Oh, and ask Irving if he can put together a bunch of songs with Pastor Oscar singing."

Mae-June nodded. Poor Oscar. Poor Cora. Poor, poor, poor Cora. Mae-June began to cry. Sobs from far down in her soul. She regretted ever thinking ill of Aunt Betty's secret recipe.

CHAPTER THIRTY-TWO

Mae-June called Wilfred about Pastor Oscar.

"Oscar? Gone? I can't believe it. He was doing so well. Pastor Joe said he was. Supposed to have rehab and come home. I don't understand." Wilfred's voice trailed off.

"Big loss," Mae-June said. "Big, big loss to the church. Came by to see Pastor Joe last week. I heard them when I walked by the office. Mentoring, I'd say. Now the whole shebang is up to me."

"The Pastor's doing a fine job, Mae-June. You're too hard on him."

"Speaking of the pastor," Mae-June interrupted. "Suzanne Simms stopped by. Her daughter Rita is a nurse up in Knoxville."

When Wilfred mhmmed, Mae-June went on. "She says she has a patient by the name of Joseph Decker. Name sound familiar? And he came in as a result of a car accident. AND, get this, he's engaged to be married in a few weeks. Coincidence?"

When Wilfred didn't answer right away, Mae-June prodded, "Are you there?"

"Yeah, I'm here. Just trying to figure out if we'll get arrested for having private information on somebody in the hospital. You know, they've got this HIPPA thing now."

"We won't get arrested," Mae-June said, impatiently. "Anyway, that's not the point. What do you think?"

"What do *you* think?" Wilfred answered.

"I want to hear what you think," she said.

"I think we should drive up to Knoxville Hospital tomorrow to investigate."

"Agreed," Mae-June answered.

Even as Mae-June sat beside Wilfred in his beat-up, noisy, pickup truck bucking and bouncing its way up the highway to Knoxville, she wondered why she'd agreed to his invitation. She was, of course, curious about the Joe Decker in Knoxville Hospital, but was fulfilling her curiosity worth spending a day with Wilfred? She'd vowed never to be alone with the man lest he make more of it than it was. That Pastor Joe. He'd only been in Wilsons Corner a short time and look what havoc he'd wreaked. Which brought her back to the point of this trip. If Joe Decker in Knoxville Hospital was Pastor Joe, who was the Joe Decker residing in the parsonage?

"Nice takin' a little road trip with you, Mae." Wilfred eyed her instead of the road.

"Keep your eyes on the road," she said. "And it's Mae-June." She sniffed and instantly regretted it. The overwhelming aroma of Aqua Velva infiltrated every molecule of air in the cab of the pick-up.

"Mae-June, then," Wilfred said with a slight tip of his bald head. "Nice bein' with you and all. P'rhaps we can stop for a bite to eat on our way home."

Just as Mae-June thought. Give him a minute and he thought he could take over her life. "We'll see," she said. "I'm not very hungry."

"Yes," Wilfred said, his voice perky and hopeful. "We'll see. You just might work up an appetite with this spy mission we're on."

"No need to over-exaggerate."

"Seriously, that's how I feel. How do you feel?"

"Achy." She rubbed her shoulders. "I'm not taking too kindly to this truck of yours."

"Now, now," Wilfred said. "No need to insult the old girl. And you know what I meant. About this mission we're on." Wilfred flicked on the blinker, pulled around a Toyota, returned to the middle lane. "You've got to admit, this is the most excitement we've had in the church in years."

"I wouldn't go to that extreme," Mae-June said. She knew plenty more than Wilfred about the goings on behind the scenes. She was sworn to confidentiality, of course, and nobody but nobody was going to pry the details out of her. "Truth be told, I can't get my mind off Pastor Oscar. I feel guilty leaving Cora alone."

"There's no rule about visiting only one person in a day," Wilfred said. "We can head to Cora's house once we finish up here in Knoxville."

Mae-June regretted saying a thing about Cora. She decided it was safer to say nothing at all. Seemed Wilfred could turn around anything she said to prolong the agony of sitting beside him and smelling that retched Aqua Velva. She stared straight ahead at the belching black smoke pouring out of the tailpipe of the semi in front of them. That was more pleasant than paying attention to Wilfred.

"There's the sign." Mae-June pointed to a blue sign with a big white H in the middle. Wilfred swung off the exit and followed signs for parking. Mae-June grew more and more impatient as he circled higher and higher in the parking garage before finding a spot on the fifth level, section B1. Mae-June jotted down 5-B-1 on the miniature notebook she kept in her purse for emergencies such as this.

"Quite a big hospital they have here," Wilfred said. "Must be three times our little County Hospital back in Wilsons Corner." He paused, seemed to stare through Mae-June.

With a hand on the door handle, she waited for him to speak. He remained transfixed and she said, "Well? What are you thinking?"

Wilfred shook his head and his eyes slowly focused on her. "Do you think?" he asked. "Do you think if Pastor Oscar had been at *this* hospital, he would have lived?"

Mae-June huffed and shoved open the door to the truck. "The good book says there's a time to live and a time to die. The Lord…" She pointed upwards "…is under control. You're not doubting His time, are you? Now come on. We've got a mystery to solve."

She stepped out of the truck and headed in one direction, while Wilfred headed in the other. "This way," she said, then noticed he was heading toward the elevator sign. "Wait up!" she called.

When she caught up with Wilfred, he placed a gentle hand on her lower back to guide her in the direction of the elevators. She swatted it off. "I've been walking since I was less than two," she said. "I'm sure I can manage from here to there."

She quickened her pace, but not fast enough. Wilfred caught up in no time.

The elevator dropped them on the first floor of the hospital in a round-shaped lobby enclosed by windows. One section of windows looked out onto a busy round-about. Young men in blue shirts greeted drivers who handed over their keys and dollar bills.

"Looks like you could have sprung for valet parking," Mae-June said, her eyes at half-mast.

"Never been here," Wilfred said. "If I'd known, I certainly would have saved you some steps."

Mae-June took a few more extra steps towards the information desk. "Joseph Decker," she stated before the receptionist looked up or Wilfred caught up. "We're here to visit Joseph Decker. Do you have his room number?"

An older gentleman, bald on top with white hair curling around his ears, tapped a keyboard. He touched the screen with an arthritic index finger, scrunched his forehead, turned to a younger man beside him and pointed to the screen. "What's this mean? Name's here but no room number."

The younger man rolled his chair closer to the senior citizen and studied the screen. He clicked a few buttons, pointed back at the screen. "See this? That means he was discharged." He looked up at Mae-June and smiled. "The computer says he was discharged."

"Are you sure?" Mae-June inquired forcefully. She stood on tiptoes and tried to lean over the counter to see the computer screen, but it was still out of her view. She couldn't accept she'd made this more than an hour-long journey with Wilfred for nothing.

"Yes, quite sure," the man said.

"Does it have his address there? Do you know where he went?"

"Wilsons Corner," the older man said, peering at the screen.

The younger man glared at the older man. "That's confidential. You aren't supposed to give any information. Not even to kin."

Wilfred popped his head over Mae-June's shoulder. "Thank you," he said. "You've been a big help." He placed his hand on her upper arm and attempted to guide her away. She struggled to free herself from his grasp.

"Leave me alone," she said. "I could have gotten more information if you'd left me alone."

"You heard the man. We got more than we should have."

Finally freeing herself, Mae-June strode across the lobby. "Come all this way on a wild goose chase," she said.

Wilfred hurried to catch up. "Now don't get your feathers ruffled, Mae."

She raised her arm so her pocketbook swung in front of her like a pendulum and turned her back on him.

"Mae-June," he corrected. "It wasn't a waste. I reckon we figured out one thing. This isn't our guy because if Pastor Joe isn't Pastor Joe and this was Pastor Joe, he would have shown up at the church by now."

"What are you talking about? If Pastor Joe isn't Pastor Joe? Your mind could use a bit of a tune-up, Wilfred Wheeler." Mae-June plopped onto a cushioned chair beside a window.

He took the seat across from her, eyes alight. "Think about it. If our Pastor Joe was one and the same with this patient and now is out of the hospital, wouldn't he have called? Wouldn't he have shown up?"

She thought about it. "Maybe." She wasn't ready to concede her point to Wilfred. "They said he went to Wilsons Corner. Doesn't that sound suspicious to you? Of all the places he could have gone, he comes to our corner?"

"Mystery solved." Wilfred slapped his knees. "Coincidence in names, that's all. Now, let's go get us some grits."

"The mystery is not solved," Mae-June persisted. "Nowhere near solved."

Wilfred sighed deep and long. "Aren't you as hungry as you are curious?"

Mae-June thought he looked like a forlorn hound dog. As much as she hated to admit it, she was hungry. "Why don't you be a gentleman and bring the truck around to the front door?"

He sprang from his chair like a jack-in-the-box. "Cracker Barrel?"

"Oh, all right," she said, refusing to smile, yet anticipating their corn muffins with blackberry jam.

CHAPTER THIRTY-THREE

I think you'll like it here if you give it a chance," Joe Decker said. He was sitting on the couch in the parsonage. When he chose his seat, he hoped Roxanne would sit beside him, but instead, she positioned herself in one of the rockers across the room. He liked what he'd seen so far in Wilsons Corner. Granted, he hadn't seen much, but it was less hectic than Boston. It would be a better place to raise children. Yet, he was confused. Was Tennessee God's will for him? He wasn't sure. Roxanne had been distant since her arrival. He hoped they could talk privately this evening while Pastor Joe was at the calling hours for Pastor Oscar.

"Maybe," Roxanne answered. "What are my choices— Tennessee and you or Boston alone? Is that it?"

Her comment stung. "I don't want to lose you," he said.

"Then perhaps you should have consulted me first." Her eyes glistened. Her fingers gripped the armrests.

"I'm sorry," he said. He reached across the divide separating them, beckoned her to come sit beside him. She did not move. "I really am sorry. You have to understand. I'm confused, too."

"Is this the way it's going to be, Joe?" She loosened her grip and laced her fingers through the spindles of the rocking chair. "You don't know what you're doing so you make a rash decision, tell me afterward with an apology, but still expect me to change my whole life?"

"No," he said. "No." The silence that followed nearly killed him. What would he do without Roxanne? He truly loved her. But what about God? What if this whole Wilsons Corner thing was God's plan for his life? And what about God's plan for Roxanne? How could he know?

"There are some things I know for sure," he said. "There are other things I'm confused about."

"And they are?" Roxanne asked.

"I could picture myself raising a family here. It's more peaceful than Boston."

Roxanne's face grew tight. She crossed her arms over her chest. "In Podunkville, USA?"

"They could play outside," Joe said.

"What kind of education would they get here?"

"Hold on." Joe held his palm facing her. "I'm certain I want you as my life partner, as the mother of my children. If Wilsons Corner will not work for you, I'll call Gordon Conwell. I'll see if they have other leads for me. The wedding is only a few weeks away. Let's get that behind us before we deal with where we are going to settle down. Or begin a ministry."

Roxanne stood, turned her back to him, gazed out the window above the bookcases. He silently watched her, gave her time to process his suggestion. She walked to the back of the rocker, leaned her elbows on top of the backrest. *"I'm* not beginning ministry anywhere," she said. *"You are."*

"True," he said.

"And then what?" she asked. "You're asking me to marry you and then we'll decide where we live? I'm not sure I trust you. What assurances will I have if I go through with the wedding?"

"What do you mean?" He reached for his can of Coke on the coffee table, took a long swallow, and placed it back on the coaster.

"I want a marriage where I count," she said.

"Of course, you count. Why would you think you don't count?" He laughed. When she didn't respond, he ceased in the middle of a 'ha.'

Roxanne pushed herself away from the rocker. It rocked back and forth four or five times, each time a slower rotation. She shoved her hands into the front pockets of her jeans. "I get the feeling you think what you want is more important than what I want. You think because you've been in school longer than me, you're better than me. Let me tell you, Joe Decker …" She pulled her hands out of her pockets, tapped her index finger into the palm of her other hand. "I've been out in the workforce while you've been in school. I've supported myself. I've got an apartment. Sure, it was tiny. But it was mine. I figured out how to live on a budget. I paid rent. I ate food I purchased and cooked myself. I sacrificed. You haven't done any of those things. You don't understand real life. What I know matters. What I think matters. If I marry you—"

"What do you mean—*if?*" He sat up as straight as he was able.

"You can't make decisions for the both of us without input from me." She shook her head, walked to the front of the rocker, plopped down. She crossed her arms and looked away. Her cheeks were pinker than usual. She blinked rapidly, tears slid from her eyes to the corners of her mouth.

That darn leg! Joe wanted to leap up, hug her close, tell her it would work out. Unfortunately, there was no leaping for him. For that matter, he had no right to say things would work out. How could he know for sure? Things didn't work out for plenty of people. The words were borderline manipulative. "I'm sorry," he said, and he meant it.

When they were in Boston dating, the future shone like a beacon. He would finally be out of school, getting on with his life, engaged in the career he'd dreamed of most of his life. Growing up in the Congo River Basin with missionary parents, he sat through night after night of sermons sitting on benches with no backs listening to his father's voice with the trumpeting of elephants in the background along with the high-pitched, *he-he-he* of chimpanzees, and the squawk of parrots.

For a while, he considered a career in wildlife management or large animal veterinary care. He pictured himself zipping through the bush in a Land Rover releasing elephants from snares, tending to their wounds. Then when he was about ten, an injured elephant nearly trampled one of the missionaries living in the compound. Joe joined the crowd listening to the missionary tell his story of scrambling to safety behind a tree while the elephant charged. His mother found him sitting on the ground with the group hanging on every word of the story. She made him come home immediately. He never heard the end of the story, but from that point on, he decided to be a preacher like his father. Maybe return to Africa. Observe big game from a safe distance. He crossed the ocean to attend undergrad in Texas, then moved to Boston for seminary training. When he met Roxanne, he changed his plans. In comparison to the Congo, Tennessee didn't seem far at all from Boston.

Roxanne's face softened. "I don't know if I can do it," she said.

"Do what?" Joe asked.

"Joe, you chose a career that involves me. I didn't choose it. There will be expectations. They will want me to—I don't know. Play the piano. Entertain guests. Be on committees."

He thought back to seminary. They had gatherings of spouses to answer questions such as Roxanne posed. It had never occurred to him to invite her to those gatherings. They weren't engaged at the time. "I don't know what they will expect," he said. "But I promise you this. You will not have to do anything you don't want to do. And I promise you something else. I will consult you on any decision that involves both of us. Money, where we live, kids. Everything."

Roxanne was silent for a bit. Joe waited.

"I need time to think about it," she said. "But first, I'd like you to call the seminary, as you said, and see if there are leads for churches closer to Boston. Anywhere in Massachusetts. Maybe New Hampshire or Maine even. When the time comes, I want my parents to have a chance to be every-day grandparents."

"Okay," he said. "I have a counter-proposal. We go to church this Sunday to see how we feel about Wilsons Corner."

"Deal," she said.

CHAPTER THIRTY-FOUR

At Dymant Funeral Home, Grady took the steps to the side porch two at a time. His robe billowed about him like a sail in a gale. He wasn't sure what he was supposed to wear to the calling hours for Pastor Oscar. After carefully analyzing his closet, he decided the robe was his best bet. If nothing else, it gave him confidence, a sense he was above everyone else.

A solemn-faced man with gray hair, gray glasses, and a black suit greeted him inside the door. "Petronella or Sullivan?" he asked.

"Petronella," Grady said. "Oscar Petronella."

"Down the hall to the left."

Grady headed in the direction the man pointed. One side of the wall was a glass cage with several small tan and orange birds chirping and flitting from one artificial branch to the other. On the other side, an aquarium was built into the wall. Striped blue neons zigzagged through plastic plants, and orange swordfish nibbled on food at the surface. Grady shook his head. Odd, he thought. But then again, he'd never been in a funeral home so he didn't know what to expect. Maybe all funeral homes doubled as aviaries and aquariums.

From the room just beyond the birdcage and fish hallway, a line of people extended out the door. Grady recognized a few from the congregation. He didn't know their names yet, but at least he knew he was in the right place. They nodded at him, solemn faced, lips a taut smile.

He breezed past them into the room and spotted Miss Cora in a black dress standing beside the coffin. Music flowed softly from a speaker. *Amazing grace, how sweet the sound.* A song he had never heard before coming to Wilsons Corner; a song he had come to appreciate.

The robe wrapped awkwardly around Grady's legs as he approached Miss Cora. She grabbed his arm. "Oh, pastor, pastor, pastor." Her eyes glistened with tears but her smile was genuine. "I've been waiting for you." She clutched his arm tight enough to leave bruises.

Pastor Oscar looked more alive in the casket than he had at the hospital. Grady thought the man might sit up any minute, wave, and say, "Just a joke, folks." In fact, Grady stared, expecting something to happen, hoping it would happen, praying it would happen.

He felt he might hurl. What did he know about death or grief? How could he offer comfort to Miss Cora and everyone else who was grieving? You had to love someone in order to grieve and Grady had never loved anyone except in a surface kind of way. The room began to spin.

"Pastor? Are you all right?"

From somewhere down a long tube, Grady heard Wilfred Wheeler's voice. "Pastor?" The voice seemed further away.

"Pas —"

Grady awoke on a Victorian-style couch, all dark wood except for a velvet maroon cushion built into the back and a velvet maroon seat on which he was sprawled. Wilfred Wheeler stood guard. Grady blinked a few times before he weakly sat up. "What happened?" he asked, dropping his throbbing head to his hands.

"You fainted," Wilfred said. "Out cold. You were heading straight for the casket but Irving caught ya. Your lucky day. Feeling any better?"

The answer was no, but Grady didn't want to admit it, and he hardly considered this his lucky day. "Yeah," he said. "I guess I'm feeling a little better. Could you get me some water?"

Wilfred yanked the door open to the hallway and Grady caught sight of the line waiting to pay their respects. A woman covered her mouth, pointed at him, whispered to her husband. Grady wondered how he was supposed to maintain the respect of the congregation after this. Surely, he'd be the laughingstock. He looked away as Wilfred closed the door again.

Grady's cell phone vibrated and without checking the screen, he answered.

"Matt is livid!" His mother didn't seem much less so.

"So what else is new," Grady said in the sullen voice of Grady the teenager from Orlando. *Why now? Why had she called before he was back to his whole self?*

"He wants the car, Grady. Bring it home." She was begging now. Groveling.

"How was I supposed to escape without taking the car? Huh, Ma, huh?"

"Escape? Why do you think you needed to escape?"

"You're kidding, right? He never liked me, and you know it. I was tired of him always yelling at me … and you, for that matter."

Wilfred returned with a paper cup of water and handed it to Grady. Grady mouthed a thank you and reverted to his Pastor Joe voice. "Tell him not to worry," he said into the phone. "I have a good job. I'll pay him for the car. I'll look it up online. Pay more than the Blue Book value even, if that's what he wants."

She lowered her voice. "You could never afford that, Grady. And besides, that car is more valuable to him than—"

"Go ahead and say it … me and you."

"That's not—"

"Is that Grady? Gimme that phone!" Matt the Rat's voice boomed through the phone as loud as if he were in Dymant Funeral Home.

Grady stood, walked closer to the windows, away from Wilfred, and covered the side of his mouth. "Look, Ma," he whispered. "I can't deal with this now. A man died."

"You've killed a man?" Matt had obviously grabbed the phone. "I'm not surprised. I always knew it would come to this."

"I didn't kill anybody. I just said somebody died and I'm dealing with it."

"Why would you be dealing with it if you weren't responsible for it? Don't play me for a fool, Grady. Don't expect me to bail you out."

Forget Orlando Grady. He was Tennessee Pastor Joe now. Tennessee Pastor Joe was strong. He didn't wimp out from a bully. In his strongest Pastor Joe voice, Grady spoke with conviction. "I'm not in jail. I didn't kill anyone. I'm the pastor of a church in Wilsons Corner, Tennessee, and I've got to perform this man's funeral."

Grady gagged on the last words. He couldn't believe he'd said it. Said where he was. Said what he was doing. He pounded his forehead with the palm of his hand.

A torrent of cuss words flung from the kitchen in Orlando reached Tennessee faster than the speed of light. "You stole my car to become a pastor? A classic car I worked years to restore? You're quite a case. Quite a case. What do you know about running a church, you imbecile? I'm prosecuting. I've had it with you."

"Matt, don't! Give me the phone. Let me talk to him." His mother's voice was loud at first, then faded away. Matt must have pushed her aside.

Silence on the other end. Grady waited for Matt to speak. When he did, the words were gruff with a tad bit of the edge shaved off. "Get that car back here now or I'm coming to get it." The phone went dead.

Grady turned around slowly. He felt cold, empty, dazed. How had he let it slip where he was?

"You all right, Pastor?" Wilfred stood across the room, frozen in place, eyes half afraid, half curious.

"Yeah," Grady said. "No. But I'll be all right. Just need some time alone."

"Sure, sure." Wilfred jabbed a thumb over his shoulder. "I'll go back in. Just holler if you need me."

"Thanks," Grady said. He stayed in the private room long after Wilfred returned to the viewing. Partly because he was embarrassed. Partly because he needed to do some soul-searching. Partly because he was stunned at his own words and Matt's threat.

Grady took off the robe, placed it on the couch, ripped off the clerical collar, tossed it on top of the robe. Who was he kidding? Matt was right. He was an imbecile, a liar, a deceiver. Why did he think he could give marital advice? Why did he think he could have teenagers perform praise music in a church that didn't want it? Why did he think he could speak at a funeral?

People expected him to have all the answers ... even to know what God thought. He didn't even have answers for half his own problems, never mind other people's problems. And how was he supposed to know if the answers he came up with were answers from God?

These people needed someone who could lead them, give them the spiritual direction they came to church looking for. He didn't even know where he was going, never mind where other people were supposed to go. They needed someone who had been taught what to do at funerals besides faint. What to say to an overbearing husband who said his wife didn't respect him. They needed someone who at least had read the Bible and prayed with more variety than, "Help me, help me, help me."

They needed the real Pastor Joe.

Grady crossed the room, pushed aside the heavy maroon velvet drapes, and looked out into the night. The moon shone brightly above the trees. Another few days and it would be full. What would he be doing in another few days?

He wished he could google it, but there were some questions even Google couldn't answer.

Grady trudged up the steps to the yellow cottage. He noticed lights on in the living room. He didn't remember leaving the lights on. Strange. When he put the key in the lock, the door swung open. His heart beat faster. Had someone broken in while he was at the calling hours?

"Hey, how'd it go tonight?"

Grady recognized the voice of Pastor Jay from the couch. He'd forgotten about bringing him home today. The last thing he needed was to face the real pastor. The trained one. Not now after making a fool of himself by fainting and having the worst conversation yet with his mother and Matt. He stepped over the threshold and sat down heavily in the rocking chair with his legs out straight and his arms draped over the chair arms. "Not good," he said.

"Really?" Pastor Jay leaned forward, concern in his eyes. "What happened?"

Grady contemplated spilling his guts. Telling Pastor Jay the whole story. Coming clean, handing over the reins, packing up, and heading north. "How cold is it in Boston?" he asked.

The concern in Pastor Jay's eyes disappeared and humor replaced it. "What? What does that have to do with tonight?"

"I'm thinking of going there. How cold does it get?"

Pastor Jay leaned back, tossed an arm over the back of the couch. "Coming into the cold season now. Leaves have fallen. Probably 40s or high 30s. Gray sky. Wind chill in a few weeks could bring it below freezing. Come on, Joe, your evening couldn't have been so bad you'd leave without another job to go to. Trust me, if there was an opening up there right now, I'd beat you to it!"

"I don't think I'm cut out for this." Grady scanned the room. He didn't want to leave, but he could foresee a train wreck headed his way. Better to bail before the train left the tracks. Today or Sunday. What difference would a couple of days make?

"You're tired," Pastor Jay said. "You're coming from the viewing hours of a good man. Death is the worst you'll deal with. You know that. Of course, you're depressed."

Grady wanted to ask more about death. Where was Pastor Oscar now or was he anywhere, but he held it back. If he asked the question, it would be, pardon the pun, a dead giveaway he wasn't a real pastor. "I don't even know what I'm going to say tomorrow. I mean, as a pastor, I've got to say something." With his elbow on the chair arm, he rested his chin in his hand. "What am I going to do?"

"I'll write it," Pastor Jay said. "It's the least I can do after all you've done for me—filled in after the accident, picked me up today. What time is the funeral tomorrow?"

"11:00."

"I'll have it done tonight. Go get some rest. You'll feel better in the morning."

Grady stood, shoulders drooped, studied Pastor Jay. He regretted thinking of him as pompous. The guy had wisdom and compassion. He wished he didn't have to leave. He could learn from Pastor Jay. "We didn't talk about your evening," he said. "What'd you do you first night in the personage?"

"That's another story." Pastor Jay shook his head.

"I have time," Grady said. "You listened to me. I can take time." He returned to the rocker and sat with his forearms on his knees, intent on whatever Pastor Jay was about to reveal.

"Roxanne came over. She's extremely unhappy. About moving here and me making the decision without consulting her. She went so far as to say she was reconsidering the marriage."

Grady's mood immediately shifted. Maybe Pastor Jay would leave and no one would be the wiser. Things could stay as they were. He'd figure out a way to cope with it all. "What'd you say?" Grady heard the happiness in his own voice and toned it down as best he could. "What are you going to do?"

"Good question." Pastor Jay stared at the top corner of the cut-out into the kitchen. He didn't speak for so long Grady glanced up at the corner to see if something might actually be up there. Finally, Pastor Jay said, "I promised I'd call Gordon Conwell and see if any churches in New England are looking for a pastor."

Grady could almost feel a light bulb appear above his head. What if Pastor Jay did get a position in New England? The guy could go back North and no one would even know he'd been here. There was still the problem of shouldering so many burdens, but he felt he could learn to cope with it. And of course, there was Matt the Rat. Now he knew where Grady was.

"I wish you the best, bro," Grady said. "I really do. You've got a real mess on your hands."

CHAPTER THIRTY-FIVE

A small pulpit with a carving of a cross stood angled so that whoever stood behind it would not be looking at the casket. Grady couldn't help but wonder if the placement was for his benefit. Over a dozen floral arrangements ringed the casket—a small vase of roses on a short white column, a large fan-shaped spray of white carnations mixed with a purple flower. An arrangement of pink, blue and white draped the bottom half of the casket. A silk ribbon crisscrossed it with the words "Husband" in gold. Directly behind it on a silver stand was a floral display of white and yellow lilies. The ribbon on that arrangement said, "Beloved Pastor." Mae-June must have ordered it.

When Miss Cora spotted Grady, she rushed to greet him. She wrapped her arms around him and momentarily leaned her head against his chest. She pushed away, her hands still gripping his upper arms. "I'm so glad to see you. Are you all right? I was so concerned after last night." She pulled him towards a chair in the front row and sat beside him. The pulpit blocked the view of the casket, and Grady was relieved.

"I'm okay," he said. "Okay. Felt a bit queasy last night. Probably ate something that didn't agree with me."

"Oh," she said.

Grady couldn't tell if she believed him or not. He turned around to see how many people were in attendance. He estimated seventy-five people filled the padded metal chairs. He recognized Wilfred Wheeler, Officer Irving Welch, Mae-June, and a dozen or so others from the church. He guessed the rest must be neighbors or relatives or friends.

Music started softly from a speaker up front, then someone must have turned up the volume because Grady felt the music sweep over him. He recognized the baritone voice as Pastor Oscar.

On a hill far away stood an old rugged cross …

Miss Cora sniffed. A woman behind her sniffed. Miss Cora sobbed. The woman behind her sobbed. Grady handed Miss Cora a handkerchief. She dabbed at her eyes and nose. Grady heard the crinkle of a tissue pulled from a purse-size package. He didn't think he could take much more before he'd be boo-hooing. At long last, Pastor Oscar's recorded voice dragged out the last note and faded away.

The people shouted, *Amen!*

A man Grady did not know stood and walked to the pulpit. He had an air of authority about him. Dark suit with a Noah's Ark tie. Salt and pepper hair. Tall. Walked totally straight, no slouching at all.

Miss Cora leaned over and whispered, "That's Bud McNeilus. He's the pastor of St. Luke's over in Ballston Creek. He and Oscar became great friends and prayer partners through the Interfaith Pastor's Guild."

Bud McNeilus reached inside his suit jacket and withdrew a paper. He unfolded it slowly and smoothed out the wrinkles before he looked up and surveyed the group. Only when his eyes rested on Grady did he smile. He referred to his notes and began to read.

"Oscar James Petronella was born in Savannah, Georgia, to Betsy Falmouth Petronella and James Morton Petronella. He had two older brothers, Melvin and Maurice. In 1941, Melvin and Maurice joined the Army. The brothers were assigned to the USS Jacob Jones. In February of 1942, off Cape May, New Jersey, the ship was sunk by German U-boat 578 and Pastor Oscar's two brothers perished.

"Oscar was born a number of years after his brothers died, but he heard about them daily from his parents who never recovered from the loss of their sons. He grew up in a home with distant, emotionally uninvolved parents.

"Miss Cora lived on the same block as Pastor Oscar. They were childhood friends, then married, and were devoted to each other for 42 years. He attended Gordon Conwell Theological Seminary in Massachusetts and pastored churches in Connecticut, New Jersey, and Missouri before retiring to Wilsons Corner. He was a dedicated member of the Wilsons Corner Bible Believing Congregation. He and his great baritone singing voice will be greatly missed by all who knew him."

Bud McNeilus folded the paper, returned it to the inside pocket of his suit coat and nodded at Grady. "Pastor Joe Decker, current pastor of Wilsons Corner Bible Believing Congregation, will now share a few words."

Grady stood and walked confidently to the pulpit with Pastor Jay's sermon in hand. He grasped the edges of the pulpit and scanned the audience with a smile. His eyes lit on a familiar looking woman who was just now walking in the door. She had shiny black hair, a little wavy. She wore a professional navy suit and navy heels with a cut-out in the toe. She smiled at him and took a seat in the last row. Only then did it compute—it was Roxanne. *What was she doing here? Was Pastor Jay far behind?* She looked out of place—as if she, like Grady, had taken a wrong turn and wound up here by accident. Grady kept his eye on the door, but Pastor Jay did not enter.

"Good morning." After seeing Roxanne, Grady's confidence waned. The words stuck in his throat. He coughed and tried again. "Good morning." He paused, looked down at his notes. "Thank you for being here today." He continued to read without looking up. "Miss Cora recognizes that you don't have to be here. Your presence today is an affirmation of your love and support for her. Although she may not remember every word shared today, she will remember your presence here for the rest of her life.

"Jesus once said, 'Let us not love in word or talk but in deed and in truth' (1 John 3:17-19 ESV). Your presence today shows your love in deed, but do not end it here today. One week, one month, one year from now Miss Cora is still going to need you.

"So how do we help her in her time of need?

"When we feel powerless and don't know what to say, some of the best advice I have ever heard is three simple words that begin with the letter 'H.'

"<u>Hush</u>: Don't feel you have to give answers for Pastor Oscar's death. Don't feel the pressure. There are some answers we will never receive on this side of eternity. Even if we did have a full explanation, it wouldn't bring Pastor Oscar back to us or heal the pain in our hearts.

"<u>Hear</u>: Listen to Miss Cora. Listen to her stories of her husband. Listen to her hurt, her memories and her pain. Calmly, patiently, listen.

"<u>Hug</u>: Give her a shoulder to cry on. A hug to help her through. There once was an elderly gentleman who lost his wife. Upon seeing the man cry, a 4-year-old boy who lived next door climbed onto the man's lap, and just sat there. Later, when his mother asked the boy what he said to his neighbor, the little boy said, 'Nothing, I just helped him cry.' Sometimes the best we can do is help others cry.

"Hush. Hear. Hug. That is some of the best advice I have ever heard.[1]

"The ladies of the church prepared a luncheon for everyone here today. We invite you to join us."

Grady folded the papers in half and returned to his seat, his hands trembling.

Someone prayed. They listened to more recordings of Pastor Oscar singing. Everyone filed by to gawk into the casket one more time. Grady survived it all by zoning out.

---

[1] www.propreacher.com/free-funeral-sermon/

When it came his time to leave the planet, Grady decided he'd be cremated immediately and his ashes sprinkled somewhere. He wasn't sure where yet, but he figured he had plenty of time to find a meaningful place.

In the foyer, members of the congregation circled him. Some thanked him for being there for the living and the dead. Some just wanted to stand with others who happened to be near him. On the edge of the crowd, he noticed Roxanne. A moment later, she was gone.

The decorating committee had transformed the fellowship hall with white tablecloths and votive candles floating in small goblets of water. Someone had brought half a dozen floral arrangements from the funeral home and set the larger ones on the floor beside a long table filled end to end with all sorts of steaming dishes.

Mae-June met Grady at the door. "A beautiful young woman just walked in," she said. "Asking for you."

Grady's heart stopped. He was sure it literally stopped. His face paled and the room blurred. "Really?" He hoped his voice didn't sound as squeaky to Mae-June as it sounded to him. "What did you tell her?"

Mae-June raised her chin and Grady had a clear view up her nostrils. "Nothing. She just asked for you. She's over there by that table." Mae-June pointed to a table halfway across the room.

He scanned the area and spotted Roxanne carrying on a conversation with Dixie Talbot. He made it across the room in no time. He faced Roxanne and kept his back to Dixie. "It's good to see you. Why didn't you let me know you were coming?" He put a hand across Roxanne's shoulders and pulled out the chair so her back would be to the room. She didn't take the hint and sit.

"We were just about to introduce ourselves," Dixie Talbot said.

"Plenty of time for that later," Grady said. "Tomorrow, next week, next month, plenty of time."

"Mommy! Betty Lou took a cookie!" Betty Jean ran across the room from the dessert table. She crossed her arms and lifted her chin, obviously proud of herself for being the good twin.

"I'd better go," Dixie said. "Later. We'll chat later." She hurried to the dessert table.

"If I'd known you were coming," Grady said to Roxanne, "I would have prepared you."

"Prepared me for what?"

Two worlds colliding, he wanted to say. How was he supposed to talk to Roxanne without making her feel uncomfortable that he was being too forward? If Mae-June hadn't figured out this was Roxanne, he doubted anyone else had. He decided he'd better get her out of there before people started asking questions.

"You know what?" he said. "My duties are done here. Why don't I walk you to your car?"

She looked stunned. "Why don't you want these people to know me? Have you already figured out I'm not cut out to be a minister's wife?"

Come up with a plan, Grady told himself. *Quick. Anything.* "That's not it," he said. "This food … not much here … how about we go where we can get a regular meal, not these snacky things. What do you say?" He noticed Wilfred Wheeler approaching and strode across the room to meet him.

"Miss Cora asked if you would offer grace so we can begin," Wilfred said.

"Certainly," Grady said. "But listen, I really need to leave after that."

"Is that Roxanne?" Wilfred leaned to the right to look past Grady.

"I just need to leave." Grady placed a trembling arm across Wilfred's shoulder and guided him towards the microphone. "You go ahead. Quiet them down."

Wilfred whistled into the microphone. "Pastor will have the blessing and then the guests of honor can form the line first."

Grady led the prayer, then rushed Roxanne to the parking lot.

"That was awfully nice of that man to take charge and let you leave," Roxanne said. "I feel bad, though. I guess it's all part of your duties until Joe takes over."

Grady opened the door to the Pontiac and Roxanne leaned over to check it out. "*This* is your car?" she asked. "*How* in the world did you afford it?"

"Lucky break," Grady said. He waited until she got in and fastened her seatbelt before dashing around to the driver's side, hopping in, and squealing towards the exit. He braked at the end of the driveway trying to remember any restaurants in the area.

"Left," he said aloud. "We'll get on the highway and head north. If we don't see anything before the mall, there are a few places near it." He hoped he sounded confident, like someone who knew his way around the area. He pulled out of the driveway and turned left.

"So how long have you been in the ministry?" Roxanne asked.

"Not long," Grady answered.

"I'm just wondering why they didn't ask you to be the senior pastor. I mean, Joe's just getting out of the seminary."

"They knew I wouldn't accept it," Grady said. "So they didn't waste time asking." Partially true so he only felt partially guilty. He studied the terrain whizzing by the window. Fields and occasional houses. Small, rundown homes. Some with rusted tin roofs. Some with old cars up on blocks. Some with pens of chickens in a side yard. Each home represented a family. For all he knew, a family that belonged to Wilsons Corner Bible Believing Congregation.

He noticed a billboard for an Italian restaurant off the next exit. Supposedly it had earned the title of Best in Central Tennessee. "How about Italian?" he asked.

"What?" She sounded confused.

"Food," he said. "You like Italian?"

"Sure," she said. "I thought we were talking about duties of a pastor, and I didn't know what Italian duties were!" She laughed and the sound tickled Grady's gut.

He took the exit and circled the large lot until he found a place far from the door. "Must be good," he said. "Lot's full."

The *maître d'* seated them in a booth near a stone fireplace. The only other lights were votive candles on the table. Grady picked up a candle and held it close to the menu. "Sheesh," he said. "What's the deal? What is it they don't want us to see?"

Roxanne chuckled. "My thoughts exactly. I can't see a thing on the menu, but most Italian restaurants have eggplant parm. But it all depends on how they make it if it's good or not.

Sometimes the skin gets tough. An Italian woman once told me that you prepare eggplant by cutting it in rounds, sprinkling a lot of salt on it, then layer by layer you do that and the bitterness comes out. It's actually like a brown liquid. You have to dab up the liquid with a paper towel. Anyway, that's what I'm ordering. Eggplant parm." She set the menu on the edge of the table and sipped her water.

Grady had opened his mouth to comment at least three times. He kept thinking she was done speaking, then she'd start up again, and he didn't even like eggplant. He set his menu on top of hers. "I'll go with chicken parm," he said.

He made it through dipping herbed bread in olive oil listening to Roxanne chitchat about nothing, really, but by the time he was cutting into a cherry tomato and stabbing romaine, he couldn't hold back any longer. "Why did you come to the funeral?"

In the dim light, he watched her sit back in the vinyl booth seat. He couldn't be certain, but she seemed deflated. The confident, happy, professional person disappeared, replaced by a scared, uncertain young woman. Someone being pulled against her will.

"I'm sorry," he said. "You probably just wanted to be friendly. Get to know the people before you took on the official duties."

Immediately she drew forward and pressed against the table. "I shouldn't be dragging you into the middle of this."

"Careful, the dishes are hot." The waiter placed an oblong platter in front of each of them.

Roxanne pointed at her plate. "I'll never eat all this." She laughed. "We should have gone halves."

"You can always take leftovers home," the waiter said, holding up a grater. "Cheese?"

They both nodded and the waiter rained down parmesan cheese on their plates. When the waiter left, Roxanne cut a bite-size piece of eggplant. "Delicious! This is perfect." She pointed her fork at the platter.

Grady hadn't taken a bite yet. Instead, he held his knife in one hand and fork in the other over his plate. "In the middle of what?" he asked, although he had an idea. "You said you shouldn't be dragging me into the middle. The middle of what?"

Roxanne took a small bite of eggplant and chewed slowly. Grady waited, utensils poised.

"I don't know if I can do it," Roxanne said.

"You don't have to eat it all."

"I'm not talking about this food. I'm talking about being a pastor's wife. I didn't know who to talk to and you're a pastor. I hoped to make an appointment if I saw you after the funeral. Sometime. Maybe this week. You counsel people. I just need to know—how does your fiancée feel about it?"

Grady squinted into the dimness. "My fiancée? I don't have a fiancée."

"Mae-June says you do."

Grady couldn't believe how convoluted the whole situation had become. A song came to mind that he heard when he was a kid. Something about a guy being his own grandpa. "I don't have a fiancée," he said with emphasis on the last word. "There are certain members of this congregation who think they know me, but they don't."

"Mae-June was so certain," she said. "She actually said you were getting married in just a couple of weeks."

"Forget Mae-June," he said. "But you. I don't understand. I thought you and Joe were getting married in a couple of weeks."

Roxanne picked up the napkin from her lap and dabbed at her lips. There might have been tears in her eyes. In the dim light, Grady couldn't be sure.

"I do love him," Roxanne said softly. "That's the problem. But marrying a pastor was never in my plan. Then I met Joe. What do you do when you fall in love with a person, but not his profession? I thought we'd live in Boston. That's where my job is. That's where my family is. Joe said we wouldn't move after we got married. I don't want to uproot my whole life and begin again somewhere else."

She stabbed a large bit of eggplant with a passion that made Grady think she was trying to kill it. She chewed and he waited for her to continue.

"He's chosen a career that is as much about me as it is about him. They're going to expect me to lead a children's division. Kids are great, but I don't want to lead them in anything."

"If it makes you feel any better, there aren't kids in the church," Grady said. "Well, just a couple."

"They'll probably expect me to have people over for dinner and I have no interest in opening up my private life for the world to see."

"Not a problem there either," Grady said. "They have this schedule. You'll be eating at a different member's house after church every week."

"What if I want to plan my own Sunday afternoons?"

"I don't know," Grady said. "I never thought of that. Every week they've assigned me a family and off I went."

"How long has this been going on?"

"A couple … ever since I got here," he said. He dabbed his fork at a glob of sauce that had dripped off the side of his plate.

"I have my own dreams," she said. "I want him to go to work and me to go to my job and we sit around the dinner table like normal people without being interrupted by some random person dying or someone needing counseling. You know it's not a 9 to 5 job, Joe."

For some reason, he expected her to call him Grady. Like she knew the real him. When she said *Joe*, he blinked, confused.

"How do you handle it?" Her eyes begged for an honest answer. How could he answer with anything other than the truth?

"How do I handle it," he repeated. He cut a piece of chicken and chewed slowly. She waited for an answer. He balanced the knife and fork on the edge of his plate, placed his elbows on the table, interlocked his fingers. "By the seat of my pants," he said. "Let me tell you about the last few days."

He told her about Ralph and Rose in his office; about the big deal over water fountains; about Pastor Oscar's death. "I had never been to a funeral before," he said. "And then I had to present one, or whatever you call doing a funeral. Officiate. I think that's what Joe said last night. Officiate."

Roxanne jumped in immediately. "You'd never been to a funeral?" She pointed her fork at him. "Not even in seminary? Joe had to attend three funerals for some class or another, and then officiate at two. That was an excellent talk you gave, by the way."

Grady laughed wryly. "Of course it was good. Joe wrote it."

Roxanne picked up her napkin and covered her mouth. She leaned her head back and laughed until both of them became aware other diners were staring. When she regained control, she said, "I thought all seminaries taught about funerals. What seminary did you go to?"

Grady cut off a too-big piece of chicken parm and stuffed it into his mouth so he wouldn't have to answer. He chewed slowly while he thought. Everyone thought he went to Gordon Conwell because they thought he was Pastor Joe who *had* gone to Gordon Conwell. She'd know he was a fake if he said Gordon Conwell. *What was he supposed to say? What was it that Pastor Oscar had said about Gordon Conwell? Oh yeah, that professor. What was his name? Dr. Our Something. Ouerbach! That was it!* He was aware of Roxanne's eyes upon him. He put off swallowing as long as he could.

"Gordon Conwell," he said. "Do you know anything about Dr. Ouerbach retiring? He was one of my favorite professors. I'd hate to see the school lose him."

"He died," Roxanne said. "Didn't you know?"

Grady choked and coughed until his face turned red. He grabbed the cloth napkin he'd left beside his plate and gagged into it. "No," he squeaked. "I didn't know."

"That's strange," she said. "I thought an email went out to all alums a few days ago."

Grady gulped in air, wiped the napkin across his lips. "Ooh, ooh," he said. "I haven't been in my email in a while. Too busy. You know how it is."

"I suppose," she said slowly. "Don't you have to answer e-mail every day? Joe is tied to his."

"Nah," Grady said. "Not here."

Her brow wrinkled. "Everybody's been talking Ouerbach dying. I'm surprised you hadn't heard it from one of the alums."

"I don't keep in touch with many of them," Grady answered.

"Why not?" Roxanne asked. "Joe emails his classmates all the time."

Even in the dim light of the restaurant, Grady watched suspicion creep into Roxanne's eyes. He was going to have to be careful around her. Of anyone, she could blow his cover if he slipped up with a word or two.

"Did your fiancée attend workshops for pastor's wives?"

Roxanne had changed the subject so abruptly, for a second, Grady didn't know what she was talking about. "I told you, I don't have a fiancée."

Again, Roxanne pointed her fork at him, almost in a threatening way this time. "You'd better get one fast. They want you to be married." She rolled her eyes and spoke mockingly. "So, if he counsels females, the wife has to be present. And I'm supposed to cook meals for people he wants to have over." She leaned back into the booth, sighed heavily. "See my dilemma? If I back out, there goes Joe's job. I can't do that to someone I love. But I can't give up my whole life either."

Grady remembered his conversation with Pastor Jay the night before. About the possibility of Roxanne calling off the wedding. "Have you talked to him about it?" he asked.

"I tried, but he doesn't seem to get it."

All Grady could think was all three of them were kindred spirits, caught in a web that had grown so big it encompassed them all.

CHAPTER THIRTY-SIX

J oe Decker settled his good leg on the coffee table, picked up the remote, and flipped from channel to channel. Car chases. Robots. Murders. Nothing at all behooving of a man of the cloth. Even the ads would have embarrassed him if anyone else had been present. He clicked the television off and tried Roxanne's phone again. Voicemail. Where was she? She hadn't mentioned any plans for the day. What if she'd been in an accident? What if the paramedics couldn't find his number in her cell phone? What if she hadn't earmarked him as her emergency contact?

With great effort, Joe lifted himself from the couch, steadied himself with his good leg hugging the coffee table, and stood looking over the living room of the parsonage. Not bad, but not good either. He doubted Roxanne would want to live this close to the church. He'd spoken to recent seminary graduates whose parsonages were situated on church grounds. Parishioners didn't understand boundaries. Burst in without knocking. One pastor, Charles Wells, had just awoken one morning, come downstairs bare-chested in his boxers and there was Mrs. Whatever-Her-Name-Was, a big gossip to hear Charles tell it. She was arranging blueberry muffins on a platter.

"I was livid," Charles told Joe. "But what was I supposed to do? I'm standing there in my underwear and there she was bringing us blueberry muffins. How was I supposed bawl her out?"

"So what did you do?" Joe asked, not only because he was interested, but also because he wanted to know how to retain his dignity should he encounter such an experience.

"I don't remember," Charles said.

"And no room for guests," Joe said aloud, drawing his attention back to the parsonage. Only a two-seater table in the kitchen. He wouldn't invite guests to eat on trays on their laps, elbow to elbow on the couch. Not professional and too many spills.

The yellow cottage would do temporarily. On the other hand, maybe they should look for a place now. Then Associate Pastor Joe wouldn't have to move out. He seemed pretty settled and happy here. It would be awkward to overlap and have the three of them under one roof. Joe wondered where Associate Pastor Joe had been living before he moved into the parsonage, and what was the story about him moving in now.

Thinking about size, now that his insurance money had been deposited into his account, he'd look for a bigger car that could accommodate children. Maybe a van. They hadn't talked about children, but he didn't plan to wait too long to start a family.

Joe ambled to the kitchen, opened the refrigerator, pushed aside a gallon of milk, a head of lettuce, a package of tomatoes.

He could use a snack more substantial than the carton of vanilla yogurt he found behind the ketchup. He closed the door, opened a cabinet, pushed aside the Rice Chex, a can of peaches, a box of ziti. Aha! Peanut butter crackers. He ripped open the package, took one out, sat at the table and finished the crackers in no time.

Where was Roxanne? She said she wouldn't be gone long. It was after 2:30, and he was bored. Roxanne left before 11:00. Where was she? He picked up his cell phone to call her again when there came a knock on the door. Strange. He doubted Roxanne would knock. He'd told her Pastor Joe had a funeral today and he would be alone. He hobbled to the door and pulled it open. "Where have you—"

"Who are you?" a little girl with blond hair and freckles demanded with a hand on her hip.

"Yeah," said an identical child beside her. "This isn't your house."

"Yeah," said the first. "Pastor Joe lives here."

"Are you a *buglar*?" asked the second. "If you're a buglar, we're telling our mommy."

Joe grinned, then laughed aloud. "No," he said. "I'm not a burglar, and there's no need to tell your mommy."

"What's your name?"

"My name is also Joe, and I'm also a pastor. You can call me Pastor Jay."

The girls giggled. "Two pastor Joes?" one asked.

"Are you twins?" asked the second one.

"No," Joe said, "not twins." He opened the door wider, stepped out, and sat on the stoop. "Do you ladies mind if I sit down?"

"We ain't ladies," said one. "We're girls."

Joe lowered himself onto the top step. "And very cute girls at that. Are you going to tell me your names?"

"Betty Jean." She slapped her belly with both hands.

"Betty Lou," said the other, mimicking the gesture of her sister.

"So, I take it you two are twins." Joe crossed his hands over his good knee.

They smiled at each other. "Twins means you have the same birthday," Betty Jean said.

"And you look alike," Betty Lou said.

Betty Jean brushed a hair from her bangs. "Not always. Emma and Ernest are twins and one's a girl and one's a boy."

If Roxanne met these two little munchkins, she'd want to start a family as quickly as he did, Joe thought.

"What happened to your leg?" Betty Lou pointed to his cast.

"I broke it," he said simply.

Betty Lou's eyes widened. "In half? How did they put it back together?"

"Did they glue it?" Betty Jean asked. "Mommy has glue. She fixed the vase. Betty Lou bumped it."

"It wasn't my fault! You chased me!"

"Where's your mommy?" Joe decided it was best to divert their attention from the broken vase.

"Over there." Betty Jean pointed in the direction of the church.

"Cleaning up," said Betty Lou. "They had a party. But no balloons."

"It wasn't a party!" Betty Jean insisted. "It was a *foonal.*"

"What's a foonal?" Betty Lou asked.

Betty Jean shrugged.

"Does your mommy know where you are?" Joe asked.

Both girls focused their eyes on their shoes, then cast a guilty look at each other. Betty Lou provided the answer. "She said to stay close."

"She said to stay where we could hear her voice," Betty Jean said.

"I think she must be very worried about you," Joe said.

From far down the parking lot, around the corner of the church, Joe heard a voice calling.

"Is that your mommy?" he asked.

Betty Jean inhaled sharply.

"We better go!" Betty Lou said.

They grasped hands and skipped across the parking lot, steps in unison, giggling and chattering words Joe could not hear. He rose from the steps and returned to the house, smiling.

CHAPTER THIRTY-SEVEN

The funeral luncheon had wound down, and Mae-June was clearing the tables and collecting the decorations. Across the room, she heard Dixie Talbot calling for her girls. Mae-June looked the other way, not surprised she lost those kids. Not surprised at anything that woman did.

"I told them to stay nearby." Dixie scurried about the fellowship hall looking under tables, behind furniture, in the broom closet. "Betty Jean! Betty Lou! I told them they had to stay where they could hear my voice."

Mae-June heard the panic rise in Dixie's voice. She watched her barge into the kitchen and ask if anyone had seen them. The answer was apparently no because Dixie dashed across the fellowship hall and out into the parking lot. Even with the door closed, Mae-June heard her shrieks. "Betty Jean! Betty Lou!" In an instant, Dixie was back in the fellowship hall. "Has anyone seen the girls?"

Mae-June shook her head, as did Irving who was securing the sound system, as did Chipper Mangrove who was stuffing tablecloths into a plastic bag to take them home to wash. Dixie dashed into the sanctuary, and a second later the girls skipped into the fellowship hall laughing and singing.

Out of the goodness of her heart, Mae-June opened her mouth to call Dixie when she heard what the girls were telling Chipper Mangrove.

"We met another Pastor Joe."

"He hurt his leg."

"He lives with our Pastor Joe."

"But they aren't twins."

Mae-June felt her face fade to white, then flush to pink. Another Pastor Joe? With a hurt leg? Could it possibly be the mystery Joe who had been in Knoxville Hospital? That old man at the reception desk had let it leak that a Joe Decker had been discharged to an address in Wilsons Corner. Too many coincidences added up to it wasn't a coincidence. She had seen Pastor Joe leave with that lovely woman. She doubted they were back. Besides, the twins knew Pastor Joe. They said this man was a different Pastor Joe.

"Irving," she called. "Have you seen Wilfred?"

Irving looked up from his squatting position in front of an amplifier. He held a coil of black cord in his hand. "I haven't seen him," he said. "Can I help?"

Maybe it was better this way, Mae-June thought. Not to involve anyone else until she'd figured out what was going on. "No," she called to him. "Never mind." She headed for the door and practically bumped into Dixie Talbot who had just sighted her children. "Watch where you're going," Mae-June said.

Dixie shot Mae-June a disgusted look. "Same to you," she said.

Sticks and stones, Mae-June thought and slipped out the door. Wilfred's battered truck was parked beside her car in the lot. Of all places to park, why did the man park near her? Never mind. She was on a mission. A mission she would complete without the help of Wilfred. She felt strange walking the length of the parking lot, turning to the right when she passed the church, hesitating before she climbed the few steps and knocked on the door.

She'd only been in the parsonage a handful of times in all her years as church secretary. She felt the pastor and his family deserved privacy, and she was not one to overstep a boundary. Plenty of other people took care of that. Besides, by the end of the workday, she'd had enough. Why would she want to spend time with her boss, if you wanted to call him that. She thought of the two of them as a team, working in tandem, like two Clydesdales pulling a load.

She heard some rustling, then a heavy foot interspersed by a lighter footstep. The door flung open.

"Yes?" A handsome young man stood holding the door. He was tall, dark hair, actually looked a bit like Pastor Joe. "May I help you?" the man asked when Mae-June did not immediately respond.

Mae-June breathed in deeply and let it out. "I hope so," she said. "Who are you?"

He laughed, his cheeks crinkling, his eyes watering. "And who might you be?" he asked pleasantly.

"Mae-June," she said. "Church secretary."

His face lit up and he opened the door wider. "Mae-June! Finally, we meet in person. Come in! Come right in. I'm Joe Decker. I've been eager to meet you."

He stepped aside, but she stood frozen to the spot. Even though she'd been suspicious of the other Pastor Joe from the beginning, this didn't make sense. Who was the other Pastor Joe and why was this Joe Decker living in the parsonage with the other Pastor Joe? Were two men playing a sick joke on the church?

"Is there a problem?" Joe Decker asked.

"I'm just confused," Mae-June said.

"Come on in and let's talk about it."

Mae-June stepped over the threshold feeling uneasy. Outside these doors, she was under control—of her life, of the church, of understanding people and their motives. Here in the parsonage, who knew what was going on. She chose to sit in the nearest chair—a rocker near the front window. He sat on the couch and took a minute or two to find a comfortable position for his leg.

"You know, I was getting concerned about Roxanne. She told me she had some kind of appointment this morning. Said she'd be back around 1:00. I haven't seen or heard from her all day. Have you seen her?"

Mae-June thought back to the attractive woman Joe, or what's his name, had left with. Could she possibly be Roxanne? How would the two of them even know each other? "Maybe," she said. "Let's talk about you first. Are you sure you're Joe Decker?"

Pastor Joe chuckled. "Positive," he said. "Want to see my driver's license?"

Mae-June realized they'd never asked the other Joe Decker for identification. He'd sent information ahead of his arrival. She shook her head. "How long have you been living in the parsonage?"

"A few days," Joe said. "I thought you knew. Do you mind explaining to me what's going on?"

"I was just going to ask the same of you," Mae-June said.

"O-K." He drew out each letter. "This church, Wilsons Corner, invited me to be the pastor."

"I know that part." She was losing patience with the whole situation. Tired of trying to figure out who to trust.

"I was driving here a couple of weeks ago and had an accident. They sent me to Knoxville Hospital and Rehab. When I was discharged, Pastor Joe brought me here." He paused, then said, "I thought Roxanne asked you about me moving into the parsonage."

Mae-June tilted her head, pursed her lips. "She did, but I thought she was talking about the other … who do you think you live here with?"

"The associate pastor. See that's why I'm going to be called Pastor Jay so everyone won't be as confused as you are right now. I wasn't sure if he'd told you or not, that's why I said Pastor Joe just now. But you've proven the point, all right."

"We—don't—have—an—associate—pastor."

"I don't understand," Pastor Joe said. "Who lives in this parsonage?" He chuckled then asked, "and calls it a personage?"

"That would be Pastor Joe."

Pastor Joe closed his eyes and rubbed his forehead. "I thought you said you didn't have a Pastor Joe."

"He showed up the night we were expecting you, said he was Pastor Joe. We thought he was you. He's been preaching, visiting the old folks, counseling people. Why he did a funeral this afternoon and spoke a wonderful talk about three H's."

"I wrote that talk," Joe said.

"Why would you do that for someone who is impersonating you?"

"I had no idea he was impersonating me! He told me he was the associate pastor."

"I told you we don't have an associate pastor!"

"I know that now, but I had no way of knowing it up until this moment."

They sat silent for a few minutes, each mulling through the new information each had received from the other.

"What does Roxanne look like?" Mae-June asked.

"Black hair. Very shiny. Brown eyes. Italian nose."

Before he could go any further, Mae-June interrupted. "I believe she attended the funeral today. She left with ... I don't know what to call him. We thought he was you. For now, I'm going to call him Fraud Joe. Roxanne left with Fraud Joe."

A few more seconds of silence, then Mae-June asked, almost mournfully, "What are we going to do?"

"*We* aren't going to do anything," Pastor Joe answered. "*I'm* going to take care of it. On Sunday. I'll sit in the back, see how the service goes, and confront him. Just sit tight, Mae-June. I don't want you breathing a word of this to anybody."

Grady roared into the church parking lot and skidded to a halt beside Roxanne's Mini Cooper. She opened the door of the

Pontiac, stepped out on one leg, then turned her head to him. "Our secret," she said. "I don't want anyone to know I've been speaking to you."

"Our secret," he answered.

"I don't think I can face Joe right now," Roxanne said. "I'll call and say I'm not feeling well, I'll see him tomorrow."

"Good idea," Grady said. He waited while Roxanne settled in her Mini Cooper and started the engine before shifting to first gear. Then he noticed Wilfred's beat-up truck parked beside him.

What had Dixie told him about somebody named Zeke and his wife Magnolia? They were related to someone and somebody lived upstairs from somebody. *Whatever.* The important part was Wilfred might know where Mae-June's son Jimmy was. He spied Wilfred locking up the church and called to him. "Hey, what's up?"

Wilfred turned the key and checked the door to be sure it was locked. His serious face brightened into his characteristic grin. "Pastor! That was a great homily at the funeral. Three H's. I'll remember that."

"Thank you," Grady said. "Have a minute? I've got a question for ya."

Wilfred folded his arms across his ample belly, keys dangling from one hand. "Sure, what's up?"

Grady dispensed with the niceties. "I have reason to believe you know where Jimmy Yearling is."

Wilfred dropped his head and didn't say a word.

"I guess you just confirmed it. Why haven't you told Mae-June? You know she's been missing him all these years."

Still, Wilfred did not respond or look up.

"Well?" Grady pressed.

"A promise is a promise."

"Who did you promise what?" Grady tilted his head trying to catch Wilfred's eye, but the man didn't look up. "Look, Wilfred, this is important. Who did you promise what?"

Without raising his head, Wilfred peeked from beneath his lids at Grady. "Jimmy. I promised I wouldn't tell Mae-June or Dixie."

Grady straightened up and stood as tall and as intimidating as he could. "I'm not Mae-June. I'm not Dixie. I'm your pastor. Joe Decker. And I'm insisting you give me contact information."

"All's I know is he works at Zellwood Furniture. He calls me from time to time to check up on Mae-June and Dixie."

Joe Decker hobbled from the kitchen to the living room and back again. He reached the two-seater table, turned around and hobbled to the couch. Over and over and over. This day was turning out to be miserable. The news from Mae-June was more than he could bear. More than he could comprehend. Roxanne. He thought he knew her. Knew her well enough to believe she'd make a good pastor's wife. Knew her to be an honest, caring, trustworthy human being. If she had been in contact with Fraud Joe, as Mae-June named him, what was that all about? Why would she be keeping that from him? And Fraud Joe. What was he up to? Why would someone pass themselves off as someone they were not? What kind of spell could he have on Roxanne to convince her to go along with it?

More than his car had been wrecked when he lost control in Knoxville. His whole life was wrecked. Driving south, Joe had been totally confident he was living out God's will for him. He was convinced God had arranged for him to meet Roxanne on the Duck tour. Their love was destiny. If all that were true, why would God want him to be in an auto accident? If God had brought Roxanne to him, why would He want her to lie? God couldn't possibly approve, never mind plan for, the deception of Fraud Joe.

Joe remembered a seminary discussion in Dr. Snyder's class. *You will encounter problems. You will encounter people with problems. You cannot take them on as your problems.* Is that what he was doing … taking on a problem that belonged to someone else? No, this was his problem. And not only that, it was a problem for Wilsons Corner Bible Believing Congregation and he was the leader of that congregation. He needed to protect his flock, but first, he had to find out who and what he was dealing with.

CHAPTER THIRTY-EIGHT

J oe Decker had been waiting over an hour to quiz Fraud Joe and had grown impatient. Finally, in the late afternoon he heard a car door slam. He peered out the window and watched Fraud Joe shuffle across the parking lot kicking up dried leaves, shoulders drooping, chin on chest, heading for the woods. The guy looked defeated, hopeless. If Joe Decker hadn't known what was going on, he would have felt sorry for him.

Grady sat on his favorite stump in the woods near where he had seen the deer. For reasons he couldn't express, this had become his sanctuary. The place to think about his life, about his choices, about his next steps. The first next step was his sermon. The question had been bouncing around in his head for the last couple of days and he still wasn't sure. Joe Decker would probably volunteer to write it, but it didn't seem the right thing to do. He should officially say goodbye even though the congregation wouldn't know it was a goodbye. He would know and that made a difference.

He wondered if Suzanne Simms knew Melissa would be singing this Sunday or if she'd be surprised to see her daughter taking part in the service, never mind being in church. He wondered how the Praise Team would be received. In a way, he was glad he wouldn't be around to pick up the pieces. In another way, he knew he'd always and forever wonder what happened to the Wilsons Corner Bible Believing Congregation once the real Pastor Joe took over the helm. He wondered what would happen to Roxanne and Joe as a couple. If they would marry. If Joe would take care of the congregation with as much care as he had.

Mae-June said she'd have his check ready over the weekend. He thought about taking it on Saturday and leaving right then and there. But what about the Praise Team who had practiced and were actually excited to sing? Myra Mosely had called to tell him she'd found someone to help her dress and bring her to church. How could he disappoint her and not be there? And what about the family expecting to have him over for dinner? He wasn't sure who it was, but the wife was probably planning a menu or shopping or cooking right now. How could he disappoint so many people?

Besides all that, he was close to finding Jimmy Yearling. Bringing Jimmy home would be his parting gift to Mae-June. Do something nice for her. Have her remember him as the good guy.

And then the most problematic item of all. Taking the check. How did he want people to remember him? Someone who listened, he decided. Someone who made a difference. Not someone who had masqueraded as someone else, stolen a check, and then hightailed it out of the place.

In the beginning, impersonating a pastor was a coincidence, an accident … or was it fate or God that brought him here? He didn't choose to deceive a congregation or have them fall in love with him. Back then, he didn't care about them. They were just a sea of unknown faces, random people, supporting actors in the script of his life. Somewhere along the line, all that changed. He couldn't pinpoint the moment the sea parted and he saw them as individual people with real lives. Now he cared about them.

Would it be better to continue the charade somehow? Even if he could think of a way to pull it off, it didn't seem right now he had learned to see beyond himself. All these weeks he had given without caring; now that he cared, was he supposed to stop giving?

Maybe he should make up a story about why he was leaving. Say a relative was in a car accident and no one else was available to help out. But that was an intentional lie to cover up an unintentional lie. The truth? Was that the only way out of it? To break people's hearts, to shatter their faith in him, humankind, and maybe even God? It didn't seem kind. It didn't seem necessary. It didn't seem humane. Why hurt because you had come to love?

It was easier before he had a conscience. Better when nobody else mattered. Better when his life was much smaller and uncomplicated.

What he wouldn't give to be back home in Orlando, lounging on the couch playing video games, listening to Matt the Rat bitch about why Grady flunked out of UCF. It all seemed petty and another lifetime ago compared to what was happening now. He needed to turn off his brain and just concentrate on the next couple of days. Find Mae-June's son and write a sermon.

Having made a plan, Grady slowly plodded through the woods back to the safety of the little yellow cottage.

"How was the funeral?" Joe asked when Fraud Joe returned.

Fraud Joe dropped into the rocking chair, raised his chin skyward, and closed his eyes. "I hope I never have to do that again as long as I live."

Way to make an inroad in the conversation. Joe laughed, hobbled across the room, patted Fraud Joe on the shoulder, kept a firm hand long enough to establish himself as the top dog. "You're just getting started, my boy. Get ready for funerals more difficult than this. Children drowning, crib deaths, car accidents. Toughen up."

Fraud Joe opened his eyes and now Joe could read more into them. Terror. Sorrow. A sinking man, or rather, a sinking boy. How old was this young man? He looked too innocent to be a con artist. "Let me get you a drink of water. You look shot. Joe shuffled into the kitchen. "Tell me about it."

"A bunch of people appreciated your sermon."

"That's good." Joe retrieved a glass from the cabinet. Turned on the faucet.

"Dead bodies, though. I have a hard time. You know I was visiting Pastor Oscar when he died. Left the room for a while and next thing I know, dozens of people are running in. A nurse, or somebody, said I was the only one who could do any good and told me to go in. Can you imagine? What a responsibility. Then Miss Cora came down the hall. She told me Pastor Oscar really liked me. You know, they never told anyone they lost twins at birth. He actually told her if they'd lived, he wished they would have been like me. The whole thing was a nightmare."

Joe returned with a glass of water and placed it on a stone coaster on the coffee table. Etched on the glass was the word *Grace*. "Why would it be a nightmare that someone wanted their children to be like you?" Joe asked, returning to the couch.

Fraud Joe picked up the glass and downed three-quarters of the water in three gulps. He placed the glass back on the coaster, sighed deeply, and pushed his feet into the carpet so the chair rocked slowly. "Just not a good idea," he said. "And now I've got to come up with some sort of memorable sermon."

"All sermons should be memorable," Joe said. "Why are you concerned about this one?"

"This is the last …"

Joe sat up straight, laser-focused on how Fraud Joe would finish, perhaps give himself away, but he stopped speaking and rocked a little faster.

"I'd better get started," Fraud Joe said.

"Any ideas on topic?"

"Not a clue," Fraud Joe said. "Not a clue."

"Why don't I write it for you?" Joe volunteered.

"I need to take care of this myself." Fraud Joe rubbed the condensation from his water glass. "Easy or not, they deserve it. You'll be taking over soon enough."

"We need to talk about that," Joe said. "I'm good to go actually. I could speak this Sunday if you want."

Fraud Joe placed his hands on the armrests and shoved himself to a standing position. "No, I'm good. I've got this."

"Don't leave so soon," Joe said. "I've been alone all day. We've hardly talked about your experience running the day-to-day operations of the church. Or the people."

The muscles in Fraud Joe's arms tightened. Joe noticed it immediately. "I mean if you have time," he rushed to add.

Fraud Joe seemed to relax. He sat back down. Rocked slowly. "There's this woman," he said. "She has twins."

"Really? Twins?" Joe's interest piqued. He had wondered about them ever since their afternoon visit.

"About four or five. Anyway, their father is Mae-June's son, but they don't know she's their grandmother."

"Why not?" Joe couldn't imagine overlapping lives and not knowing you were related.

"Mae-June says their mother, Dixie Talbot, seduced her son who skipped town and hasn't been seen since. But I'm telling you," Fraud Joe pointed a firm finger at Pastor Joe. "I'm telling you. Dixie Talbot is an excellent mother to those girls. Don't you think people should get a second chance, Joe? If someone makes a mistake … on purpose or not, are they marked for life?"

"Grace," Joe said. "Like on your glass."

Fraud Joe looked confused, then turned his glass to read the word etched there. "I don't even know what grace is. There's a book about it in the bookcase. Something about it being amazing."

"Grace is forgiveness even if you don't deserve it. The slate is wiped clean."

"Okay, we'll call it grace," Fraud Joe said. "I think Dixie deserves grace. I think I've got a lead on Jimmy."

"Who's Jimmy?"

"Mae-June's son and the father of the twins. I'm gonna look into it. And then there's this old lady … not the oldest I've seen, believe me. Anyway, she's old. She married this guy Norman when she was young. He was killed in a war less than a year later. It's been, I don't know, at least half a century, and she tells the story like it was yesterday. She says it was the best time of her life. Can you imagine it? The best time of your life was fifty years ago? I want my best times to be happening all the time."

"Mindfulness," Joe said. He watched Fraud Joe try to grasp the concept.

"What?"

"It means living in the now. Not overthinking the past or the future."

"Okay, yeah, what'd you call it?"

"Mindfulness."

"I like that! Living in the now. Then there's Mae-June." Fraud Joe smirked. "Talk about a piece of work."

"I'm sure she has her reasons."

"Her way or no way," Fraud Joe said. "She treats me as if I'm her kid."

"Was she on the search committee?"

"What?"

"When you interviewed, was Mae-June on the search committee?" Joe probed. He hated acting like a friend who was interested, when in fact he was fishing for clues as to who Fraud Joe really was.

The light dimmed in Fraud Joe's eyes. He stumbled over his words. "I don't remember."

"How'd you happen to come to Wilsons Corner anyway?"

Fraud Joe's eyes darted to Pastor Joe's face, then down at the area carpet between them. "What do you mean?"

"How long have you been here? What was your interview process like? Why'd you choose this church above others?"

Fraud Joe stood. "I didn't," he said. "It chose me. I need to write a sermon," he said and headed to the guest bedroom.

CHAPTER THIRTY-NINE

E arly Saturday morning, Mae-June placed three eggs and an unsalted stick of butter beside her KitchenAid mixer. She ate a bowl of cereal, washed the bowl, and brushed her teeth. She gently pushed a finger on the top of the butter and determined it was soft enough. She placed it in the bowl of the mixer with one and a half cups of sugar and set the machine to cream the two ingredients together. When they formed ribbons of batter, she cracked the room temperature eggs, one by one, into the creamed ingredients with the mixer on low. She sifted the flour, baking soda, and salt into a smaller bowl, then combined milk and pure vanilla extract she ordered from Mexico.

She poured half the dry ingredients into the mixing bowl, then half the milk mixture, then the second half of each. This was an important part of the process. Don't undermix or overmix. Years of baking exquisite cakes had trained her eye to know the exact moment to press the Off button on the mixer.

She ripped off a piece of waxed paper and used it to dip into another stick of butter and grease the pans. No artificial spray stuff for her cakes. She could easily detect a chemical taste when she used it once many years ago. Pour the batter into the pans, then into the oven they went.

Now *that* was the way to make a cake. It wouldn't be like last time when whoever the baker was baked the cake for Fraud Joe. This would be a cake everyone would be talking about for years to come. She felt sorry for whoever made the cake for Fraud Joe with the letters formed by a kindergartener and obviously a boxed mix. Whoever it was would certainly be embarrassed after seeing what a cake was supposed to look like and taste like. For a moment she felt sorry for that person. How embarrassed she would be. But what could Mae-June do about that? Lower her standards to make someone else feel better?

When the cakes were baked, she let them cool for ten minutes in the pans, then carefully ran a knife around the edges, removing both layers from the pans without so much as a morsel sticking and breaking off. Then she wrapped them in plastic wrap and placed them in her freezer. That was another of her secret techniques. Freeze the cake before frosting it to prevent crumbs from mixing in with the frosting.

She dabbed dishwashing liquid on the cake pans and scrubbed, humming in harmony with the words in her head. *The love of God is greater far.*[2] She placed the first pan in the drainer and then the second. *Than tongue or pen can ever tell.* She dried the pans, stacked them in the cupboard with her baking supplies, wiped down the countertops, then brewed herself a cup of coffee. *It goes beyond the highest star and reaches to the lowest hell.*

Mae-June brought her coffee to the living room, sat on the couch, and slipped off her shoes. She adjusted the pillows and

---

[2] *The Love of God*, by Frederick Lehman

relaxed into them. "Ahhhh." It had been a busy morning, but it would be worth it to see the look on Pastor Joe's face when he spied the cake. During closing remarks at church this week, she'd have Wilfred make an announcement inviting everyone into the fellowship hall to meet the real Pastor Joe and enjoy a piece of cake.

The guilty pair bowed down in despair. Mae-June propped herself on the couch with pillows and snapped on the television.

On Saturday morning, Joe Decker and Roxanne sat in the Honda salesman's office waiting while he fetched copies of the papers for Joe to sign for a fire engine red Honda Odyssey minivan.

"I can't see it," Roxanne said. "You don't need a big vehicle. I don't need a big vehicle. It's too much money."

Joe beamed as though it were his first two-wheeler on Christmas morning. "Just think of the fun we'll have. Bring a bunch of people with us. Teen-agers and kids …"

"Joe says there aren't any kids in the church. Hardly anyone within ten years of our age."

"Joe says? When were you talking to Joe?" He felt worse about attempting to entrap Roxanne than he had when he tried the same tactic on Fraud Joe.

"I told you. At the funeral." She folded her hands on the oversized Mexican purse in her lap and looked the other way.

"How could you find time to talk about the church at the funeral? Certainly, he was busy conducting the service."

The corner of her mouth twitched. "He just said it, that's all."

Joe waited for more, but nothing else was forthcoming. "A Christmas tree," he said. "How would we get a Christmas tree home? This van is going to come in handy."

"Whatever," she said, crossed her arms, and suddenly found the ceiling very interesting.

"I've got the papers." The salesman burst through the door with a sheaf of papers in his hands. He was a roundish man with a cherry red face, sparkling blue eyes, and a smile trained to dissuade anyone from walking out the door without a purchase. He wore a name badge that identified him as Albert. Albert slapped the agreement on his desk and placed two pens on top, positioned within reach of Joe and Roxanne.

"It's not me buying the car." Roxanne stood and walked to the window, her body language displaying her displeasure.

Albert chuckled. "My mistake," he said. "My mistake. But I'll bet you'll be the one captaining this baby all over town."

"We don't have a baby." Her eyes drilled into Albert.

Joe cut in. "Honey, he's referring to the van as a baby. Albert, give us a minute?" Albert shot out of his chair with such force, the chair rolled backward and hit the wall behind him. He extended both hands like a construction cop indicating *Slow down, slow down.* "Of course. I could use a cup of coffee. Call me when you're ready." He pointed to the showroom outside the glass wall of his office and then back to the papers on his desk.

"Thank you," Joe said to Albert's retreating back. He turned his attention to Roxanne. "I don't know why he put down two pens. The van is only in my name ..."

"That is not the problem. I don't know why we're here. It's what it represents."

"What does it represent?"

"Control," Roxanne said. "You made the decision to move here without telling me. You decided we should have a child. You decided …"

"I never decided we would have a child. I assume some day we will, but that will be between the two of us." Joe stood and extended his hand to Roxanne. "Come on. We're leaving. You are more important to me than a stupid van."

Roxanne hesitated. "If you want a van …"

"What I want is a happy wife. Come on. We're leaving." Joe opened the door and Albert nearly knocked into him.

The coffee in Albert's cup sloshed onto his hand. "Whoa," Albert said, wincing. "Whoa, that's hot." He set the cup on his desk and turned around with his smile pasted back on. "So, where were we?"

"Actually, I've decided not to take the van," Joe said. He nodded to the door. Roxanne went through and he hobbled behind.

"What?" Albert objected. "I've got the papers—"

Joe hurried as best he could behind Roxanne through the showroom without responding to Albert's footsteps or his calls. "I can make the deal sweeter! This is the perfect vehicle for you. Safer than the Grand Caravan. Better gas mileage. Come on back. Let's just talk about this. You won't get a sweeter deal anywhere."

Out the door into the parking lot they could still hear Albert. His voice tone had changed to accusatory. "Wasted my time. You said you were buying a car today. Well, don't …"

Roxanne helped Joe position his leg in the car, then she slid into the driver's seat.

"Albert!" A second man stood in the doorway, a manager Joe presumed. "Get back to your office. Sorry, folks. You're welcome back anytime. We'll work this out."

Joe laughed. "Did you see that guy's attitude change? I'll bet if we come back tomorrow, we'll get a better deal with that manager just because of how Albert acted."

"Are you kidding me?" Roxanne slammed on the brakes at the parking lot exit and swiveled to face Joe.

Immediately his face changed. "No, I didn't say we were coming back. I'm just making an observation. Anyway, that's how you walk out on a deal. We hadn't signed anything. We were not obligated to stay and be forced against our will. I'm not buying a van, Roxanne. You and I will talk."

Shortly after Pastor Jay left with Roxanne to go car shopping, Grady pulled out his duffel bag and began packing all of his things except what he would need for church tomorrow—his khakis, a button-down shirt, socks, underwear, shoes he had acquired by way of the church credit card. Mae-June hadn't said anything, so the bill must not have come in yet.

He scrounged in the cupboards for snacks on the road. Not many possibilities. He'd forgotten until that moment that he had to replenish the food he and Pastor Joe had eaten from the stockpile. The pickings were slim, but he did manage to find a box of Rice Chex. He could stick his hand in the box while he was driving. In the refrigerator, he located an apple behind the milk on the first shelf. He'd wait until tomorrow to grab some cheese. Didn't want it to go bad overnight.

Grady was placing the apple in a small cooler he'd found in a closet when the doorbell rang. Almost no one visited him in the parsonage, and definitely not on Saturday. He jogged to the door and opened it to a young man he had never seen before. Grady guessed the man was a few years older than himself. He wore a nice pair of jeans, no rips or stains, a green t-shirt with a long-sleeved flannel shirt over it. His faded blond hair had a slight wave. He was lean and clean shaven.

"I hear you was lookin' for me," the man said. "Jimmy. Jimmy Yearling."

On Saturday afternoon, Mae-June removed the cake from the freezer and carefully set the two layers on waxed paper on her counter. She measured out two cups of dark chocolate chips and poured them into a bowl with one cup heavy cream. With her KitchenAid, she mixed the two ingredients for just the right amount of time. Then she spread the mixture on one cake and placed the other layer on top of it. With her thin frosting spatula, she spread the remaining ganache frosting on the top and sides of the cake. She mixed white chips with cream and spooned it into a piping bag. She squeezed with just the right pressure and formed the words, "Welcome, Pastor Joe." She had wanted to mention the church name somehow, but that wouldn't work. *Wilsons Corner Bible Believing Congregation.* You'd need a pretty big cake or write in tiny letters to fit that on!

When she was finished, Mae-June stepped back and declared it was good.

Grady's eyebrows raised in surprise. For some reason, he had pegged Jimmy Yearling as an irresponsible redneck. The guy standing before him was put together and confident. He opened the door all the way. "Come on in, Jimmy," he said. "I wasn't sure I'd hear from you. Definitely not so soon."

Jimmy stepped inside and glanced around like someone who had dreaded a day of reckoning but was relieved it was finally here.

Now that Jimmy was standing before him, Grady wasn't sure what to say.

"I got two messages," Jimmy said, rocking front and back on his sneakers. "Thought it must be urgent. Some kinda bad news or somethin'. I couldn't get ahold of Mr. Wheeler and all, so's I decided to come on by."

"No, nothing bad," Grady said, regaining his wits. "Have a seat. Just wanted to talk a little. Figure some stuff out, is all. Two times. You said two messages from me."

Jimmy spied the rocking chair and sat down heavily on the edge of the seat, feet flat on the floor, elbows on his knees. "Facebook and Wheeler. Yeah, I got that Facebook message. I said it wasn't me. Didn't want no lectures or nothin'. You know how it is with guys like you to guys like me." He placed his hands on the chair arms. "Then Wheeler told me you weren't a bad guy. I didn't even know they had a new pastor. And a young one."

"I'm no one to judge," Grady said.

"Yeah, well, most guys in your position are. So why'd you want to see me? Somethin' about Dixie or my Mom, I presume. Or the girls."

"All of the above," Grady said. He'd taken a seat in the other rocking chair and angled it to face Jimmy. The sun shone brightly through the window behind Jimmy. It formed a sort of halo over his head. Grady stared at it a minute musing on the irony of it. He tapped his foot and the action put the rocker into motion. "Dixie's a good mother," he said.

"So's my Mom." Jimmy lowered his lashes.

Grady hadn't expected that reply. All along, he thought Jimmy might think of Mae-June in the way he did—as a control freak. Or maybe the way he looked at Matt the Rat—critical, demanding, insisting on his own way.

His surprise must have reflected in his face because Jimmy looked at him quizzically. "Don't you think she is ... a good mother?"

Grady thought about this a moment. "I've never known her as a mother. Just a ... just a ..." He wrestled to make his answer as truthful as possible. "She's very knowledgeable," he said.

"Has a good heart," Jimmy said in a voice not to be challenged.

Grady bobbed his head and mulled over Mae-June's heart. He supposed Jimmy was right. Had never considered it.

"Yeah," Jimmy said. "Does everybody around here think I'm some bad guy or somethin'?" Jimmy rolled his head towards the church and around the room.

Grady shrugged. "Not really. Don't talk about you at all, that I've heard."

"You lyin' to me, Pastor?"

"No." Grady shook his head. He felt he had to tread lightly with this guy or he might bolt, and at this point, Grady *was* wondering why he left and never looked back.

"I'll tell you why I left." Jimmy launched himself into a standing position. He towered over Grady now, and Grady wasn't sure whether to stay seated or stand also. He decided to stay seated.

"I left because they are both good women. Good moms. Good people. They don't need the likes of me around. Embarrassing them. Better I left. Those kids don't need me messing up their lives." He turned his back on Grady and strode towards the door.

"Don't leave," Grady said. "What you said. It's not true. Kids need a father. And a mother needs her son." The minute Grady heard his own words, he felt a pang in his heart. What about his own mother? What did she need from him? "Assurance," he said aloud. "A mother needs to know her son is okay. That you're making it in this world. That you remember all she taught you. She needs an occasional shout out."

Grady stood, and the two men stood face to face, quietly musing on Grady's words.

"Too late," Jimmy said. "Been too long."

"I don't think so," Grady said. "It's never too late. Not for turning around. Not for going forward. I think being stuck with regrets is the worst thing."

"Maybe," Jimmy said. "You think Dixie wants me back?"

"Couldn't say," Grady answered. "But I'd be willing to bet your mom does. And those daughters of yours are the cutest things under the sun!"

Jimmy didn't move for a minute or two. Then he turned slightly towards Grady and his countenance had brightened. "Riddle tells me you play basketball. Wanna do a quick one on one?"

"Love to," Grady said, leaping to his feet so fast the rocking chair banged into the wall, ricocheted off, and banged again before slowing its rotation.

They strode out the door like two friends who had just unloaded a burden they'd been carrying for a long time.

CHAPTER FORTY

Mornin', Pastor." James Lambert greeted Grady on the steps of the church on Sunday morning. Four children, from preschool to preteen, followed him in a straight line like ducklings following a parent. A woman dressed in yellow—yellow suit, yellow felt hat, yellow shoes, yellow purse—took up the rear. Grady half expected them all to quack.

"I've been meaning to thank you for the note of support you sent me this week," Grady said, doing his best imitation of Pastor Joe.

The children caught up, the youngest two wrapped around Mr. Lambert's legs like anchors. Mrs. Lambert stood a respectable distance away and kept her eyes on the Bible in her hands. James Lambert blushed. "It was nothing," he said. "Nothing at all."

"It was something to me," Grady said. "I think you'll be pleased with the service today."

James Lambert disentangled himself from the kids and opened the door to the church. "I look forward to it," he said.

"And so do the kids." The children followed their dad into the church, and Mrs. Lambert nodded her head as she passed.

Cletus Jackson caught up to Grady as he reached for the door handle. "My wife and I were blessed by your visit last week, Pastor. We talked about it all week. Blessed. That's what we kept saying to each other. We felt blessed."

"Thank you, Brother Jackson." Grady liked the affectionate titles of Brother and Sister the church had adopted. When he used them, it gave him confidence that he was, in fact, a real pastor. "Where is your wife today?"

"Down with a cold," Cletus said. "Sneezing up a storm. Using a box of tissues in the morning. Another box in the afternoon."

"You tell her we'll be praying for her." The words slipped from Grady's lips before he had time to vet them.

"Thank you," Cletus said. "I'll be sure to tell her." He nodded in appreciation and entered the church.

Grady stood outside the door and contemplated his own words. Maybe he *would* pray for Mrs. Jackson. What harm could it do? He entered the church and straightaway unlocked Mae-June's office. One envelope lay in the corner of Mae-June's desk. A window envelope through which he read the words *Joseph Decker*. His heart fluttered and his hand trembled as he reached for it, then drew his hand away and listened to two voices in his head. *You earned it* and *It wasn't intended for you.* He heard muffled voices in the hallway. Was one of them Mae-June? He couldn't tell. Quickly, he made his decision on which voice he'd listen to, grabbed the envelope, and proceeded to his office to don his preaching robe.

When Grady entered his office, Wilfred waited with the silver robe. He shook it and helped Grady place his arms in the long, billowing sleeves. "Looking forward to another good one," Wilfred said.

"You'll remember it," Grady promised. "Every bit of the service."

Wilfred ceremoniously clasped the two snaps beneath the neckline and velcroed on the collar. He smoothed the fabric on Grady's shoulders. Grady followed every movement of Wilfred's hands. He would miss this robe and the feeling of authority it brought.

"I hear Roxanne's in town," Wilfred said. "Where is the lovely lady?"

Grady jerked around to face Wilfred, the moment of respect and authority dissipated. "Where'd you hear that?"

Wilfred's belly bounced up and down as he laughed from its depths. "Everybody knows, son. That pretty young woman at the funeral?" He winked and peeked around Grady as if she had magically appeared.

"Wasn't feeling well enough to come." Grady stumbled over the words.

"Sorry to hear that." Wilfred patted Grady's shoulder. "Tell her I'll be praying for her."

"Thanks," Grady answered.

"Are you all right, Pastor?" Wilfred's eyes conveyed his concern. "You seem nervous as a long-tailed cat in a room full of rocking chairs."

"I'm okay," Grady said in a voice that didn't convince even himself. *Just get through this morning*, he told himself. *You'll be better off away from here and they'll be better off without you.* The words sounded familiar in his head. Jimmy Yearling had said Dixie and Mae-June were better without him. Grady had disagreed. What about himself? Were this church and his mother better off without him? He didn't have time for that type of deep thought. He strode down the hall and waited for the *da* DA Dracula music to cue him for his entry. He had a sermon to preach and a tambourine to bang against his leg.

Pastor Joe hated to do it, but he didn't have a choice. He slit his suit trousers up the inseam to his knee. With great effort, he pulled them over his cast. Normally, he would have sent his white dress shirt out to be pressed with a perfect crease down the sleeves and a starched collar. A semi-pressed shirt would have to do. At least it was clean. A cell phone rang and he pulled it out of his pocket. The screen was dark. Odd someone would only let it ring once and hang up. Then he heard it again and again. It wasn't his phone. He limped across the hall into the living room and noticed a cell phone on top of the coffee table. Fraud Joe must have left his phone. Answer it or let it go to voicemail? Maybe it was important. Or maybe the call would be another clue as to who his roommate was. He picked up the phone and pressed answer. "Hello?"

"Grady?" The voice was that of a frantic woman.

As tempted as he was to answer in the affirmative, Joe's conscience won out. "No," he said. "This is his roommate. May I help you?"

"Oh." Her voice became soft, almost imperceptible. "He didn't say he had a roommate."

"Actually, I only moved in with him recently. Do you want to leave a message?"

"Will you be seeing him soon?" Her breath was heavy.

"Yes. In a few minutes actually."

"This is his mother. Tell him I just found out Matt—he'll know who that is—is on a bus heading that way. He left here yesterday. Grady needs to be prepared. Matt is the maddest I've ever seen him. Tell Grady."

Grady. So, the guy's name was Grady. Joe hobbled to his bedroom, plucked a black tie with a red dot from where he'd placed it on the bureau. He stood in front of the mirror and draped the tie around his neck, making sure the wide part hung a foot longer than the narrow part.

Grady. What was Grady up to? He turned the wide end of the tie around the narrow end, wrapped and crossed until he'd formed a perfect knot. He pulled the knot tight and stepped back to examine the results.

"Joe? Are you here?" He heard the front door open and Roxanne call out to him. "Out in a minute, Roxanne. Have a seat."

He slipped one arm, then the other into his suit jacket, threw his shoulders back and marched into the living room. "Are you ready?" he asked Roxanne. She nodded and they headed out the door for church.

The first part of the service blurred past Grady. When Wilfred announced the sermon time, he ambled to the pulpit, unfolded the papers with his scribbled sermon, and grasped the smooth wooden edges. He waited until most eyes were focused on him, then he began to preach. "Today I'm going to talk about praising God." He paused, his head nodding, his lips upturned. "I wondered about this—how do you praise God, so I spent time this week studying the topic. I found Psalm 150:1-6." He'd googled the word 'music' and this is one of the texts that had come up, but he wasn't going to reveal exactly how he'd studied up on it or why.

"Have you ever thought about it? How do we praise God?"

"Oh yeah."

"You preach it, brother."

"Let's praise him now."

Grady continued. "This text in Psalms answers the question of how we praise God. It says, 'Praise the Lord! Praise God in his sanctuary.' Sanctuary is another word for church." *Thank God for Google.* "So here we are in the sanctuary, in the church, and we are praising God. Next, it says praise Him in His mighty heavens. I thought about that one a lot and concluded it must mean after we die. I mean, really, I don't think Wilsons Corner, Tennessee, classifies as a mighty heaven."

Chuckles rippled throughout the congregation.

A door in the back opened and Joe Decker hobbled in wearing a black suit, one pant leg flapped up to his knee. Roxanne followed him in.

Grady choked. He coughed. Irving rushed up with a bottle of water. Grady unscrewed the top, took a long swig, replaced the cap. He watched Mae-June twist around at the sound of the door opening and closing. Mae-June examined Joe and Roxanne up and down and up again. She turned back to the front with her chin a little higher, her lips upturned, her eyes sparkling. *What was that about?*

Grady looked down at his notes. The words flew around on the page like fleas in a windstorm. He blinked until they came into focus. No choice but to keep on preaching. Keep on doing what he was doing. Figure out the Joe situation later. "Praise Him for His mighty deeds," he shouted. His voice cracked on the last word. "What mighty deeds has God done?" he shouted louder.

Responses pinged from one side of the church to the other.

"Saved Daniel from the lions."

"Parted the Red Sea."

"Sent Jesus to die on the cross."

Jesus dying on the cross. That was still a mystery to Grady. Why couldn't God have snapped his fingers to right whatever was wrong in the world? If God had done that, Matt the Rat wouldn't have been so mean. Grady wouldn't have had to flee Orlando. He wouldn't be in this mess right now.

"All good answers," Grady said. "God has done a lot of good stuff so we praise Him. Let's go on to the next verses. 'Praise Him with the sound of the trumpet: praise Him with the psaltery and harp. Praise Him with the timbrel and dance: praise Him with stringed instruments and organs.'" He smiled at Miss Cora sitting a few pews away from the organ, Pastor Oscar's spot beside her empty. "Every week we enjoy Miss Cora's organ playing, don't we? Let's thank her." He clapped slowly, and little by little, some members of the congregation joined in. He increased the pace once, twice, three times, until the sound was deafening. He stopped abruptly and waited for the clappers to cease, then he spoke again.

"'Praise Him upon the loud cymbals: praise Him upon the high-sounding cymbals.' Wow! Trumpets and harps and stringed instruments and cymbals. And dance even!"

Some people nodded their heads and smiled. A few to the left waved their arms in the air. Some looked confused. A few crossed their arms over their chests and glared.

Grady had most of them right where he wanted—open, vulnerable, ready to accept what was to come next.

"In keeping with the Bible," Grady shouted, "May I present to you the Wilsons Corner Bible Believing Congregation's Praise Team!"

The curtains behind him slowly parted. Alex McAllister came into view sitting behind a drum set. Chains draped his neck like a scarf. The curtains expanded further to reveal Michael Turner poised with a bass guitar. A chain circled his waist like a belt and hung to his knees. Keith Swanson loped across the stage dragging chains wrapped around his ankles. He planted his feet behind his keyboard and played a few rousing scales.

Suzanne Simms' daughter Melissa stepped from the wings, a cordless microphone in her hand, chains dripping from her wrists. She wore a black skirt four or five inches above her knee and a white blouse slit too low for a Mae-June standard.

From the audience came a sound halfway between a scream and a gasp. Grady searched for the source and wasn't surprised to find Suzanne Simms wide-eyed, covering her mouth with a trembling hand.

Grady reached beneath the pulpit to the basket of chains he'd noticed the first time he stood before the congregation. He grabbed the last remaining strand and whipped it around his shoulders. He strode across the stage, picked up the tambourine, and stood behind Alex waiting with Keith and Michael. Alex played an elaborate chord on the keyboard and they began playing and singing. Grady beamed until he thought his face would split.

Melissa raised the microphone to her lips and belted out, *"If you've been walking the same old road for miles and miles!"*[3] She raised her left hand and punched the air. *"If you've been hearing the same old voice tell the same old lies … "*

Michael strummed his guitar faster and louder, raised the fretboard to the heavens, closed his eyes and shook his head in unison to the beat.

There's a better life
There's a better life

The rusty-hair kid in the third row stood, swayed, clapped his hands. His father grabbed the boy's arm and shoved him back into the pew. The eyes of an older woman in the middle were cartoonish. Grady half expected them to bulge out on springs.

If you've got pain
He's a pain taker
If you've got chains
He's a chain breaker

Michael Turner grasped the chains from around his waist and tossed them. They bounced across the stage, adding to the percussion of the song. The group sang on, gaining confidence with each succeeding verse.

If you've got chains
He's a chain breaker

---

[3] Chain Breaker by Zach Williams

Faster they played their instruments. Louder became their voices.

One by one, they sent their chains clattering across the stage. Melissa held the last note longer than Grady thought possible anyone could go without a gulp of air. Michael played the last chord. Alex ended with a boom-boota-bang on the drums.

The jingles of Grady's instrument reverberated throughout the sanctuary for a full minute past the others.

Grady was on a high. They'd pulled it off. The team did great! He was proud of his sermon, proud of the kids. He awaited a response.

Silence descended upon the church. A profound silence. A silence quieter than silence. And then Grady heard it—the clump of steel-toed boots on the tiled floor. His Adam's apple ballooned and temporarily shut off his air supply. Only one man could walk like that—heavy, commanding, announcing to the world *I am the boss*. Matt the Rat. Grady hadn't figured Matt into the equation. Sure, he had accidentally revealed where he was, but for Matt to come all this distance, on this particular day, at this particular moment? Grady's low was lower than his high had been high.

The footsteps drew closer—clump, clump, clump. They paused. Matt stopped beside the second pew. He shook his head, leaned heavily on his left leg, his right knee bent. "What kind of a charade are you up to this time, Grady?" he demanded.

CHAPTER FORTY-ONE

Grady dropped his head and peeked through his eyelashes at the man's wrinkled khakis, at the rumpled plaid shirt, at the pointed jaw, at the day's growth of a beard, at the condemning eyes. He felt eyes bore into his skull—the Praise Team, the congregation, Matt the Rat who tapped his steel-toed boot in a cadence that rivaled the Praise Team's performance.

"Who's Grady?" Alex whispered.

"I don't know," Grady said. And it wasn't a lie. In that moment, he didn't know who he was—the boy Grady who had lived under the iron rule of Matt the Rat or Pastor Joe who had garnered the respect of many of the people sitting before them. Or maybe he was someone else entirely.

Irving Welch, dressed in his police uniform, jumped up from his pew and rushed to Matt. He grabbed him by his upper arm and whispered loud enough for all to hear, "We've got a church service going on here. Come with me."

Matt shook off Irving's hand. "And who's leading this sham?"

"It isn't a sham," Irving commanded. "Our pastor, Joseph Decker." He pointed to Grady. "Now come with me."

"I don't know who Joseph Decker is," Matt hollered. He pointed at Grady. "But that isn't him. That's my stepson, Grady Gilbert, and he stole my car."

A collective gasp rose like steam from the audience to the peak of the ceiling. Grady reached out, felt the edge of the drum, steadied himself. Black spots clouded his vision. He heard footsteps approach. He felt Irving Welch guide him to the pulpit chair the Praise Team had moved to the side before church began. He sank into the chair. His robe puffed out, then floated down onto his legs.

"We need to know what's going on here." Irving Welch spoke kindly, yet firmly. Grady breathed slowly in and out. He raised his head and opened his eyes. Beside the second row on the right, Matt had his hands on his hips, tapping his foot.

"I'll tell you what's going on." An elderly man in the back stood. He leaned heavily on his cane with both hands. "That music was sacrilegious, and Pastor Joe should be fired here and now."

Irving rolled his eyes. "Sit down, Hilton. There's more going on here than music."

"That boy there is Grady Gilbert," bellowed Matt. "And I'd like to know who you think he is and what he thinks he's doing up there."

Grady felt awkward in his shiny silver robe, but no one asked him to take it off. He was glad. It felt like armor. He remembered a story in the Bible from his grandmother's church. A boy going up against a giant. He wished he'd googled the story. Maybe he would have had a better idea how his own situation would play out.

Wilfred joined Irving and stood on the other side of Grady. He said, "The Bible says if someone wrongs you, you must first go to him and discuss it. I believe we owe it to Pastor Joe … I mean Grady, if this man is to be believed. We owe it to Grady to let him explain what appears to be some kind of mistake."

Wilfred's hand on Grady's shoulder drawing him to the microphone was firm this time. If Grady had entertained any thought of escaping, the window of opportunity had slammed shut. If only Pastor Oscar hadn't died. Pastor Oscar would have understood and would have known what to do.

"I never lied," Grady said.

Whispering and rustling spread throughout the church. "Actually, Wilfred, it was you who first called me Pastor Joe," Grady continued.

Wilfred's face reddened and his chin dropped.

"I ran out of gas and walked down the driveway to ask for help. You all thought I was Pastor Joe." Grady shrugged one shoulder. "And I decided, why not?"

The rumble of Matt's deep laughter reached Grady. "How gullible are you people?"

Matt's comment cut Grady. His congregation was not gullible, and he was ashamed of himself for not standing up for himself or defending them. He thought with all that had happened, he should have built up some sort of emotional protection from Matt. If Matt would only let him explain all he had accomplished over the last several weeks, the man might even be proud.

"That's enough," Wilfred said firmly. "We're only dealing with the facts here …"

"Those are the facts!" Matt called.

"Have a seat, sir," Irving said. "Or I'm going to force you to leave."

Grady couldn't believe anyone could or would speak to Matt that way. He raised his head long enough to watch Matt hesitate, then the family in the second row pushed closer to the middle to give him room, and Matt sat down.

Chipper Mangrove stood. "It is partially our fault," she said. "I remember when Pastor … I mean Grady arrived. We never asked who he was. We just drew him in and let him lead. I brought him a glass of punch … with melting lime sherbet." She raised her chin slightly and glanced at Mae-June out of the corner of her eyes.

"What's going on?" Myra Mosely asked the person to her left, then to her right. Neither supplied an answer. "I don't understand. What's going on?"

Joe Decker kept his eyes on the unfolding scene, waiting for the right moment to intercede.

Alex, Keith, and Michael circled Grady. Melissa faced the audience. "Lighten up, people," she said. Michael stuck two fingers inside his cheeks and whistled which did the job of quieting the group.

"Oscar." The voice was soft, but somehow everyone heard Miss Cora. "I couldn't have made it through without Pastor Joe." Her voice cracked and Sally Greenwood hurried over and placed an arm around her waist. "Other ways, too. He helped me in other ways. I felt guilty. He told me it wasn't a lack of faith. Thank you, Pastor Joe … Grady … for helping me to see things differently." She sat and sobbed.

"What's happening?" Myra Mosely said. "Why's everybody upset?" She grabbed her cane and the back of the pew in front of her. With great effort, she stood. "Who cares what his name is? Grady. Joe. What's a name got to do with it? He visited me." She let go with the hand holding the back of the pew and pointed to Grady. She teetered back and forth and came near to falling until she grabbed the pew again. "He listened to me. That's all I've got to say. He listened."

"He taught us about baseball," Ralph Riddle said. He and Rose exchanged shy glances.

"I made you frosted brownies," Rose said. "They're in the car. I think you'll like them even better than the welcome cake."

Mae-June's eyes bulged. *Welcome cake.* Mystery solved. Rose made the original welcome cake.

Grady managed a thank you nod and a weak smile.

Mrs. Lambert stood. Her eyes darted this way and that as she spoke. "This might seem small, but it was big to me. I didn't want my children getting sick, and this Pastor Joe …" She pointed at Grady. "He fixed the horrible water fountains in the church." The last word was barely out of her mouth when she abruptly sat down.

Grady stared in surprise. He had never heard her speak before.

Dixie leaped from her seat and spoke loudly, almost a shout. "When I had these babies, very few of you accepted me." For half a minute she did not say a word and kept her gaze fixed on Mae-June. "But Grady did. He listened to me. He respected me. He didn't look at me as some sinner or … or … a whore." Some in the congregation rustled paper, others cleared their throat, a few whispered to someone beside them. Dixie let the word hang in the air until they quieted. "He's a good man. I don't know Pastor Joe yet, but he's going to have some big shoes to fill after Grady."

"Nonsense!" There was no mistaking Mae-June's voice or the disgust dripping from it. "I knew something was wrong from the very beginning. I tried to say, but nobody listened. It wasn't me who had the problem—it was him! All that ridiculousness at the board meeting. All that sneaking away he did. All the things he didn't know. Sometimes it felt like I was babysitting."

Sometimes Grady felt the same about her.

Roxanne stood. Her eyes scanned the congregation. "My name is Roxanne Newman," she said. "I only met ... Grady ... a few days ago. "He may not be your traditional pastor. He may not be trained in Biblical theology or homiletics or eschatology or any of the rest of it, but he has a way with people. We talked, Grady and me. He's a good listener. He talked me through my options, which helped me tremendously to get my thoughts in order."

"I've been on a stinkin' bus all night," Matt said. "Where're my keys? I'm driving home and your mother insists I bring you—"

Grady remained silent. The congregation stared from Matt to Grady to Pastor Joe to Roxanne to Irving.

Mae-June stood. "What about the real Pastor Joe?" she asked. "We haven't even greeted him properly with that imposter taking center stage. I made a welcome cake." She cast a pitying glance at Rose. "You're all welcome to meet Pastor Joe in the fellowship hall after and enjoy a piece of moist cake."

From the back of the church, a loud voice commanded attention. "My name is Pastor Joseph Decker. As pastor of this church, it is my duty to step in and take over from here."

A collective gasp ricocheted from the front of the church to the back and from the east wall to the west. The rustle of people changing positions to see who had spoken was nearly deafening.

With all the attention on Pastor Joe limping to the front, Grady inched toward the door. Baby step by baby step. He stopped momentarily when he perceived someone looking his way. A few feet from the door to the hallway, he turned and ran. The last thing he heard was Betty Jean and Betty Lou giggling. Down the hall, out the entry door, down the steps, through the parking lot. His robe shimmered in the sunlight, billowed on the sides, and wrapped around his legs. The Pontiac. Where had he parked the car? With so many cars in the lot, the Pontiac was hidden from view.

Pastor Joe limped to the front, climbed the three steps to the stage, tripped on a set of chains. Wilfred grabbed him on one side and Irving on the other.

"You mean she goes with him …" From the back of the church, Hilton Alabaster pointed to Roxanne and then to Pastor Joe. "And not with him?" He pointed to the place where Grady had been standing.

All eyes followed Hilton's pointed finger.

"Where is he?" Wilfred yelled.

"That way!" Betty Lou pointed. Wilfred and Irving dashed out the door while Pastor Joe folded his hands on the pulpit and waited until one by one each member of the congregation noticed him and quieted. They stared at him expectantly, yet confused, hoping for answers. Joe smiled and held them in suspense a minute longer.

"Good morning," he said. "My name is Pastor Joseph Decker. Your pastor." He spoke slowly, calmly, warmly, gradually making eye contact with each member. The tension in the room eased. "We've all experienced a shock today, haven't we? On Thursday, I learned Grady had presented himself as me, and I came in here this morning with the intention of calling him out on it. I decided to wait until the end of the service to see how everything went …"

Grady spied the Pontiac dwarfed between a pickup truck and a Dodge Caravan, almost hidden from view. He ran towards it and jumped in, turned the key. His hands trembled on the steering wheel. His foot, leaden, refused to make contact with the gas pedal. His brain divided in two and argued with itself.

Go! Go! Go!

But Miss Cora needs you!

They all hate you now!

I doubt it. The Praise Team. Four teens came to church.

Mae-June hates you.

But wait 'til Jimmy contacts her. You did that!

Across the parking lot, Grady watched as the Riddles, Suzanne and Melissa Simms, Dixie and the twins, and a host of others swarmed out of the church.

"Grady, come back!" Wilfred called.

Irving stood behind Wilfred facing away from Grady. He appeared to be talking into something he held in his hand. He turned to face Wilfred and whispered something to him. Grady could neither hear the conversation nor see what he held in his hand.

Finally, Grady's foot came to life. He gunned the engine and dodged parked cars on his way to the exit. He didn't pause at the end of the driveway, just pressed harder on the gas pedal and grappled with the wheel to turn left. Past where he'd run out of gas all those weeks ago. Onto the freeway ramp heading west. *Was it safe to slow down? Was it safe to look in the rearview mirror? Was it safe to breathe or think? What now? What now? What now? Keep driving! Get away, get away, far away.*

The last Grady glanced at the speedometer, it registered 80. Shortly after, he heard the siren behind him. He glanced in his rearview mirror, and sure enough, flashing red lights and a cop gesturing for him to pull over. Disgusted with himself, Grady changed lanes, then inched into the breakdown lane.

The officer stepped out of his car, adjusted his belt and strode towards Grady.

"You again?" the officer asked. The same officer that had issued him the ticket on his way to see Joe Decker in the hospital. "Do you know how fast you were going this time?"

"Not sure," Grady mumbled, refusing eye contact.

"License and registration, please."

Grady reached into the glove compartment. The registration was on top where he'd shoved it after the last speeding ticket. He handed it over along with his license.

"Thank you," the officer said and returned to his squad car.

Grady slouched until his knees touched the dash below the steering wheel. He felt alone and ashamed. Ashamed of deceiving the congregation. Ashamed of getting another speeding ticket. Alone in the world with no one to complain to about his predicament. He missed them all, maybe even a teensy bit, he missed Matt the Rat.

He glanced in the mirror to see what was taking the officer so long. The guy was talking on a radio. He nodded his head, spoke a few more words, replaced the speaker to its cradle and exited the car.

"Lucky for you, Mr. Gilbert," the officer said. "This time I can say *yes* I know Officer Irving Welch." He handed back the documents. "You are a wanted man."

Grady's vision blurred. He dropped his head until his forehead rested on the steering wheel. *Irving Welch had put him on the Most Wanted List?* He could hardly believe it.

The officer's serious demeanor faded, and he smiled. "You are wanted by Joseph Decker, Wilfred Wheeler, Roxanne Newman, Miss Cora, Ralph Riddle, and a host of others at Wilsons Corner Bible Believing Congregation. They want you back."

The words refused to compute. Grady's brain could not switch from speeding ticket to the image of his face on a Most Wanted poster to going back from where he had just run from. "I don't understand," he said to the officer.

"Let me get the exact wording Officer Irving Welch sent." The officer read from a paper in his hands. "'There's a place for you here. We will work it out. We want you back at Wilsons Corner Bible Believing Congregation.' And then there's a whole bunch of names. And something about a Miss Cora having room."